Wiping my face, I feel half-dried trails from tears I don't remember shedding. Where am I? I close my eyes against the throbbing pain in my head, leaning against the wall behind me. Think Mae, think. What the hell happened last night?

Life has never been easy for DonnaMae. After losing her mom as a young girl, she learns to navigate a world full of uncertainty with her dad and brother. Just when she begins to find her footing, a devastating betrayal from someone she trusted turns her world upside down.

Left grappling with the aftermath, DonnaMae faces the ultimate question: Will she let what happened define her, or will she fight to reclaim her life?

Through every twist and turn, you'll laugh, cry, and root for her as she finds her way. DonnaMae is a powerful story about finding light in the darkest moments and the unbreakable spirit it takes to fight for your future.

Donna Mae

AJ SPRINGER

E&E BOOK TIME PUBLISHING CO.

Titles By

AJ SPRINGER

DonnaMae

MaryLou

SPRINGER

AJ grew up in the small town of Aberdeen, Washington, where she discovered her love for family, community, and the thrill of adventure.

Her unstoppable drive has fueled her journey to write her second novel, even when others told her it wasn't possible. Whether it's overcoming challenges or chasing dreams, AJ is living proof that persistence and heart can turn the impossible into reality.

Above all, AJ treasures her roles as a wife and mom to two wonderful children—a part of her life she cherishes most. She rises before the sun to write, fueled by tea, chocolate, and her love for storytelling. Writing may not yet be her full-time career, but it is her truest passion and a way to share stories of resilience and hope.

DonnaMae is AJ's second book in her series, continuing the heartfelt, inspiring timeline that began with **MaryLou**. Through her books, AJ invites readers into stories of strength, love, and never giving up, just as she strives to do every day.

Published by E&E Book Time Books

March 8th, 20025

Hillsboro, OR, United States

Cover by: Rob Hugo (portnw.com) & Sara Crowell

Editor: Railee Bradshaw (raileebradshaw.com)

Railee, you are truly amazing, and both of my books wouldn't be the same without you! You have been my rock through this entire journey—thank you.

A heartfelt thank you to everyone who supported me along the way—you know who you are, and I truly appreciate every bit of encouragement, guidance, and love you've shared.

Thank you to all my Beta readers—your feedback, and insights, have been invaluable.

An extra big shoutout to my Crew Chief, the head of my book pit crew, Abigail. Thank you for riding this wave with me, for helping me fine-tune and polish my work, and for caring about DonnaMae as much as I do.

To my sister—my number one fan—thank you for always listening to my wild ideas and cheering me on. Your belief in me means the world.

Thank you to my husband for always standing by my side through every adventure.

Dedicated to:

Hick Chicks:

There's no mountain I wouldn't climb, no river I wouldn't cross, and no ass I wouldn't kick for you. Here's to life-long friendships.

My Stepmom:

The one who never sought credit but has given more than I could ever ask for. Thank you for always being there for me, even when I didn't realize it.

My Coaches:

Boxing saved my life. You'll never fully know the impact you've had on me, but you saved me. Thank you.

To everyone who has been knocked down by life so hard that getting back up felt impossible:

Know this—you can rise again. You can punch back. And you can win.

Don't give up. Keep fighting.

Shadow Boxing

What happens when the bad guys staring back at you
    Mirror image of animosity
    Became something that resembles an atrocity
    Lost myself because the faith that you had lost in me
    Couldn't accept my flaws
    But I personified it
    Couldn't stand up to fear
    So I stood behind it
    Many mistakes but life isn't something
    that lets you rewind it
    No but you will pay your dues
    Karma always gets her check
    Got an L and I thought I wore it well
    But it was just the abundance of my misfortune
    That to myself I wouldn't tell
    You lose when you chose wrong
    Lost when you moved on
    Made so many mistakes
    they all paired up like a Groupon
    Buy one get one free
    Thought I was the savior just to become the enemy
    Lost my energy
    Life isn't feeling like it used to
    Feeling used by you, the wells run dry
    No tears for years that I had let go by
    I sit in silence
    Darkness consumes my thoughts
    You know the game is over when
    you feel like you have lost

Thought I had all the moves
End up the one that was crossed
The one who stares back in the mirror
Always in my way
Life's a match but lately I don't wanna play
Lose to come back strong
Win when you admit wrong
But all these wrongdoings
Seems I can't get right
Say a prayer for the demons that keep me up at night
The face of the one that looks back at me
Forever throwing punches at a phantom
Whom I'll never hit but is always hitting me

— WILLIAM ROBERT LOWE —
EMOTIONS OVER CLARITY

DonnaMae

CHAPTER 1

June 15th, 2002

My tears blur the surrounding darkness.

The smells of mildew and bleach curl through my nose as I peel my face from a cold tile floor. Sitting up, I feel the floor's chill through my sweatpants, prickling my skin with goosebumps. I pull my knees to my chest and rub my legs for warmth. A memory of putting on my sweatpants flashes through my mind.

Where am I?

My heart races as I strain to see through the dark.

My head is pounding and I feel slightly dizzy, like I just stepped off a fast-spinning carnival ride. I close my eyes against the throbbing pain in my head, leaning against the wall behind me, my hand bracing against the floor for support. The last thing I remember is... nothing.

Think Mae, think. What the hell happened last night?

Wiping my face, I feel half-dried trails from tears I don't remember shedding. A sob escapes me, its rawness and familiarity letting me know it's just one from a series of many I've already cried.

I let out a slow breath and struggled to push myself up to stand. My trembling and unsteady arm gives out — my fingers slip into a warm liquid. "What the hell?" Nausea overwhelms me, and I collapse back against the icy wall.

My heart pounds. My body aches as I tremble with fear.

I close my eyes and begin counting to slow my breathing. One... two ... three... pause... One... two... three... It's like I'm a little girl again. I can almost hear my dad's voice saying, "It's ok, Mae. Just breathe. One... two... three..."

A repugnant odor invades my focus, and I gag. "What is that smell?" I pull my shirt up over my nose.

Ok Mae, get it together. Think! Where are you? What happened? How did you get here?

My head throbs. The urge to vomit becomes unbearable, as I strain to remember where I am and how I got here. But it's no use. My memory is as dark as this unfamiliar room.

CHAPTER 2

December 26th, 1990

DonnaMae gripped the handle of her basket as she wandered through the Howard Mason Hall. "Daddy?"

A loud clanking noise startled her. DonnaMae spun around just as warm air blew on her legs, carrying with it a smell like moldy burnt toast. Someone must have turned on the heaters, she realized. The heaters at her grandpa's shop made the same noise and had the same smell. She turned back.

"Daddy!" DonnaMae said, a little louder this time.

She had arrived a few hours ago with her dad and her brother Allan to prepare for the service. While the grown-ups set up tables and flowers, DonnaMae had been allowed to run around and explore, then Auntie Jo said she was supposed to get ready to welcome guests as they arrived. But now DonnaMae didn't know where her daddy was.

She wandered into a spacious room filled with tables and chairs, almost like her school lunchroom, but these tables were covered with black tablecloths. The wooden floors creaked under DonnaMae's feet. Tall, narrow windows with thick, dark, ugly curtains lined the back wall, flooding the room with soft morning light. Above her, three big crystal chandeliers caught the light, casting tiny rainbows along the walls. Despite the rainbows, a heavy sadness weighed on DonnaMae. She was about to leave when she found her dad standing in front of one of the large windows, his back to her, shoulders slumped. Rays of sun delicately dusted the top of his light brown hair.

DonnaMae squinted, trying to see what had captured her dad's attention out the window.

Outside, frosted rooftops stretched out in all directions, but her dad was looking past these at an open field of vibrant green with a rocky driveway leading to a big old yellow house. DonnaMae knew that house. It was her grandma and grandpa's house, where her mom had grown up. DonnaMae loved going there for sleepovers and playing in that field. She knew exactly where she was. Last week, she had stood on the street below with her family, mesmerized by a parade of big trucks and floats decorated with twinkling Christmas lights. She could almost taste the hot chocolate that her grandpa had given her with a candy cane in it. But now, even with the giant Christmas wreaths and red bows hanging from lampposts, the small town of Howard was quiet and uneventful.

As DonnaMae leaned forward to see if the hot chocolate stand was still on the corner, her basket brushed gently against her leg. Remembering her quest, she skipped to her dad's side.

"Daddy, Daddy, Daddy!" She held out her basket filled with perfectly folded papers to show him.

When her dad faced her, DonnaMae noticed the sadness in his bright blue eyes, rimmed with tears. This had been happening a lot in the last few days, and she hated seeing him sad. It made her feel sad.

Determined to bring a smile to his face, DonnaMae laughed. "Look, Daddy, look at my basket!" Her laughter filled the air as she twirled in her light blue floral dress, the white wicker basket with a matching blue ribbon swinging in her hand.

"Sis!"

Startled by her brother Allan's voice, DonnaMae stopped twirling.

"You're supposed to be getting ready to hand those out at the front door," Allan said as he walked in. "Auntie Jo is looking for you."

DonnaMae dropped her basket. Feeling like the world was still spinning, she crossed her arms and tried to focus on her brother. He was only a year and a half older, but a lot taller. At six years old, it seemed to DonnaMae that everyone was taller than she was. People often asked if she and Allan were twins and that always made her laugh, because how could they be twins if he was taller? One of her soft blonde curls dropped in front of her scrunched-up face. "I don't want to give people papers with Mommy on them. They don't want pictures of her, they want Mommy."

Allan picked up the basket. "I want to see Mommy too, and so do all these people. That's why we're handing these out."

"Daaa—" DonnaMae whined, but before she could finish, her dad bent down on one knee between the two of them.

He gently uncrossed one of DonnaMae's arms, letting her little fingers fall into his big, rough hand. Then he reached for Allan's hand. "I love you both so much," he said, "and I know today won't be easy for us, but I'm right here, and I'm not going anywhere." Leaning forward, he kissed them each on the head. "Let's go say hi to all our family and friends. Let's go celebrate Mom." He stood, still holding their hands. "And then after, we'll all come to this room for some food and your grandma's famous chocolate chip cookies."

"Can I have a cookie now?" DonnaMae asked, giving her dad's arm a slight tug.

He smiled. "Not yet, love."

Allan held out the basket of pamphlets to DonnaMae. "You better take this, Sis. It doesn't match my dress."

DonnaMae giggled, taking back the basket. "You're not wearing a dress, silly boose!"

"Boose?"

"Yeah, you're a silly boose!"

"I think you mean goose."

DonnaMae saw the beginnings of a smile on her daddy's face. She loved it when she made him happy. She let out another loud belly laugh, "You are both silly booses, and we should get a pet goose."

"What?" Allan laughed.

As she giggled, DonnaMae's gaze fell on the pamphlets in her basket, where her mother's pretty face smiled up at her. "Wait, Daddy, you and Brother both need a Mommy paper before I give them all out." She pulled her hand free, took a pamphlet from her basket, and held it up to him.

Her dad's face softened as his hand hovered over the picture of DonnaMae's mom. Her mommy's soft brown hair curled around her picture-perfect face. Joy and life filled her brilliant blue eyes, and her smile was so bright that it made DonnaMae smile just by looking at it. But the picture seemed to have the opposite effect on DonnaMae's dad. Tears slipped down his cheeks. He wiped his face, cleared his throat, and quietly read the words across the top: "Celebrating MaryLou. December twenty-sixth, 1955 — that was when Mom was born — to December twenty-first, 1990, when Mommy..." he coughed and cleared his throat again.

"That's the day we said goodbye to Mommy," Allan said, putting his arm around DonnaMae.

DonnaMae leaned her head towards her brother. She was glad he was there, because she suddenly wanted her mom to be holding her and giving her one of her big bear hugs. Mommy gave the best hugs. "Hugs can make everything better," her mom used to tell her.

DonnaMae fought back the urge to cry, not wanting to bring sadness to her dad or brother once again. Why did she always have to ask so many questions? No matter how hard she tried, she always seemed to make her dad sad. She'd thought for sure the paper would've made him happy. That's what it was supposed to do for everyone: share Mommy's smile so they could smile.

"Come on, you two," DonnaMae said, taking the paper from her dad and placing it back in her basket so he couldn't read any further. With a gentle pull of his hand and a firm grip on her brother's, she led them back towards the Mason Hall entrance.

After what felt like an eternity of handing out pamphlets to an endless line of people, DonnaMae's feet ached. Glancing around at the growing sea of guests, she felt as if she was being tossed among waves of happiness and sadness, bouncing from one feeling to the other. She didn't know what she was supposed to be feeling. As everyone greeted her with gentle smiles, their eyes held a sadness that seemed to be specifically for her.

She did her best to keep smiling. DonnaMae's mom always told her that one smile could create a hundred others as long as she was willing to share it. Her dad kept telling her that Mom was here with them today and would always be with them. In case her mom was sad and missing her, DonnaMae wanted to have a smile on her face.

It was only a few days ago that DonnaMae's mom was at home, lying in bed. The memory of that morning remained vivid in DonnaMae's mind — her brother and her dad with tear-streaked faces, her mom looking as though she were simply asleep. DonnaMae had climbed onto the bed and rested her head on her mom's chest, clutching her troll doll tightly as she whispered good-bye. "Where is Mom going?" she'd asked her dad. "Can Trolley and I go, too? We don't want Mom to go."

Allan had crawled up next to her and wrapped an arm around her. He'd seemed to know what was going on. "Trolley can hang out with me and you, Sis," he'd said. "Mom is going somewhere we can't go, but I'm here. I'm not going anywhere."

DonnaMae handed out the last paper and stepped behind her brother. She didn't want to be seen anymore. She wanted to hide. There were so many people and she didn't know most of them. They were all slowly disappearing into a big room with a stage and rows of benches. Maybe she could just stay here until it was time for the cookies, she thought as she slid down the wall to sit on the floor.

"Come on, guys," Auntie Jo said, "let's go sit with your sister Carmel. And after this is over, we can get you some hot cocoa and one of your grandma Joyce's famous chocolate chip cookies."

DonnaMae didn't want to go sit with all those people she didn't know. "I want my mom's cookies," she said. "They're the best."

Auntie Jo knelt down beside DonnaMae and wrapped her in a tight hug. In her aunt's embrace, for a few precious moments, she felt safe.

"It's going to be ok, baby girl," Jo whispered, releasing the hug, but DonnaMae clung on tighter. "You have so many people here who love you. You're going to be ok. It's going to be ok."

"No! It's not!" DonnaMae said. The pain in her heart felt so big she couldn't breathe. "Nothing's ok! I want to go home. I need Mommy!" She sobbed and gasped for air.

"I know, baby girl, I know," Jo said, pulling DonnaMae back into her arms as DonnaMae let her tears fall freely for the first time all day.

Allan stood behind her with his hand on her shoulder. "Mae, we have to go inside now. They're waiting for us to start the celebration for Mom."

DonnaMae turned around to face her brother. He was being brave and strong, and she could be, too. She stood up and wiped away her tears.

Auntie Jo kissed her on the forehead.

"Ok," DonnaMae said, wrapping her fingers around her

brother's hand. "Let's go." She took her aunt's hand, and they walked inside to find their seats.

Row upon row of benches filled the enormous space. They sat near the front with Carmel, DonnaMae's big sister from her dad's first marriage. A balcony crowded with people encircled the center stage from above. Red poinsettias surrounded a giant framed picture of DonnaMae's mom on stage. Her mom loved poinsettias this time of year, and sunflowers in the summer.

A few minutes later, the song "When You Wish Upon a Star" filled the air, and the room fell silent. DonnaMae had never seen so many people in one place before, and they were all here to say goodbye to her mom.

A man spoke on the stage. The rustling of people around her kept catching DonnaMae's attention. Now and then, she was sure she heard her name being whispered.

DonnaMae understood her mom had been sick, but she didn't understand why she'd had to leave, or why she wasn't coming back. When DonnaMae got sick, her mommy always made her better. Why couldn't someone make her mommy better?

A choir got up on stage and sang some songs that DonnaMae didn't know. A group of Rainbow Girls, not wearing rainbows, talked, and DonnaMae thought that was strange. They all seemed to have funny things to say that made everyone laugh.

The choir sang another song, and more people said nice things about her mommy. It felt like a party, but she didn't want to have a party without her mommy. Everyone was crying, so she figured they felt the same way.

Frustration and confusion swirled inside DonnaMae as she let her thoughts wander again. Her mommy loved Christmas, but she had missed it. Santa came, and he left her stocking empty. DonnaMae wondered if Santa had brought presents to her mom wherever she was and that's why he didn't leave anything for her at the house.

Suddenly, everyone stood up, and DonnaMae's dad walked up to the stage.

"Where is Daddy going?" DonnaMae asked, looking up at her sister.

Carmel bent down and picked her up. "Dad's just going to say a few words to thank everyone for coming, and then we get to go have some food, ok?"

"Oh, are we going to that big lunchroom with the rainbows on the wall?" DonnaMae asked. Carmel gave her a blank stare, but before she could say anything else, a hand touched DonnaMae's leg.

"Are you ready for hot cocoa and cookies, Mae?" Allan asked. His eyes were red and glossy. If she had only been a better listener, she could have told him one of those jokes the Rainbow Girls told to make him smile, she thought.

DonnaMae leaned from her sister's arms towards her brother and wrapped her little arms around him. "Don't be sad, Brother," she whispered in his ear. "I won't eat all the cookies. I'll share a few of them."

Allan laughed and hugged her back. A comforting warmth filled DonnaMae, making her think that Auntie Jo was right -- everything would be ok as long as DonnaMae had her brother.

Chocolate melted on DonnaMae's fingers and in her mouth as she slid down behind a table full of delicious treats. All she wanted was chocolate chip cookies and a place to be alone. She'd tried to play and laugh with her cousins, but wherever she went, she could hear people whispering about her, their faces filled with sadness.

"That poor little girl is going to be raised without her mommy."

"She needs a mommy."

"... And how is he supposed to raise her? She's going to need a mommy."

"... She was such a brilliant teacher and mother, such a sad loss for their family. What will they do without her?"

It was like they thought DonnaMae had lost her ears.

Finishing the last bite of the gooey cookie in her right hand, DonnaMae looked at the fresh one in her left. The long black tablecloth shielded her from everyone's staring eyes and sad words. She would have crawled all the way under the table to hide, but she wanted her daddy to be able to find her if he needed to, and she had gotten in trouble once for hiding under tables, so this seemed to be the best option. Her thoughts melted together with the last of the chocolate in her mouth.

Her mom was dead. She wasn't coming back because she got sick and died. DonnaMae wanted so badly to go back in time and lay with her mommy a little longer, to tell her she loved her and that she was the best mommy ever. She wanted to promise to be a good little girl and help her daddy and brother so her mommy wouldn't have to worry.

A tear slipped down her face as she took a bite of her second cookie. Sadness filled her heart, and it sank to her stomach as she pieced things together. Her mommy had died and that meant she was gone forever. But why was everyone so sad that her daddy had to take care of DonnaMae and her brother? Her daddy was a good daddy, and she was glad she had him.

"Mae?"

DonnaMae looked up in surprise to see her daddy standing over her. She quickly brushed away the tears on her cheeks. "Hi," she said, crumbs falling from her mouth.

Her dad slid down the wall and sat next to her on the floor behind the table. "This is the perfect hiding spot," he said, leaning over to take a bite of her cookie. "And that is the perfect hiding spot snack."

DonnaMae giggled. "I'm full. My heart is sad, and it's not

making me feel better like I thought it would."

"Oh, Mae," he said, wrapping his arm around her shoulders and hugging her close. "My heart is sad, too. It's ok to be sad, and it's ok to want to hide from all of this." He kissed the top of her head. "I kinda wish I could just hide from it all, too."

DonnaMae giggled again. "You're kinda hiding right now, Daddy."

He smiled. "Well, I guess I am. What do you say we just sit here for a few minutes, then we go find Brother, say our goodbyes, and head home?"

DonnaMae snuggled tighter into her daddy. "I think that's a great idea. Trolley is probably worried we've been gone for a long time. I don't want her to think I'm dead."

He gave her a tight squeeze, and she noticed he had tears trying to escape like hers, so she held out her cookie for him to take another bite, and he did.

The next morning, the house was quiet and dark aside from the soft glow of holiday lights as DonnaMae crept down the hall in her pink robe.

Allan had beaten her to the idea of sneaking downstairs for some cookies. He was already in the living room.

DonnaMae sat at the top of the stairs to watch him.

The floor was still littered with stockings from two days before, with small remnants of wrapping paper and ribbons scattered beneath the tree. The bed where her mom once lay had been folded back into a couch. Her daddy lay there now, fast asleep beside a plate of cookies, a bottle of what looked like apple juice and a glass that still had a little of the drink in it.

Allan tiptoed over to their dad. He made it to the table in front of the couch, but he didn't reach for the cookies. He picked up the bottle of juice. The bottle had a big "VO" on the side, and the label looked like it said "Sea-something." Maybe it was a seaman's apple juice, DonnaMae thought.

Allan took a sip, then immediately spat the juice out all over the table. "Spicy!" he yelled.

DonnaMae slapped a hand over her mouth to hold in her giggles as her daddy jumped up and ripped the bottle out of Allan's hand. "No, no, no, that is not for kids," he said, and patted the top of Allan's head before rubbing his own.

"Why can't I have it, Dad?" Allan asked, wiping his lips with the back of his hand. "It was just spicy. I can handle spicy."

"Because it'll make you sick 'til you're older. It'll hurt your tummy, son." Daddy knelt next to Allan and opened his mouth. "Did you drink it?"

"Ouch, Daddy, no, I spit it out. Then you took it from me."

"Ok, son, let's go get you some breakfast. We can have cereal today as a morning snack and then we can watch the *Frosty the Snowman* movie."

DonnaMae leaped up and bounded down the stairs. "I want cereal and to watch the Frosty movie!" She came to a screeching halt on the kitchen tiles to keep from crashing into her dad and Allan. "But no rotten Sea-man's juice for me."

Her dad turned around, a chuckle in his voice. "What did you just say?"

"The rotten apple juice stuff Brother just drank." DonnaMae tried to sound out the words as she remembered them, "It said, Sea-something on it.'"

"Yeah, let's leave it at rotten apple juice," said her dad. "You shouldn't drink it 'til you're an old man."

"Daddy, you're not an old man?" DonnaMae giggled. "You should probably give your Sea-man's juice to grandpa."

Her dad let out a loud laugh. "Ok, let's stop talking about Sea-man's juice." He turned and walked to the sink. "I should for sure get rid of it, though," he said, rubbing the side of his head.

DonnaMae and her brother sat at the kitchen table while their daddy got the milk from the fridge. The refrigerator was so packed with food people had brought over that he had to take things out just to find the milk. Casseroles and baked goods from friends and family overflowed the kitchen, covering every surface and creating chaos and frustration for her dad as he tried to get bowls out of the cupboard but had nowhere to set them. In his attempt to scoot one plate of food over to make room, he accidentally dropped it on the floor.

DonnaMae thought her dad would get mad. She would have gotten mad. But he just laughed.

"Well, that's one way to get rid of some of this food," he said as he brought the milk to the table and filled their bowls of cereal. Then he cleaned up the mess and didn't stop cleaning for the rest of the morning while DonnaMae and her brother sat at the table coloring.

By noon, the house finally felt almost back to normal. DonnaMae loved Christmas and all the fun decorations, but things had been so chaotic that it was nice to have everything put away.

Her dad set another tray of freshly baked chocolate chip cookies on the table. "I guess we better eat these while they're warm," he said. "Mom's friend Brenda just brought them over, and there's not one spot left on the counters to put them." He glanced around the room. "We need to get out of this house, get some fresh air." He paused, staring out the window. Then, with a sudden burst of energy, he said, "I have an idea," and darted out of the kitchen. They heard him running up the stairs.

DonnaMae picked up a cookie. "Daddy said we could eat them." As she dipped the cookie into her milk, her daddy danced his way back into the kitchen and placed a pile of snow clothes on the table.

"One, two, three, four," her dad said, "everyone stand up and put your feet on the floor. Daddy has a surprise."

"Where are we going, Daddy?" DonnaMae asked, setting her

pink crayon down next to her drawing of a little pig she had turned into a princess pig with curly brown hair and a pink dress.

"Let's get dressed and go on an adventure."

"We're going on an adventure," DonnaMae giggled.

"Come on! One, two, three, four... pants, socks, shoes and head to the door," he sang.

"Wait! What?" Allan was still shading in HeMan's brown boots, which he had carefully outlined in a darker brown. "Where are we going?"

"If I told you, it wouldn't be a surprise now, would it?" Dad laughed.

"You say that every time you have a surprise," DonnaMae giggled, pushing her chair back to get up.

"Well, it must be true, then. Come on, you guys get dressed and I'll pack snacks."

DonnaMae jumped up from the table and began pulling on her snow clothes. For the first time in what seemed like a long time, she felt a spark of joy from her daddy. As she bundled up, she thought about how much her mommy would have loved to join them. She whispered to herself, "I hope you're watching, Mommy. We're going to have so much fun today."

Allan raised an eyebrow at their dad. "Snacks? What kind of snacks?"

Dad let out a deep chuckle. "Well for sure none of this crap," he said, picking up one of the endless trays of crackers and tossing it in the garbage before heading to the back pantry.

DonnaMae followed. Her daddy held up a yellow bag. "I just bought your mom a fresh bag of chocolate chips and a fresh jar of peanut butter, but she never got to use them." He scooped DonnaMae up into his arms. "I used to find her right over there," he pointed to the back wall under the small window. "She would take a spoon and dip it in a jar of peanut butter and then in the bag of chocolate chips and eat it."

DonnaMae smiled up at him. "She showed me that trick once.

It's sooo yummy."

He packed the chocolate chips, the jar of peanut butter, a canister of Planters cheese balls, and three bottles of Cherry Squeezits into a plastic bag.

DonnaMae and her family lived in a small town called Aridian, which was right next to another small town called Henwood, where her dad had gone to school. DonnaMae loved driving through her dad's old hometown. Sometimes they would even stop and get burgers at the burger place across the way from his old high school. Today they drove right by it. They lived an hour away from the beach and they went often. The drive was long and windy and covered by evergreen trees that stood out beautifully against the winter sky. Raffi's "Down By the Sea" played through the car speakers and DonnaMae sang along with her brother in the back seat of their mom's old station wagon.

"Daddy, have you ever seen a llama eating its pajamas?" DonnaMae sang and then busted up with laughter.

"No, but I've seen a whale with a polka-dot tail," he replied, laughing with her in the rearview mirror.

As they pulled onto a long, deserted sandy gravel road, DonnaMae rolled down her window just enough to hear the ocean before they could see it. This was something her mom always used to do for them as they approached the beach. Soon the tall grass transitioned into dunes of sand and they drove onto the sand and down the beach.

"THE BEACH!" DonnaMae squealed, clapping her hands.

"But it's winter," Allan said, scrunching his face. "Isn't it the wrong time of year for the beach?"

Dad parked the car. "Your mom taught me there is never a wrong time for the beach." He reached over to the passenger seat, where a bag of supplies sat instead of DonnaMae's mom. He dug around in the bag, then held up a green thermos. "And that is why we have this — hot chocolate, and stuff to build a fire."

"YAY!" both kids cheered.

The beach was the perfect escape for everyone, a place where they could wash their worries away. DonnaMae and her brother ran around playing tag in their snow clothes while their dad unloaded the car and built the fire.

DonnaMae yelped with laughter as her daddy picked her up and ran after her brother, tackling him to the sand. The three of them held hands as they walked to warm themselves by the fire.

They roasted marshmallow cookie bars someone had made for them. The smell of campfire and saltwater swirled around as DonnaMae snuggled up next to her daddy and they looked out over the ocean.

"You know what I loved the most about your mom?" Dad asked.

"What, Daddy?" DonnaMae kept her gaze on the ocean.

"She was all the things of the ocean: strong, beautiful, free, and true to herself. Just like you and your brother."

"I'm strong like the ocean," Allan said, flexing his right arm to show it off like he had big muscles.

"I'm beautiful like the ocean," said DonnaMae, placing her hands under her face.

"And never forget to be authentic and free, like the ocean," her Dad said.

DonnaMae turned to her Daddy, but before she could ask him what he meant, he explained, "That means be yourself. Don't let anyone hold you back from being who you want to be."

The flames flickered in her daddy's eyes as he stared out at the ocean, and DonnaMae's heart longed for her mommy. But it ached even more for the pain she saw in her dad, knowing he missed her, too. She closed her eyes and could still see her mom standing on the beach, her hair blowing in the breeze, her perfect smile. DonnaMae could feel her mom there with them.

"I promise, Mom," DonnaMae whispered as the sound of waves crashed on the shore, "I will be strong for Daddy. I will be brave, and I will always be here with a smile for you if you need it."

CHAPTER 3

February 1991

DonnaMae's heart hammered in her chest, the sound filling her ears as she peered out from her bedroom door down the dark hallway. She thought getting older would make things less scary, but she had just turned seven and the upstairs hallway still terrified her at night. The faint glow from her room barely touched the edges of spooky shadows on the walls. She just needed to get to her daddy's room and she would be ok.

All the bedrooms were upstairs. Her room was at the end of the hall, while her brother's room was next to the stairs, directly opposite their dad's. As her eyes adjusted, DonnaMae saw both bedroom doors ajar and set her focus on her daddy's. Taking a deep breath, she quickly tiptoed down the hall. The cool wooden floors creaked softly beneath her feet. She made it safely to her dad's room. His bedside table lamp cast a soft glow on her mom's box, giving DonnaMae a small sense of comfort in the dark room. But the bed was untouched, and DonnaMae's dad was not there.

DonnaMae stood in the doorway, scanning the room for any sign of her dad. His bathrobe hung over her mom's old rocking chair. Staring at the chair, she was sure it moved. Without hesitation, she dashed across the hall to her brother's room.

Allan's eyes snapped open as DonnaMae placed her icy fingers on his warm arm. "Scoot over please, Brother," she said, climbing into his bed. Allan shifted against the wall, making room for her. "I had the bad dream again, and I can't fall back asleep."

"The fire one?"

"Yeah, and Grandpa was on the other side of the door. I could see him through the flames, but he couldn't open it to save us." DonnaMae's heart was still racing as the images returned to haunt her. "He watched us burn in the house. I screamed, and I screamed, but no one came to save us."

Allan propped himself up on his elbows and wrapped an arm around her as he squinted at his Mickey Mouse clock. Mickey's white-gloved hand hovered over the four. "It's not wake-up time yet." His words were a gentle whisper.

DonnaMae snuggled next to him and pulled the covers up to her chin, her gaze on her brother. "Daddy wasn't in his room, just Mommy's box on his nightstand."

"Did you tell her 'hi?'" Allan asked, sliding back down onto his side, facing her.

"She's not really in the box, Brother."

"Her ashes are, so she kinda is in the box. But you're right. She is here," he placed his hand over his heart, "not just in the box."

"I know." That's what their daddy always said when DonnaMae missed her mother. DonnaMae yawned.

"Did you check downstairs for dad?" Allan asked. "Maybe he fell asleep on the couch again."

They both went quiet and listened for sounds of the TV downstairs, but all DonnaMae could hear was her own breathing.

"I'm sure he's just asleep on the couch," Allan said, rolling onto his back.

DonnaMae watched him close his eyes before closing her own.

When she awoke, DonnaMae blinked away the grogginess, comforted by the familiarity of her brother's room. Allan was still beside her.

The memory of last night's unsettling dream crept into her thoughts, sending a shiver down her spine. Then she remembered her dad not being in his bed. She jumped up to check if he was there now.

Daddy's bed was still made perfectly, just like it had been last night. But that didn't tell DonnaMae much — her dad always made his bed and was always the first one up. Turning to head down the stairs, she remembered Trolley was still in her brother's room and ran back to get her.

Trolley was trapped under Allan's sprawled-out legs on the bed, leaving only the doll's scrunched-up face and light pink hair visible. "Oh, no!" DonnaMae whispered. "I'm sorry, Trolley. I'll save you!" She gave her doll's head a light tug, trying not to wake up her brother, but Trolley was stuck. DonnaMae pulled harder this time with both hands and yanked the troll out from under Allan's leg, sending her and Trolley to the floor with a thud.

"I can run faster!" Allan mumbled in his sleep, rolling over.

DonnaMae quickly covered her mouth as giggles escaped her. Then she jumped back to her feet and headed downstairs to find her daddy.

The smell of warm pancakes filled the air as she descended the stairs. Her tummy grumbled, and she felt relieved, knowing her daddy was downstairs cooking breakfast. They had pancakes and eggs or French toast almost every morning for breakfast, except on weekends when they got to have cereal while their dad slept in.

DonnaMae skipped into the kitchen, excited to tell her dad about her brother talking in his sleep. "Daddy, Daddy, you're not going to believe what just —"

"Shhh, Mae, not so loud," Dad said, rubbing the side of his head without taking his eyes off the pancake on the frying pan. "Daddy has a headache."

"Sorry." DonnaMae dropped her voice to almost a whisper, "I was upstairs and Trolley was stuck under Brother's legs and I —"

"Is your brother awake?"

"No, he's still cuttin' logs," she giggled. "That's what I was trying to tell you. When I pulled —"

"That sounds very silly, Mae." Her dad let out a small chuckle and turned to her. "It's 'sawing' logs. Can you please go get your brother?"

"But Daddy, that wasn't the funny part, I —"

"Don't make me ask you again, DonnaMae. Go get your brother, please."

DonnaMae gripped Trolley tight in her hand. "You're not even listening to me!" she growled as she stomped off.

"If you keep up that attitude, young lady, you are going to start your morning off with the belt!"

By the time she was back upstairs, tears threatened to spill over, and DonnaMae clenched her fists in anger. She'd been so happy to see her daddy, and now she wished she hadn't. She would rather eat Frosted Flakes than his stupid pancakes. She was so mad she could punch the door to her brother's room.

"Wake up, Brother!" she yelled from the doorway. "Dad said you have to get up!"

Allan rolled over and pulled the blankets over his head. "No, thanks!"

"Fine! I don't care. Let him offer you the belt for breakfast too!"

DonnaMae stomped off to get ready for school, her cheeks burning. Her Dad always told them to get dressed after breakfast. Well, she was going to get dressed before breakfast! That would show him, she thought.

For the rest of the morning, DonnaMae remained silent. However, when her dad dropped her off at school and said, "I love you," she felt compelled to respond. Their family had a rule that no matter how upset they were, they always expressed love before parting.

"I love you," she grumbled in reply before getting out of the car.

DonnaMae trailed behind her brother through the playground gate. Sadness and anger swirled inside her. She disliked feeling angry with her dad and couldn't grasp why he was so grumpy. She had done nothing to deserve it. If anything, she should be angry with him for not being there when she needed him last night. Lost in her thoughts, she didn't realize her brother had stopped and turned around until she bumped into him.

"You ok?" Allan asked, placing his hand on her shoulder.

"Yeah, sorry, I was just thinking about..." she trailed off, not wanting to talk about it.

"Cheer up and have fun today. Maybe *outside* of the library."

She groaned, "You sound like —"

A kid cut her off before she could finish. "Hey Allan, come check this out!"

Allan's focus shifted to the kid, and he dashed off. Glancing back at DonnaMae, he gave her a quick wave and mouthed "Love you," before vanishing into the covered area.

DonnaMae paused at the playground gate, taking in the loud laughter and shouts around her. She scanned the playground for Miss Jenny, her favorite recess aide known for her big hugs and kind smile. Instead, all she saw was Mrs. Arminius, the strict aide who always seemed to be yelling at everyone.

DonnaMae noticed Allan darting through an area where running wasn't allowed and she worried that he would get yelled at. But Allan quickly slowed to a walk as he joined some kids playing four square. The kid who had called him over showed him a new move, then handed the ball to Allan. Allan repeated the move with perfection before joining the game.

DonnaMae rolled her eyes. *Of course Allan picked up the new move immediately*, she thought. *What doesn't he do perfectly?*

Shaking off her feelings, DonnaMae told herself to make the best of the day. She spotted a group of girls from her class sitting in a corner under the covered area with Lisa Frank stickers and mini erasers spread out between them. Excitement bubbled up in DonnaMae. She couldn't wait to show them the new Lisa Frank erasers her grandma had just bought her. With a bright smile, she skipped over to join them.

"Hey, DonnaMae, did you bring your erasers today?" one girl asked as DonnaMae approached.

"Yeah, I got the new set of unicorns and rainbows!" DonnaMae eagerly pulled off her backpack to fish out the erasers. "It also has fun fruits. Maybe we can play—" Just as she was about to show them, the bell rang.

The girls groaned and started lining up for class. As DonnaMae followed them, she eyed their long, beautiful braids, pretty curls, and cute dresses. She looked down at her baggy jeans and oversized t-shirt with a sinking feeling in her heart. Her long curls had recently been cut into a short, shaggy hairstyle that she thought made her look more like the boys who teased her than the girls she wanted to be friends with.

DonnaMae loved attending the school where her mom used to teach, because all the teachers had known and loved her mom. But she also hated it, because the school was so far from home that DonnaMae didn't really have many friends here. She thought about the library, her usual hideout during recess. The boys couldn't find her there, and she could lose herself in the endless rows of books. She didn't really read the books — she just looked at the pictures and made up her own stories. It was safe in the library, and she didn't have to worry about being teased. But today, she really wanted to play with the girls. She wanted to show them her new erasers and maybe, just maybe, make some friends. Maybe the boys wouldn't see her today.

A light shove to her backpack made DonnaMae stumble out of line. "Watch out, little boy, you're in my way," a boy named Cory sneered. He was tall and always dressed in the latest, coolest clothes, and he was the ringleader of the teasing.

A whistle blew, and Mrs. Arminius's voice echoed through the covered area. "DonnaMae, get back in line!"

DonnaMae's cheeks burned with embarrassment as the playground went quiet. She walked to the back of the line. Today was not her day.

As she walked into the classroom, DonnaMae clutched her box of erasers tightly. Maybe tomorrow she would show them to her soon-to-be new friends. Today, the library sounded like a better plan for recess than the playground. She tucked the box safely back into her bag before hanging it on a hook and sliding into her chair.

The morning passed in a blur, and DonnaMae tried to focus, but her mind kept drifting to the idea of playing with the girls at recess. When the bell finally rang, she hesitated. Should she head to the library or take a chance? If she went outside for recess, she would have to wait in line with the other kids to get back in afterwards, and she would have to pass the classroom where her mom used to teach. Getting to stand in line outside her mom's classroom door used to be DonnaMae's favorite part of the day. She would wave at her mom and see her smile before going into class. Back then, DonnaMae felt like the cool kid, because her mom was the best teacher at her school. But now DonnaMae hated standing by that classroom door. It no longer looked like her mom's classroom. All the decorations were gone, and so was her mom. The library was in the other direction, so if she spent recess there, she never had to even see her mom's old room or the new teacher who'd taken her place.

Lily, one of the girls from earlier that morning, smiled at DonnaMae. "Hey, are you coming to play with us?"

DonnaMae's heart skipped a beat. "Yeah, I'm coming!" she said, pulling her erasers from her bag and hurrying after the girls. Maybe today would be a good day.

They regrouped under the covered area of the playground, and DonnaMae gently opened her box of erasers.

"Wow, those are so cool!" Lily said, pointing at the unicorn ones.

DonnaMae's smile widened. "Thanks!"

"We should make this a club," Lily said.

"Yeah, a Lisa Frank Eraser Club!" DonnaMae said, trying to keep her voice steady, though inside she was practically bouncing with excitement.

Another girl said, "Girls only!"

All the girls burst into giggles and cheered, "Yay!"

They spent the rest of recess trading erasers and making up stories.

Just as the bell rang, Cory and a couple of his friends walked by. Cory sneered at DonnaMae again, but before he could tease her, DonnaMae quickly stepped in front of her new friends. Thinking of the saying, "If you can't beat 'em, join 'em," she made fun of herself before Cory had the chance. Throwing her arms up and waving them around, she shouted, "I have boy cooties. You better watch out!"

The other girls burst into laughter and joined in, chanting, "Oh no, boy cooties, watch out, Cory!"

The boys rolled their eyes, ignored the girls, and headed to line up.

DonnaMae was so proud of herself, and so excited about her new club, that she didn't even notice she was standing next to her mom's old classroom.

The rest of the day went by smoothly, and she couldn't wait to tell her dad about it.

After school, she spotted her dad waiting in his truck and ran to him. "Bicycle Race" by Queen spilled out of the truck when she opened the passenger side door. This song always made her laugh — a grown man singing about wanting to ride his bicycle and not believing in Peter Pan or Superman, and he got other people to sing with him.

"Daddy, Daddy, guess what?" she said as she jumped into the truck. "I started a Lisa Frank Eraser Club today!" She paused and looked right at him. "At recess, outside!"

He smiled, his face lighting up. "That's great, Mae. I'm so proud of you."

DonnaMae's heart swelled at her dad's reaction. She'd hoped it would make him happy to hear she'd spent recess outside. He was always trying to encourage her to do so. She hadn't told him about how the boys teased her, but she had told him she'd rather spend recess in the library than play outside. It felt good to hear him say he was proud of her. She would need to do this more often.

"Maybe this weekend we can get you a few more of those eraser things for your new club," he suggested.

"Yes, please!" DonnaMae decided to just forget about how mad she was at him. She had his full attention now and the last thing she wanted to do was ruin it. "How was your day, Daddy?" she asked as she spotted Allan running to the truck.

"It was a long, dirty one!" her dad replied, glancing down at the white mud and dust that covered his pants. "But one day closer to finishing your mom's dream."

Allan opened the truck door and jumped in just in time to bust out the last few lines of the bicycle song with some upper body dance moves.

"Wow, you should go pro!" their dad laughed, glancing over his shoulder.

Allan settled into his seat. "Are we going to the old grange today or are we going home?" he asked, eyeing his dad's work clothes.

Before their mom got sick, DonnaMae's dad had surprised them all by buying the old grange hall. It used to be where the small town held big events years ago. Built in the 1930's, it needed some renovations. Her dad originally planned to knock it down and build them a new home close to the school where her mom taught, but when they first visited, DonnaMae's mom fell in love with the old building, and DonnaMae understood why. The grange had big double doors that opened into a spacious room lined on both sides with floor-to-ceiling windows that flooded the space with natural light. Dark wood floors complemented the white walls and tall ceilings. There was an upper area that looked like a stage, with a large kitchen off to the side. The building also had a creepy basement and an attic that no one ventured into. When DonnaMae's mom saw the place for the first time, she declared it the perfect spot for her dream daycare and preschool. After she passed away, the building sat unused for a while, but over the past year, DonnaMae's dad had been there every day, working hard to complete her mom's dream.

Some days DonnaMae hated the place, like last week when she was sick and she'd had to lie on the carpet samples and her dad's coats on the office floor while a plumber worked. It felt like the project took all of her dad's attention. But other days, she loved it because she got to help her dad build and paint, contributing to her mom's dream. When they weren't helping, she and Allan played in the woods across the street, hiking, building forts, and creating adventures together. That was her favorite part.

DonnaMae's dad chuckled at Allan. "Hi, son. How was your day?"

"It was great," Allan said. "We don't have any homework, which makes it a fantastic day in my book!"

"Well," their dad said, "to answer your question, we're going home. I forgot to pull meat out of the freezer for dinner, so we'll stop at the store on the way and make it a TV dinner kind of night."

"YAY!" DonnaMae and Allan cheered.

"And can we watch *The Simpsons*?" Allan asked. "It is a weekend!"

"As long as we do some reading first," their dad said as he pulled out of the school parking lot and onto the road.

At the mention of the weekend, DonnaMae became even more excited. Not only was she feeling better about the day, but her sister Carmel was coming to visit tomorrow. Last time her sister came over, they'd crafted puppets and put on a big puppet show for their dad. DonnaMae couldn't wait to do it again. She could already picture them sitting around the kitchen table, scissors and glue in hand, creating new characters for their next performance.

DonnaMae talked the whole way home, telling her dad and brother every detail of her new club, her friends, and all the ideas she had for activities they could do together.

The next morning, DonnaMae shook her brother awake. "Brother, Carmel is on her way over to play with us all day!"

Allan groaned, "Right, so we get to sleep in!" He rolled over and pulled the covers over his head.

"Hellooo! Earth to planet brother, you awake in there?" DonnaMae poked her head under the covers. "Beeboop, beeboop, I-am-an-alien-from-planet-sister-and-I-am   calling-for-you-to-play with me... beeboop."

DonnaMae's favorite movie was *ET*, and she loved pretending that she had an alien friend. She could always get her brother to play with her.

Allan bolted upright in bed, reaching an arm out and pointing a finger towards her. "Brother-T phone home," he said in a silly ET voice.

DonnaMae copied him. "Sister-T phone home."

Carmel burst through the doorway, pointing her finger in the air towards them, "Big Sister-T phoned home," she said in an almost perfect ET voice, "and is here to play with you."

DonnaMae and Allan ran to their big sister, wrapping their little arms around her.

Carmel rubbed both their heads and put her arms out like a

zombie. "Let's eat breakfast and play after," she said in her ET voice again.

"ET would play with its breakfast," DonnaMae giggled.

"And you look like a monster, not an alien," Allan added.

Carmel kept her arms outstretched and turned to walk out the door. "Well then, follow me, and we shall have a monster mash kind of breakfast," she said, switching her voice to a deep, scary monster tone.

DonnaMae loved it when their big sister came to visit. Carmel was their half-sister, but that didn't matter to DonnaMae — a sister was a sister. They were family. Carmel was from their dad's first marriage. DonnaMae had heard the story plenty of times, about how their dad had a baby right out of high school with a woman named Dory, and Grandpa Frank made him marry Dory. But Daddy and Dory were not in love with each other, although they were in love with Carmel. The marriage didn't work out because love is so important. Later, their daddy fell in love with DonnaMae's mommy, MaryLou, who was his best friend in the entire world. It was like they had their own Disney fairytale. Now they were all one big family and lived happily ever after. They used to see Dory on the holidays, but now that Carmel lived in Seattle for school and had a big-girl job, they didn't ever really see Dory. Carmel still came to visit once in a while, and when she did, it was DonnaMae's favorite time. Despite being much older, Carmel played with them as if she were their age.

After breakfast, Carmel brought the big crafting box to the table. DonnaMae leaned in eagerly, her elbows resting on the round, solid oak table top. Sunlight filtered through the floral curtains, casting a warm glow on the pushed-aside plates with syrup smears and pancake crumbs. The aroma of bacon still lingered in the air.

"Ok, pick out what you want to use to draw the story as I tell it!" Carmel said with a smile.

Carmel always told her famous "Itty-Bitty, Teeny-Weeny"

stories when she came over, and DonnaMae eagerly tried to imagine what today's adventure would be as she and Allan rummaged through the box filled with markers, crayons, pipe cleaners, and other random craft supplies.

"Do I have to draw?" DonnaMae asked. "Can I use the Play-Doh? Pleeease?!" She held up a bright yellow container.

Carmel laughed. "Of course you can! You can create the characters however you like." She winked at DonnaMae. "And what about you, Allan? What's your choice?"

Allan looked up, his face brightening. "I'll use the smelly markers," he said, pulling out a bright blue Mr. Sketch box with strawberries, lemons, and a chocolate bar on it.

Soon the table was covered with paper, markers, little piles of different colored Play-Doh, and tipped over empty containers.

Carmel put the last dish from the table in the sink. "Perfect. Now, let's get started with today's adventure of 'Itty-Bitty, Teeny-Weeny.'" She sat down between DonnaMae and Allan, her voice softening. "Once upon a time, not very long ago..."

DonnaMae and Allan leaned in closer.

"I was playing all alone upstairs, when I heard the very faint sound of music playing."

"Oh no, why were you playing all alone?" DonnaMae asked, turning to her sister. "I'm sorry you were alone. Sometimes it's hard to be all alone."

"Mae, it's just a story," Allan said, rolling his eyes at her.

"It's ok," said Carmel. "At first, I was scared, because I knew that no one else was home, so where was the music coming from? But it was such a happy little tune that I became curious. So, very quietly, I got up and followed the sound..." Carmel opened her eyes wide, turning her head slowly from side to side like she was searching for the source of the sound. "I followed the music, tiptoeing down the hallway to the top of the stairs. When I got to the top of the stairs, I saw it."

"Saw what?" DonnaMae perked up in her seat. "What did you

see?" She knew it was just a story, but sometimes she thought maybe her sister really had seen the little people. Where else would she have gotten all these stories from?

Carmel continued, "There was an itty-bitty, teeny-weeny hole at the base of the wall right next to Allan's bedroom, and that was for sure where the music was coming from."

DonnaMae glanced at her brother as he drew a large half circle on his paper.

DonnaMae squeezed her dough. It was harder than she thought it would be to make things out of dough and pay attention to the story.

"How had I not noticed this before?" Carmel continued. "I crouched down so that I could look inside. And what did I see?"

"The itty-bitty, teeny-weeny people!" DonnaMae shouted in excitement. She loved the tiny people. Sometimes she wished one would live in her dollhouse. She liked to think that maybe they did, and they only came out when she was sleeping.

"That's right," said Carmel. "I saw the itty-bitty, teeny-weeny people, and they were having a party!" She did a little dance in her seat.

"What kind of a party?" Allan asked. "Everyone loves a good party!"

"It was an itty-bitty, teeny-weeny birthday party for an itty-bitty, teeny-weeny little girl."

"How did you know it was a birthday party for a girl?" DonnaMae asked, looking over to see if her brother had drawn a girl yet. "What made her look like a girl, not a boy?"

"Well, there was an itty-bitty, teeny-weeny little girl, with two long, itty-bitty, teeny-weeny braids, sitting at an itty-bitty, teeny-weeny table, with an itty-bitty, teeny-weeny, bright pink birthday crown on her itty-bitty, teeny-weeny head." Carmel made a crown shape with her hands and placed them on her head.

DonnaMae rolled three pieces of dough and twisted them together like braids. She was good at doing hair. They had a Play-

Doh set where she could style the Play-Doh people's hair and she loved it. Maybe she would be a hairdresser when she grew up. Then she could make sure all little girls had haircuts that made them look like girls, not boys.

Her sister was still talking about the decorations for the party, but DonnaMae wasn't listening. She wanted to know more about this little girl. As curiosity filled her, she interrupted, tilting her head towards Carmel, "Was she wearing a dress? What color was it?" She couldn't help but wonder if the little girl was like her — kinda boyish? Or was she super girly like DonnaMae wished to be? DonnaMae rolled some pink Play-Doh between her fingers. "And did she have lots of friends at her party? Were her itty-bitty, teeny-weeny friends girls?"

"Yes!" Carmel said, "All kinds of itty-bitty, teeny-weeny friends, both boys and girls."

This made DonnaMae happy that the girl had friends, and lots of them. She couldn't help but wonder what her life was like. Did she have a mom and a dad? Was she popular at school? Did she have a brother? Did she like race cars? Thoughts swirled around as she molded a cake out of Play-Doh.

"Happy Birthday to you…" Carmel's singing brought DonnaMae back to the story. "And just before the itty-bitty, teeny-weeny girl could blow out the itty-bitty, teeny-weeny candles on her itty-bitty, teeny-weeny cake, I accidentally let out a not-so itty-bitty, teeny-weeny sneeze. In fact, it was gigantic!" Carmel scrunched up her face and let out a long and dramatic, "Ahh… ahh… ahh-CHOO!"

DonnaMae sat frozen and held her breath, waiting to find out what was going to happen next.

"The itty-bitty, teeny-weeny birthday party immediately fell silent." Carmel paused.

"Did you get snot all over them?" Allan asked, laughing. "Itty-bitty, teeny-weeny deaths by giant boogers and snot."

"You are so gross!" DonnaMae squealed.

Laughter and footsteps echoed from the other room. DonnaMae looked up as her dad rounded the corner with his friends Barney and Mark. "What's so gross?" her dad inquired.

"The new waitress at the cafe," Barney muttered to Mark, who let out a hearty chuckle.

"Right, or —"

"Daddy!" DonnaMae said, jumping up from her seat.

"Hellooo," her daddy said, bending over to give DonnaMae a quick hug before turning to Allan. "We're going to work on the race car. Just seein' if you wanted to help, Allan?"

DonnaMae's heart sank. She just wanted her daddy to come hang out with them, not take her brother away. "Daddy, Carmel was telling us a story, and we're crafting!"

"Well, when you guys are done," her dad surveyed the table, "with your 'booger' story, you're welcome to come out to the garage."

DonnaMae felt a spark of anger. Her dad couldn't just come in here and ruin all their plans. "No, thank you," she said quickly. "We have lots of things to do! Allan has plans with us."

"Or," Barney suggested gruffly, "you can come be a man in the garage." He turned to head out the door, Mark following behind.

DonnaMae tightened her grip on the dough in her hand. She didn't like her dad's friends and their dumb jokes. "Daddy, we're doing things and —" she cut herself off when she caught the excitement on her brother's face. He clearly wanted to work on cars with the guys in the garage. She surrendered. If it made her dad and brother happy, she told herself, she was ok with it. Anything to make them happy. And it would be nice to spend some girl time with Carmel. "Yeah," she said. "That's a great idea."

DonnaMae wasn't mad at her brother. Maybe his plans weren't the same as her plans. Even though Barney's "come be a man" comment made her blood boil, DonnaMae knew it was important to her brother to get to spend time with their dad. She turned to Carmel. "Want to go play with Barbies?" She pushed her

Play-Doh back into its yellow container. "Maybe we can finish our story time tonight," she said to Allan.

Carmel smiled, "That works for me."

But they wouldn't get to finish the story. Allan spent the rest of the day in the garage with the men and then Carmel had to leave.

That night, sadness filled DonnaMae as she curled up in her bed. She missed Carmel already. It felt like a piece of her heart was missing, not just because she didn't get to hear what happened to the little girl or where all the little people went, but because she was alone yet again.

She hugged Trolley tighter, wishing Carmel was still there to cuddle with her. It seemed like Carmel's visits were getting shorter and fewer, and now DonnaMae wouldn't see her again for a long time because Carmel was going away to school.

Carmel was always really good about writing letters, but it wasn't the same. Without her sister there, what would DonnaMae do the next time she couldn't join in on the "man" things? When she came second to race cars and her dad's friends?

CHAPTER 4

December, 1992

Guns N' Roses' "Welcome to the Jungle" seeped into DonnaMae's sleep, stirring her awake. She rubbed her eyes in the darkness. Crawling out of bed, she reached for her pink fuzzy robe hanging on the bedpost. Her mom had given it to her when she turned five, and now at eight it no longer felt big and comfy. Instead, it hugged her snugly, making her feel like her mom was hugging her every time she wore it. As Axl Rose's raspy voice echoed through the floorboards from downstairs, DonnaMae realized she wasn't the only one in need of a comforting hug tonight.

She slid into the fuzzy troll slippers from her auntie Jo before making her way downstairs. Before she even reached the bottom of the stairs, she spotted her daddy fast asleep on the couch, a half-empty glass of "old man juice" on the floor.

Shortly after DonnaMae's mom died, her dad had purchased a new stereo system with speakers that rivaled DonnaMae in size, a tribute to her mom's love for music. They had the best dance parties, filled with her mom and dad's favorite songs. The song playing now and Tom Petty were two of DonnaMae's favorites, but one in the morning was not the ideal time to enjoy them. Well, not for DonnaMae anyway. Her dad seemed to think it was a great idea, and every time he did it, she would find him with the "old man juice." She figured the drink was like candy. She knew it wasn't good for her, but sometimes when no one was paying attention, she would hide it in her room and taste some. But she had never actually seen her dad drink the stuff — she had only ever seen the aftermath.

DonnaMae walked over to the stereo and pressed each button until the music stopped playing.

The living room glowed with holiday lights, casting a warm and festive ambiance on the not-so-happy picture of her dad. DonnaMae knew this time of year was when her dad missed Mom the most. Christmas had been her mom's favorite holiday, and her dad always went all out to celebrate it in her memory. DonnaMae and her brother each had their own Christmas trees. Their dad was always there for them, keeping them busy and making sure they were ok. But who was taking care of him?

DonnaMae walked up to her tree, tucked neatly under the stairs, and paused to admire her decorations. This year, she had chosen blue and white lights, and carefully placed her hand-strung Froot Loops in front of them. The effect was magical — the cereal looked like it was glowing. She smiled. Her tree was perfect.

DonnaMae turned and walked to where her dad lay on the coach, next to her brother's tree. Her brother had made ornaments out of Legos, which was super cool, but DonnaMae secretly believed her tree was prettier. She would never tell him that.

She bent down and picked up the stinky-smelling glass on the floor, wrinkling her nose as she carried it to the kitchen sink. "Old man juice smells like pickle juice and feet," she muttered, grimacing. She returned to the living room and pulled a blanket from behind the couch, careful not to disturb the mountain of laundry that must have been her dad's project for the night. She draped the blanket over her daddy and tucked him in.

"I love you forever, and always daddy," she whispered, before kissing his forehead. She couldn't help but giggle when he snored loudly in response, like a bear.

Heading back upstairs, she stepped on a stray LEGO. "Fart-butt!" she grunted, hopping on one foot. "Damnit!" She wasn't sure what that even meant, but she'd heard her dad use it before when he hit his head in the shop. It didn't really help, but it made her giggle. She sounded nothing like he did.

Most of the time, it was pretty easy to fall right back asleep. But tonight, she laid in bed staring at the Care Bear cutouts her mom had made on her ceiling. She tried to imagine what life would be like if her mom were still alive.

She pictured her mom joining in their late-night dance parties, showing off some ridiculous moves that made them all laugh until their sides hurt. Maybe her mom would be the one to deal with the pickle-juice-smelling glasses. And her mom would be there to tuck her in at night.

DonnaMae smiled at the thought and finally drifted back to sleep, dreaming of Care Bears and family dance-offs.

The next morning, DonnaMae watched as her dad finished washing the last dish from breakfast and placed it on the drying rack with a flourish, as if he'd just completed a grand performance. He was the same dad she saw every morning, going through his routine like a well-oiled machine.

He paused, looked up at the ceiling, and began his daily ramble of the checklist: "Breakfast, check... lunches, check... teeth brushed, check... kids getting dressed..."

DonnaMae had to bite her lip to keep from giggling. *Kids getting dressed?* she thought as she looked down at her mismatched socks.

It had been two years since her mom had passed away, and since then, she and her dad and brother had created a new way of life. Her dad was even getting better at doing DonnaMae's hair for school.

Her hair had grown long and girly and now it was almost the perfect length. She'd used her money at last year's book fair to buy a book titled *25 Different Ways to Style Your Hair*, which had everything from side ponytails to braids, and it came with a tool called the Topsy Tail that did even more cool things, and her dad was getting pretty good at figuring out how to do the different styles on her.

Dad released a long breath and leaned against the sink — his gaze remained fixed on the beautiful ceramic light cover above him.

DonnaMae gathered up her hair supplies and carried them to him. "Daddy?"

He turned around to face her, his eyes glistening with unshed tears.

DonnaMae hesitated. "I'm sorry, I didn't mean to scare you. I just wanted you to braid my hair, please."

"You didn't scare me, Mae," he said, bending down to scoop her into his arms. "Daddy was just thinking about Mommy and the time we all went to Disneyland. Remember?"

DonnaMae shook her head no.

His smile grew. "Well, you puked all over the car, and we had to stop at a run-down hotel to clean up and stay the night." He pointed above the sink. "And that's when we found that light cover."

"Someone forgot their light cover at a hotel?" DonnaMae asked, tilting her head and crinkling her little nose as she looked up at the light.

"Something like that," he chuckled. "Now, what'd you want me to do with your hair?"

"Tell me more stories, Daddy." It wasn't very often that DonnaMae's dad shared memories of her mom, and she had stopped asking because she didn't want to make him sad. But when he did share, she never wanted him to stop.

He ran his fingers through her long, wavy blonde hair. "We'll have to save that for another day, Miss Mae. We've gotta do something with this rat's nest on your head."

"Hey! Rats don't nest on my head."

"Should we shave you bald?" he asked, setting her back down.

DonnaMae giggled. "No, silly! Just one braid, please."

"Perfect," her dad said with a smile, taking the supplies from her. He expertly gathered her hair, securing it with the rubber band before carefully braiding it.

As he worked, DonnaMae felt a mix of pride and sadness. Even though her dad had become a hair-styling pro, complete with his own special techniques, she still wished she knew more about her mom. Had her mom ever worn braids?

He finished off the braid. "All done," he said, stepping back. "One beautiful braid for my beautiful girl."

DonnaMae beamed up at him. "Thanks, Daddy."

"Go get your brother, please, and let's hit the road to school."

DonnaMae skipped out of the kitchen singing "Hit the Road, Jack."

After school that day, Grandma Joyce picked up DonnaMae and Allan to go to their weekly swim lessons at the Natatorium. DonnaMae enjoyed the lessons, but dreaded the drive home after. Despite her grandma making the car nice and warm, DonnaMae always felt cold to the bone. Shivering in the backseat of Grandma Joyce's car, DonnaMae couldn't wait to get home and have the hot cup of tea she knew her dad would have waiting for her.

Ever since DonnaMae had told her dad that the school provided milk and graham crackers to students after swim lessons, he'd started doing the same for her and her brother after their evening lessons at the Natatorium. Once, when she'd complained that she couldn't get warm, he'd swapped her milk for warm tea with a splash of milk, just like her mom used to have. Now, it was DonnaMae's favorite treat.

When they pulled up to the house, DonnaMae was surprised to see a mountain of furniture piled high in the yard, blocking the porch stairs. Sofas, chairs, and tables all stacked on top of one another. There was even a lamp teetering on top of the pile.

As Grandma Joyce parked the car, DonnaMae spotted her daddy climbing over the porch railing like he was on a playground. He leaped to the ground and stood in the front yard for a moment, hands on his hips, admiring the pile with a satisfied grin. Then, he turned and waved at DonnaMae through the car window, his face beaming.

DonnaMae giggled, thinking he looked just like the Little Mermaid in her cave of gadgets.

She and Allan leapt from the car, DonnaMae dancing and singing "Part of Your World" from the Disney movie.

"Why is all the furniture in the yard?" Allan asked, furrowing his brow and scanning the scattered chairs and tables.

DonnaMae stopped singing when she realized it was all *their* furniture.

Allan wasted no time waiting for an answer and climbed the makeshift mountain. Their dad was always thinking up crazy ideas of games to play and they had for sure made obstacle courses in the yard before, but never with the furniture from the house.

DonnaMae figured this must be another game, and her tea and crackers must be waiting on the other side of this new challenge. Following her brother, she climbed, gripping the edges of a coffee table to hoist herself up. "Is this the new way into the house?" she called down, laughing.

Their daddy chuckled, watching her. "Well, it's certainly one way in!"

DonnaMae slid back down on the underside of a sofa. "Or is it a new playground?" she asked, landing at her grandma's feet.

"What on earth!" Grandma Joyce said, her voice full of disapproval. DonnaMae recognized that voice all too well — it was the same one her grandma had used when DonnaMae and her brother made mud pies in the yard using the fancy pie dishes from the china cabinet.

DonnaMae's dad kept his gaze fixed on the pile of furniture. "Thought I'd give the house a little refresh." He walked to Donna-Mae, scooped her up with a grin, and said, "Let's just say we're trying something new!"

"And what about all the furniture my daughter loved so much? What do you plan to do with that?" Grandma Joyce asked, hands on her hips.

"Would you like it?" Dad asked, turning to face Grandma with DonnaMae still in his arms.

DonnaMae didn't want their furniture to go, but she also didn't want her daddy to get in trouble. And her grandma did not look happy.

"Dale, I —"

"Grandma always says we should try new things," DonnaMae interjected, hoping to defuse the anger. "Right, Grandma?" She didn't really want to try new things, but she trusted her daddy had a plan. There wasn't a single Christmas decoration outside, so maybe he was just going extra, extra big this year for the holidays and he needed to make room for it all.

"I am King of the Mountain!" Allan cried from the top of the pile.

DonnaMae let out a big laugh and squirmed from her daddy's arms to climb the pile some more. When she reached the leg of the coffee table, she paused and skipped back to her grandma. "Love you, Grandma. Thank you for taking us swimming," she said, giving her grandma's legs a big squeeze.

"WOW," Allan yelled from inside the house, "this is gnarly! The house is basically empty!"

"Yep," Dad smiled, "perfect for fort-building with Christmas lights."

Grandma Joyce kissed the top of DonnaMae's head. "I love you too, Mae. Go have fun building forts with your brother and daddy. I'll see you Tuesday after school." She reached into her purse and pulled out a book. "And don't forget your book. You need to practice your reading so you can grow up and be a schoolteacher like your mom."

DonnaMae gave her grandma one more good squeeze. Everyone always told her she would be a teacher like her mom, so she was used to this comment, but she wasn't sure if that was what she wanted to be. She really enjoyed doing her dolls' hair, and maybe she wanted to be a hairstylist, but she didn't want to hurt her grandma's feelings. "Maybe I'll be a schoolteacher for hair-styling people," DonnaMae grinned as she grabbed her book and then bolted back to start her big climb into Fort Land.

"Be careful," was the last thing DonnaMae heard her grandma say before she sprinted into the house, leaving her dad to defend himself against her slightly less angry-looking grandma.

The house felt like a blank canvas. Allan had already staked his claim for fort-building, and DonnaMae's excitement bubbled up. This was going to be the best Christmas yet. She claimed her tree as her home base and looked around. Everything was gone.

"What do you think Daddy's going to do with our stuff?" she asked, turning to her brother, who was dragging a pile of blankets to the center of the room. Last night's laundry was still in the basket, unfolded, sitting on the floor.

"He's going to put it at the daycare for now," her dad said, walking back into the house. "The big truck will be here in the morning."

DonnaMae stared at her daddy. The daycare was almost finished, and it made sense that it would need a couch, but this couch was hers. Why did she have to share everything that was hers? "Daddy, did you make my tea?"

"I'll go put the kettle on right now!"

No tea. He forgot her tea. He was changing everything. She

had to share her daddy every day, and now she was going to have to share him with other kids. And those kids would get to have more of her things. She wanted to scream. Suddenly, she didn't feel like building forts — she wanted things to be the way they were this morning. She wanted things to be the way they were before her mom died. Though she didn't even remember what that was like, she knew it had to be better than this.

Her brother was laying blankets out on the floor. He didn't seem to have a care in the world, and she felt like she couldn't breathe.

DonnaMae went up to her room and laid on her bed. "At least you still love me," she whispered, pulling her Trolley doll up under her arm and rolling to her side. She didn't want to be angry. She didn't want to cry. Why couldn't she just be like her brother and never care about anything?

A few minutes later, she heard a soft knock on her door. Her daddy came to sit beside her on the bed. "Oh Mae," he whispered, brushing a strand of hair out of her face. "Are you upset about the furniture being gone?"

DonnaMae nodded, not trusting herself to not cry.

"I know everything keeps changing, and I know that's really hard." Her dad took a deep breath. "I miss your mom every day, too. But even with her gone, we're still a family. That'll never change."

DonnaMae squeezed her doll tighter. "But why do we have to change everything?" Her heart felt like a tangled mess. She was so mad at her dad for making things change but also felt sad for him, and she just wanted to have fun, just the three of them.

"Change is a part of life, sweetheart," he said, placing his hand on her arm. "It's not always easy, but sometimes it brings good things, too. Change doesn't mean I love you any less. You and Allan are my world."

"But you forgot my tea," she said, her voice trembling. "And you're giving away our couch."

Her dad sighed and scooped her into a warm hug. "I'm so sorry, Mae. I didn't mean to forget your tea. How about we go make it together now?"

DonnaMae broke the hug and sat up on her bed. There was something about her dad that seemed different — she didn't know what it was, but he seemed happy.

"And the couch, well, it's just a thing. We'll make new memories with a new one." He stood from the bed. "And you know what? You can keep some special things just for you, maybe the lamp for your nightstand. How does that sound?"

DonnaMae thought for a moment and then nodded slowly. "Ok. But can we still put out more Christmas decorations this weekend, like we planned?"

Her dad smiled and kissed her forehead. "Absolutely. We'll make the house look amazing for Christmas. Just you, me, and Allan." He raised his right hand. "We are the Three Musketeers! All for one and one for all."

DonnaMae felt the knot in her chest untangle. "Ok, Daddy. Let's go make tea."

CHAPTER 5

July, 1993

DonnaMae sat on the new gray couch in the living room, wrapped in a light purple handmade afghan blanket. Her painted pink toes poked out from the blanket and she wiggled them as she flipped the pages of her *Boxcar Children* book. Some days, she missed the old brown couches, which had been so soft that when she sat down, she sank right into them. But today, she felt extra comfy with her book and a steaming cup of tea beside her, and she didn't mind the new furniture. It made her feel sophisticated, like she was twelve or thirteen instead of just nine; especially the round wood end tables that had little drawers for her to keep her book in, and the little coaster she set her tea on.

Her dad had read *The Boxcar Children* to her last night, so she already knew what happened, but she loved the way the characters came to life in her mind, and how the four children were always working together as a team to solve problems. She also liked to practice her reading and memorizing the words in case she had to read out loud in class.

As much as DonnaMae enjoyed reading, she also hated it because it was a challenge for her. Some days it felt like playing Scrabble. If she got the letters in the right order, she could make a guess at what word fit the sentence best. Once she memorized what each word looked like, it became easier. She took pride in her progress, feeling a small victory each time she recognized a word without hesitation. Then, when her daddy asked her to read a part of the book, she could say yes and he would be proud of her too.

DonnaMae knew she should probably get ready to go camping with her grandparents, but the adventure of the Blue Bay Mystery in her book was too tempting to resist. Maybe she could read just one more chapter first. She nestled back into the blanket.

Maybe she would grow up and go on big adventures like the boxcar children, and then she could teach others about her adventures. Being a teacher would make her family happy and she could also do something she loved. She turned the page and got lost in the adventure, imagining she was Benny Alden in the book.

The back door slammed, pulling DonnaMae back to reality. Allan dashed through the house and up the stairs. He was wearing jeans and a white T-shirt that was no longer white, covered in dirt and grease from working on the race car in the garage with their dad.

Jealousy stirred in DonnaMae's chest. Allan had a special connection with their dad that DonnaMae lacked. They bonded over the roar of engines and the smell of oil, two aspects of racing DonnaMae actually found appealing, but she couldn't share in their love of the sport. She loved her brother and her dad, and she always tried to join them in the garage, hoping to share their passion for racing. Her family made sure to remind DonnaMae that she was named after a famous race car driver, and that her mom had loved the sport. DonnaMae felt she should love it too, but somehow, she just didn't. Perhaps it was because the cars constantly hogged her daddy's attention, attracting all his annoying friends who seemed to think they were hilarious. Or perhaps it was because racing seemed like a boys' club where DonnaMae simply couldn't find her place as a girl.

Fighting off her feelings of jealousy, she turned her attention back to her book: a world she could belong to, where her imagination could run wild and she didn't have to compete for attention. But before DonnaMae read another word, a loud roar filled the house from the garage. She liked the sound of the race car engines.

Changing her mind about the book, DonnaMae jumped up, tossing her book and blanket aside, and ran out the back door the way her brother had come in. The ground rumbled beneath her feet as she sprinted over the driveway towards the garage. This was part of what she liked about the loud motors. It was so cool that something so small could bring that much thunder. She wished she was like that.

When she reached the open garage door, it felt like her whole body was shaking. The race car was halfway backed out of the garage door a few feet from DonnaMae, with her dad sitting inside. "Daddy!" she yelled, but her voice was drowned out by the roaring motor.

Standing there and taking it all in, DonnaMae could see why her dad loved race cars so much. His sprint car, low to the ground with large wide tires, looked incredibly fast. He always took pride in keeping his things in great shape and looking their best. No one would ever guess this car raced on a muddy track every weekend, the way its polished white body and baby blue roll cage shone against the dark grays of the garage. The big wing on top had the number fifty-seven — a combination of her parents' favorite numbers — in the same blue as the roll cage, with a smaller front wing that read "MaryLou" in baby blue.

Despite her distaste for racing, DonnaMae knew a lot about it. Her dad had once told her that his racing was like her Barbies: he just liked to play with the cars and he could get lost doing it for hours. But that didn't make DonnaMae feel better, because she couldn't play with him, only his friends could. And she wanted him to play Barbies with her. She would love it if he did that. She wouldn't be annoyed or feel like he got in the way. She would be so excited.

DonnaMae yelled again, "Daaaaaaaaaaaaa —" the motor cut out "— aaaaaaadddddddy!"

Her dad crawled halfway out of the race car. "Are you ok, Mae?" Worry flashed across his face.

DonnaMae stood still. She had her daddy's attention all to herself. There was no one else here yet to play with him and his car. None of his friends were here to tease her. It was just her daddy. "I think I have the flu," she said quickly, hugging her tummy.

"Shit," he said, pulling himself the rest of the way through the window of the car and jumping to the ground. "Did you get sick? Are you ok?" her dad placed his hand on her forehead. "You don't feel warm?"

DonnaMae gave a small cough. "I don't feel good. I think I've got the bad bug," she murmured, leaning her head against his stomach and forcing out another cough.

"What doesn't feel good, Mae?" He ran his hand over her head.

She had to think about that. She hadn't planned that far ahead. "Um, my head hurts, Daddy. Maybe we can just stay home tonight and watch boxing or *The Simpsons*."

"Mae, why are you holding your tummy if your head hurts?"

"Because thinking about my tummy hurting makes my head hurt," she said, now rubbing the side of her head.

"Oh, I see." Her dad bent down and hoisted his not-so-little girl up into his arms. "Well, I guess we had better take you inside and put you right back to bed and call the doctor to come check you out. It sounds like you have a cough too, so this must be very serious."

As they left the garage, Allan burst from the house. He had changed his clothes to all black with a black snow cap on his head. "DAD!" he said, "I have a great idea. If I wear this," he pulled the snow cap over his face and peered out through two tiny holes he'd cut for his eyes, "I can sneak into the pits and no one will see me and I can be with you in the pits and help with the..." He pointed at DonnaMae in her dad's arms. "Wait, what's wrong with her?"

"Sis is not feeling well. She might have the flu."

"Wait — what? She was fine earlier when she was jumping on my bed."

DonnaMae laid her head on her dad's shoulder and stuck her tongue out at her brother. "I have the flu bug. Dad can't go racing now."

"What? Nooooo, Dad, I have the best plan ever. It'll work. Look, I even used a black marker to color over the little white tag on my black pants." Allan twisted to show off his handiwork.

Dad continued towards the house while DonnaMae stuck her tongue out at her brother. "We're going inside to call the doctor right now. Allan, you can join us."

"Dad, she's not —"

"I don't need a doctor, Daddy. I'm feeling a little better, but I don't think I should go anywhere."

Allan threw his hands in the air. "Oh, what! No! She's always doing this. You're always such a —"

"Allan, that's enough," Dad said. "Go change your clothes and pack to go camping. Your grandparents will be here in a few hours."

"But Dad, I —"

"Now!"

Allan dropped his hands and hung his head with a defeated sigh.

DonnaMae felt bad about her brother getting yelled at. She loved him, and he looked really cool in his all-black, secret ninja, sneak-into-the-pits costume he made. Maybe he would make her one if she said sorry, but probably not, because he stuck his tongue out at her as he walked past. She wasn't sure why she was lying and she knew it was wrong, but she wanted her daddy's attention and being sick or injured always worked.

Daddy set her down on the couch in the living room and sat next to her. "Mae, do you really not feel good?"

"No, Daddy, but I feel sad, and that makes me not feel good."

"Why are you sad?"

"Because I don't want to go to the races. They're so boring. It's just a bunch of cars going in a circle on a dirt track, and it would be way more fun to stay home and spend time with you."

"I see. Well, Daddy made a commitment to do something, and I have to follow through with that commitment or I'll let other people down. Besides, you're going camping with your grandparents and that's your favorite thing to do."

"Yes, but we're also going to the races and it gets cold, and it's boring."

"But you get to eat peanuts with Grandpa, and we can pack an extra blanket. And when I drive by the stands, if you watch real close, I will wave at you."

DonnaMae sighed and dropped her head back against the couch.

"Did you know you're named after Donna Mae Mims?" Dad asked with a big smile. "She was the first woman to win an SCCA National Championship in 1963, driving a pink car."

DonnaMae had heard the story a thousand times of how her dad had woken up in the middle of the night before her parents had even talked about having kids, and how he'd known what he was going to call his little girl if they had one, because she was going to be a race car driver, because it ran in her blood.

"You know, your mom used to love going to the races," Dad said, pushing hair out of DonnaMae's face.

DonnaMae wanted to be just like her mom, and she wanted her dad to be happy. What she really wanted was just to spend time with her dad. But she loved spending time with her grandpa too, and eating the salty peanuts out of the shells and dropping them on the ground and not having to clean up her mess. Grandpa always took her to get a hot chocolate at the booth when he got his beer.

DonnaMae gave in. "Can I have some money to buy a treat from the confession stands?"

Her dad laughed. "You mean concession stands?" He reached into his pocket and pulled out a five-dollar bill. "Yes, you can have five dollars, but don't lose it."

DonnaMae jumped up, grabbed the five-dollar bill and took off running towards the stairs. She stopped at the bottom and turned back to her dad. "Thank you, Daddy. Sorry for not being honest about my tummy." When she saw his smile, she knew it was ok, and she took off upstairs to tell her brother sorry and that she would buy him a treat too.

The campfire cast a cozy warmth on DonnaMae's face as the smell of bacon and smoke wafted through the air. Her grandpa expertly tossed the bacon around in a pan. The sizzle was music to Donna-Mae's ears.

Camping with her grandparents was one of DonnaMae's favorite things. They owned a spacious lot at Wynoochee Wild-Wood Campgrounds, right by the river. It was perfect — their own little slice of wilderness paradise.

Grandpa Delmar had built a massive rectangular fire pit out of cement, complete with a sturdy grate that he placed over the flames for cooking in his giant square cast-iron pan. DonnaMae loved being his assistant, especially in the early morning when they were the first ones up. She'd crinkle up the newspaper and help him build the fire, a ritual that made her feel like she could be one of her boxcar characters. While the fire crackled and sparked to life, her grandpa would brew a pot of coffee in the percolator and boil water in a kettle for her tea. Then, nestled by the warmth of the fire, he'd tell her stories.

Sometimes, he'd recount his days as head chef in the Korean War, or tales of how he met Grandma Joyce before heading off to war. DonnaMae cherished these stories, especially the ones about her mom. Her favorite was the one where her mom defied the norm by building her own boxcar to race with her brother, despite girls not being allowed. Though she hadn't raced in the official competition, her dad had taken them to the outskirts of town to race down big hills, and DonnaMae's mom wouldn't just race the boys — she'd win.

"Right, Miss Mae!"

Grandpa's voice brought DonnaMae back from her reverie. "What, Grandpa?" she asked, blinking.

"Your grandma was asking what kind of pancakes we wanted, and I said you and I picked fresh blueberries for blueberry pancakes yesterday." He sipped his coffee.

DonnaMae squeezed her mug of tea, then took a long drink. "Yes, please," she said, glancing up at her grandma, who was still standing nearby. "Oh, would you like some help? I can go get the berries."

"Yes, child, that's what I was asking," her grandma said with a chuckle. Then, sharing a glance with Grandpa, "I told you she was still too young to be staying up that late at those races."

"Don't worry, Grandma, I slept through the whole second half on Grandpa's lap," DonnaMae said.

Her grandpa almost spit out his coffee, he laughed so hard.

"I'm not sleepy." DonnaMae jumped from her chair. "I was just thinking about the story Grandpa told me about how he knew you were going to be his wife the moment he saw you."

Grandma's smile lit up her face. "Oh, he said that, did he?" Her eyes twinkled with fond memories. But before any more was said, DonnaMae was in full sprint to retrieve the berries from the barn, and to make extra noise while doing so to wake up her brother, who was still sleeping in the loft.

CHAPTER 6

September, 1995

DonnaMae sat alone on her pink carpet in her bedroom, eagerly pressing the rewind button on her new karaoke machine. It was a gift for her eleventh birthday, but with her busy summer helping out at her grandparents' shop, the Flying A, she'd barely had a chance to use it. Today she was home early and not at the daycare because her dad was busy prepping the car for the final race of the season, and her brother was off somewhere. Since starting junior high, he had made new friends in the neighborhood and was rarely home, leaving DonnaMae with the house all to herself.

As she adjusted the microphone and prepared to sing, a thrill surged through her. She embraced her new dream of becoming a famous singer. That dream was the very reason she had asked for the karaoke machine. She pictured herself on a grand stage, under the spotlight, with a crowd cheering just for her. Her heart fluttered with excitement. Today, with the freedom of an empty house, she could let her imagination run wild and sing as loudly as she wanted.

The best gift from her birthday was the stage her dad had created. He'd transformed an old closet connecting to his room into a cozy bed nook for her by removing the wall and sealing off the connection to his room, and together he and DonnaMae had decorated it with glow in the dark stars, hung a net for her stuffed animals, and added new bedding. Moving her bed to this nook had opened up her room and revealed her large, full-length mirror. They'd framed it with white Christmas lights to create a stage-like feel when she stood in front of it.

While waiting for the cassette tape to rewind, DonnaMae flipped the case and admired Whitney Houston's radiant beauty in a white tank top, her flawless smile showcasing perfect teeth.

DonnaMae glanced in her mirror at her own smile with straight teeth, a feature that her brother did not have. Despite this difference, they still looked almost like twins.

The rewind button on her karaoke machine clicked and popped up. DonnaMae pressed play, gripped the microphone, and jumped to her feet, ready to belt out Whitney's "I Want To Dance With Somebody." As the music filled the room, her heart filled with butterflies as she pretended she was about to walk onto a real stage. DonnaMae watched herself in the mirror as she danced and sang.

By the end of the song, she had worked up a sweat and was thirsty. Hovering her finger over the pause button, she debated whether to let the next song play so she could get to "Love Will Save The Day," or play "I Want To Dance With Somebody" one more time. Deciding to take a break, she set the mic down on top of the speaker, letting the song play as she headed downstairs for water. She had to be fast. She didn't want to deal with rewinding to find the start of the song if it played past it.

She dashed into the kitchen and didn't even notice her dad's friend Barney standing at the fridge until she crashed into him.

"Oh, sorry! I didn't see you. I —"

"Was that you singing upstairs?" Barney asked, cutting her off. A smile took over DonnaMae's face, but before she could respond, he continued, "Or do you have a dying cow up there you're trying to save?"

Her smile vanished instantly as he burst into laughter. She dropped her gaze.

"You'd better get back to your cow, Miss Mae. I don't hear her. Maybe she died." Barney chuckled as he walked out of the kitchen.

DonnaMae stood frozen until she heard the back door shut. *Dying cow? Did I really sound that bad?* The comment shouldn't have surprised her. Her dad's friends always said the stupidest things and thought they were so funny. But this one felt different. She couldn't just laugh and make fun of herself with him. This felt like a punch right in the gut.

DonnaMae walked to the sink, took a glass from the cabinet, and turned on the faucet. As her glass filled with water, her excitement drained. She stared at the water, feeling the sting of Barney's words replaying in her mind.

Back upstairs, Whitney had already started singing "Love Will Save The Day." DonnaMae dropped on the floor next to her karaoke machine and hit the stop button. "Ain't no love saving my day," she said with a huff, throwing herself onto the floor and staring at her ceiling. *I sound like a dying cow! Whitney, how did you get so good? Why do I suck at everything I do?* Sadness and frustration built up inside her. She closed her eyes and squeezed them tight, trying to hold everything in.

"Don't be weak. So, you can't sing. Who cares?" she told herself, trying to sound brave. "Don't be so mean. You can still dance. You're the best at crafting and ..." DonnaMae paused, fighting back tears. She wanted to give herself the kind of love her mom would have given her if she were here, but right now, she felt so alone and couldn't think of anything.

Now she wished she wasn't alone. She wished her brother was in his room next door to hers, but he was out with his stupid new friends. If she knew her sister Carmel's new phone number, she would call her, but her sister had moved again. It didn't matter — DonnaMae was used to being alone, or with a bunch of dumb guys and her dad. Sometimes her dad would bring a female friend over, and DonnaMae would get excited to meet another girl, but they never stayed long, and she would never see them again. His male friends always seemed to stay.

"MOM, why did you have to leave me? Why do I have to face all this alone? No one understands me, and I hate being the only girl." As these words escaped her, so did a single tear. No matter how hard she tried, she couldn't fight the sadness of missing the mom she never knew. When it hit her, she couldn't seem to stop it.

"And that's a wrap for the summer of ninety-five, brought to you by yours truly, on your favorite station, KIX 95.3," a cheerful voice announced over the radio, just as Tim McGraw's "Don't Take the Girl" filled DonnaMae's room through the speaker of her small radio alarm clock. DonnaMae hit the button on top of the clock, turning it off, and pulled the covers over her head. Barney's words, *Dying cow*, echoed through her mind. She let out a low groan and pulled the covers tighter around her ears, trying to block out the memory.

Under her blanket, the air became thick and hard to breathe. Annoyed, DonnaMae tossed the covers back and sat up in bed. "I'm awake now, I might as well get up," she grumbled as she swung her legs over the side of her bed. Ignoring her fuzzy slippers, she stumbled to the light and flicked it on. As she turned back around, the first thing she noticed was the karaoke machine left in the middle of the room, its shiny buttons glinting in the morning light, mocking her. The events of yesterday played vividly in her mind. DonnaMae sighed deeply and moved the karaoke machine back under the rack of cassettes, her fingers tracing its edges. She couldn't help but wonder if she should just throw it away. It wasn't like she had any plans to sing into it again. She bent down, picked up her treasured Whitney Houston cassette case, and carefully removed the tape from the player.

Placing it back in its case, she slid it into the only open slot on the rack.

Running her hand over the neatly organized tapes, she whispered to herself, "Go help your dying cow... Err, you're a dying cow!" she growled, her hands balling into fists.

The bright white title *The Judds* caught her eye. Her favorite album, "Rockin' with the Rhythm," with its first song "Have Mercy," always lifted her spirits.

At her grandparents' car shop, DonnaMae loved working in the stereo room, where cassettes lined the walls from floor to ceiling. This cassette was special for her and her grandma; they would always sing and dance to it together. Every time DonnaMae helped at the shop, her grandma would let her pick out a few new cassettes, which was how she'd acquired her extensive collection. Her grandpa had once found an extra wall mount for cassettes at the shop. It had a little crack at the top, and he was going to toss it out, but DonnaMae asked him for it, and he let her have it. She was so short she couldn't even see the broken part, and now it held all of her favorite cassettes.

As DonnaMae looked at her collection, memories of happy moments with her grandparents made her smile. She put on "Rockin' with the Rhythm" and let the music wash over her, hoping it would help her forget Barney's cruel words and remember the joy singing brought her.

DonnaMae pulled *The Judds* cassette from its slot. Wynonna and her mom looked more like sisters than mother and daughter. They were both so pretty. How cool would it be to be a famous singer with your mom? She let out a small laugh. "How cool would it be to just have a mom?" she said, her voice filled with longing.

"Rise and shine, monkey butt," DonnaMae's dad called, popping his head into her room.

DonnaMae turned to face him, forcing a smile. She wanted to be mad at him for what Barney had said, but it wasn't his fault. He didn't even know. What was she supposed to do? Tell on his friend? If she told him now, she would get the "love yourself for who you are" speech, or the "just look in a mirror, you are just like your mom — she was so strong and didn't care what anyone thought" lecture. So, she knew exactly what to do: paint a smile on her face and move on like everything was perfect.

"Or should I say the monkey butt has rised and is already shining?" Dad added with a grin.

"I don't think 'rised' is a word, Dad," DonnaMae said, giving him a half eye roll. "I think it would be 'risen' or 'raised' or... I don't actually know."

"It's a word in my book today," he laughed. "Come on downstairs and I will make —"

"Pancakes!" she finished for him.

"Maybe I was going to make meatloaf?"

"Eww, not for breakfast!"

"Hey, you never know, it might be good. Breakfast in ten minutes, ok?" He disappeared back down the hallway.

DonnaMae took a deep breath, trying to shake off the lingering hurt. As she stepped out of her room, she heard the faint sound of music coming from Allan's room. She knocked on his door. "Allan, are you up?"

"Yeah, yeah, I'm up," he said, opening the door. Allan stood in just his boxers, his hair sticking up in all directions, and a song she hadn't heard before swirled around her, making her want to dance.

"Who is this?" a real smile spread on her face as she bobbed her head to the beat. "I like it."

He rubbed his hand over his messy hair. "It's Hootie and the Blowfish, 'Hold my Hand.'" He chuckled, "If you weren't always listening to that country shit, you would know this song." Then he closed the door.

DonnaMae tapped to the beat on the door. "Hurry up, Dad's making pancakes," she said, trying to sound enthusiastic.

"No shit? Pancakes?" Allan yelled back at her through the

door.

DonnaMae laughed and headed downstairs to the kitchen, where the smell of sizzling bacon and freshly brewed coffee filled the air. Her dad was at the stove, humming a tune as he cooked.

"Good morning again," he said with a warm smile. "Orange juice is on the table."

"Thanks, Daddy," she said, pouring herself a glass.

A few minutes later, Allan shuffled into the kitchen, fully dressed but still looking half-asleep, and plopped down at the table.

"Order up," their dad announced, sliding a plate of hot dog buns in front of them. "Eat up. We've got to leave for school soon." With a smirk, he strolled away from the table.

"Can't wait," Allan said sarcastically, but DonnaMae's gaze lingered on the glossy golden-brown buns.

"Um, are those hot dog buns?"

Returning to the table with a jar of peanut butter and a bowl of strawberries, Dad declared in a thick French accent, "They are French buns." He sat down, grabbing a bun. He spread peanut butter on each side, and placed a row of strawberries where one would normally lay a hot dog, before closing it up and taking a big bite. "What are you two waiting for? This is delicious!"

Following suit, DonnaMae and Allan assembled their own French buns. "Wow, this is really good!" DonnaMae said through a mouthful.

Allan devoured one in record time and was already on to his second. Their dad chuckled, looking at the plate with only a few buns left. "I was getting tired of pancakes, and we needed to use these buns before they went bad, so...!" He waved his hand dramatically over his creation.

After breakfast, the three of them grabbed their stuff and headed out to Dad's old white truck.

"Shotgun!" DonnaMae called, racing to the passenger door.

"I'm walking to school, so you don't have to call shotgun every day," Allan laughed.

"Fine," DonnaMae said, sticking her tongue out at Allan before climbing into the truck. She rolled down the window, "Have a good day. Love you, Brother."

"Love ya, too," Allan said. He waved before beginning his walk to junior high.

Dad started the truck and "Who'll Stop the Rain" by John Fogerty played on the radio. Normally, this song would have been a perfect fit for their little hometown in the rainy Pacific Northwest, but today it wasn't raining, so Dad sang, "Someone has stopped the rain."

DonnaMae cherished these drives to school with her dad, with the windows down and the morning breeze ruffling their hair, Dad singing along to the radio, making up lyrics and cracking jokes. He was such a dork, but DonnaMae loved it. This time felt special to her, because it was just the two of them with no distractions. She had her dad all to herself, and she was the center of his attention.

"Want to stop at Jack in the Box and get a tea?" Dad asked as the song came to an end. "I could go for a coffee today."

"Yes, please!" DonnaMae laughed as her dad turned into the drive-thru before she even finished answering. This was one of her favorite things about driving to school with her dad. Sometimes they would stop and get a donut, but today, tea was the comfort she needed.

After they pulled out of the drive-thru, Dad handed DonnaMae his coffee and held her cup of tea out the window as he drove. The tea was always too hot for her to drink right away, so this was his way of cooling it down for her.

"Careful, Daddy," DonnaMae said, watching tea splash out of the cup into the wind, missing her dad's hand by inches. "Don't burn yourself like last time."

"And *you* don't drink all my coffee this time," Dad said, flashing her a smile.

"Gross." DonnaMae made a gagging sound. "I don't even like

the smell of it."

Her dad pulled his arm back in. "Well then, I guess we had better trade drinks."

"Gladly." DonnaMae's tea had cooled to the perfect temperature. She took her first sip, feeling the warmth spread from the inside out.

Dad rolled up the window. "So, what's on the agenda for today? Any Lisa Frank club meetings?"

"Dad, we don't have that anymore," DonnaMae said. She still had all her Lisa Frank erasers, stationery, and stickers — she had even asked for the bed set for Christmas. But the club had fizzled out. DonnaMae still hung out with the girls at school, but she wasn't that close with them. It was hard not living close to the school. After weekends and summers, she always felt like she was coming into a book series without having read the first book, not knowing half the things going on. Now that her dad's daycare was up and running, she always walked there after school. She had some kids she walked with and knew well enough because they grew up together, but she was only really friends with Kat. Even then, Kat had more friends she was closer to than DonnaMae.

"Do you have any new kids coming to the daycare today?" DonnaMae asked, changing the subject.

"Let's hope so, but none are scheduled to come in," her dad said. The daycare had started to pick up. Initially, parents were hesitant to bring their kids to a man-owned, man-run facility, but after a newspaper article highlighted it as his late wife's dream, things began to improve. The all-female staff also probably helped.

DonnaMae nodded, taking another sip of her tea. She admired her dad's determination and the love he put into running the daycare. Despite the challenges, he made it work, and she felt proud of him for keeping her mom's dream alive. The thought of her mom's legacy brought a smile to her face as they pulled up to the school.

Her dad parked and turned to her with a warm smile. "Have a

great day, I love you."

"Thanks, Dad." She jumped out of the truck, leaving the rest of her tea in the cup holder. She wished she could take it with her. Especially because she'd have to spend the day sitting next to Rachael again at their group table.

Rachael was mean. And, as usual, she spent most of the day making fun of DonnaMae.

By the end of the day, DonnaMae anxiously watched the clock from her desk. School would be out in fifteen minutes, and she couldn't wait to walk to the daycare with the other kids. She loved that they got to adventure out on their own, like the boxcar children.

"We have two weeks until our Valentine's Day party," the teacher said as she took a stack of papers off her desk and walked around the room to hand them out, "so before we go home today we are going to make our classmates list and draw out our plans for our mailboxes."

"Can my mom come to our party?" a girl asked from the other side of the room.

"Oh, I want mine to come too," Kat whispered across the table to DonnaMae.

"Oh, maybe mine too," DonnaMae said, then giggled. "Well, my da—"

"Your mom is dead," Rachael said, staring at DonnaMae. "How is she going to come?"

"My mom might be dead," DonnaMae shot back, "but your mom is ugly and — "

Rachael slapped DonnaMae hard across the face.

DonnaMae froze. She had never been hit before, other than from her brother. She slowly touched her cheek and her other hand formed a tight fist as rage filled her. *Hit her back or tell the teacher*, repeated rapidly in her mind. DonnaMae's hand shot straight into the air and she blurted as loudly as she could, "Miss Quinn, Rachael just slapped me in the face."

"I did not!" Rachael yelled back.

"Yes, you did," DonnaMae said.

"Ok, ok children, settle down and keep your hands to your-self," Miss Quinn said, giving them both a frustrated glare.

"What?" DonnaMae cried in disbelief. "She just slapped me hard in the –"

"That's enough, Mae, you are disrupting the class." Miss Quinn's voice was stern.

"So much for doing the right thing and telling the teacher," DonnaMae grumbled. *She didn't even bother to look at me*, she thought, her anger growing.

"Hit her back," Matt said on the other side of DonnaMae.

"Hit me back and I will kick your ass," said Rachael. "Plus, Mae is too much of a wimp to do anything but tattle."

The other kids at her table kept talking, but DonnaMae stopped listening. *You're a wimp, a dying cow. Your mom is dead. You look like a little boy.* She had heard it all, and it was getting old.

DING, DING, DING

The bell ringing brought DonnaMae back to her surround-ings. Kids were heading out the door and DonnaMae grabbed her things and headed out herself. There was a huddle of kids outside the doors. They slowly surrounded DonnaMae when she walked out, all chattering to her at the same time. She only caught pieces of what everyone was saying.

"Fight —"

"After school —"

"She won't show —"

"Meet here at three-thirty —"

"Playground —"

"Wait, stop, what are you all talking about?" DonnaMae finally shouted above everyone else.

Matt stepped forward, "You meeting Rachael here to kick her ass."

DonnaMae looked around. More than half her class

surrounded her. *A fight?* Her heart raced. She was tired of being picked on and pushed around, laughing along while others laughed at her. Maybe this was the answer. Maybe it was time she stood up for herself.

"FINE!" she said, "I'll do it!"

Everyone got excited, reaching out and touching her arms and shoulders with random words of encouragement.

"I'll go tell her to meet on the playground at three-thirty." Then she amended, "Make it three-forty-five. I need to run and ask my dad if I can first."

"What?" Kat laughed. "You're going to ask your dad if you can fight a girl after school?"

"Yeah, he needs to know where I am and what I'm doing and —" DonnaMae stopped when she realized everyone was looking at her funny.

"Ok, well, let's start walking," Matt said, throwing his backpack over his shoulder to lead the group of friends on their way.

They walked so fast that they beat the bus that dropped off the after school kids to the daycare. DonnaMae opened the front doors and waved her friends in to follow. From the end of the front hall walkway she could see straight through the building to where her dad was alone on the upper level, getting a snack ready for the kids. "Come on guys, follow me."

All six kids followed DonnaMae through the daycare.

"Daddy!" she hollered as she got closer. She picked up her pace when she had his attention, but didn't run. She knew better. *Walking feet inside, please*, she imagined him saying.

"Dad, Daddy... Dad."

"Mae, DonnaMae, Mae," he replied as she reached him.

"I have something to ask you and — well, tell you — and, um... Well, I guess I need your help." She spoke so quickly that she wasn't even sure what she'd said.

"Does it have anything to do with the gang of kids you have

following you? Cause if you all just came for snacks, I need to go get more."

"Ohh I am hungry. Lunch today wasn't pizza like they said. It was some —"

"Mae," her dad cut her off.

"Oh yeah, sorry. Ok, so today in class a girl made a joke about mom being dead, so I called her mom ugly and she slapped me across the face... Like, hard, Dad... It hurt! But I didn't cry or say ouch. I did the right thing."

"You punched her in the face?" her dad asked, setting down the snack tray before giving her his full attention.

"Umm, no, Dad. Ohh, can I have an apple slice, please?" She held out her hand. "I raised my hand and told the teacher. And then she told us to keep our hands to ourselves and did nothing."

"Yeah, the teacher did nothing about it," Matt jumped in, "so Rachael said to meet her at the school at three-thirty and she was going to kick Mae's butt."

DonnaMae reached over and grabbed an apple slice since her dad was not giving her one. "Yeah, something like that. Anyway, so what do I do?"

"Well, you had better get your ass back down to that school and kick her ass," her dad said. He picked up the tray of sliced apples and gram crackers and held it out for DonnaMae and all her friends to take some.

"Wait, what? You're going to send me back down to the school to fight?"

"You can't not show up. You will be the laughingstock of your class. And if you say you're going to show up to something, you had better show up."

"Ok, but Dad, there's one problem... I don't know how to fight!"

"Sure, you do. You fight with your brother all the time. Keep your hands up, always protect yourself, and this is how you make a proper fist so you don't go breaking your thumb," her dad demonstrated by closing his hand into a tight fist, fingers curled into the palm, thumb outside the fingers to create a solid structure. "Knuckles aligned to the front, and the wrist remains straight," he said, punching the air.

With her friends high-fiving and cheering, DonnaMae's heart raced. She wasn't sure if she should be excited or terrified.

"Just don't throw the first punch, and then it's self-defense," her dad said. "But you guys have fifteen minutes until 3:30, so you better run and come back after."

DonnaMae gave her dad a big hug, not really wanting to let go, but also ready to go kick someone's ass. She snatched one more apple slice before going. Her friends followed her out the door and with each step, her fear created a nervous energy that made her walk faster.

***

"BROOOOOOOOOOOOTHER!" DonnaMae came crashing through the house, her voice echoing off the walls before her dad even stepped inside.

"I'm right here," Allan said before she could reach the stairs.

DonnaMae spun around to find her brother on the couch, his eyes wide with surprise. "You are not going to believe my day. I got slapped by a girl in class and —"

"Wait, what?" Allan's notebook dropped from his hand to the coffee table with a dull thud, next to an unopened box of Gobstoppers.

DonnaMae had his full attention. Too excited to sit down, she paced back and forth in front of the coffee table, her hands gesturing wildly as she spilled every detail of her story.

"Mae," her dad's voice cut in, "you left the back door wide —" DonnaMae stopped mid-stride and turned to look at her dad, a frown creasing his forehead. "You ok, Son?"

DonnaMae glanced back at her brother. Allan's arms were

crossed tightly over his chest, his knuckles white from the pressure.

"No, Dad, I'm not ok!" Allan threw his hands out towards DonnaMae in frustration. "I can't believe you sent Mae back down to the school to fight some girl. What if —"

"Let me finish the story," DonnaMae cut him off, her voice firm but still tinged with excitement. She resumed her pacing, trying to remember where she left off. "So... We walked to the school. I was so excited, but nervous, and well, you name it, I was feeling it. I think at one point I wanted to puke, but I didn't." She paused with a wide smile, hands on her hips, still holding her dad's and brothers' attention, even though her dad already knew what happened. "We all got to school and waited, but she never showed up. I was ready, though!" She resumed pacing. "I would've punched her right in the throat just like Dad says," she said, throwing a wild air punch that sent a jolt up her arm and made her smile even bigger. "Kat had her watch on, so we just played on the playground but she never came. Over half my class showed up, and I can't wait for tomorrow when everyone asks her where she was. She wanted to kick my ass and didn't even show! Now she'll be the laughingstock!"

Allan's brows furrowed deeper, his lips pressing into a thin line. "What was your plan if she showed up, Mae?" he asked, crossing his arms again.

"I was going to kick her ass," she said, shadow-fighting her invisible opponent, "just like Dad said. I would have pulled her hair right out of her head and kicked her in the — well — ok, she doesn't have a 'where the sun don't shine' spot, but I would have still kicked her there."

"I think you might need to learn how to fight first before you go around picking fights with people, Mae," Allan said, glaring at her.

She stopped and stared at him, "I'm always being picked on, and this time she wasn't just picking on me, but Mom. It was time I stood up for myself." Her smile was gone now.

"This just doesn't sound like you, Mae. You don't like it when people get made fun of, and you don't like hurting —"

Their dad cut Allan off, "I'm proud of you, Sis. Now, how does meatloaf and mashed potatoes sound for dinner?"

"That sounds perfect, Daddy," DonnaMae said in her baby voice, a tone she knew Allan couldn't stand. "Thanks. I'm gonna go do my homework."

As her dad and Allan headed towards the kitchen, DonnaMae felt a flicker of anger that her brother wasn't proud of her, but she knew he was just worried. He would eventually tell her how proud he was, and he might even share some Gobstoppers. She decided to ask him for help with her punching practice, at least as much as he could offer. She figured he didn't know much about fighting either, but he must know more than she did. After all, he was a boy.

In truth, DonnaMae was relieved that Rachael hadn't shown up. The thought of hurting anyone made her feel queasy. She actually felt sad for Rachael. Why was she so mean? She must have learned it from somewhere. Someone in her life was probably treating her poorly, and that was sad. But DonnaMae didn't want her dad or her brother to know that. She wanted them to think she was just as tough as they were.

As DonnaMae climbed the stairs to her room, the muffled voices of her dad and Allan drifted from the kitchen. She paused to listen.

"Damn, Son, did you drink half the milk after school? Maybe try having water. Milk is expensive — have a glass, not the whole thing. Geez."

Relieved that she wasn't the topic of their conversation, DonnaMae laughed quietly. As she continued up the stairs, her thoughts raced.

What would I have done if Rachael had shown up? Could I have taken a punch? Could I have thrown a punch? Would I ever really hurt anyone?

CHAPTER 7

October, 1996

"I can't believe this still fits me!" DonnaMae said, twirling in a circle so her skirt flew up around her.

"You haven't changed much since fifth grade, Mae," Allan said, carrying his empty cereal bowl to the sink. "That was only last year."

"Almost two years is a long time, Allan," DonnaMae said, hands on her hips. "I was ten when I wore this last, and I'm almost twelve now. That's a big difference."

"Right," Allan said, shaking his head, "I'm not sure it works like that, but whatever. It's a felt circle with the center cut out and some Velcro. I think you could be a fifties girl for the next ten Halloweens if you wanted to be." He laughed.

Grandma Joyce had made the skirt for the fifties social that their grade school put on every year. A few of the teachers had a band, and they played 1950's music all night while DonnaMae and Allan danced until their feet hurt. "Rockin Robin", was her favorite song. DonnaMae had worn the skirt that her mom had made for her until she could no longer get it around her hips, then Grandma made her this red one with a white poodle and black music notes on it.

"At least I'm dressing up," DonnaMae said. "What are you going to be, Mr. Middle Schooler, too-cool-for-Halloween?" She straightened her skirt, picked up the box of Cheerios, and poured some into a bowl, singing "Rockin' Robin" as she went.

"I put the blueberries in the fridge," Allan told her. "There's a hard-boiled egg for you, too. And I love Halloween just as much as you, if not more. You'll see." He walked out of the kitchen.

DonnaMae chuckled softly to herself as she finished preparing her breakfast and settled down to eat. She whispered to the ceiling, "He's your son."

In December, it would be eight years since her mom's passing, yet DonnaMae still spoke to her. Sometimes, she caught her dad doing the same thing and wondered if it was normal. However, she questioned what truly defined "normal." Their life was far from normal, but they made it work, and she liked it.

DonnaMae tipped her bowl back and drank the last of the blueberry-flavored milk just as her dad yelled, "Heeellooo," in the silliest girly voice she had ever heard.

Walking over to the sink she hollered back, "Heeellooo, anyone home?"

"Heeellooo, I think I'm going to need some help puttin' on my bra." Dad poked his head into the kitchen.

At the sight of him, DonnaMae busted out with laughter. She'd known what he was dressing up as for Halloween because they'd all gone shopping at Salvation Army together for costume parts, but she hadn't seen his costume yet.

Halloween was a big deal for their family and they always went all out. DonnaMae's mom had adored all holidays and celebrated them with great enthusiasm, and Halloween was no exception. Dad's favorite story to tell Allan and DonnaMae was about when their mom dressed them up as little old people. He had made a mini walker for DonnaMae and a small cane for Allan, and their mom sprayed their hair gray and white. They were only five and seven at the time. It was their last real Halloween together as a family, because the next year Mom was too sick to do anything. Dad promised her he would continue their traditions and her love for the holidays, and he definitely fulfilled that promise.

He walked into the kitchen now, wearing a frilly floral blouse, a skirt, and pantyhose, and holding a bra in one hand and high heels and a clutch in the other. "I have no idea how you ladies wear these pantyhose," he said, twisting his waist back and forth in his skirt. "Wow, they are so itchy."

"Well, we shave our legs and, umm, well, we don't have, umm, you know..." DonnaMae let out a little giggle and covered her mouth.

"You mean you don't have any balls," Allan said, reappearing in a cut-up and bloody shirt. He patted his dad on the shoulder as he walked by. "Looking good, old man. Or should I say, old woman."

"Well, this woman has little to no experience putting on bras and makeup," Dad said in his girly voice. "Sooo, can you help a poor little lady out?"

"Dad, I think you need to work on your Mimi voice," DonnaMae said, walking over to him and taking the bra out of his hand. "Maybe you should watch an episode of The Drew Carey Show before you go to work. Also, you need to take your shirt off before you put your bra on."

Her dad removed the frilly blouse before slipping his arms through the bra straps, and DonnaMae fastened it behind him. "Brother, will you get the pudding balloons out of the fridge so we can give our dad some boobs?"

"I can't believe you thought of this, Sis," Allan said, pulling out two water balloons filled with pudding from the fridge.

"Oh, it's not my idea, it's from the movie *Now and Then*. Teeny says that Jell-O is too jiggly and pudding has a heavier, more realistic texture."

"Dad, who is going to be feeling your pudding boobies?" Allan said, handing over the vanilla balloon boobs.

"Ain't nobody gonna be touching my vanilla boobies, or I will kick them where the sun don't shine," Dad said, still perfecting his Mimi voice.

"There you go Dad, all set, now we just need to paint your eyelids with so much blue eyeshadow you look like a clown." DonnaMae picked up the little plastic bag of makeup.

"Yeah, there's just one problem." Allan smirked at DonnaMae. "None of us know how to put on makeup."

"I can try, Dad," DonnaMae said. "It can't be that hard. I mean, I read lots of girl magazines that show you how to do it."

"Remember when you wanted to be a hairdresser?" Allan laughed, "Not sure that turned out so well for a few of your barbies."

"Just because I don't wear it doesn't mean I don't know how, Brother," DonnaMae snapped back. "Also, I was like five. Every girl wants to be a hairstylist and do their dolls' hair."

"Ok!" their dad said, giving them both the "that's enough" look. "Your sister doesn't wear makeup because she is perfect and beautiful just the way she is."

"I'm not sure about the perfect part, Dad, but yeah, Sis, you are fine without it." Allan gave one more laugh, "But I would still protect your face, Dad."

"Oooooohhh, I know I am fine," DonnaMae said with a quick twist. "Do you see this fifties skirt?" She turned to look at her dad and then burst out laughing. "And dad, I can't take you seriously looking like this."

"Hey, I've always said when you need me to be your mom, I'll put on my high heels and do the best I can." Her dad slipped his feet into his very large, bright blue high heel shoes. "Oh wow, but I also never said I would walk in them. Maybe just put them on."

They all burst out laughing as he tried to walk around the kitchen in his high heels and pudding-balloon-filled bra with no shirt.

"Someone... please..." Allan gasped through his laughter, "go get... a camera!"

"I think I have a little film left on my keychain camera!" DonnaMae darted from the kitchen to get it.

After school that day, DonnaMae skipped up the steps of the Kids Place Daycare. She loved that her dad had finished her mom's dream, and she loved the daycare even more on holidays. Her dad had outdone himself this year for Halloween. A mound of dirt in the front parking lot had been transformed into a burial ground with handmade headstones. Plastic jack-o'-lanterns replaced the shades on the giant lamp posts that framed the building, casting a warm, orange glow, and cobwebs hung everywhere, adding to the spooky but fun atmosphere.

As she entered the building, DonnaMae's excitement grew with the sounds of laughter and the smell of freshly popped popcorn mingled with a hint of caramel. She couldn't wait to find out what her dad had planned for snacks. She was starving, and it was sure to be a yummy treat.

The main hall looked like a haunted house for little kids, strewn with cobwebs and spooky decorations. DonnaMae grinned when she spotted a group of kids dressed as witches, superheroes, and ghosts, all giggling and showing off their costumes. There was even a little Barney the dinosaur.

Halloween music grew louder as DonnaMae approached the side door that lead to the play area outside. When she opened the door, she couldn't believe her eyes. Her dad had transformed the whole play area into a carnival. There was a popcorn ball-making booth, a bobbing-for-apples station, a caramel apple-making area, a ring toss, and someone serving punch out of a giant cauldron. Dad had even turned the grassy area into a pumpkin patch. She spotted him there, sitting on the ground in his skirt and frilly blouse with a woman DonnaMae had never seen before. Beside them, the cutest little girl in a ladybug costume was tapping on a pumpkin. The little girl looked to be about three years old.

DonnaMae thought the woman and the little girl must be new to the daycare. A few parents were there volunteering, but DonnaMae recognized every one of them — it was always the same group that showed up for the fun events her dad held at the daycare.

The play area was filled with laughter and kids running around in their costumes. DonnaMae inhaled the delicious scents of caramel and popcorn mixed with the crisp autumn air as she passed the popcorn ball-making booth and watched as kids shaped the sticky, sweet popcorn into balls, their faces lit with excitement. Her stomach growled and her mouth salivated at the thought of making one to eat for herself.

Ignoring her hunger, she continued to the pumpkin patch. "Hey, Dad!" she called out as she neared.

Her dad looked up from his conversation with the new woman and smiled warmly at DonnaMae. The little girl in the ladybug costume looked up too, her big eyes curious and full of wonder.

"Mae!" Dad called out in the same silly voice he'd used that morning. "What do you think?" He spread his arms wide to encompass the carnival.

"It's amazing," said DonnaMae. "You really outdid yourself this year! And it sounds like you're getting your girly voice down." She pointed towards his heels, no longer on his feet but resting next to the pumpkin on the ground. "The heels, however?"

The woman next to her dad guffawed and quickly covered her mouth, almost knocking off her thick round glasses, but not before a snort escaped.

DonnaMae held back her laughter, not wanting the woman to think she was laughing at her.

Dad laughed. "Yeah, my feet are killing me!" He indicated the woman beside him. "Mae, this is Elise. Elise, this is my daughter Mae."

Elise dropped her hand from her mouth and extended the other towards DonnaMae. "Nice to meet you. Your dad has told me a lot about you." She had wispy, shoulder-length brown hair, and no costume. Who didn't dress up on Halloween? DonnaMae thought.

DonnaMae raised an eyebrow at her dad as she shook Elise's hand.

He smiled, gesturing to the little girl beside him. "And this is Adaline," he said, resting a hand on the girl's shoulder.

DonnaMae bent down on one knee to join them on the ground. "Well, hello, little miss ladybug. I sure do love your costume."

Adaline only responded with a smile, but her big eyes and rosy cheeks were better than words. They warmed DonnaMae to the core.

"Today is their first day," Dad explained. "Elise was just picking up Adaline, but they had to get a pumpkin first."

DonnaMae turned to Elise. "Yes, and you have to paint it!" she pointed towards the pumpkin painting booth. Glancing back at Adaline, she said, "Your daughter looks just like you, except as a ladybug."

"I think it's just a mother-daughter thing. I look just like my mom as well."

DonnaMae stood. "I wouldn't know. Mine is dead."

Elise's face turned red.

DonnaMae knew that was her cue to get out of there before she got the "Oh gosh, you poor thing," and pity eyes. She shrugged, "I'm starving. I'm going to go try out the caramel apple booth. It was nice meeting you." She spun off towards the booth, but not before hearing Elise apologize profusely to her dad.

"Oh gosh, I am so sorry."

DonnaMae knew Elise meant nothing by saying it was a mother-daughter thing, and Elise probably knew DonnaMae's mom was dead. Everyone knew her dad had started the daycare in his late wife's memory. DonnaMae had even seen women fall for him because of it. It was probably the big article the newspaper had done on her dad and the daycare. Small town news travels fast, she thought. She had met a few of those women as her dad's new friends, but they didn't stick around. It actually made DonnaMae laugh when she thought about it.

But why was she just mean to the new woman and her adorable little girl? It wasn't like that woman would want anything to do with DonnaMae's dad, who was wearing a full face of makeup and a skirt with high heels. DonnaMae had no idea why she was rude, and she honestly didn't care, but she was excited to get to see more of that little lady bug at the daycare. She made a mental note to remind her dad to touch up his lipstick and eyeshadow later. But for now, she was famished and couldn't wait to sink her teeth into one of those caramel apples.

CHAPTER 8

September, 1997

DonnaMae sat cross legged on the floor in front of the expansive mirror in her bedroom, eyes fixed on the cover of a well-worn *Seventeen Magazine* from 1994. She had stumbled upon it a few weeks ago, tucked away in a box belonging to her older sister. The girl featured on the cover was gorgeous, wearing a cropped black-and-white striped turtleneck with short sleeves and white pants. She had a flat and muscular tummy, perfectly styled long, dirty blonde hair, and sun-kissed skin. Beside her, a featured article titled "When the worst happens: my mom died" caught DonnaMae's eye. Was this why Carmel had saved this issue? Did she feel like she'd lost a mother, too, even though her mom was still alive? DonnaMae shook the thoughts away. She didn't want to read that article, she had already lived it. It was the article featured above it in bold pink letters that had enticed her to pick up the magazine: "Makeovers." The magazine was only three years old, so DonnaMae figured the stuff inside couldn't be that outdated. She flipped it open to page thirty-six, on how to have the girl on the cover's perfect face. Leaving her finger there to hold her place, she returned to the cover. The model's eyeliner was on point — that was what DonnaMae wanted to learn.

She wondered if she might want to be a model when she grew up, like the girl on the magazine cover. Everyone would know her, love her, and think she was perfect. She imagined strutting down runways, posing for photo shoots, and basking in the crowd's applause. The idea thrilled her. It would be like being a famous singer, but without the need to sing or even speak. She wouldn't have to worry about being compared to a dying cow.

Today was her first day of middle school and DonnaMae felt excited, but also nervous. Her brother had made new friends who lived close by and she couldn't wait to walk to school with all of them. She wanted to look her best so she could make new friends and be cool.

DonnaMae eagerly returned to her marked page and began reading aloud, "How to Get Your Best Friend's Hair." As she scanned the page, she didn't find any information about makeup, let alone eyeliner. "Ugh, that's not helpful," she groaned, tossing the magazine aside.

On the floor in front of her was a little kids' pink makeup kit she'd gotten for Christmas a few years ago. It had some overly pink blush with a small brush and some clear lip gloss, but no eyeliner. She faced her reflection. Her eyes were what she loved most about herself. They were a vibrant shade of blue with tiny streaks that resembled lightning bolts. People always complimented her eyes. If she had eyeliner, she could make them even more noticeable, just like the girl on the cover of the magazine.

Struck by an idea, she leaped up and rushed to her small desk filled with craft materials. She rummaged until she found a black permanent marker. She paused, then quickly went back to grab the entire box of art supplies.

She dropped back down in front of her mirror, set the box on top of the magazine, and pulled the lid off the black permanent marker. Using one hand to hold her eye closed, she delicately traced a thin line with the marker just above her eyelashes.

Her dad's words rang in her thoughts: *If you want to see what your mother was like, just look at yourself in the mirror.* She exhaled slowly, fogging her mirror. *A lot of good that does,* she replied to herself, wiping off the fog and switching eyes.

She blinked and refocused on her handiwork. "Not bad. I think you're supposed to do the bottom, but —"

A wave of sadness cut her sentence short, and her reflection blurred as tears threatened to surface. *How in the hell is looking at myself in a mirror supposed to replace the fact that I don't have a mom to teach me this shit?* she thought as she fanned her face and blinked back her tears.

She knew her dad's response would be, "You don't need to wear makeup. Your mom never did. You are beautiful just the way you are!" But he didn't understand. DonnaMae liked the way she looked — she just wanted to be more of a girl, and to fit in.

When her vision cleared, she saw how much her eyes stood out with just a hint of eyeliner and satisfaction bloomed, outweighing all other emotions. She lifted her chest and pulled the magazine up close to inspect the cover girl's face. She couldn't think of anything she could use for eye shadow, but she might have something that would work for her lips. In her craft box, she found a pallet of watercolor paints. Scratching her fingernail over the light pink, she created a dust that she pinched up and rubbed between her fingers. It lightly stained her finger pink, giving her an idea.

She took the clear lip gloss from her kids' makeup kit and squeezed a little on top of her hand, then scratched some powder from the blush and tapped it beside the gloss. Using her hand as a pallet, she mixed dust from the brown and bright red watercolor paints with the blush and swirled it all together with the gloss, creating a chocolaty red color like the girl in the magazine wore. Carefully, DonnaMae applied a touch of the mixture to her lips with her finger and then rubbed her lips together to smooth it out.

"Now for just a little blush," she said with a smile, and dusted her kids' blush over her cheeks. "Oww," she cringed at the pink streaks on her pale complexion. "Well, this is for sure not my color," she laughed, dropping the brush and rubbing her hands in circles on her face to spread the color or even remove it.

Now her cheeks were bright red, but she wasn't sure if it was from the blush or from her rubbing.

Deciding to give it a minute while she got dressed, DonnaMae quickly cleaned everything up. "Everything has a place, and every place has a thing," she said in a deep voice, mimicking her dad.

She slipped out of her dad's oversized shirt and put on her bra. She had no boobs at all, but one of her childhood memories was of watching her mom put on a bra backwards, and then spin it around, lean over, slip her arms through the straps, and stand up, pulling the bra up to lift her boobs into the cups. DonnaMae's bras didn't latch in the back like her mom's had; they were more like a swimsuit. But she still put her bra on backwards first and spun it around just like her mom used to do. She figured she was just practicing for one day when she had a real bra and real boobs.

DonnaMae pulled on a tight fitted black shirt with a water-color painting of a butterfly, and black spandex pants to match. She slipped into her brand-new pair of black loafer-style platform shoes and walked back to the mirror to inspect her outfit. Turning her foot side to side in the mirror, she was glad she had decided to go with no socks. The shoes looked way better than when she had tried them on at K-Mart with the socks on. Her rosy cheeks had faded, yet a hint of blush remained. "Perfect," she said, admiring her transformation, feeling like an entirely new person. If only her stomach would stop cramping. She didn't think she was that nervous, but it was the first day of middle school.

On her way down the hall, she knocked on her brother's door. "You ready?"

"Yeah, I'm coming!" Allan said, pushing his feet into his shoes.

"Are you so lazy you can't untie your shoes?" DonnaMae asked in her best Dad voice.

"Thanks, Dad, they're not meant to be untied. I'm not

walking on the heels of the shoe. Look, my feet slide right in." Allan pulled his foot in and out of the shoe to demonstrate.

DonnaMae continued to the stairs. "If you say so. Come on, let's —"

"You guys ready for school?" Dad called up from the bottom of the stairs. "I still want to get your pictures before I — Donna-Mae, what the hell is all over your face? You look like a clown! Go wash your face right now!"

DonnaMae blushed, and suddenly a wave of nausea joined the nervous cramping in her belly. "Dad, I —"

Her dad cut her off, "You're twelve years old, not eighteen, and you look... Just go wash your face."

DonnaMae dropped her head and turned towards her brother.

"Dad, come on, that's a little —"

"Allan. Not another word. This does not involve you."

"No, but you don't have to be so —"

"Allan, ENOUGH!" Dad barked back. "Mae, you don't need that shit on your face. You're beautiful without it."

DonnaMae was almost back to her room, but her dad was loud enough she feared the whole town could hear him. On her way to the mirror, she stopped to grab a box of tissues from her dresser. She plucked out a few and dried the tears that filled the corners of her eyes. As she blotted the gloss from her lips, she examined her makeup. Her cheeks were overly pink, but she didn't think she looked like a clown. She really didn't even have much makeup on.

Allan walked into her room. "Hey, just ignore him. You don't look bad at all, you just had too much pink on your cheeks. After he leaves, you can put it back on, he'll never —"

"Just leave, please," DonnaMae whispered, holding back her tears.

"Sis —"

"LEAVE! I'm fine. It's whatever, I don't care."

"Oook," Allan said, backing out of her room, hands up in surrender.

What was wrong with her today? One minute she wanted to cry, the next she was happy, then angry, then happy, then sad and now angry again. She loved her brother, worshiped the ground he walked on, wished she was more like him. Everyone loved him. All their family, all their friends, all her Dad's friends, her grandparents... Allan, Allan, Allan... it was always all about Allan. DonnaMae didn't hate Allan for it; she loved him. She just wished she could be more like him, but now she was angry with him because of it. All she wanted was for everyone to like her, to laugh with her instead of at her, to think she was pretty and funny.

She couldn't get the marker off her eyes, but she managed to remove everything else. It looked like she might have to tell her dad that the stain wasn't coming off, or perhaps her eyelids were so red from rubbing that she couldn't see any remaining traces. Now she looked like a clown — one that had been crying and had some kind of eye infection.

DonnaMae stood staring at her reflection for a few minutes. She didn't hate herself or think she was ugly, but right now, she didn't love herself or the way she looked. She noticed things she didn't like: the little freckles lined up over her nose, the indent on her upper lip... and then she stopped. This scrutiny wasn't helping her mood. In fact, it was making everything worse.

She imagined what her mom would say to make her feel better. She would remind DonnaMae of all the things she loved about her little girl. DonnaMae focused on the tiny bolts of lightning in her eyes. What else did she love about herself? DonnaMae stepped back. She was short but lean, and although often described as short and stocky, she didn't see herself that way; she loved her body. Running her fingers through her hair, she loved its length and the varying shades of blonde. *There*, she thought, *three things I love about myself*.

She could still be a model, maybe just a hair model or a clothing model. She laughed at herself. *Wait, models have people who do their makeup for them, right?* This thought gave her a little boost of confidence, just enough to put a smile back on her face and head back downstairs to face the day.

Allan was sitting at the kitchen table trying to fold the back page of one of his *MAD* magazines to see what the image was, and her dad was leaning against the kitchen sink, drinking a cup of coffee.

"Ok, can we please just take this picture so we can go?" DonnaMae asked, head hanging low, eyes locked on her feet.

"Sorry I yelled at you, Mae. It's just that you looked —"

"It's fine, I'm fine. Let's take the picture." DonnaMae lifted her head and forced a smile. "I'm just excited about school and I'm ready to go." She knew her dad felt bad enough that he wouldn't say anything about what was left on her still-red face.

"Maybe we can do it tomorrow and just pretend that it's the first day of school then," Allan suggested, standing from the table. "Today can be the practice run."

"It's whatever, I'm fine," DonnaMae said.

"Do you want me to drive you?" her dad asked.

"I don't care." She really didn't care anymore. She was just ready to be out of the house.

"It's cool, Dad," Allan said. "We'll walk so I can show her where to meet me after school to come home together, and she might meet new friends walking in like I did, and that helps on your first day."

"Ok, let's go to the front porch," their dad said. "I'll take your picture and I'll leave you both to it."

DonnaMae was great at faking it and painting on a smile, even when she didn't feel like smiling. It had always been easier for her to pretend everything was fine rather than confront anything painful. But today, faking it hadn't been as easy.

Surprisingly, her makeup turned out better than expected. After her skin calmed down, her lips retained a slight tint, her cheeks were no longer too pink, and her eyeliner looked real. She even received a few compliments from girls she didn't know. But the rest of her day was a disaster!

She started off by walking into the wrong classroom for her first period and had to be escorted to the right one. Her feet were nearly raw from walking in new shoes without socks, and her stomach and emotions were in knots all day.

Her brother and all his friends walked ahead of her on the way home from school. She was fairly certain she was limping, and she was grateful they couldn't see her because she wasn't sure she could handle being teased. Seeing her house in the distance gave her the strength to push through the pain and walk faster until she was just a few steps behind the boys. She brushed past them to get home sooner.

"Mae, wait up! I have the house key," Allan said as she passed.

DonnaMae turned to tell him to toss her the keys, but before she could speak, her heel caught the edge of the pavement. She tripped and landed backwards on her backpack.

Allan and his friend hurried over. "You ok, Mae?" Allan asked, extending his hand to help her up.

"I'm fine. Just got tripped up in these dumb shoes," she said, accepting his help.

"We're going to Paul's house," Luka said to Allan as DonnaMae dusted herself off.

"Cool, see you later," Allan said, bumping knuckles with them.

As they started to walk away, Luka paused and turned back. "See you later, Allan's little sister."

Ugh, DonnaMae thought. There it was, *Allan's little sister.* That name would probably stick with her throughout her school years and for the rest of her life. She would forever walk in the shadows of her big brother, forever just Allan's little sister.

When she got home, DonnaMae changed out of her clothes and into her dad's oversized t-shirt and fuzzy blue pajama pants. Wrapped in a big blanket, she curled up on the couch to read the next book in her new series, *The Babysitters Club*, book twelve, *Claudia and The New Girl*.

Apart from her stomach pains, the aches of the day melted away for DonnaMae as she lost herself in her book.

When her dad came home, he walked into the living room and then walked back out without a word. If she or Allan were reading, he never bothered them.

DonnaMae stretched her legs and creased the upper corner of page fifty-six. *Wow, how long have I been reading?* Feeling a sudden urge to pee, she jumped up and dashed into the bathroom.

DonnaMae doubled over on the toilet seat, realizing that she had held it for far too long as her stomach cramped even harder. When the cramping subsided, she mustered the strength to stand and was met with a chilling sight: blood swirling in the toilet.

Memories of her class on the menstrual cycle came rushing back to DonnaMae as she made the connection. This signified her transition into womanhood, and something about her body naturally disposing of the lining and unused eggs on a monthly basis. Tears streamed down her face as she stood over the blood-filled toilet. *Here I am again, wishing I had a mom to help me figure out what to do.*

As another wave of cramps hit her, DonnaMae sat down on the toilet, gripping her midsection, afraid she might shatter if she released her grip. *Ugh, I have to do this every damn month forever. Being a woman sucks!* she thought, fighting back a wave of nausea.

DonnaMae thought back to her class when the teachers had handed out some pad thing to go in her underwear. She couldn't remember what she had done with it. As far as she knew, her brother had taken it and turned it into a float for lighting fireworks in the river at camp. The image of her brother placing firecrackers on top of a large plastic pad to ignite them and make them explode on the river made her burst into laughter.

Laughing, crying. Why did she feel so out of whack? She muttered to herself while stuffing a wad of toilet paper into her underwear, then stood and pulled up her pants. She wiped away her tears with the back of her hand, leaving behind a faint trail of moisture. "You can figure this out," she told herself. She quickly washed her hands and glanced at her reflection in the mirror, ensuring her face didn't betray any signs of tears. Inhaling deeply, she counted to three in her head before exhaling slowly and feeling a sense of calm wash over her. "Mom, be in dad's ear and guide him," she whispered, making her way to the door.

"Daddy!" DonnaMae approached her dad, who was stirring a pot of something that smelled like burnt milk. "What are you making?"

"Mashed potatoes," he said, holding up a red Betty Crocker box that read "Scalloped Potatoes" on it.

"Umm, Dad, that doesn't say mashed potatoes," DonnaMae said.

"Yeah, I know. I was trying to make something different, but I think I overcooked them and, well, now I'm making cheesy mashed potatoes." He laughed and went back to stirring and mashing in the pot.

"Umm, Daddy," DonnaMae said, again in her baby voice. She hated that she talked in a baby voice, but it just happened, and when she started, she couldn't stop. Sometimes she didn't even know she was doing it. "I, um, well, I just went to the bathroom and I... umm... well, I think I... Well, there was... um... blood." She kept her gaze on the stove.

Her dad dropped the spoon in the pot. "What? Are you ok? Do you need —"

"I'm fine. Well, other than these tummy cramps. They hurt. But I think I just, um... you know..."

It was like a bulb went on behind her dad's eyes. "Oh, yes, well." He dried his hands on the towel hanging on the stove. "Your mom used to get the worst cramps. We have a heating pad around here somewhere. I think it's in the back laundry room. Let me get it for you."

"Thanks, Daddy, but I, um... Well, I'm bleeding, so I need, um... Well, I don't have anything, and —"

"Oh, yes, yes," Dad said, reaching into his pocket and pulling out some cash. "Here, go to the store and get whatever you need."

DonnaMae's eyes widened. A twenty-dollar bill! They lived across the street from the store and she walked there often with her brother. Allan was the last person she wanted to walk to the store with right now, though. Going alone sounded perfect.

"Thanks, I'll be back," she said, taking the twenty from her dad's hand.

At the store, DonnaMae stood in the middle of the aisle, overwhelmed by all the different options. An array of multicolored boxes and bags filled the aisle with whimsical designs. Always, Maxi, Stay Free, Kotex, so many different names. She carefully examined the price tags. Despite knowing she had a twenty-dollar bill, her habit of always searching for the most affordable option compelled her. She reached for a small bag of pads with a moon and stars design, advertised for nighttime use. Then she grabbed a bag of maxi pads with wings. *What? Why would you want a pad to have wings?* she wondered.

Straightening, DonnaMae pretended to know what she was doing. "I need one of these," she said, pulling a small box of OB tampons from the shelf, not even sure how they were supposed to fit in her underwear. "And this. Oh, and two of these." Reassuring herself of her choices, she grabbed one bag of pads with wings.

I don't need anyone's help, she thought, scanning her full basket with approval. *I got this.*

As DonnaMae walked towards the checkout, she spotted the makeup aisle and couldn't resist. The shelves were a treasure trove of beauty products. There were pastel eyeshadows from Maybelline, all the colors reminding her of her grandmother's spring garden; CoverGirl's jars of creamy liquid foundation and Revlon blushes in compact metallic cases. Bonnie Bell lip glosses glimmered with flavors hinting at a candy store. DonnaMae stopped at the mascara section, spotting several enticing options: Maybelline's Great Lash, with its classic pink and green tube, CoverGirl's Professional Mascara in sleek black, and L'Oréal's Voluminous Mascara in striking gold. Each one promised to enhance lashes with a glamorous, eye-catching effect.

DonnaMae's gaze fixed on a slender, dark blue tube that perfectly matched the one she had seen in a glossy magazine ad. It claimed to provide a natural look. She picked it up, along with a new clear lip gloss from the same line which shimmered in the light, and dropped both items into her basket with a satisfied smile. With more than enough money to cover her little indulgence and the assurance that her dad wouldn't be asking to see her purchases, DonnaMae felt confident and deserving of her new womanly purchase.

The next morning, DonnaMae reached over and turned off her alarm clock before she could even make out what the radio announcer was saying. She was already awake, and had been for a while. Her stomach churned like she was strapped into a vice at her grandpa's workshop, twisting relentlessly. She clutched the heating pad tighter around her midsection while sitting on the edge of her bed in one of her dad's t-shirts. A loud knock jolted her. Glancing up, she saw her dad in the doorway. She wasn't prepared for a heartfelt conversation, but the pleading look in his eyes left her no choice.

"Well, good morning, monkey butt," he said, walking to her bed.

"Morning, Dad." She rubbed the sleep from her eyes. "The heating pad helped my tummy, thanks." She managed a small smile.

"Thank your mom for that," he said, then paused, shifting uncomfortably on the bed. "Speaking of your mom, I know I'm not her. I could wear high heels and try to fill that role, but I can't truly be her."

The thought of her dad in heels made DonnaMae laugh. "Except for that one time, and you did a pretty good job with them, Mimi."

"Ok, I might look good in heels," he said, flashing her a silly grin, "but I can't be your mom." His smile faded. "I'm not a girl, and I don't know the first thing about being one." His face hardened as he spoke. "But I am a guy, and I do know what guys think of girls." He shifted his weight to one side. "I overreacted yesterday about you wanting to wear makeup. I talked to my friend, and they would like to take you shopping for makeup at a place where they can teach you how to do it right."

DonnaMae felt a pang of guilt for her purchase last night, which was safely tucked away under her pillow. "It's ok, Daddy," she said, wrapping herself into a hug to relieve the new wave of cramps and the guilt. She really just wanted this conversation to be over.

"It's not ok, Mae. I need you to know a lot of things. I just don't know how to tell them all to you." His expression softened. "I don't want you to grow up and become just another notch on some guy's belt. I want you to be the porcelain doll in the glass case on a shelf, the one all the guys respect and want but can't have."

"You want me to be a porcelain doll? What? Don't they break easily?" DonnaMae cocked her head to the side. "Why would I be a notch on a belt?" She wasn't sure what kind of lecture he was trying to give her, but it wasn't making any sense, and she was hungry.

Suddenly, she realized that when her dad said one of his friends had offered to take her out to look at makeup, he didn't mean one of his guy friends. "Wait, do you have a girlfriend who wants to take me to get makeup?"

Her dad laughed. "Yes, she's one of the moms at the daycare. We've been talking, and yesterday —"

"Why are you talking about me to one of the kids' moms at the daycare?" DonnaMae felt a swirl of emotions. Was she supposed to be upset or happy that her dad was talking about her? Suddenly, she didn't feel guilty about last night's purchase anymore.

"You know her, Mae. It's Adaline's mom, Elise."

"My little ladybug?" DonnaMae perked up. She loved that little girl and her adorable baby blanket. She didn't know Elise well, but now that she thought about it, Elise did hang around at pick-up time, and Dad would talk to her longer than most parents. "Are you dating Elise?"

"No!" Her dad rocked back on his heels. "But I do think she's someone you'd like, and maybe going shopping with her would be fun." He smirked. "You know, a girl for you to talk to about things?"

DonnaMae felt some relief, knowing her dad wasn't dating anyone. "Ok, we can talk about this another time." She shook her head, trying not to laugh about her dad trying to play matchmaker for her with other moms. Other than the makeup and her starting her period, they had been doing fine. She didn't need a mom. She hadn't had one for the last seven years. Why would she need one now? "I am, however, really hungry," she said.

Her dad laughed. "Right, you're a growing girl. We should feed you." He started to leave her room but paused and turned back to her. "Mae, you're growing into a very beautiful young woman, and I want you to love yourself. It doesn't matter what anyone thinks. Just be yourself, because you are wonderful."

"I am pretty cool, aren't I?" she said with a genuine smile. There were things she didn't like about herself or her life, but over-all, DonnaMae really did love who she was and she loved her little family of three, even if she was the only girl.

"Yes, you are. So today, just enjoy your new school and don't worry about what people think. Learn and have fun."

"Ok, but Daddy, can I please learn how to shave my legs? My

leg hair is poking through my black stretch pants, and it looks like I have hairy pants."

"Well, maybe we won't do that this morning. Let's just not wear those pants for now." A big smile grew on his face. "Daddy loves you, Mae."

"I love you too, Daddy. Forever and always."

"I sure hope so," he said as he turned and left her room.

CHAPTER 9

March 1998

DonnaMae stood in the middle of her room, a place once full of all her childhood memories, now an empty shell. The light pink walls were bare, and the curtainless windows let daylight flood the room, making the emptiness feel even more pronounced. There were indentations in the carpet from where her dresser once sat. The bookshelves, once packed with the adventures of *The Boxcar Children* and *The Babysitters Club*, were now empty. Only two holes remained where her cassette tape rack once hung. It felt unreal to see the room like this, so lifeless. DonnaMae stared at her last box, labeled "Barbies" in big bold letters, her heart heavy. She wasn't sure what to do with her Barbies. She didn't play with them anymore, but the thought of parting with them completely made her stomach churn. But it would be one less thing for her brother's friends to tease her about, and there wouldn't be room for them in the new house. She didn't need her Barbies. She was fourteen, and teenagers shouldn't play with Barbies anymore.

She pulled the cap off the black marker and, with a deep breath, wrote "storage" on the box.

"You ready, Mae?" Her dad walked into the room. "Is that the last box?"

"Yes, that's everything." She looked around her room, taking it in one last time. They were moving to a rental house because her dad was on another one of his "everything needs to change" kicks, but this time the house remodel had gone too far.

A few weeks ago, DonnaMae and her brother had come home to find their dad on the front porch with half the furniture in the yard, yet again. This time, he had a sledgehammer in his hand and had knocked out walls. That was when the remodeling began. It kept going, and her dad decided it would be better if they moved out for a few months, which was a good thing, because the house didn't have water after Dad cut into a pipe he didn't know was in the wall.

DonnaMae had mixed feelings about the move. This house was all she had ever known and her room had been a place where she laughed, dreamed, and spent countless hours playing. At the same time, she felt excited about the new place and the fresh start it represented.

Her gaze landed on the large mirror. Staring back at her was a girl who looked older than she felt, her face touched with the makeup she'd bought with Elise. The light coat of mascara and shimmer of lip gloss gave her a sense of sophistication. Her long, wavy blonde hair was pulled back into a tight ponytail. She wore her favorite denim jacket over a plain green t-shirt and white jean shorts. She smiled. "I wish we could keep my big mirror," she said as she struck a pose in front of it, imagining her empty room as a stage one last time.

"We can get you a different mirror when —"

"Wait," DonnaMae cut her dad off, turning to face the slanted ceiling. "We have to take the Care Bears Mom made." She had left the handmade Care Bear cutouts on her ceiling tiles all these years. She didn't want to leave them behind.

Her dad reached up and gently pulled the pins out, handing them to DonnaMae one by one. Something about packing them up felt like she was also packing away her mom.

"Ok, now are we ready?" Her dad glanced around the room one more time before picking up the last box.

As they walked past her brother's room, DonnaMae and her dad spotted Allan, standing still with his hand resting on the image of Mickey Mouse and Goofy racing go-karts that their mom had painted on his wall.

Dad's face fell, and he quietly set the box down. Without a word, he wrapped his arm around DonnaMae's shoulder and gently guided her into Allan's room.

Allan turned around, a single tear tracing down his cheek. He rarely cried — he was always the tough one. DonnaMae had seen him cry when they were younger if he got hurt, but otherwise, he was always her rock. He never talked about missing their mom or feeling sad. DonnaMae often felt alone in her grief, like she missed her mom so much because she was left with all boys. But now, seeing the pain in her brother's eyes, she realized she wasn't the only one. She turned to her dad, who also had tears.

"Son, I..." her dad started, but didn't finish.

Allan turned back to the wall. "I miss her," he said, his voice breaking the silence. "I will miss this." He traced the outline of Mickey's ear, just like DonnaMae had done so many times.

DonnaMae joined her brother, placing her hand next to his on the wall. She instantly felt that connection to her mom she always felt, and followed his hand as they traced the painting together one last time. She slowly leaned her head on her brother's shoulder. "I will miss this too, but I'm here. I'm not going anywhere." Allan had said those same words to her the day their mom died. Now it was her turn to support him.

Her brother wrapped his arm around her, and she turned in, hugging him tightly. DonnaMae didn't want to cry — she wanted to be strong for Allan. But there was something about her big brother holding her tightly, his tears falling freely, that made her own tears come without control. They stood there holding each other until their dad came over and wrapped them both in his arms.

"Change is hard," he said, "but change is good, and as long as we have each other, we will always be alright."

Allan stepped back from the hug and wiped his eyes. "Well then, I guess we'd better get started on these changes." He bent down and picked up his last box, labeled "Storage."

DonnaMae wasn't ready for that moment to end — she wasn't ready for the change. But she also knew there was no choice. She took a deep breath and followed her brother out, and did not look back.

They spent the weekend moving into the rental house. With over half the school year still ahead, DonnaMae was adjusting to all the changes. She had been enjoying junior high so far. It was fun having different classes and meeting new kids. She loved being in a real choir and walking home from school every day. But now, living too far from the school, she would have to ride the bus instead.

DonnaMae pulled another shirt from one of the boxes in her new room. She had unpacked everything except her clothes, but her new room still lacked personality and warmth. Unlike her old room with its light pink walls and big window, this room had plain white walls and a small window covered with beige blinds. It felt small, cramped. The carpet was a dirty brown. There were no bookshelves or cassette racks here, just a simple, empty closet. The only things that felt like home were her dresser and her bed.

Savage Garden's "Truly, Madly, Deeply" played softly in the background as DonnaMae rummaged through her clothes. When they'd moved, she had dumped everything from her drawers into boxes without thinking. She had over an hour to get ready for school, but at this rate, it might take her the whole hour just to find her socks. More shirts, more pants, plenty of underwear, but no socks. How did that even happen?

Feeling hot, DonnaMae went to let in some fresh air. Her window overlooked the driveway. As she opened it, she saw Elise's car backing out. *Huh? Why was Elise here?* Her dad and Elise were just friends. *Right?* Or was she his girlfriend now? Had she spent the night at the house?

Anger filled DonnaMae. A new house, a new school, and now a new girlfriend? It was all too much. She slammed the window shut, her mind racing with questions. The changes in her life felt overwhelming, and the thought of Elise being more than just a friend to her dad was —

She tripped over the box she'd been digging through. "UGH!" DonnaMae groaned and kicked the box in frustration.

"Hmm, that doesn't sound like my little morning sunshine girl," her dad said, walking into her room with a mug in his hand. "Maybe a cup of hot tea and some pancakes will turn that frown upside down."

"No thanks, Dad. I'm not hungry."

"You have to eat, Mae. And if you don't drink this, it will just get cold and turn into your first science experiment in this house," he said, setting the cup of tea on her dresser.

DonnaMae stared at the little yellow Lipton tea bag swaying in front of Mickey Mouse's face on the side of what was once one of her mom's mugs. A slow smile spread across her face as she thought of all the cups of tea she had forgotten about in her room. They would grow mold, and her dad would find them and ask about her science experiments. He never got mad at her, he always just laughed about it. He said that her mom was just as bad and he would find her dirty tea cups everywhere. One time, he even found one in her classroom that was so disgusting she actually claimed it was a science experiment.

"Aww, see? A cup of tea makes everything better. It's what

your mom used to say." He picked the cup back up and handed it to her.

"Thanks, Dad. I just…" She paused and swallowed the lump in her throat. Maybe it was more than the socks. Maybe she wasn't ready to ride the new bus to school. She missed her old house, the one she'd grown up in, the one her mom had died in, the only home she'd ever known.

"What's the matter, Mae?" Dad walked over and sat on her bed, patting the space next to him. "Come talk to your wise Old Man. Maybe I can help."

DonnaMae turned around and sat beside him. She took a sip of tea, but her hope of preventing tears from falling faded as her eyes filled with them anyway.

"OUCH!" she cried. "Daddy, that was hot!"

"Oh man, I'm sorry. I put an ice cube in it, but I didn't test it." Her dad jumped up and ran out the door. "I'll get you some ice," he hollered back as he ran to the kitchen.

The tea wasn't really that hot, but pretending to burn her tongue was a way to hide her true feelings, ones that made her feel weak. She didn't want to be weak — she wanted to be strong and not cry over a silly bus, or school, or missing her mom — the mom she didn't even know.

Her dad returned and handed her an ice cube. "Ok, put this in your mouth and it will help. I'm so sorry, Mae. I should have checked it." He wiped his hand on his pant leg. "So much for a cup of tea fixing everything," he said with a short laugh.

This time, DonnaMae didn't fight it. She let the tears slide down her warm cheeks. "I… it… I'm sorry, Daddy," DonnaMae whimpered as she folded into her dad's chest and he wrapped his arms around her.

"Mae, why are you sorry?"

"I'm just having a rough start to my day. You were just trying to make it better and now I'm being a big baby."

Her dad hugged her tight. "Mae, it's ok. Was it really that hot? Maybe I should take a look at it?"

"It was just my tongue. It'll be ok. I'm also just..." She paused, not wanting to say anything that would make him upset with her. She liked the attention from him and didn't want to say the wrong thing to lose it. But now she felt like she had no choice. "I miss my room and I'm kinda worried about riding the bus and I can't find my socks anywhere and, well..." She paused again, hoping her dad would cut in and she could get away with not saying anything else. When he stayed quiet, she let out a deep breath and finished. "I don't want you to remodel our house. I don't want you to take away the only thing I have of my mom."

"Oh, Mae." Her dad pulled her into him and wrapped his arms around her again. A slow breath escaped him.

Witnessing her dad in pain was something DonnaMae despised. She hated talking about her mom or upsetting him, but she also hated that he was seeing someone new. She could ask him about Elise later. Elise had looked ready for work, anyway, not like she had just had a sleepover. Maybe she was just dropping something off. She had been helping with the move this weekend — lots of people had.

"Mae, not a day goes by that I don't miss your mom. I loved her so much, and I know you don't have many memories of her because you were so young. But you know what? You're so much like her. All you have to do is look in the mirror, and there she is. I see her in you every day: in your heart, your strength, your creativity, your passion, your drive, your love for everyone. You don't need a house, Mae — you just need a mirror." He sat up tall and held her hands in his. "I know we're making some changes. I know it's difficult. But I also know you are one of the bravest girls in the world. I also know your mom is right here." With her hand in his, he placed it over her heart. "She's watching over us, and she'll always be with us. A house is just a house. We make it a home, and Mom will always be a part of our 'we.'"

DonnaMae had heard all of this before. She honestly wasn't sure what she wanted her dad to say to her. Nothing was going to bring her mom back. Sure, she wanted her dad to finish the house — she was ready to have a real bathroom again. She also knew that her dad needed the change. Buying all the new furniture wasn't enough. He needed the remodel to help him move on from Mom, but DonnaMae also didn't want him to move on. She didn't want to move on. She barely had anything to hold on to to begin with.

DonnaMae slid her hand from under her dad's to wipe away any remaining tears. "Thanks, Daddy. Sorry, I'm such a mess this morning. I think it's all just a lot."

Dad stood and motioned for her to join him. "Mae, change can be good. Maybe you'll even make some new friends in this part of town. You're so outgoing and friendly. This is going to be good for all of us. Remember, this move is only for a few months."

She stood and gave him a hug. "Ok, thanks, Daddy. Now if I could just find my —"

Before she could finish her sentence, Allan walked in with a small box in his hands. "Mae, I have a box of your stuff."

"Well, good morning, Son. I was just about to get a glass of water to dump on you." Dad laughed.

"What? Why? I'm up. I had to find my clothes for school and..." Allan paused, meeting DonnaMae's gaze. "What's wrong with you?"

"I think you solved it," DonnaMae said, walking over and pulling socks from the small box he was holding.

"You're crying over socks?"

"ALLAN," Dad snapped.

"What? Geez. They're just socks. You'd think someone died!"

"Really, Allan," Dad said, his voice full of annoyance. "I have to get to work. Breakfast is on the table. Allan, stay with your sister and make sure you get on the bus together to and from school today."

"Great, I'm starving. Thanks, Dad." Allan dropped the box on the floor and walked out of the room.

"Sis, you'll be fine," said Dad to DonnaMae. "You got this. I would be more worried about your brother missing the bus than anything else." He laughed again. "Call me at the daycare when you get home from school. The new phone is all set up on the kitchen counter. I didn't mount it to the wall yet, so if you walk too far from the counter, you'll pull the phone off."

DonnaMae laughed, since she had a habit of stretching the phone cord as far as it would go while walking around the kitchen and talking on the phone. "Ok, thanks, Daddy. Have a good day at work. Love you!"

"I sure am glad it's not raining," DonnaMae said, turning towards her brother. "Do you think we're in the right spot?" She reached up and pulled her brother's headphones off his ears, letting the sounds of "Peaches" by The Presidents of the United States of America, pour out of them. "Hello, turn off your disc-man. I'm talking to you."

"Hey, that's a good song." Allan glared at her. "I could hear you just fine. I'm ignoring you."

"Why? That's not nice."

"Because I'm trying to listen to my music."

"You aren't supposed to have those at school, anyway." She scowled.

"I can have it in my bag, don't freak out."

The bus pulled up before DonnaMae could respond. She had imagined a cute yellow school bus, like the ones in movies, but this was a city bus, large and unfriendly. DonnaMae stepped up and smiled at the driver, who returned her smile. "Heading to the junior high?" DonnaMae asked, just to be sure before getting on.

"Yep, come on," the driver said cheerfully, waving her aboard.

Allan stepped past her and got on the bus, pulling his head-phones back over his ears. He didn't even acknowledge the driver, just walked right past. DonnaMae shuffled behind him onto the bus, but she paused to say, "Good morning. Thank you for picking us up."

DonnaMae had never been on a bus like this before. The front seats faced each other like two sofas in a living room, and the back of the bus had a similar setup, but with a seat that ran along the back. The middle had rows of seats like she expected to see on a bus. She quickly found her brother sliding into one of these seats near the back and slid in next to him.

Three boys sat in the back of the bus, and one girl who had her head down. DonnaMae wondered why the girl looked sad.

As the bus pulled forward, one of the boys said something DonnaMae didn't quite catch, but she knew it wasn't nice by the way the other boys laughed in response. She turned her head slightly so she could hear better.

"Casper, where are you? We can't see you," one boy cackled at his own stupid joke.

"Yeah," said a bigger boy, "but she can't be Casper the Friendly Ghost, because she's so white no one can see her to be her friend." He laughed so hard he started coughing.

DonnaMae turned around in her seat to see the girl they were laughing at. She was more red in her face than pale. DonnaMae's heart hurt for her. She never understood the point in kids being mean. It reminded her of the days not long after her mom died, when she had a boy haircut and the kids at school laughed at her and said she had cooties. DonnaMae had learned to laugh it off, pretending it didn't bother her, but it did. She just got good at hiding it, knowing that if they didn't see her cry, they couldn't hurt her anymore. But these boys were not little kids, and this girl looked like she was about to cry. If she did, DonnaMae knew it would be the end for her — she'd be labeled as the crybaby ghost next. DonnaMae sighed, stood, and went to sit next to her. "Hi, my name is DonnaMae, but my friends call me Mae. What's your name?"

The girl tilted her head up towards DonnaMae. "Hi, I'm Ella."

"Oh look," one of the boys taunted, "Casper found a friend —"

Before he could say any more, DonnaMae glared at him. "Hey, that's not nice!"

The bigger boy shifted in his seat and started sniffing the air. "Do you smell that?"

"Smell what, man?" the other boy asked, now sniffing the air with an eyebrow raised.

"Tuna," the bigger boy said with a very serious voice. "I smell tuna fish!"

DonnaMae felt her face grow hot. Her dad had packed her a tuna sandwich for lunch today. *Oh no, is it me?* She tried to breathe through her nose without making it noticeable.

"Looks like we got ourselves a Tuna Girl!" The boy stared at DonnaMae, making it clear he was talking about her.

Shoot. How can he smell my sandwich? Before she could react, the other boys started laughing and one pointed at her and said, "Can you please close your legs? You're killing us over here, Tuna Girl."

HUH? Close my legs? What the hell are they talking about? My sandwich is in my lunch box in my bag, not in my pants!

DonnaMae glanced at Ella, who was staring at the ground. DonnaMae was glad Ella wasn't looking at her, because her face was probably as red as the bigger boy's shorts.

The boys were rolling with laughter and chanting "Tuna Girl" over and over between laughs.

DonnaMae looked at her brother, who was staring out the window with his headphones on, bobbing his head to the rhythm of his music. She turned back to the boys. "I'm not sure what's so funny about my dad packing me a tuna sandwich for lunch. I don't know how you can even smell it, but you guys are really not that funny."

This sent the boys into a full-on laughing fit. "She said it's her sandwich," one finally let out, and they all laughed more.

DonnaMae gave up and just started laughing with them, because sometimes it was easier to make fun of herself with others than to actually care. "I can ask him to pack you one tomorrow if you love tuna that much." She laughed as hard as she could, and before she knew it, the bus came to a stop and she realized they were at the school.

DonnaMae stood and quickly shuffled off the bus. Her brother was gone before she could get to him, and Ella was still behind her with the group of laughing boys. She didn't want to leave Ella alone, so she stopped and waited by the school doors.

"Hey, where's your locker?" DonnaMae asked Ella as they entered the school. "I can walk with you."

Ella kept going without answering, but once they were inside, she steered DonnaMae to the side of the noisy hallway and stopped. "You are nuts. Do you even have a tuna fish sandwich in your lunch?"

"Yes. What else would they have been talking about?"

Ella giggled. "You know, your..." she paused and glanced around the hall before leaning in closer. "You know, between your legs. Your girly parts."

"What?" DonnaMae scrunched up her face. She was so confused. Girly parts? What did a tuna fish sandwich have to do with her girly parts?

"They were saying you smell bad down there!" Ella nodded towards DonnaMae's crotch.

"EWWW! What?! Are you talking about my vagi—"

"Yuck! Don't say that word! And shhhh! Gosh, don't draw attention to us." Ella was giggling like a little girl. "They're going to call you Tuna Girl forever now. Maybe they'll forget about me."

"Forget about calling you Casper? Why do they call you

Casper, anyway?" DonnaMae changed the subject to push aside her embarrassment.

"Because I'm so pale. I have dealt with it forever. My skin is so white it's almost see-through." Ella held up her arm and pulled back the sleeve of her blue shirt. "I try to hide it as much as I can, but it really doesn't matter. We all went to grade school together, and they all know how white I am. I don't tan. I just burn. And then they just call me Lobster or something like that."

"Casper the Ghost Lobster," DonnaMae said, causing them to both giggle. "That's not very creative of them. They're just dumb boys, and honestly, I feel sad for them. If they're making fun of us, it means they learned it from somewhere. Someone in their life probably makes fun of them a lot."

"Or they're just mean!" Ella said, hurt bleeding from her words.

DonnaMae threaded her arm through Ella's and started walking. "Let's just forget about them. Where is your locker, and who do you have for first period? My locker is — *Oooph.*" She smacked into the back of a girl with thick, curly red hair. Startled, she stumbled forward and inadvertently got a mouthful of curls. Dropping Ella's arm, DonnaMae instinctively brushed at her face. "Ugh, I'm so sorry. I wasn't even looking. I just —"

DonnaMae's words caught in her throat as the girl turned around to face them, holding a half-empty bottle of SunnyD. The sticky liquid dripped from her hair and onto a poster she held in her other hand, soaking it. The red-haired girl adjusted her thick coke-bottle glasses, her face flushing. "Great, just what I needed today," she said, sarcastically.

DonnaMae felt awful. This was her fault — she hadn't been paying attention.

Ella quickly dropped her bag and pulled out a small pack of tissues. "Here, let me help clean that up," she said, offering the tissues to the red-haired girl.

"You carry tissues in your backpack?" DonnaMae asked.

"Um, yeah," Ella said, "you should always be prepared for anything. I even have Band-Aids."

The red-headed girl let out a deep laugh, grabbing their attention. "I don't think Band-Aids are going to help this shitshow," she said, wringing orange juice out of her hair with her free hand.

"I'm really sorry," DonnaMae said, "I should have been more careful."

Ella handed the girl a new tissue. "My name is Ella."

"I'm DonnaMae, the girl that created the shitshow," DonnaMae cut in. "And I'm really sorry. How can I help?"

The red-haired girl glanced up at DonnaMae, her expression softening slightly. "It's fine," she said, her tone less harsh. "I can just add it to the list of things I'll get teased about today."

This made DonnaMae feel even worse — she didn't want to be the reason someone was teased. She could see it on Ella's face that she felt the same way. DonnaMae grabbed a tissue and tried to help dry off the wet flyer in the girl's hand. "What was your name?" she asked.

"Izzy," the girl replied, letting DonnaMae take the soggy flyer.

"CHEERLEADING TRYOUTS" the flyer read in big, bold, blue letters.

"Are you going to try out for cheerleading?" DonnaMae asked.

"I was thinking about it. Are you guys?" Izzy asked.

Ella burst into laughter. "Um, NO!"

DonnaMae stood frozen, her gaze glued to the flyer. "Cheerleading?"

"Yeah, tryouts are next Friday after school," Izzy said, her voice filling with pep.

DonnaMae had always loved the idea of performing. Being a cheerleader seemed like the perfect way to entertain people. She enjoyed making others smile and laugh, even if sometimes she was the butt of the joke. But cheerleading? That was about school spirit, bringing energy, and leading cheers. A spark of excitement flickered inside her, reigniting the flame of her desire to be on stage once more, without the fear of sounding like a dying cow. If Izzy had the courage to do it, why couldn't DonnaMae?

"YES! I will be there!" DonnaMae blurted out, not realizing the other two girls had started their own conversation.

"What? Be where?" Ella asked.

"I'll be at cheerleading tryouts. Are you going to join us, Ella?" DonnaMae asked.

Izzy laughed. "Um, wow, did you check out for the last few minutes?" She placed her hand on DonnaMae's shoulder. "I do that all the time, find myself in my own world. We were just talking about how Ella doesn't want to do it, but she can come watch the tryouts, if her mom lets her."

Before DonnaMae could respond, the intercom crackled loudly and the whole hallway went quiet.

The principal's voice came over the intercom. "This is just a reminder that all first-period science classes will be meeting outside today in front of the school. Outdoor Science starts today!" He paused and cleared his throat. "Again, all first-period science classes will be meeting outside today in front of the school. Thank you, that is all."

"Shoot, that's me," DonnaMae said, giving both girls an apologetic smile. "I better go."

"That's me too!" Ella smiled back.

"And me!" Izzy said with excitement. "I just got my schedule switched so I could be in band."

"You're in band?" DonnaMae asked, turning to face Izzy.

"Yep, band geek at your service," Izzy gave a salute and stood at attention. "But maybe after I get this stickiness off me..." Izzy took off towards the bathrooms.

Ella crumpled up all the tissues in her hands and held out the small tissue bag with only one perfectly folded tissue left. "Guess I'm going to need to have my mom get me more."

"Yeah, I might have to ask my dad to get me some. Those were handy, thank you!" DonnaMae folded up the cheerleading flyer and tucked it into her backpack. "I felt so bad. She seems like a nice person."

"I think she was ok. Seemed like she was just happy we didn't make fun of her."

Sounds like we all have that in common, DonnaMae thought before responding. "Right. Now, where was your locker?"

DonnaMae and Ella stuck together for the rest of the morning. As they made their way outside, Ella stopped before the line of kids waiting to load three buses, "I forgot we had to take the bus to the wetlands today."

"Yeah, I think it's only today that we have to take a bus," DonnaMae said, not really remembering what they were doing but glad to be outside. "Don't we walk to the fields tomorrow?"

"Let's get on the last bus," Izzy said, running up behind DonnaMae and Ella and not stopping as she headed to the last bus. "There's no line, so maybe no one will be on that bus."

"Wow, where did you come from?" DonnaMae laughed and grabbed Ella's arm. "Come on," she said. They jogged after Izzy and the three of them climbed onto the bus.

Inside, it smelled of old lunches. Izzy was right — there were very few people on the bus, and they all shuffled to the back. One girl with long, dark brown hair in a messy ponytail was sitting all alone, staring out the window. The hum of conversations buzzed behind DonnaMae as other kids entered behind her, but she couldn't peel her eyes off the girl. She considered sitting beside her. But what if she wanted to be left alone? DonnaMae's heart pounded as she remembered the countless times she had sat alone, feeling invisible, wishing someone would notice her. But she also remembered the times when she was glad to be left alone.

"Let's sit here," Izzy said, stopping a few seats in front of the girl.

DonnaMae hesitated and glanced at her new friends, drawing strength from their presence. She felt like they all kind of needed a friend today. Ella, behind DonnaMae, shrugged her shoulders at

Izzy. DonnaMae knew they were waiting for her to answer. She took a few steps past Izzy and then noticed the sadness on the girl's face as she stared out the window. She glanced back to Ella one more time before making up her mind and walking towards the girl in the second-to-last seat on the right side.

"Or not?" Izzy said, still standing by the seat she had picked.

"Hi," DonnaMae said to the girl.

The girl raised her eyebrows. "Hi?"

"My name is DonnaMae. That's Izzy and Ella." She half-turned, pointing to the other girls, who had followed DonnaMae's lead and stood behind her.

"My name is Hazel," the girl said, staring at DonnaMae.

DonnaMae knew at that moment she had made the right decision. "Is this seat taken?" Before Hazel could respond, DonnaMae slid into the seat next to her and waved to her friends to join them. "Or are you waiting for friends?"

"Today is my first day here. So, no, not waiting on friends."

"Like, you just moved here?" DonnaMae asked. "Or like your first day in science class? They seem to have moved people around. Izzy just got switched to morning science today, too." She knew she was talking too fast. Her dad always told her to slow down when she got excited, and she usually didn't think she was talking too fast, but this time she knew she was. She was nervous. But why would she be nervous? She was meeting new people and making friends. That's what she wanted to do, right?

Hazel let out a small laugh, "No, like I just moved here to live with my dad this weekend. I'm from Oregon." She smiled. "I do really like science though, so I'm excited about being in this class."

DonnaMae reminded herself to slow down. "Well, it rains a lot around here, so outside might not be that much fun tomorrow, but —"

"Who's the new girl?" Izzy interrupted from the other side of the aisle, leaning so far over that she looked like she might fall right out of her seat.

"Izzy, meet Hazel." DonnaMae pressed herself as far back into her seat as she could so Izzy could see past her. "Hazel, meet Izzy."

"Nice to meet you!" Hazel said, leaning forward.

Izzy tugged on Ella's shirt sleeve, pulling her almost onto her lap so they were both leaning out of the seat. "This is Ella!"

Hazel laughed. "Nice to meet you, Ella." She gave a small wave before sitting back in her seat and looking at DonnaMae. "Have you all been friends since grade school?"

DonnaMae couldn't help but laugh at her comment. She only talked to a few of her friends this year from grade school. There was one she shared a locker with. But the rest, well, she wasn't sure she really fit in with them. "Oh no. We all just met this morning. I met Ella on the bus on my way to school. Ella and I ran into Izzy, ok well, I *literally* ran into Izzy who was looking at a — hey, do you want to go to cheerleader tryouts with us tomorrow after school?"

Hazel sat wide-eyed, staring at DonnaMae. "Wow! That was a lot. Did you have too many cups of coffee this morning?"

"Eww, no. Coffee is gross. I drink tea," DonnaMae said with a serious tone, making Hazel laugh again.

"I love tea!" Hazel said.

"You do? I don't think I know anyone else my age who drinks tea."

Izzy leaned over to join the conversation. "I like tea!"

Ella leaned over Izzy's back. "I like hot chocolate."

All four girls busted out with laughter.

"So... do you want to go to cheerleading tryouts with us?" DonnaMae asked again, breathless from laughing.

"I can come watch, but I was a cheerleader last year back home and I don't really want to do it again this year," Hazel said.

"I'm just going to watch too, if my mom says I can," Ella said, still leaning onto Izzy.

"Perfect. Sounds like a date. Izzy and I can try out for cheerleading and you guys can cheer us on," DonnaMae said.

The next Friday after school, DonnaMae stepped into the auditorium of her soon-to-be high school for cheerleading tryouts, her heart pounding with a mix of excitement and nerves. The room buzzed with the chatter of other girls. The high school cheerleaders stood on the stage, chatting effortlessly, looking perfect. DonnaMae lifted her chin and pulled her shoulders back, unsure if she was going at this alone or if her friends would really show up. But she knew she couldn't let that matter anymore. She had to stand on her own, and if no one came, she wasn't going to let it slow her down.

The girls had only just met, but they hit it off quickly, finding so much in common. They ate lunch together every day. She and Ella even rode the bus home together every day, ignoring the boys who tried to get their attention. It was easier being Tuna Girl and Casper together than alone.

DonnaMae scanned the chairs in the auditorium, trying not to get her hopes up too much. She knew it was common for people to say they'd be somewhere and then have a reason not to show.

But then she spotted them: her friends, their faces beaming with excitement as they waved her over. Standing even taller, DonnaMae made her way towards them.

As she shuffled her way to her seat among her new friends, DonnaMae felt a sense of relief wash over her. They had all shown up, even Hazel and Ella, who were not even trying out.

"Hey there!" Izzy leaned over Hazel's lap before DonnaMae could even sit all the way back in her seat. "Did ya snag a number when ya walked in?" Izzy held up a square white piece of paper with bold black numbers on it and two safety pins. "I'm fifteen!"

DonnaMae held up her piece of paper. "I'm fourteen. What are the odds of that?"

"They said to pin the number to your shirt," Ella whispered just loud enough for the four of them to hear her.

"I don't think they gave me safety pins." DonnaMae leaned in a little closer. "Why are we whispering?"

"We're not whispering." Izzy jumped up and threw her arms in the air. "We are cheering!" she yelled at the top of her lungs. Her voice echoed around the room and grabbed the attention of the other girls.

Ella swatted at her. "Shhhhh, you are crazy, sit back down."

But it was too late, the whole room had already caught on and everyone let out a whooping cheer.

DonnaMae stood to join in. It felt amazing to be part of this enormous room filled with whoops and hollers and so much cheering. She wanted so badly to be part of the reason for others to cheer and to bring them entertainment. All Izzy did was jump up and yell. DonnaMae could do that.

DonnaMae and Izzy sat back down. Hazel and Ella sat between them. "Hey," DonnaMae said, leaning forward in her seat, "do you guys want to have a sleepover this weekend at my grandparent's house?" The rec room at her grandparents' house was legendary in their family for having parties. DonnaMae had heard all about how her mom used to host amazing girls' nights there, and she was about to have her first one if her friends said yes. "My grandparents have a really cool rec room above their garage, it has a pool table and a bar and —"

"Hell yeah!" Izzy cut her off. "You fixin' to throw a shindig to celebrate us bein' cheerleaders?"

"I'm down," said Hazel. "I can bring some fun magazines."

"Umm, I'll have to ask my mom first," said Ella, "and she'll probably want to talk to your grandparents."

The lights dimmed and a group of senior cheerleaders rallied on the stage, their energetic presence sending a wave of excitement through DonnaMae's body. She was ready to take on this challenge, even though she was nervous. The cheerleaders gave a quick demo and rundown of how tryouts were going to work. Each girl was to introduce herself and say why she wanted to be a cheerleader, and to do the following jumps and exercises. They shouted out a bunch of cheers and had everyone join in and call back at them. The room was so full of energy DonnaMae couldn't wait to be at a real pep rally – not just be at one, but lead one!

The cheerleaders called out a few numbers and one of the girls jumped off the stage to take the girls with the corresponding numbers to go warm up.

Izzy leaned over to DonnaMae. "Are you nervous?"

"Yeah, kinda, but I'm also excited. How about you?"

"I'm so nervous I might shit myself!" Izzy laughed loudly.

"Izzy! Oh my gosh!" Ella crinkled her nose. "That's soooo gross... stop... just stop!"

They all laughed at Ella and before anyone else could respond the next numbers were called out. DonnaMae loved that she actually had someone to talk to. She never knew what her brother was thinking or feeling. Hell, half the time she wasn't even sure he was actually human. She never understood why she had so many feelings, and her dad and brother never really seemed to care about anything. She wasn't sure why she felt ok to show her feelings with her new friends, but she was glad she was honest and didn't just say her normal, "I'm fine!"

DonnaMae's thoughts were interrupted by another group of numbers, "Thirteen, Fourteen, Fifteen, Sixteen and Seventeen. You are with me, Molly." A tall, lean girl with her blonde hair pulled back into a flawless ponytail did a perfect kick jump and then bounced her way off the stage. As she jogged down the aisle, DonnaMae and Izzy joined the other girls jogging after her.

"Good luck!" Ella yelled after them.

"You got this!" cheered Hazel.

After tryouts, Izzy's arm hung over DonnaMae's shoulder as they walked out of the auditorium. "Damn girl, I didn't even know you had a set of pipes. Ya sure can get a crowd amped up!" She linked her arm around DonnaMae's other side. "We just need to teach you left from right."

"Yeah, I've never been good at the whole dance routine, with a group thing." DonnaMae laughed at the thought of herself as a little girl in dance classes, getting flustered, giving up, and doing her own dance and waving to her dad instead of following along with everyone else. Everyone thought that was cute when she was little but that would not work now. She would have her work cut out for her with the routines, but right now she didn't care. She felt so alive. During tryouts, she didn't just get the other girls to respond, she got them to stand up and clap with her. She didn't stop encouraging them to join her until she had every last person in that room on their feet. It helped that Izzy jumped up next to her and joined in when it had stopped with only half the audience. It lit her fire, and the next thing she knew she was doing star jumps and high kicks she didn't even know her body could do and bouncing around like a jackrabbit. The more they cheered back, the more energy she had!

"So, tomorrow night? Meet at my place and I'll have my grandma pick us up?" DonnaMae said as they sat down on the stairs in front of the auditorium to wait for their parents. "If you all write down your numbers, I can give you each a call when I get home to give you my address."

"I see my mom," Ella said, tipping her head in the direction of a light blue car parked across the street. "I'd better go, but I'll call you, Mae. I've got your number."

"Yeah, my dad will be here soon," DonnaMae said, glancing around anxiously. "Does anyone have paper?" She was really excited to see her dad and tell him everything.

"I have a pen," Hazel said.

"Just write it on your hand," Izzy suggested.

"No way. My dad will be pissed. He hates it when my brother draws on his hands."

"I'll do it," Hazel said, pulling off the cap. "We can do a three-way call tonight." As Hazel scribbled their numbers on her hand, DonnaMae scanned the street again. *Where is my dad?*

Hazel and Izzy ran off at the same time when their parents showed up. Just as DonnaMae was starting to feel the panic rise, thinking her dad had forgotten her and she was going to have to walk home or find a payphone, a little red Honda pulled up right in front of her and rolled the window down. "How did it go?" Elise called out from the driver's seat.

No freaking way. What the hell was she doing here? DonnaMae looked over her shoulder to see if Elise might be talking to someone behind her. There was no one but DonnaMae. Of course, who else would Elise be talking to unless she had a friend at tryouts? DonnaMae laughed inwardly at the thought. Elise was probably young enough to have friends here.

"Donna?" Elise called out from the car.

DonnaMae rolled her eyes. No one called her Donna. She stood up and walked to the car.

"Hi! How did it go?" Elise repeated, as if DonnaMae must not have heard her the first time.

"Thanks for stopping by, but my dad is on his way to get me." DonnaMae looked up and down the street. "I don't want to miss him."

"Donna, your dad asked me to come get you. He was working on the house and I was there, and he asked if —"

"Oh." DonnaMae's heart sank. She pulled the door open and dropped into the passenger seat, her excitement deflating like a balloon.

"I was thinking maybe we could get some ice cream to celebrate," Elise said, trying to sound cheerful.

"I haven't had dinner yet," DonnaMae said, keeping her eyes on the road as Elise pulled away from the curb. Ice cream after events was her and her dad's thing. The thought of doing it with Elise without her dad made DonnaMae's stomach knot up.

"I won't tell if you don't tell," Elise said, raising her finger to her lips.

"No, thank you. I need to eat dinner," DonnaMae said, facing the window, blinking back the sting of tears. The house, the cars, everything was more important to her dad than she was.

"Ok, well, what should we pick up for dinner?"

DonnaMae felt a flush creep up her neck. Dinner? It was one thing for Elise to pick her up as a favor to her dad, but dinner? Why was she coming over for dinner? DonnaMae hadn't seen Elise all week and had allowed herself to believe that Elise had just dropped something off the other morning and left. Honestly, DonnaMae had forgotten Elise was even around. And now she was eating dinner with them, like she was part of their family?

DonnaMae crossed her arms tightly and leaned back in her seat, the lump in her throat growing. "I'm not hungry!" she said, her voice sharp. This girl was definitely more than just her dad's friend.

CHAPTER 10

August, 1998

The warmth of the afternoon sun poured down DonnaMae's back as she watched an oversized backyard slowly being transformed into a wedding venue. She unzipped her hooded sweatshirt, letting a breeze cool her skin. It was her first time at her soon-to-be step-grandparents' house. The lawn was bordered by wild hedges and clusters of trees in the back that looked like a secret forest. She pulled her bag from the car trunk and tossed a light blue dress wrapped in clear plastic over her shoulder, taking in the scene as she walked towards the house.

People she didn't know walked around tables draped in ivory cloths, arranging settings and centerpieces. The air was thick with the scent of fresh cut grass and sweet pea flowers, their delicate blossoms arrayed in mason jars. To her left, a small band was setting up under a canopy of shimmering fairy lights, their instruments glistening in the last rays of the sun. A wooden arch stood at the end of the yard in a nook bordering the secret forest, draped with more sweet pea flowers and ivy. It all seemed like something from a Disney fairytale. All it needed was a talking rabbit to hop out from the forest, or some birds to fly out and tie a ribbon around the top of the arch. But for DonnaMae it didn't feel like a fairytale. It didn't even feel real.

Her dad, dressed in a light gray suit – more formal than she'd ever seen him – was laughing with a woman she barely knew. Elise, his bride-to-be, stood beside him in a beautiful floral sundress, her wavy dark brown hair brushing the tops of her shoulders with every movement.

Feeling a swirl of emotions, DonnaMae wasn't sure where she fit in this moment. She glanced around again. Where was her brother?

Her eyes landed on a table lined with half-frozen bottles of water, their labels color-coordinated with the soft pastel and ivory theme of the wedding. She wandered over and picked one up, the condensation cool and slippery in her hand. As she opened the bottle and took a sip, she watched her dad and Elise share a quiet, loving moment, their heads bent close together in laughter.

DonnaMae couldn't help but wonder why Elise was different. What did she have that the other girls her dad had dated, or the "friends" he brought home, didn't? DonnaMae had grown to like those women, only for them to disappear one day, just like her mom. But not Elise. Why her? And why after only six months?

DonnaMae had learned not to get attached to her dad's female friends, because they always ended up leaving. So, she'd mostly avoided Elise. But now, Elise was about to become her new mom. After tonight, they were supposed to be one big happy family, the five of them. The thought of little Adeline, at least, almost made DonnaMae smile.

Sometimes, DonnaMae wondered if maybe her mom had something to do with all of this. Maybe, after seeing her dad send DonnaMae to the grocery store alone when she started her period, her mom decided it was time DonnaMae had a woman in her life. Maybe there were going to be more moments when she'd need a mom, not just a dad. DonnaMae thought they'd already made it through the hard parts. The only thing left was dating, and honestly, she had no interest in that. What else was there that she'd need a mom for?

"You must be Donna."

DonnaMae spun around, accidentally spilling some water from her bottle onto her chest. The tall woman standing before her cast a long shadow. She could have been Elise's twin, but was much taller and had blonde hair. "Yes – well, no, it's DonnaMae, but my friends call me Mae."

"I'm Jenny," the woman said, extending her hand to Donna-Mae. "Elise's older sister."

"I can tell. You look a lot alike."

"People say that a lot," Jenny said with a warm, welcoming smile.

Elise had three sisters, which DonnaMae found amusing, because her dad had three sisters and her mom had three brothers. She could only dream of having such a large family.

"I'm not sure where I'm supposed to get ready," DonnaMae said, glancing towards the house. "And I'm doing Adeline's hair."

"Yes, she's been asking for you, and I think your brother is inside having lunch."

"That sounds about right, just watch out for his drink. It will most likely not be a rootbeer." DonnaMae laughed.

"Typical for his age," Jenny laughed. "Well let's go inside and get you set up." DonnaMae nodded and followed, giving her dad one last glance.

***

DonnaMae's fingers weaved through Adeline's fine, light brown hair, creating a beautiful braid. "You are going to be the prettiest little flower girl in the world," DonnaMae said.

Adeline sat taller in her chair. She clutched onto her little blanket pressed against her chest, with a smile that lit up her face. "T'ank you, MaeMae!"

"But you must sit still so I can finish."

"Ohhhh-Tay, MaeMae!" Adeline had an abundance of spunk and intelligence that made her seem older than her years, but her little voice made DonnaMae want to wrap her up into a hug every time she said her name.

DonnaMae's emotions about her dad's marriage to Elise knotted in her chest, but one thing was certain: Adeline had captured her heart, and now she had the joy of being an older sister, she was going to be the best big sister ever. DonnaMae had the best big sister in the world, but just like everyone else, Carmel wasn't physically around anymore, leaving DonnaMae alone in a world full of men. She knew it was the age difference, and that Carmel had moved away for school. They still wrote letters, but DonnaMae couldn't help wishing things were different. She wanted to be the kind of big sister to Adeline that Carmel had once been to her.

"Ouchy," Adeline whispered softly.

DonnaMae quickly loosened her grip on the little girl's hair. "I'm sorry, little one," she said, focusing all her attention back on Adeline. She tied a rubber band around the end of the braid that ran across Adeline's head like a headband. "Perfect!" she said. "Ok, time to add the flowers!"

"I all 'urple ones."

"Let's see what we can do, ok," DonnaMae said, turning around to find the glass filled with fresh-cut sweet peas and a few other wild flowers. She spotted a single, vibrant purple sweet pea and carefully plucked it and wove it into the braid. "Does that work?"

"Good," Adeline said, her smile stretching from one ear to the other.

DonnaMae couldn't help but smile back at how adorable she was.

As she weaved flowers into Adeline's hair, DonnaMae couldn't shake the unsettling feeling of her dad marrying someone she barely knew. Elise would be a permanent part of their lives. The house was newly remodeled, with a new bedroom and bathroom added upstairs, squeezing DonnaMae into a room half the size of her old one. All the artwork her mom had painted was gone. There was nothing left of her in the house, just fading memories.

This wasn't how things were supposed to go. They were supposed to be the Three Musketeers, just her, her brother, and her dad. One day her dad was going on a date, and the next, he was marrying Elise.

"How's it going in here?" Jenny asked, poking her head into the big bathroom and pulling DonnaMae back to reality once again.

"We are just about done," DonnaMae said, keeping her eyes on what she was doing.

"Wow, it looks amazing! You should be a hairstylist!" Jenny's cheerful voice filled DonnaMae with warmth.

Elise's family was really nice. Elise had shared stories with DonnaMae about their family traditions — gingerbread house decorating parties, giant Easter egg hunts with money in the eggs, and fondue nights where they sat around for hours, dipping bread and meat into melted cheese while talking or reading. The fondue nights especially sounded amazing. DonnaMae couldn't help but feel a twinge of excitement at the thought of being part of those experiences.

"Seriously, this turned out perfect!" Jenny said, standing next to DonnaMae, examining Adeline's braid as DonnaMae tucked in the last flower.

"Thank you. I practiced on my dolls, and little Adeline lets me do her hair often."

"Well, you are very good at it."

"And done!" DonnaMae said, giving Adeline a nod in the mirror. "You are free to go, but be extra careful to not mess it up until after the pictures."

"I will teep it un-messed" Adeline said, jumping down from her chair and striking a pose.

"Shall we go get you a snack?" Jenny said to Adeline, who happily galloped out of the room, clutching her baby blanket tightly in one hand and Jenny's hand in the other.

DonnaMae tidied up the vanity, gathering her hair tools to style her own hair. She had invited her friends to the wedding and to an after-party at her grandparents' house. She laughed inwardly at the thought of going to her mom's parents' house after her dad's wedding with someone else. "Mom, you don't have to worry," she whispered. "She'll never be my real mom, just my stepmom."

Saying "mom" filled her with a mix of emotions. She hoped Elise would like her and that their relationship would grow. But what if they had nothing in common? What if Elise didn't even want to be her mom? After all, she already had Adeline.

DonnaMae ran the curling iron through her hair, staring at her reflection. In just a year, everything had changed — new house, new school, new family. She wanted to embrace it all, but at the same time, it felt like she was losing everything familiar.

She envied her brother's carefree attitude. He lived his life focusing solely on his happiness. These things never seemed to bother him. But as much as she tried to be just "one of the guys," she was a girl with feelings and emotions that were becoming harder and harder to lock away. Some days, she felt like the pressure cooker at her grandma's, ready to burst. She needed to open up and let out some steam, but she didn't know how.

The scent of heated hair filled the room as she wrapped strands around the barrel of her curling iron, releasing them into loose curls. Each curl felt like a small victory, a piece of control in her life she had no control over. DonnaMae paused and took a deep breath. She was determined to make the best of the day, to embrace the new changes, even if they scared her. She carefully placed the curling iron back on the vanity and smoothed down her dress, feeling the soft fabric under her fingers. It was time to face the music, as her grandpa would say.

———

Wildflowers popped against the backdrop of the evening sky as the sound of dancing and loud music echoed through the air. DonnaMae was left bewildered, unable to recall what had just transpired. The wedding festivities went by in a whirlwind, with family members from both sides all around, each one wanting to embrace her, and offer their heartfelt congratulations. She was not sure why they were saying it to her. *Congrats, your dad finally found you a mom?* DonnaMae half laughed at this thought.

"Mae, are you ready to go? Your mom — err, your step— umm..." Ella paused, giving Hazel just enough time to swoop in and save her.

"Elise said she got us a limo, and it's here to take us to the rec room, and she said we can take more food and dessert with us."

"Oh yeah, we should for sure bring food and maybe they won't notice if we take some drinks?" Izzy laughed.

"We have drinks in the rec room?" DonnaMae said, looping her arms through Hazels and Ella's. "And I'm sure we're stacked on food. My grandma Joyce is known for hosting parties!"

"Not those kinds of drinks," Izzy said, nodding her head towards the keg and cooler full of adult drinks. "Those kinds of drinks," she said, lowering her voice.

"Oh my god! NO!" Ella said, scolding Izzy as she pulled her arm to join their chain. "Come on, let's go!"

Izzy shrugged. "I mean, it could be a good time?"

They all laughed. DonnaMae glanced back to the dance floor, where her dad twirled his new wife around. She couldn't help but smile at the sight of him, even as sadness tugged at her heart. "Yeah, I'm ready to go," DonnaMae said, forcing her feelings away with thoughts of the fun night they had waiting for them.

When they got to the rec room, Grandma Joyce and Grandpa Delmar were already home from the wedding.

"Do you think it was weird for your grandparents to be at their dead daughter's husband's wedding?" Ella asked.

"ELLA! What the —" Izzy started to yell at Ella, but before she could finish, Ella cut her off.

"It's an honest question."

"It's fine, guys," DonnaMae said. "She's been dead for years. It's not like it just happened. I don't know, and to be honest, I thought about it too. I also thought it was funny that we were coming here after their wedding. My mom will always be my mom, dead or alive. I'm no different from you all. I have a mom." DonnaMae paused and opened the door to the shop, then turned to face them. "Mine just can't ground me or yell at me like y'all complain about."

DonnaMae laughed and jogged up the stairs to the rec room. The smell of freshly made popcorn filled the stairs as soon as she opened the door. "WOW!" DonnaMae said, scanning the room.

Her grandma had filled the room with treats and popcorn and set the table out with Monopoly on it. The bar had hot chocolate laid out, and fresh hot water was boiled in the coffee maker. There was a note on the fridge that read, "Have fun, girls! More snacks and Cool Whip in the fridge. We are just inside if you need anything."

Reading the note almost brought tears to DonnaMae's eyes. She might not have a mom that was alive, but she had the best grandparents in the world. This place held more of her mom than their house ever did. Her mom's childhood was literally on the walls, with magazine clippings she had decoupaged covering one whole wall. This place screamed MaryLou, and now DonnaMae.

"Wow," Izzy said, pulling open the fridge door and peering in with wide eyes. "She even filled the fridge with soda, including a few Surges."

"Oh no, those are probably leftovers from my brother. I think we would be up for three weeks if we drank one of those," DonnaMae said, waving her hands in a dismissive gesture at the cans of Surge.

"Yeah, no thank you. I'll stick with a Snapple," Ella said, standing over the table full of snacks and reaching for a bottle. "But I will be eating this whole can of cheese balls! And these," she said, ripping open a bag of peanut butter M&Ms and dumping them into the bowl of popcorn, "belong in here."

"Yes! The only way to eat popcorn," DonnaMae said as she walked back to the table, scanning the impressive spread. Her grandma really had stocked them with everything — she'd even gotten them each their own roll of bubble gum tape and plenty of other candy. They didn't need the Surge. They were going to be up all night just from this junk food.

"This is fabulous, there is even a veggie tray!" Hazel said, her eyes wide as she took in the spread of mixed vegetables, practically bouncing on her toes.

"*We* are fabulous!" Izzy added, a grin spreading across her face as she threw an arm around Hazel's shoulder.

"We are the Fab Four!" DonnaMae said, striking a pose with one hand on her hip and the other in the air like a pop star.

"Isn't that what the Beatles were called?" Ella asked, raising an eyebrow.

"How the hell did you know that? DonnaMae is the music girl," Izzy said with a laugh, nudging DonnaMae playfully.

"And Ella is the Queen of Random Facts!" DonnaMae added, giving Ella a bow.

"I think the Fab Four fits for now," Hazel said, shrugging and popping a baby carrot into her mouth.

"Yes, but we will have to come up with our own name at some point," DonnaMae laughed, looking at her friends. This was what she needed, a night of fun and laughter, surrounded by the people who made her feel like she belonged. DonnaMae's heart swelled with gratitude for her grandparents and for the friends who had become her second family.

"Should we start with some quizzes?" Hazel proposed, pulling out a stack of magazines. "This one is going to be good. I just got it from Seven Eleven yesterday." She held up the *Teen Magazine* with "Be Beauty Quiz" in big bold letters across the bottom, the highlighted quiz "What Your Words Say About You" down the left side.

"Wow, that's a good stack of magazines," Ella said, walking over and pulling the next two magazines off the stack. "You even got *Bop* and *YM*?"

"Well, I asked my dad to pick up a few magazines for our girls' night and this is what he came home with."

Ella glanced back down at the stack in Hazel's hand and laughed. "That explains the next one: *Theater Week*." She picked it up and burst into laughter at the sight of the next item: the July issue of *National Geographic*, "Dinosaurs Take Wing: The Origin of Birds," featuring a striking cover image of a feathered dinosaur. "*National Geographic*?" Ella said. "Do they have quizzes?"

Hazel hugged the magazine stack to her chest. "No, this one is mine. I'm going to be a geologist someday." A smile spread across her face and DonnaMae felt a twinge of jealousy that Hazel knew what she wanted to be when she grew up. Hazel released her embrace on the stack of magazines and gazed down at them like they were decadent desserts. "This will be my late night reading after you all pass out from your sugar high," she laughed. "As for the *Theater Week*, it's one my dad subscribes to, and he just added it to the pile." Hazel's eyes widened at the cover of the magazine, "But hey, *Rent* is a great musical." She started to sing, "Five-hundred, twenty-five thousand, six-hundred minutes —"

"Oh no, not a musical song!" Izzy said, walking to the cutout shelf in the wall where the stereo system sat.

"For the record," said DonnaMae, "I think being a geologist is so cool." She had no idea what she wanted to do or become and she wasn't sure what everyone would think of that. She figured it would be best to keep the conversation going in another direction. "But I have to know: what does that song even mean?" She had heard Hazel sing it several times before.

"Well, there are 365 days in a year and twenty-four hours in a day and sixty minutes in every hour, so that means there are 525,600 minutes in a year, so —"

"So, you are making my brain hurt," Ella cut in, now flipping through the pages of the *Bop* Magazine.

Izzy closed her eyes and rubbed an imaginary crystal ball. "I'm not seeing a mathematician in your future," she said in a soft, creepy fortune teller's voice.

Ella laughed and pushed Izzy lightly on the shoulder.

Izzy opened her eyes and giggled as she regained her balance.

"I'm going to be a schoolteacher," Ella said. "I already have a plan."

"A teacher and a plan, that sounds just like my mom," DonnaMae said with a short laugh, realizing too late that she'd spoken out loud when all the girls grew quiet and stared at her with the "we feel sorry for you" expression she hated so much. "You know what helps hurt brains?" she said quickly before anyone could pity her, or even worse, ask her what her plan was going to be, or if she was going to be a teacher like her mom. She hated that shit. She walked over to join Izzy by the old record player, pulled one of the records off the stack on the shelf, and placed it on the record player. Van Morrison singing "Brown Eyed Girl" crackled through the speakers and DonnaMae turned it up. She loved this song. "Dancing makes everything better."

"I love this song," Izzy said, dancing around with DonnaMae.

"It's not bad, but maybe we'll listen to something more up to date for the next one," Ella said, walking to the stack of tapes and CDs that DonnaMae and Allan had added to the wall of music from over the years. She searched through them while the girls danced and sang along to Van Morrison. As the song ended, Ella held up an orange and yellow CD case. "You have *The Hansons* up here. How do you play a CD on this thing?" Ella ran her hand over the front of the record player.

"Um, you don't," DonnaMae said, dancing her way over to Ella with a laugh. Her uncle had recently wired in a new deck that played CDs and cassette tapes, but she had to unplug the record player and plug in the new stereo. DonnaMae loved the sound of records and old music. Her dad played records often in the garage and always told her when a song her mom loved was on. She had her own collection of "oldies" from working at the shop, but she also loved the new stuff. There was just something about listening to a record player that made her feel good. She knew her friends didn't feel the same, and she also liked the Hanson Brothers. She wasn't the biggest fan of their long hair, but she loved the song "MMMBop."

"Ok, Ella, you had better dance with us!" DonnaMae said as the Hanson Brothers filled the room, and the girls "mmmbopped" right along with them, dancing and laughing. Before the song was over, DonnaMae knew she had been right: Music was the trick. The worries of the day melted away with the sounds of the music, and the more she danced and laughed, the better she felt.

The room was alive with energy. *Who needs the Three Musketeers when I have The Fab Four?* she thought. Ella danced, holding her Snapple in one hand and a few Red Vines in the other, while Hazel showed Izzy some twisting dance moves from one of her musicals, and Izzy tried to replicate them. *Seriously, what could ever go wrong in life with friends like these?* she thought as she joined in on the dancing with a handful of popcorn.

CHAPTER 11

June 14th, 2002

I feel like I'm in a fog — heavy, sinking, drowning. Or have I already drowned?

His breath is hot on my neck, his body pinning me so I can't move. I open my mouth to scream, but nothing comes out. I want to pull away, but it's as if I'm frozen in place. His hand moves over me like a snake trying to find its prey, smooth and quick, striking without warning.

This can't really be happening.

I'm screaming, "Stop, please stop!" but no sound escapes my mouth. The urge to punch and kick grows weak. The drive to fight for my freedom fades. It's as if his venomous strike has paralyzed me. I cannot escape this snake's grasp. My body feels as heavy as a bag of bricks.

His embrace tightens. His breathing is so loud it almost masks the sound of crashing waves from the ocean outside.

The ocean, my ocean. I can hear the ocean. With each tightening embrace, I let the crashing waves grow louder in my mind. This is my escape. My ocean is here to save me, here to carry me away. I let the sound of the ocean swallow me whole.

• • •

I drift to the bottom of the dark ocean, lost in its nothingness. It is just me and the sound of my ocean.

CHAPTER 12

September, 1998

DonnaMae sat on the edge of her bed, threading a needle. In the whirlwind of moving, school, and constant changes, she had forgotten to finish the skirt she'd planned to wear on her first day of high school. After unpacking the last box and finding her sewing supplies, she remembered the unfinished project. Though it was now more than a month into her freshman year, today felt like the perfect day to finally wear it for advanced choir tryouts. The teacher had personally asked DonnaMae to audition, and DonnaMae wanted to look her best. Maybe if she told the teacher she made the skirt herself, it would distract her teacher from DonnaMae's imperfect voice when she sang solo. She had even bought a new white three-quarter-sleeved top to layer over a dark blue tank, perfectly matching the colors in the skirt.

The plush gray carpet in DonnaMae's new bedroom felt soft beneath her bare feet as she sewed the zipper into her skirt. Light blue walls met a ceiling three shades darker with a purple undertone. Her brother had painted fluffy white clouds on the ceiling for a dreamy daytime sky. At night, countless glow-in-the-dark stars turned it into a breathtaking night sky. When she turned on her black lights, the clouds glowed like a sunset with twinkling stars, her favorite thing.

Though DonnaMae sometimes missed her old room, she loved that the Three Musketeers had designed this one together. She only had four years left in it before she'd be going off to college, anyway. Skipping college wasn't an option, which added to the pressure she felt to choose a career.

Just as DonnaMae pushed her needle through the fabric's thickest section, she heard her dad honk his horn twice. That meant he and Adeline were on their way to the Daycare, and soon Elise would be right behind them on her way to work. DonnaMae chuckled as she wondered if this was what living in a college dorm would feel like, everyone doing their own thing, occasionally crossing paths at meals.

Her new family dynamic wasn't bad. She liked having her little sister around. But everything felt so unfamiliar, and DonnaMae struggled with how to fit in. It felt like upstairs, where all the kids' bedrooms were, belonged to one family, while the downstairs was a completely different world, ruled by her dad, Elise, and Adaline. The thought of one day living on her own was starting to sound more and more exciting.

As DonnaMae pulled her needle through a final knot to ensure it was secure, she admired how the light blue thread perfectly matched the skirt fabric. She ran her fingers over the knot, remembering her grandmother's advice about adding a latch at the top, but that would mean starting over, since she hadn't left enough room at the top of the skirt. Eager to wear the skirt, she decided against the latch. She held the skirt out in front of her and smiled at the finished product. Dark blue dragonflies traced in silver sparkled in the morning light.

Over the summer, DonnaMae had taught herself to sew on her mom's old sewing machine. Sometimes when things got too complicated, her dad directed her to seek help from her grandmother, but more often than not, he would help her find a solution. One time, to patch a hole she somehow cut into the side of a purse she'd just finished making, they ended up buying some kind of melting glue she had to iron to make the fabric stick together. It actually turned out better than when she had started. "Sometimes mistakes are the best thing that can happen," her dad told her. The purse even ended up having an extra little pocket she could put her house key in. But she didn't want to have to buy glue for this dragonfly skirt.

DonnaMae looped the needle back through her seam one more time and tied an extra knot to make sure it was good and secure. She used her teeth to snap the thread. "Done," she said, hopping off her bed, "and just in time." She slipped out of her pajama pants and stepped into the skirt.

She hoped wearing the skirt today would give her the extra boost of confidence she needed for tryouts. *I mean, check out this outfit*, she thought, heading to her new full-length mirror, which she'd framed with repurposed chicken wire and painted clothespins to hang pictures. She gave herself a once-over, twisting to make sure every detail was perfect. She'd carefully scrunched her long blonde hair with gel and managed to get perfect beachy waves. The top she'd selected for the skirt looked even better than she'd hoped. "Oh yeah, the girls are going to flip!" she said.

DonnnaMae laughed at her desire to fit in at home. More than anything, she wanted to be recognized as DonnaMae, not just as MaryLou's daughter or Allan's little sister. Was that wanting to fit in, or was that wanting to be her own person?

"Stop checking yourself out," Allan said, leaning against her door frame. "We have to go. We're going to be late for school."

There was no bus that ran from their house to the high school, so every day Allan had the privilege of chauffeuring them to school in his little old man Chevy S-10 pickup truck. It had a cream-colored exterior with red, yellow, and maroon pin stripes that ran down the sides, and a matching maroon interior.

"I'm not checking myself out," said DonnaMae, "I'm checking out my handy work."

"You make that rag you're wearing?" Allan teased.

"HEY!" DonnaMae scowled. "Say three nice things about my skirt!"

"No. But I was just kidding. Good job, Sis, it looks like you bought it. Other than this string hanging down." Allan reached over and ripped a loose thread from the skirt before DonnaMae could say anything.

"Thanks," she said, anxiously lifting her shirt and inspecting the seam for any signs of unraveling. Today marked a big milestone for her: proudly wearing her first self-made skirt in public, among her peers at school. She wanted to make sure nothing went wrong.

"Maybe I'll be a fashion designer." she said. "I'm pretty good at this."

"Yes, add that to your list of things you want to be when you grow up." Allan rolled his eyes. "You look great. Can we please go?"

DonnaMae didn't want her brother's comment to sting, but it did. She had no idea what she wanted to be when she grew up, and everyone else seemed to. People expected her to become a teacher, just like her mom, but school wasn't easy for her. Why would she want to teach others when she struggled to learn herself?

Trying to shake off her brother's words, she rolled her eyes dramatically and let it go. "WOW! Normally I'm the one begging you to be ready so we're not late," she said, tilting her head with a smirk. "What's the catch? Or should I say, who's the catch?"

"Ha, I wish," Allan laughed. "We have a test in homeroom, and if you're late, you fail. If my grades tank, Dad's taking the truck keys, and we'll both be walking to school."

As if someone had flipped a switch instantly activating her turbo speed mode, DonnaMae pushed past Allan out the door. "Well, hurry up. What are you waiting for? Let's Go!" The school wasn't that far from home, but unlike the middle school it was over a bridge, and DonnaMae hated walking over that bridge.

They arrived at school earlier than usual, beating the bell for once. There wasn't enough time for DonnaMae to hang with her friends, but enough to drop off some books at her locker on the top floor of the main building, where the freshmen and sophomores hung out. The hallway buzzed with students engaged in conversations, leaning against the navy blue lockers.

"MAE!" she heard Izzy yell from somewhere at the other end of the hallway.

"IZZY!" DonnaMae hollered back, spotting Izzy's bright red curls bouncing up and down. That was one thing DonnaMae and Izzy had in common: they both had extremely loud voices.

DonnaMae weaved through the hallway and made it to her squad. "Good morning, gals." she said, striking a pose.

"You finished it!" Ella beamed, clapping her hands.

"Sure did," DonnaMae said. She dropped her blue Jansport backpack to the floor and gave a quick turn to display her skirt. As her hands brushed over the outfit, she felt an odd pulling sensation on the waistline of her skirt. She twirled again and gracefully ended with another striking pose, stealing everyone's attention.

"It turned out so great," Hazel said, giving DonnaMae an approving nod. "Perfect choice for choir auditions today."

DonnaMae grinned. "And it's Izzy's band tryouts today too!"

Izzy let out a snort, flipping her hair. "No, Sugar, that's tomorrow. My folks are ridin' me hard 'bout practicin' for both jazz and marching band, though. Think I'm gonna blow a gasket."

Ella's brow furrowed as she glanced between the girls. "Wait, how are you gonna do band and cheerleading, Izzy? And Mae, how are you gonna do cheerleading and advanced choir?"

DonnaMae and Izzy shared a look, then shrugged. "We'll figure it out," DonnaMae said with a casual wave of her hand.

Izzy winked. "Like we always do."

"Well, I'm fantastic at tryin' out for... absolutely nothin'," Ella added with an awkward grin.

DonnaMae laughed, slinging an arm around her shoulder. "Not true! You've gotta try out for my bowling team again this year."

Ella playfully pushed her off. "Psh, I'm already on your team. Besides, it's just us!"

"Nu-uh!" Hazel jumped in, hands flailing in protest. "I've got golf tryouts and weekend practices, so don't even think about askin' me to join your silly bowling team." She crossed her arms, giving them a pointed look.

Izzy chimed in, copying Hazel's move with exaggerated flair. "Yeah, y'all can keep that to the two of you. Band nerd over here doesn't do bowling."

Hazel narrowed her eyes at DonnaMae, suddenly serious. "Wait — are you not doing science club with me, Mae? You promised! We've gotta do the camps together, and next year we can —"

DonnaMae held up her hands to calm Hazel. "Yes, yes, I'm doing all the things. We'll do science camp after bowling on Saturdays. Bowling's in the morning."

Izzy burst out laughing. "Mae, what *aren't* you doing?"

DonnaMae smirked, dodging the question. "Speaking of doing things, are we still on for a sleepover this weekend in the rec room?"

But before anyone could answer, the bell rang and they all quickly grabbed their things. DonnaMae bent down to grab her bag and felt her skirt fall loose around her waist. She quickly let go of her book bag and grabbed at her side before standing up.

"What is it Mae?" Ella asked, walking up next to her.

"Bye y'all," Izzy said, closing the locker door. "I've gotta bounce. My class is in the other building." She bounced off, her red curls following suit.

"Mae?" Ella said again.

"See you both back here for lunch. I have to get to Mr. Grizzlies' class on time or he is a bear." Hazel giggled as she scampered off down the hall.

"Mae, you're not answering and you haven't moved. Are you ok?" Ella approached DonnaMae as other students bustled by in the hallway. "Did you hurt your back? One time my dad —"

"No, my back is fine," DonnaMae cut her off, yet remained frozen in place.

"Well, um... what is it, then?"

"This morning, my brother pulled a string hanging off my skirt." DonnaMae clutched her skirt tightly to her body. "I think it was connected to the zipper." She swallowed hard, whispering so softly she wasn't sure she'd actually spoken. "I'm afraid it might fall off if I stand up."

The hallway had mostly cleared, though voices still echoed from the open classroom doors. The fear of her skirt unraveling and exposing her bright blue underwear was paralyzing. DonnaMae glanced up at Ella, who was taking off her jean jacket. "Here, wrap my jacket around your waist?"

"Thank you, but how am I —"

Ella didn't give DonnaMae a chance to finish before she was standing behind DonnaMae with her jacket stretched out wide like a curtain.

DonnaMae's heart raced. Her pulse thudded in her ears. She glanced around, wishing the ground would swallow her up. She could feel the heat creeping up her neck, spreading across her face. Her friends had just praised the skirt she'd sewn herself. Now they would see that she had failed. One more thing for her to add to the list of things she wasn't good at. DonnaMae clung tighter to her skirt as she slowly stood, afraid it would disintegrate in front of everyone. *So much for being a fashion designer*, she thought, trying to laugh at herself so she wouldn't cry. *Right now, I'm more of a fashion disaster.*

"We can figure something out," Ella said, her voice calm, as if they were simply fixing a broken hair tie. She threaded her jacket sleeve through the arm DonnaMae she was using to clutch her skirt, then walked around to face her. With a smile, Ella tied the jacket securely in front of DonnaMae. "There!"

"Thanks," DonnaMae said, adjusting her hold. "But now what?"

"Yeah, I have no clue, and we're going to be late for class," Ella said.

"You should probably head to class and I'll just have to figure something out."

"I can't leave you like this." Elle bent over and picked up DonnaMae's backpack. "However, my mom will kill me if I'm tardy." She tapped her fingers against her chin. "If I remember right, last week when we were in the office, the lady at the attendance desk said she knew your mom and if you ever need anything —"

"That's right!" DonnaMae cut her off, pinching her skirt tighter around her waist. "Come on, let's go!"

Ella followed.

In the stairwell, the sound of their feet tromping down the stairs seemed loud enough to make everyone run out of their classroom and wonder what was going on. DonnaMae felt her hand grow sweaty and tightened her grip. They were almost at the bottom, and the office was not far from there. As they rounded the corner to the last set of stairs, so did a tall boy with dark hair and frosted tips. His sun-kissed skin and light blue eyes caught the attention of both girls, causing them to halt in their tracks.

"Hi, can you all tell me if I'm going in the right direction?" he asked. "It's my first day."

"Uhh," was all DonnaMae could get out of her mouth, but her head was saying plenty of other words. *Yes, you gorgeous human. Let us accompany you on your journey, leading you to your desired location. Your eyes are stunning. Hi, I'm DonnaMae, want to be friends?*

Ella coughed, clearly hiding a laugh. "You will have to excuse my friend. She... doesn't speak English."

"*Bonjour*," DonnaMae said in full confidence.

"*Salut, je m'appelle Will, ravi de faire ta connaissance*," Will said, extending his hand.

DonnaMae didn't move. If she let go of the handrail she might pass out, and if she let go of her skirt, she was going to be half naked. The jacket was covering the wrong side of her at the moment.

Ella no longer held back her laughter. "I'm pretty sure my friend just forgot how to speak altogether."

"I did not, but I actually have no clue what the hell you just said?"

"Well, it's a good thing you don't speak French," Will laughed, dropping his hand, "because that's all I know. Well, and 'cat' and a few numbers."

"Which room are you heading to?" DonnaMae asked, the words falling from her mouth before she was even sure what she was saying. Throughout her life, she had become skilled at winging it and telling others what they wanted or needed to hear, putting her own emotions on hold. At this moment, she was thankful for her ability to do so.

Will's face twisted as he searched through his pockets and scanned the surrounding area. "Crap, I must have left that paper they printed for me in the office."

"That's where we're headed," Ella said, giving DonnaMae a side smirk. "You can just come with us."

DonnaMae was not excited about this idea. She could be half naked with one wrong move and now it could be in front of what seemed to be the hottest new guy in school. She let Will and Ella walk ahead of her, so they wouldn't witness her being terrified for her life while descending the stairs.

The main office doors were open as usual, leading straight to a central reception desk. Behind the front desk, there was an open workstation lined with other offices, all of which had their doors wide open except for the one in the back. That was the principal's office, and those doors were always closed. DonnaMae could see the back of Mrs. Duhn's head through her open office door, covered with soft brown curly hair.

Will stopped at the reception desk and DonnaMae headed over to Mrs. Duhn's office. Ella turned and gave a quick wave, "Good luck, Will. Nice meeting you!" But she never stopped walking with DonnaMae.

DonnaMae knocked on the door frame. "Excuse me, Mrs. Duhn," she said in her best library voice.

Mrs. Duhn swiveled in her chair and her face filled with delight as she waved the girls in. "Come on in, sorry these new computers are going to be the death of me, I just can't seem to —" She stopped as if realizing who had knocked on her door. "Oh my, hi Mae! How are you?"

A wave of comfort washed over DonnaMae. This woman used to work with her mom at her old school. She didn't remember her, but there was something comforting about her that made DonnaMae feel like she was talking to her grandmother.

The office had no windows, and the walls were a light beige, yet it felt so full of cheer. Mrs. Duhn's desk was against the only wall with nothing on it, except for a picture of her family and a dog. The other wall had a giant cork board covered in flyers and posters.

DonnaMae pulled the door shut with her free hand. "Well, I have had better days," she said, sliding the jacket from around her waist. She let go of the skirt just enough to expose the situation, without letting the skirt slip off her hips. "I made my skirt, but my brother pulled a string this morning and, well..." She opened her hand so Mrs. Duhn could see the zipper that was only holding on by one side.

"Oh dear," Mrs. Duhn said, "I don't have any of my sewing stuff with me at school."

DonnaMae scanned Mrs. Duhn's desk as she talked, hoping to find some glue or even duct tape at this point. The second bell rang, startling them all.

"Things are about to get crazy for me with all the tardy slips and calling all the parents." Mrs. Duhn paused. "Who's class are the two of you supposed to be in? We better make sure you get excused tardy slips, and I better write it all down so you don't get marked as late, or worse, unexcused all together."

DonnaMae really didn't care about being tardy, but she knew that was a big deal for Ella, so she didn't interrupt while Mrs. Duhn talked. DonnaMae carefully took in all the items on her desk, stopping on the little container of paper clips and thumbtacks and blue wall tacky stuff. Was there a way she could MacGyver those things together to fix this? She knew both her dad and her brother would be able to figure this out. Hell, MacGyver could probably build a bomb out of the things Mrs. Duhn had on her desk. DonnaMae was about to give up and ask to call her grandma when something caught her eye. "I have an idea. Can I borrow your stapler?" she asked, reaching forward and picking it up.

"Yes, yes, of course." Mrs. Duhn waved her hand while she scribbled away on her notepad.

DonnaMae stepped to the back of the room, out of view from the small window that ran down the right side of the office door, and let the skirt fall down so she could step out of it.

"MAE!" Ella said, quickly grabbing the jacket off the chair and holding it up to shield her.

"No one can see me, and I'm sure Mrs. Duhn has seen underwear before. In fact, she has probably seen mine. Well, most likely it was a diaper, but same difference."

"Oh my gosh, that doesn't make it ok," Ella said, stretching her arms as wide as she could and shaking her head in disapproval. Laughing at how protective Ella was, DonnaMae stapled the side of the zipper on the dress, then unzipped it, stepped back into it, put it back on, and zipped it up once more. "Ok, ok, I'm dressed." DonnaMae giggled, pushing the jacket away. "Can you help me, please?"

Ella put her jacket back on. "If you promise to keep your clothes on, yes."

"Um, yes, kinda. Hold my shirt up please." DonnaMae pulled down her blue tank top and lifted the white top up for Ella to hold. She then went along the whole top of the skirt and stapled the skirt to the bottom of her tank top before pulling the white top back down and smoothing it out. Mrs. Dunh was no longer paying attention to them. She was busy typing away at her computer. DonnaMae set the stapler back down to the side of Mrs. Dunh's computer. "Thank you."

Mrs. Duhn turned to them again. "You fixed it," she said, clapping her hands together under her chin. "Well, my stapler and I will be here all day if you need us again." She picked up two pink slips of paper, "and here are your slips. I wrote that you two were helping me out." She gave them a dramatic wink and a warm smile. "And Mae, I just can't get over how much you look like your mama! Please come by anytime. It's so nice to see you."

DonnaMae opened the door and turned back one more time to say thank you before heading back off to class.

"Do you think that is going to hold all day?" Ella asked, eyeing her skirt as they walked out.

"I'm more worried about how I'm going to get out of this thing than I am about it falling apart again," DonnaMae said, running her hands over her waist line one more time.

DonnaMae's skirt held up nicely, aside from causing intense itching on her skin throughout the day. She had no doubt that her skin would appear as if she had tumbled into a blackberry patch by the time she got home.

Choir was the last class of the day, and it was the class that she wasn't sure she was ready for. She hadn't practiced at all. Actually, she never practiced for choir, except for the rare occasion when she knew no one was home to hear her. After Barney had called her a dying cow, she lost all confidence in her singing and never wanted anyone to hear her at home, just in case. Instead, she would read the music over and over until she had the words memorized.

The song for tryouts was "Ave Maria," and DonnaMae was trying out as an alto in the all-girls advanced choir. The teacher explained how tryouts would go:

first, everyone would sing the song in unison, and then she would call each auditioning student's name, and that student would step forward and sing a section solo.

DonnaMae had a strong desire to sing and be part of the advanced girl's choir. However, she didn't want to sing by herself. She loved singing with others because no one could tell that she was the girl who sounded like a dying cow.

The class completed their warm-up exercises and the teacher instructed everyone to take their positions, with auditioning students in the front row of the built-in risers so they could easily step forward when their names were called. She looked at Donna-Mae, still standing in the second row. "DonnaMae, could you please step down in front? Are you still planning to audition?"

DonnaMae stood still. Her heart raced. Her palms grew sweaty.

"DonnaMae?" the teacher said again.

DonnaMae nodded and stepped down into the front row.

The teacher approached her piano and began playing the accompaniment with one hand while using her other hand to cue everyone to start together.

DonnaMae couldn't shake the echo of the words "dying cow" in her mind, and with each passing second the walls of the room seemed to be closing in on her. The girl next to DonnaMae was chosen to go first, and everyone else fell silent. The girl sang flawlessly, hitting every note with precision, and the teacher signaled for everyone else to join back in.

The air seemed to grow thicker, making it harder for DonnaMae to breathe. She no longer heard the singing around her. Instead, her ears rang with the sound of laughter and the echoing chant of "Look, it's a dying cow." The room seemed to shrink and spin. She felt the need to find a seat, struggling to catch her breath. DonnaMae dropped back and sat on the floor, the sound of her body meeting the ground echoing through the darkening room.

Suddenly, the teacher was standing over her, repeating her name and motioning for everyone to move away. "DonnaMae, are you ok?"

DonnaMae felt relief as the room returned to its normal size and the air became more breathable. "Yeah, sorry, I just got really dizzy and light-headed."

"That can happen if you lock out your legs. Let's have you sit off to the side for this class, and we can test you out after school today if you have time." The teacher stood and addressing everyone in the room: "Let this be a lesson to you all, make sure you are not locking your knees while you are singing. She's lucky she didn't pass out and hit her head. I have seen much worse."

Being in the spotlight was something DonnaMae loved, but this experience was humiliating. How could she let Barney's mean words control her outcome in life? It dawned on her that if she wanted to sing alone, she would have to overcome this fear. She knew if her voice truly sounded as terrible as she feared, they wouldn't allow her to join the choir, and her teacher wouldn't have given her the opportunity to audition.

This week had been a lot, and today just topped it all off.

DonnaMae was more than ready for it to be over. She couldn't wait for the weekend and her sleepover with just the girls. Plus, her grandpa was working on one of his friends' race cars in the shop below the rec room and she couldn't wait to show it off to the girls. This summer she was planning on having them go with her to all the races.

CHAPTER 13

July, 1999

DonnaMae stood on the bleachers, a smile tugging at her lips. It was almost funny how at fifteen, she now loved the very atmosphere she once dreaded as a child. Dust from passing cars swirled around her, blending with the sharp scent of gasoline and the tempting smells from the concession stand. Laughter and chatter filled the bleachers, occasionally interrupted by the roar of a car engine. She wondered if her new little sister Adeline would like racing, or hate it as DonnaMae once did. Maybe she could bring Adeline along next time instead of leaving her with the grandparents.

She leaned against the railing of the bleachers. Ella, Izzy, and Hazel stood with her.

Ella adjusted her sunglasses, squinting at the sun's fading glare, while Hazel sipped on a Diet Dr. Pepper. Izzy bounced on her toes, yelling out random car numbers she thought would win tonight.

On DonnaMae's other side stood Grandpa Delmar, his face warm with a smile. She owed her love of racing to him. He had taught her everything she knew about the races, explaining why each driver might succeed or why they made mistakes on the track.

He taught her it wasn't just the driver that made the car win — it was the whole crew. Whenever she and her friends wondered who to root for, they always turned to Grandpa Delmar for insights. Between her grandpa's shop, her uncles' friends, and her dad and his crew, DonnaMae felt like she knew more than half of the drivers on the track. She couldn't imagine her life without these summer evenings at the races.

Tonight was special. It was the mid-season championship races, a highlight of the summer.

"It's still, like, totally hot out," Ella said, fanning herself with a flier from the concession stand.

"Yeah, but at least it's starting to cool down," Hazel said, taking another drink. "I *can* wait for the sun to set. It's gonna be so chilly."

DonnaMae noticed dark clouds gathering on the horizon. "Is it supposed to rain tonight?" she asked, pointing. "Those don't look like happy clouds."

"Who knows?" Izzy said, not looking away from the track. "I just wanna see the cars race! It's gonna be epic! Your uncle's modified looks brand-new."

DonnaMae smiled, forgetting about the clouds. "I helped him with it yesterday at the shop." She turned to her grandpa, "And I used to think this was so boring."

Her grandpa chuckled, patting DonnaMae on the shoulder. "You've come a long way, Kiddo. Your namesake would be proud."

The thought of Donna Mae Mims sparked a little curiosity in DonnaMae about the possibility of being out there on the track herself someday. This place, these people, and the thrill of the races had become a part of her. Before she could respond to her grandpa, the announcer came over the loudspeaker, informing everyone that the sprint cars were coming out next.

"Look! Look! There's your dad!" Ella cheered, jumping up and down and pointing as the push trucks rolled cars onto the track.

DonnaMae's gaze followed and landed on the deep cherry-red

body of her dad's sprint car. The polished bare metal of the top wing caught the sunlight, making it shine so brightly it was almost blinding. His number, 16E, was in a sparkly diamond lettering, outlined in the same rich cherry red. It seemed too beautiful to be racing on a dirt track. She thought the car looked amazing, but a part of her resented it. The number bothered her. Sixteen marked the years between her dad and Elise, with the 'E' standing for Elise. DonnaMae found it strange. Why flaunt their age gap? It just felt like another way to erase her mom's memory.

Racing was her mom and dad's thing. Now, Elise was down in the pits. DonnaMae doubted Elise even knew how to turn a wrench, let alone change a tire. Elise would make a better trophy girl, with her long legs and tan skin.

Still, DonnaMae was proud of her dad, and she was excited to be showing him off. He had earned a reputation as an amazing race car driver with his impressive talent behind the wheel, and tonight she knew he was going to win the championships. He'd been racing cars since before DonnaMae was born. He started building the light blue sprint car while her mom was alive and completed it in her memory after she passed away. DonnaMae regretted that she hadn't appreciated racing when she was younger.

"It really shines!" Ella said, turning to DonnaMae. "I bet he wins all the races tonight."

"'Cause he blinds all the other drivers, damn!" Izzy said, shielding her face.

DonnaMae laughed. "No, because he is the best driver out there."

"He is one hell of a driver!" her grandpa nodded.

The crowd erupted, and DonnaMae and her friends joined in, cheering wildly. Her dad's sprint car was neck and neck with another, both battling through the last corner towards the finish line. Her dad hugged the inside, but it looked like he was going to take second as the other driver edged ahead.

"He might be the fastest in the straight, but championships are won by who's best in the corners." DonnaMae clenched her hands into fists. "NOW!" she screamed, and just as she did, her dad dropped a little lower and punched the throttle, pulling out of the corner hot.

The checkered flag dropped, and DonnaMae's dad was the first over the finish line by a whole car's length.

The crowd went wild. DonnaMae and her friends jumped up and down, screaming with joy.

DonnaMae looked at her grandpa, who was on his feet but calm. He gave her a nod. "Like I said, one hell of a driver."

Full of pride in her dad and her cool family, DonnaMae laughed and turned toward the concession stands. "Who wants candy?" She bounded down the stands. "Last one there is a rotten egg!" she shouted, running as soon as her feet hit the cement.

"What are you, five?" Hazel said, jogging to catch up to her.

"Says the girl who is trying to catch me," DonnaMae teased, half-glancing back over her shoulder.

The races roared on, and the crowd erupted once again. With her concession snacks in hand, DonnaMae watched, heart pounding, as her Uncle Jay fought fiercely for first place, trading the lead lap after lap with two other drivers. In the final moment, his front bumper barely inched past the other car at the finish line. The stands shook with excitement. Her family was unstoppable tonight.

"Now that's racing," her grandpa said, his eyes gleaming. He looked at DonnaMae, his grin softening into a knowing smile. "Runs through your veins, kid. On both sides of the family." He winked.

DonnaMae knew racing was one of those things that was meant for boys, and that she should just be happy to watch and support from the stands. And she was. But something tugged at her, a funny feeling of wanting more, of belonging out there on the track, in the thick of the action. Why would her grandpa say what he said if he didn't think she could do it? Her brother was already down in the pits with her uncles, and they were working on her Uncle Jay's old hobby stock in the shop, getting it fixed up for Allan to take over driving.

DonnaMae glanced up at the clouds that were no longer in the distance, but looming close by. "Did you feel a rain drop?" she asked, rubbing her arms.

"No, but it feels humid," said Hazel.

"Yeah," Ella said, pulling on her jacket, "I'm warm but, like, not, at the same time."

An announcement came over the loudspeakers, letting everyone know they were going to change the order and have the sprint cars go next just in case of rain. Soon the sprints were all out on the track, warming up with hot laps.

DonnaMae turned towards her grandpa to grab a handful of peanuts from the bag. "Well, this should be interesting. I hope it doesn't rain."

"It might," he said, keeping his eyes on the track. "What the hell are they doing?"

"But also, I'm ok with getting to watch my dad win sooner." DonnaMae giggled, but her grandpa seemed not to be paying attention to her.

A loud gasp erupted from the crowd.

DonnaMae's attention was pulled back to the track just in time to watch a push truck ram into the back tire of her dad's sprint car, sending the car flying through the air. What was that push truck doing on the track during hot laps? Push trucks were supposed to help start cars that stalled or couldn't start on their own, but no cars were stalled or stopped! A loud, metallic crunch shattered the silence, echoing through the stands like a pop can being smashed as the sprint car flipped end over end. It felt as if all the air was sucked out of DonnaMae's lungs. The crunching of metal hitting the track filled the silence between gasps from the crowd. The car tumbled to a stop upside down. Fear gripped DonnaMae.

The silence was deafening. Not a sound came from the crowd, and all the cars had come to a complete stop.

With each passing moment, DonnaMae's heart raced faster, its thumping drowning out all other sounds. *My daddy, he isn't getting out of the car. How could he get out of that mess? My dad is dead.*

The mangled pile of metal that was once a car trapped her dad. An ambulance and fire truck rushed towards it from the center of the track. Men ran to the car. Flames erupted from the push truck.

The touch of Grandpa's hand on her arm jolted DonnaMae. She jumped to her feet. She couldn't just sit there and watch. She needed to be with her dad, she needed to help. She sprinted down the steps, her grandfather's voice calling out behind her, trying to stop her. Determined to reach the pits quickly, she ran as fast as she could down the paved path, adrenaline pumping through her veins.

A light mist fell and covered her skin with cool droplets. The sound of sirens filled her ears. The memory of her mom getting taken away by an ambulance consumed her. *No, I can't lose Daddy too. He's all I have left.*

She ran fast, her feet pounding the pavement to the speed of her heart. A movie of forgotten memories played back unwillingly as she ran.

DonnaMae was suddenly five again, watching her mom fall and hit her head in the classroom. She screamed for help, but teachers brushed past her. Men in uniforms rushed in with a gurney, ignoring her as they attended to her mother. "Mommy!" she cried over and over as her mom was wheeled away. A teacher held her back, leaving DonnaMae trembling and alone in the chaos, crying out desperately, "I need to be with my mommy." She wanted to run after the ambulance.

Tears streamed down her face, blurring her vision as she ran. A voice called out to her from behind. When DonnaMae turned to see who it was, her feet tangled and she hurtled forward, falling in what felt like slow motion. Her knee struck the ground. She threw her arms out to brace for impact.

"Fuck!" she screamed through gritted teeth as her face hit the wet pavement. Her hands felt as if they were on fire. Her knee throbbed, sending waves of pain through her body.

"Are you ok?" the voice sounded closer now.

Anger surged through DonnaMae's veins. "Don't come near me!" she yelled, face down. She could still hear the voice calling out, but she didn't dare look back. She didn't want them to stop her. Summoning every ounce of strength, she hoisted herself up and found her footing. Her legs throbbed. Her lungs burned as she gasped for air. Each step sent searing pain up her legs, causing her to grimace. The weight on her knee was almost unbearable, a warm trickle of blood ran down her leg.

"Mae, you need to stop. We should —"

"NO!" Clenching her hands into tight fists, she absorbed the pain, transforming it into a fuel that propelled her back into a full-force run. She locked her focus on the gate to the pits, following the wails of the ambulance. "No, no, no, not again." She ran faster, forcing the pain away, willing herself to push harder. Blood dripped down her arms as she pumped them faster to help carry her legs. She made it to the open gates to the pits and picked up her pace.

"HEY! You can't —"

"That's my dad! Fuck off!" she screamed, cutting the man off and not stopping. The ambulance was coming straight for her. She slowed down to let it pass. How would she know if it was her dad? It moved slowly towards the gate, a group of people followed behind. She strained to see her stepmom through the back windows of the ambulance as it vanished beyond the gates.

"DADDY NOOOOOOOO!" She started jogging after it, screaming, but two men forcefully held her back.

"No, stop! That's my dad! I need to be with him."

"Mae, it's alright. They're just taking your dad to make sure he's ok." She was no longer listening. She knew the men, they were her dad's friends who also raced, but she didn't hear their voices. It was her teacher's voice from all those years ago that consumed her.

"It will be alright, Mae." DonnaMae pulled away from the teacher trying to hold her. "It's not alright. My mommy needs me, but those people took her away." She screamed, "I need to help my mommy!"

But this time she was not a little girl and no one was going to stop her. She ripped her arm from their grasp. "Don't touch me!" she screamed and shoved them off her and ran.

"Mae, Mae slow down."

She knew that voice. "Brother?" DonnaMae came to a complete stop and turned towards her brother. "It's dad he — I —" She swallowed a sob, "I saw everything, he —"

"A push truck hit dad. I know. When they told me I thought it was a joke." Allan was beside her now, breathing heavy.

"I — he — what if he's dead, or he dies or —?"

"Don't think like that," Allan cut her off. He took a step back, scanning her from head to toe. "What the hell happened to you?"

DonnaMae hadn't even realized the severity of her injuries, and she didn't want to. Instead, she focused her gaze on her brother, not daring to look down. "I'm fine. Hello! Dad was just taken away in an ambulance!" *Who cares about a little scratch?*

"Um, ok, they're not just little —"

"ALLAN!" DonnaMae yelled at her brother.

"Ok, ok! They're taking him to the McCleary Hospital. Can you still run?" he asked, staring at her knee.

"Are you serious? Did you not just have to catch me?" DonnaMae threw her hands up. "Let's go!"

They took off running to Allan's truck.

The hospital felt like the scene of a scary movie. The walls and floor were a dingy, yellowish off-white, casting an eerie glow under the flickering fluorescent lights. The waiting room felt all too familiar — a place DonnaMae had been before, but this time she wasn't a little girl, unsure of what was going on. Now, she understood it all too well.

Allan stood leaning against the wall. His face held a hint of worry while DonnaMae paced the floor in front of him. The room was so quiet that the buzzing from the fluorescent lights seemed deafening. The air was thick with the scent of antiseptic, a smell that made DonnaMae's stomach churn.

When their step-mom finally emerged, she was as pale as a ghost, her eyes red and wide with unshed tears. "They said you can come see him, but just for a quick visit. He needs to get some rest, and they have to run more tests on him," she whispered, her voice trembling as much as her hands.

DonnaMae stood frozen, her breath catching in her throat, until Allan placed an arm around her shoulders and pulled her closer, offering a sense of comfort. "Come on," he said softly.

DonnaMae walked hesitantly into the room, unsure of what awaited her.

Tubes and monitors crowded around her dad's bed, their beeping and humming filling the room. Her usually lively dad now lay motionless. An image flashed in her mind of her mother lying still, peaceful, as if she were just sleeping. Her dad didn't look peaceful at all. He looked like death.

"Daddy," DonnaMae said, trying to mask her worry. As she approached the bed, she noticed bandages on his forehead and his arm. The machines around him softly beeped in rhythmic patterns, growing louder and adding to her discomfort. "Daaa —" her words stuck in her throat as she inched herself back into her brother.

"Mae, it's ok, I'm ok!" her dad said, turning his head slightly towards her, his eyes tired and full of pain.

"You aren't ok. We're in a hospital and I... I..." She couldn't speak. She would cry — not just cry, she would sob, she would break. The memories of losing her mom flooded her mind, and now, seeing her dad like this, the fear of losing him too was unbearable. The thought of being alone clawed at her heart. Overwhelmed with a mix of relief at seeing him alive and fear, she peered up at her big brother, seeking his strength to hold herself together.

Allan squeezed her shoulder, his silent assurance giving her the strength she needed to keep standing. But the fear and pain still simmered just beneath the surface, threatening to overwhelm her at any moment, not allowing her to speak.

"So, you got hit by a push truck!" Allan said with a light laugh. She could tell he was masking his own fear. He always made everything a joke.

"Yeah, but I'm ok," Dad said in a voice so raspy and quiet they could hardly hear him. "I will be ok, you guys."

DonnaMae made her way to the bed, her brother by her side every step of the way, and reached out to hold her dad's hand. "I love you, Daddy," she said, matching his soft voice. Her heavy heart could no longer fight the tear slipping down her cheek.

"I love you both so much," her dad said, his voice frail yet filled with determination. "Go on and head home. I'll be home when they're done running all the tests —"

"No, we want to stay here," DonnaMae cut him off, but before he could respond, she saw the lack of fight in his eyes and didn't want to cause him any more pain. She paused and then gently sighed, "Ok," pushing away all her fear and giving him a gentle hug. The warmth of his embrace was a reminder of how strong her dad was. Then she walked out of the room with her brother still so close they could have been one.

"He'll be ok, Mae. It's going to be ok," Allan said, and this time she heard him. Not just the words, but the unwavering belief behind them. He wasn't her teacher trying to comfort her with empty reassurances, and she was not a little girl. He was her brother, her rock, and she was older and stronger. At that moment, she knew it was going to be ok because she had him by her side. Her fear still lingered, but her courage grew a little stronger.

"I sure hope so, Brother, cause without dad, it's just you and me against the world." She sighed. She knew Elise and Adeline would still be in the picture some way, but they were not her real family. The thought of losing her dad made her want to be sick. He might have gotten married, and he might not be around as much, but he was her dad, and she didn't know what she would do without him.

CHAPTER 14

January, 2000

DonnaMae gripped the steering wheel tightly, her knuckles turning white as a car flew past her. The memory of her dad's recent race car crash played through her mind like a horror movie on repeat. As she merged onto the freeway, images flooded her thoughts. The twisted metal of his wrecked car, the crushed helmet now on display in their garage: the side of it smashed in so badly her dad shouldn't be alive. But miraculously, he was, and with only a mild concussion, a few bumps, bruises, and broken ribs.

DonnaMae loved driving, and cruising around town didn't bother her at all, but getting on the freeway for the first time after watching her dad nearly lose his life was another story. The sight of fast cars whizzing by sent her heart racing, a reminder of life's fragility and how easily one wrong move could lead to disaster. And that wrong move could be made by anyone. The push truck driver who'd hit her dad had been reckless, thinking he could outrun a sprint car and beat her dad across the track. He shouldn't have even been on the track. Even though her dad had seen the push truck and tried to avoid it by dropping low, there was nothing he could do. The truck hit his back tire and sent him flipping down the track.

DonnaMae knew that in a car, her life wasn't just in her own hands — it was also in the hands of other drivers. What if someone hit her back tire? Would she go flipping down the freeway?

"Sooo, winter formal," her dad said from the passenger seat, bringing her back from her mangled thoughts.

"Yes, winter formal," DonnaMae said, her voice a bit shaky. She added a laugh to cover it up. "Daddy."

Her dad laughed and turned towards her. "Why do you think they call it winter formal? Maybe we should buy you a snowsuit?"

"Because it's a formal dance in the winter, and NO! Dad, please, no snow suit," DonnaMae let out another small laugh, trying to push away the unsettling images in her head. "I wish Mom was here to go shopping with us," she said. It was a thought that had snuck into her mind and escaped her lips. Realizing what she'd just said, her stomach dropped. She glanced at her dad and saw a flicker of sadness in his face. Not wanting to burden her dad with her own emotions, she said, "What about some music?" The weight of her unintended words hung heavy between them. "I'm sorry, Dad. I didn't mean —"

He reached over and patted her leg gently. "It's ok, Mae. I miss her too."

She felt a knot tighten in her stomach. "Good thing I have a dad-mom who can do it all." Keeping her focus on the road, "You want to try on some high heels with me?" she laughed, forcing a bigger smile.

She glanced at her dad briefly again, his expression unreadable. The road stretched ahead. Cars raced past. DonnaMae gripped the wheel tighter, willing herself to conquer her fear of the freeway, and to not say anything else stupid.

"I am trying, Mae," her dad said, and paused for what felt like forever. "She is always here with us. She's inside of you. She's such a big part of you. Some days, I think I'm talking to her when I'm talking to you. You two are so much alike, and that will only grow as you do."

DonnaMae had so many questions. What about her was like her mom? Was she full of energy like her? Did she daydream like her? But she didn't want to upset him. She wanted to spend time with her dad, not make him sad.

As DonnaMae got older, her dad's attention had drifted, and now, with Elise in the picture, DonnaMae felt like she was competing for even less of it. Today was supposed to be special, and she didn't want to ruin it. But deep down, she wished things could go back to the way they were when she was little, when she was the center of his world, and his love and pride were always hers alone.

"Do you think we could also get lunch?" she asked. "I'm starving!"

"I'm hungry too," he said. "Do you want to get food before we go shopping?"

Just as DonnaMae was about to reply, they drove by a massive blue sign with bold red letters outlined in a vivid yellow shade that read SKIPPERS. As they exchanged glances, DonnaMae knew they had agreed on a place. Going to Skippers with her dad and brother was something she loved doing as a child.

After a lunch of fish and chips, Dad said "I'll drive," as they made their way back to the truck.

Relief washed over DonnaMae and they climbed back into the truck with full stomachs and the lingering smell of malt vinegar. They were ready to hit the road to find a dress. She closed her eyes and leaned her head against the window. "Dad wake me up when we get there. I'm so tired."

"I was just thinking the same thing," her dad said. "If you wake up before I do, wake me up." Suddenly the truck swerved hard and fast to the right.

DonnaMae sat straight up. "DAAAD! What are you doing?"

"Oh, I thought we were going to take naps," he apologized sarcastically, regaining control of the truck and continuing down the freeway.

"Ok well, I'm awake now," she laughed.

"Just in time, because we have some serious shopping to do." Her dad pulled off the freeway. "Maybe there is a place where we can get you a tea and me a coffee?"

As they entered the mall, the aroma of perfumes and fried foods wrapped around them. "Where should we go first?" DonnaMae asked as they scanned the giant map of the mall.

"We are here," her dad said, pointing to a red dot on the map. His finger glided across the map and landed on the outline of an enormous department store at the end of the mall. "Should we go to Macy's first? Yes, that looks like a good place to start. With a pit stop at Dairy Queen for a Butterscotch Dilly Bar from..." he dragged his finger along the map to the food court.

DonnaMae loved a good Butterscotch Dilly Bar, but also knew she wanted to look perfect in her dress, and that was probably not going to help. She had heard of other girls at school being on green tea only diets, or water and bagels only. Bagels had become some new health craze, but DonnaMae couldn't quite understand how they were any different from bread. What made a bagel so healthy?

Just then, her eyes caught the familiar JCPenney sign. A wave of childhood memories hit her, of shopping trips with her dad and brother at the small-town mall. She remembered standing in the dressing room, trying on pants she thought looked good, only to hear Allan and her dad outside, criticizing the fit, saying they were too tight or that she was too short for that style. Defeated, she'd end up grabbing the usual loose jeans and baggy shirts, leaving without even trying them on. Those moments had faded over time, buried beneath better memories with friends. But seeing that sign brought it all bubbling to the surface, like DonnaMae was a can of soda, shaken and ready to burst. She squeezed her eyes shut, silently pleading, *Please, don't say anything about me not looking good in these dresses, Dad. Not today. Just let today be good.*

With a slow breath, she opened her eyes and pushed the negative thoughts back down, forcing a smile. She turned to her dad, "You ready?"

It was clear upon arriving at Macy's that it was dance season everywhere, not only for DonnaMae's school. Fancy dresses filled the entire front of the store, creating a colorful and elegant display. The smells of perfumes grew stronger the further DonnaMae and her dad walked in.

DonnaMae practically skipped towards the dresses, her heart racing at the sight of the dazzling sequins and luxurious velvets in a myriad of vibrant shades. Her dad held up a long black dress with a lowcut top that was clearly made for a busty girl. "I think we're in the wrong section. I think these dresses are for women, not girls." His face crumpled as he spun the dress around, examining the slit that went up the side of the leg.

Here we go, DonnaMae thought, determined not to let his comment dampen her excitement. There were dresses here that she was eager to try on, curious to see how she would look in any of them.

"Come on, Mae," her dad said as he led the way deeper into the store. "Plus, these perfumes are too much."

DonnaMae let her hand glide down the side of a long silver sparkly dress, feeling the smooth fabric against her skin. With a sigh, she turned and followed her dad. "Ok, Dad, where should we go?"

DonnaMae couldn't help but smile as they wandered through the girls' section. The more they walked, the harder it became to hold back her laughter at the sight of her dad leading her through the racks of little dresses. Finally, she couldn't contain it anymore and burst out laughing. "Trust me, Dad, I'll always be your little girl, but I don't think any of these dresses are going to fit me!"

"I know that! I was thinking like a teenage girl section, not little —" he stopped mid-sentence. DonnaMae followed his jaw-dropping gaze.

Sure enough, there it was: the junior's section, racks overflowing with elegant hues of purples and emerald greens. Shimmering velvet dresses, satin gowns and sparkly tops lined the back wall. DonnaMae felt like she was walking on air as she approached the sea of dresses. Immersed in the waves of textures and vibrant colors, she went into a shopping frenzy.

"You'd think they'd space these racks a little —"

DonnaMae spun to find her dad right behind her with his arms full of dresses. She burst into laughter, cutting off whatever he'd been about to say.

"I found a few really cool ones," he said, holding out a few dresses. The one in front immediately grabbed DonnaMae's attention. It was a short, shimmery, cobalt blue dress, hanging by two spaghetti straps. She took it from his hand.

"WOW. I love the color of this dress, Dad, it's amazing." The dress glistened in the light as she twisted it side to side. The tag fell forward. It had a red line through the price, originally $60, with $15.95 written below it. "It's on sale," she said. She handed her dad the other dresses in her arms and only took the blue one with her as she walked towards the fitting room. Her dad followed with the rest of the dresses.

As the fitting room employee walked DonnaMae back to a room, her dad called after her, "Wait Mae, you forgot the rest of the dresses."

"Oh, actually, make that," she quickly counted, "eight," and flashed a smile at the young woman holding a door hanger with a bold white number one on it. "Actually, make that nine, please. Sorry," she added, holding up her blue dress in her other hand, as the woman walked back to the small counter to switch out the door hangers.

DonnaMae swiftly shut her door, kicked off her shoes, and

yanked her long sleeve shirt over her head in one fluid motion. She shimmied out of her pants and slipped the blue dress over her head. It cascaded smoothly down her body, settling perfectly into place. It was clearly supposed to be shorter on someone taller, but she liked that it fell just above her knees. The dress was form-fitting but not constricting, made out of stretchy material that contoured elegantly to her frame while still allowing room to breathe.

She admired herself in the mirror, the dress shimmering under the light. It was then she noticed her plain, old tan bra peeking out from under the strappy dress. She crossed her arms over her chest, considering just keeping them there the whole dance. She loved the simplicity and elegance of the dress — it didn't need extra frills to stand out, it was perfect. Yet, the bra remained a problem. She tried tucking the bra straps into her dress, but the bra slowly slid down her chest. "Well, that's definitely not going to work," she sighed. After slipping her arms back through her bra straps, she opened her door to seek her dad's opinion. Suppressing her excitement, she spun around for him. "What do you think?"

"I think you'll need a different bra?"

"Dad!"

"What? Ok, sorry, turn around one more time," he said, gesturing a circle with his hand.

She turned once, and then again the other direction. "It fits perfectly. Do you like it?"

"Yes, I do," he said, his eyes lighting up. "The fit is just right, and the color I picked is absolutely fantastic."

DonnaMae jumped up, clapping her hands. "I love it! Well, except the bra part. I don't know what to do about that, but I love it!" She paused, glancing down at her feet. "And shoes, I don't have any shoes this —"

Her dad cut her off, "Looks like we've got some accessorizing to do." His tone was oddly serious.

"Um, Dad, is that a new word in your vocabulary?"

DonnaMae laughed at her dad's suggestion. "Well, if everything goes as fast as finding this dress, we'll be home in no time!" She skipped back to the dressing room with a playful grin.

Two hours later, they had gone to every store that sold shoes in the mall without any luck. "Dad, can we just go?" DonnaMae sighed. "I'm exhausted and my feet are killing me."

"No, we have to accessorize."

"Daddy," she whined, "I don't want to accessorize anymore."

As they passed a bench, DonnaMae stopped, turned back, and dropped onto it with a huff. She couldn't believe her dad was dragging her around the mall. He, of all people, wanting to shop. He hated shopping. They'd found a bracelet and anklet at Claire's right away, but shoes were a nightmare. Every pair they tried either didn't work with the dress or cost a fortune. One pair of black shoes with thick heels had fit fine, but the crushed velvet looked awful with the dress. There was no chance they'd find shoes in the exact color, and right now, she regretted picking the dress at all. She was starting to think skipping the dance might be a better option.

"What are you thinking?" her dad asked, sitting next to DonnaMae on the bench, laying the dress on his lap.

"We go home and I go to the dance in my Romeos?"

"Umm, no, that would not be a good idea." He paused for a moment. "Unless we put some glitter on them and then we —" Her dad jumped up, pulling DonnaMae to her feet. "That's it! Come on, let's go." He practically dragged her by the arm, heading back towards one of the shoe stores they'd already gone into.

"Dad, slow down. What are we doing? Where are we going?"

"Those ugly black shoes. Come on, let's go get them. They fit you perfectly and you liked them."

"Eww no, they looked so bad with the dress. You even said no way."

"We're going to go buy them, and there is this craft store on the way home your mom used to go to all the time. We can get some Cobalt blue glitter, I can spray the shoes with tack glue and then we can dip them in the glitter and I can seal them with a light mist of a clear coat." He stopped abruptly, his gaze lost in the distance. "Well, maybe that could make them shiny, and that's not what we want. Perhaps we should apply a few layers of glue, sprinkle some glitter, and then gently brush off the excess before adding a final coat of —"

"DAD!"

"Oh sorry, I —"

"Yeah, I know, me and my shoes just became your next project and you won't stop until it's finished, and not just finished, but perfected. I know this side of you, and I trust it most of the time. Let's go get the shoes." DonnaMae smiled. She was kind of excited about her shoes being his next project. She knew they would be perfect.

Later, as they walked back to the truck, DonnaMae couldn't help but smile. Each of them carried a bag from the craft store: her dad's full of supplies to make her blue Dorothy shoes, and hers packed with new stamping gear. She'd been on a card-making kick lately, and with the store's clearance on stamps and ink pads, she couldn't resist. Though she had brought her own money, her dad had joined in, helping her choose ink colors. He even picked out something new for her to try: embossing supplies. And he promised to let her use his heat gun so they could figure it out together. It felt like they were tool shopping, but for crafts, and she was surprised at how much fun she had doing it with her dad. He really did love a good project.

One year in grade school, not long after her mom had passed, DonnaMae's teacher had turned the classroom into a little city. Each student was tasked with bringing in cardboard boxes to transform their desk into a store. But DonnaMae's dad, never one to do anything halfway, taught her how to measure her desk and sent her to school with a measuring tape. That night, they built her store out of wood. It had shutters that opened and closed, shelves for her things, and even a real mailbox. The next day, they had to take the classroom door off its hinges just to get her store inside. When it came to projects, her dad was the best. She wasn't worried about the shoes not turning out right — she was more worried about herself not looking good enough for them.

"Mae!"

Her dad's voice snapped her out of her thoughts. She had walked right past the truck. DonnaMae laughed, shaking her head. "Dad, can you drive home? I'm too exhausted to think straight, let alone drive."

"I was going to suggest the same thing," he said with a laugh as she walked back to the passenger side of the truck.

DonnaMae climbed into the truck and dropped her bag on the floor, her new blue dress spread across the bench seat between them. She couldn't stop staring at it, wrapped in the clear store bag with the hanger sticking out at the top. She loved how it fit and how it made her feel — perfect. But what was she going to do with her hair? Should she crimp it, or maybe curl it with tight rollers all day so it would be ready by —

"So, what's your plan for the dance?" her dad asked, interrupting her thoughts. "Are you going with all the girls, or...?" he trailed off, reaching for his seatbelt.

"Oh, well, Brother is going with Izzy. Hazel is going with our friend Jake, Ella is going with Brother's friend Cliff, and I think Paul is taking our cousin, which is strange because she doesn't even go to our school and she's older. But they might be dating — he seems to be at her house a lot. Marie from choir is going to join us after dinner with her date. I think she's going with that guy from —"

"Mae! Slow down," her dad laughed as he started the truck. "What are your plans for the dance? Who are you going with?"

"Well, I was kinda hoping..." DonnaMae pulled at a strand of her soft blonde hair. "You know Brother's friend, Will? I was kinda hoping he would ask me." As she spoke, she felt her cheeks heat. She had a small crush on Will, but hadn't mentioned it to anyone. "Just as friends. He's the only one out of the group not going with anyone," she spit out like rapid fire.

"Huh, well," her dad said, backing out of the parking spot. "That would be fun if you all went together."

"Well, there's also Luka, but he was kinda mean to me. I'm pretty sure he hates me," DonnaMae said, thinking about who was left in her brother's group of friends. She was pretty sure all her brother's friends thought she was annoying, but Luka was extra vocal about it. He had a way of saying things that made everyone else join in on the joke, and soon she became the joke. She had gotten good at laughing at herself, it was easier than standing up for herself or letting it hurt her.

"So, are you going to ask him, or does he have to ask you? How does that work?" her dad asked, pulling her back to their conversation.

"I'm not sure, Dad. I guess we will find out." She shrugged. "I wonder if Brother will be borrowing Grandpa's van so we can all go together." She thought out loud, trying to change the topic as quickly as possible. "If only I wasn't the only one of my friends to not have her driver's license, I would drive us."

"Well, it's not because you can't drive, or because you failed the driver's test. I know you will pass, you just have to be old enough to take the test." Her dad let out a soft laugh, "Don't try to make it go any faster, you're already growing up too fast." He gave her a heart-warming smile. "First dates with older boys at dances and then —"

"It's not a date, Dad. We're just going as friends." DonnaMae giggled. "Could you imagine Izzy and Brother dating? Ha!"

Her dad's face shifted from a warm smile to a stern frown in an instant. The sudden change in his expression was like a cold draft sweeping through the room. "Nope, and I can't imagine you dating Will. He's too old, and there's something about him I just don't like."

Frustrated, she tried to keep her tone light. "Um, Dad, I don't think you'll like any boy I date. But it's not a date, so there's nothing to worry about. Plus, he hasn't even asked me." She gave him a reassuring smile.

CHAPTER 15

February, 2000

DonnaMae sat on the ledge of the auditorium stairs, flipping a folded-up piece of paper back and forth in her fingers. Her feet dangled over the side as she kicked them back and forth. She had wanted to wear her black platform sandals today — they matched perfectly with her camo bootcut pants and black cropped tank top. However, she knew her grandpa would scold her for driving with sandals, so she opted for her black Sketchers instead. Today was the last day of driver's ed and she was glad to be done. She honestly didn't even remember what had happened in class today. She was too excited and distracted by the "love note" Will had passed her after French class. As she scanned the side streets for her grandpa's dark maroon 1989 four-door Ford Taurus, soon to be hers, excitement and impatience mingled inside her. She was ready to start driving, but she also really just wanted to get home to call her friends and to read Will's note a hundred more times. He had asked her to the dance and she could not wait. But she also knew she needed to stay focused on driving.

Today, her grandpa was helping her get ready for her test. Ever since she was five, she had been driving with her grandpa. They would cruise around the campgrounds, with her sitting on his lap, and as she grew, he would add pillows under her so she could reach the pedals and see out of the window. Being in the car business, her grandparents saw a constant influx of different cars passing through their shop, connecting them with a wide network of people in town. Once DonnaMae got her learner's permit, her grandpa wasted no time in having her drive everywhere. He'd pick her up from school, and they'd run errands for the shop or, on some days, head straight for the beach. They'd drive right onto the sand, stop for saltwater taffy, and then head back home. Those were her favorite days — she loved the beach. Some days, he would just read the newspaper, while other days he engaged in conversations about his day and the happenings at the shop. He was known for being quiet and reserved, but was different with her. They communicated effortlessly, as if they had their own special language. He listened attentively and responded honestly, avoiding sugar coating, which she found refreshing. He encouraged her to take part in activities not typically pursued by girls, providing her with her own coveralls for the shop and teaching her skills like welding, changing oil, and rotating tires on cars. He supported her ideas and always asked, "Why?" which made her rethink her choices. Last month, when she wanted to be an undercover detective because it allowed her to dress up and pretend, he didn't laugh — he just smiled. She talked herself out of it, realizing she might want to try many things and choose what she liked best to pursue as a career. Then he said, "I like that idea!" It frustrated her that she didn't have a plan like everyone else, but her grandpa never seemed to mind. In fact, he often said, "It's ok to not have a plan. Sometimes the best things happen when we drive by the seat of our pants."

With driver's ed finished, all that remained for DonnaMae was taking the test and getting her license after her sixteenth birthday. She was the youngest in her group of friends — everyone else already had their licenses and cars. Izzy was the first one to get her car. She had been working hard and saving every penny to afford it, even before getting her license. "Meet the Silver Bullet" she had said, pulling up to school with her 1981, silver Honda Civic the first day she got her license in December. Hazel was next, and her dad found an old city truck, a white '91 Chevy S10, and she of course passed both her tests with one hundred percent. She said the written one was the easiest because they covered it all in driver's ed. DonnaMae hoped that was true. She had a terrible time with tests. The questions looked like a scrambled puzzle, and she had to piece them together before she could answer them.

Still no Grandpa. *He's never late*, DonnaMae thought as she walked down the front steps, dropping her backpack and pulling on her coat.

Ella's dad got her a 1989 Mustang. It was the color of a lightly toasted marshmallow. The doors didn't open from the outside, so they had to climb in through the back, but it ran, and they drove it as often as Ella's parents allowed. Before that, DonnaMae and her friends had to convince Ella to overcome her fear of driving and get her license.

Ella was so smart. She had no problems with school at all, but there was something that always seemed to hold her back. DonnaMae could not figure it out. What was her best friend afraid of? DonnaMae had always wanted to grab life by the wheel and drive, taking every turn fast and free, trying every new thing that came her way. Ella was the opposite. Hell, half the time DonnaMae couldn't even get Ella to try a new milkshake flavor. She always got the same thing, and DonnaMae had to force her to try a bite of whatever crazy flavor she had made up. DonnaMae just didn't understand why anyone would not want to try everything. Life was too short. You could die any moment and she didn't want to miss out on anything. Maybe that was why she couldn't figure out what she wanted to be when she grew up.

Beep! Beep!

DonnaMae jumped at the sound of a honking car horn. She'd

been so lost in thoughts of her friends, she hadn't even realized her grandpa had pulled up in front of her.

"You ready to take the Delmar School of Driving test?" he asked, walking around the car and opening the passenger side door.

DonnaMae ran to him. "Hi Grandpa!" She tackled him with a hug and a kiss before he could get in the car.

"Ooffh. You're in a good mood."

"The sun is shining and I get to spend time with my favorite driving instructor."

"Ha!" He let out a low, rumbly laugh. "That's just because you didn't like driving with your dad."

DonnaMae didn't respond, because it was true. No matter what she tried, she couldn't shake the feeling that she would never measure up to her dad's driving standards, knowing that every move she made was going to be wrong. "Ok, where to today?" she asked, climbing into the driver's seat. "Maybe the beach?"

"Ha, not today." Grandpa pulled out a folded-up piece of paper and a pen from the front pocket of his work shirt. "Your grandma wrote out a list of all the things you need to pass for the test, and we are going to do them all many, many, many times."

By the time they drove up to the front of the Flying A, her grandpa's shop, DonnaMae had mastered each task. As they were getting out of the car, the door to the shop swung open and her Auntie Jo emerged, her beautiful long brown hair catching the sunlight. Her smile was infectious, and her hugs could instantly turn a terrible day around.

"I heard someone is going to be driving soon?" Jo said, walking towards DonnaMae.

"Better stay off the sidewalks," Uncle Delmar Jr. said, walking out behind his wife Jo.

"Oh, you are such a riot," DonnaMae giggled, eagerly welcoming her aunt's warm embrace. "Hey, what brings you guys here?"

"We heard you were out practicing for your test with Grandpa so we —"

"Figured we had better go somewhere off the road so we would be safe," Uncle Jr cut in, laughing at his own joke.

Grandpa stepped out of the car and closed the door. "She did fine. She will pass the test, no problem," he said, walking towards the shop doors.

A smile tugged at DonnaMae's lips. Her grandpa's faith in her warmed her heart.

"But also..." Jo said, extending her hand to reveal two stunning blue earrings. They sparkled in the sunlight, catching every ray with their delicate design. Nestled beside them was a matching necklace, an elegant chain with a teardrop blue pendant that perfectly matched DonnaMae's dress for the dance. "I thought you might need these for next weekend!"

DonnaMae was speechless, her mouth slightly open as she took in the sight of the jewelry. They were perfect, exactly what she had envisioned. She had told her aunt all about her new dress during their bowling night the week before, and now here she was, holding the most perfect gift.

Tears threatened to spill as DonnaMae reached out to touch the earrings and necklace, her throat tightening with emotion. "Auntie Jo, they're beautiful... thank you so much," she finally whispered, her voice barely steady.

She could feel the note from Will in her pocket and couldn't wait to get home to read it again. She was going to the dance and she had a date!

The gymnasium had been transformed into a winter wonderland, with twinkling fairy lights and snowflake decorations hanging from the ceiling. The lights reflected off DonnaMae's sparkly blue dress, making her feel like part of the magical scene. Her soft curls framed her face. Elise had helped her apply just the right amount of makeup, adding a touch of glitter around her eyes to match the dress. Her handmade blue Dorothy-style shoes, crafted by her dad, completed the look. With each step, DonnaMae felt like a fairy, leaving behind a trail of glittery magic.

She caught sight of Will across the room. He looked handsome in his suit, his light brown hair with frosted tips styled just right. His tie matched her dress perfectly, a small detail that made her smile and feel like he cared. He walked over to her, his blue eyes lighting up when they met hers.

"You look amazing," Will said, his voice warm and sincere. As his hand gently touched her arm, a shiver ran down her spine. She really liked him. She knew that if her mom were still alive, she would like Will too. Maybe talking to Elise about it would help soften her dad's stance on boyfriends. He didn't like Will and would never approve of them dating. DonnaMae tried to push these thoughts away.

"Thank you," DonnaMae said, feeling her cheeks flush. She glanced down at the corsage on her wrist. Will had picked out the perfect one, the blue ribbon was almost the same color as her dress and the white rose matched the one she had picked out for the boutonniere pinned to his lapel. She worried that her brother might have pressured Will into taking her to the dance and that Will didn't actually like her. But right now she didn't want to think about that, because it didn't really matter if he liked her. There was nothing to become of them other than friends.

The music transitioned to Savage Garden, "Truly Madly Deeply," and kids walked off the dance floor to make way for couples to slow dance. The lights dimmed, casting a soft, intimate glow across the gymnasium. DonnaMae's heart fluttered as Will slid his hand down her arm and took her hand, gently leading her to the center of the dance floor.

She glanced up at him, smiling down at her, showing off his perfectly straight white teeth. For a moment, the world around them seemed to blur, and all she could focus on was the feeling of being in his arms. They swayed gently to the music, their bodies moving in perfect harmony. DonnaMae's hand rested on his shoulder, and she could feel the steady rhythm of his breath.

Despite the whispers of doubt in the back of her mind, DonnaMae allowed herself to be in the moment, letting the music's soft melody wrap around them. She was dancing with Will, the boy she had a crush on, and for this brief, beautiful moment, nothing else mattered.

Will leaned in slightly, his voice soft. "You're a great dancer, DonnaMae."

"Thank you," she said, her voice barely above a whisper. Her heart soared at his words. She hoped he meant it, and just maybe he was enjoying their time together.

As the song came to an end, Will's hand lingered on her back for a moment longer than necessary, and DonnaMae couldn't help but smile. Regardless of what the future held, she knew she would cherish this night forever.

"Wannabe" by The Spice Girls erupted over the dance floor, and the mood in the gym shifted. DonnaMae and Will joined Allan and their friends, laughing, dancing and screaming the song together as a group. Izzy was laughing as she danced with Allan and Marie. Hazel looked beautiful in a sleek red dress, doing the twist with Jake. Ella and Cliff were barley dancing, but they laughed at Paul and his crazy dance moves.

DonnaMae caught her brother's eye. He gave her a thumbs up, and DonnaMae laughed. It was a night of pure joy, surrounded by friends and feeling like she was exactly where she was meant to be. She was fitting in and she was having so much fun, she never wanted to leave the dance floor.

CHAPTER 16

April, 2000

DonnaMae sat in the parking lot outside the DMV with her grandpa, her heart racing. It was finally the day of her driving test. The sky was gray and cold, typical for the Pacific Northwest, but at least it wasn't raining.

"You ready?" DonnaMae asked, glancing over at her grandpa as she opened the car door.

"Am I ready?" he chuckled, shaking his head with a smile.

DonnaMae hadn't expected to be nervous. She'd driven plenty, and her brother had passed his test on the first try, saying it was easy as long as you didn't mess up parallel parking. It must be because her family and friends all knew she was taking her test today.

Rubbing her hands together as if warming them by a campfire, she whispered to herself as she walked, "Ok, I got this."

"You'll be fine," Grandpa Delmar said, opening the glass door, making the little bell chime. "I'll be right here." He settled into one of the dark green metal chairs in the waiting area. The place was half-empty, and felt like an unfriendly doctor's office.

DonnaMae approached the reception desk where an elderly lady with gray hair pulled tightly into a bun spoke so softly that

DonnaMae had to lean in to hear. "Take a ticket, and we'll call your number."

"I'm here for my —" DonnaMae began.

"Take a number," the lady repeated, a little louder this time.

DonnaMae pulled a number off a wheel of paper — fifty-two — and went to sit by her grandpa. As she dropped to her seat, the lady's voice called number fifty-two over the loudspeaker. "Seriously," DonnaMae rolled her eyes at her grandpa, who just let out his little grumble chuckle.

She walked back to the desk. "Hi, I'm here for my driver's test. My name is DonnaMae and I have a —"

"Fill this out and your driving instructor will be out in a minute to help you," the lady said.

"Ok, thank you," DonnaMae said. *I sure hope it's not you*, she thought. DonnaMae halted. *That's not nice, Mae,* she thought. She struggled to think of three positive things about the lady. *I'm sure she is a very nice grandmother to someone.* She decided that was good enough for today and joined her grandpa to complete the paperwork.

A tall, lean man wearing dark brown suspenders over a green shirt walked out into the waiting area. "DonnaMae."

"Well, I guess I didn't need to get another number," DonnaMae laughed as she stood up. Her grandpa gave her a cheeky smirk.

Ok, here goes nothing, she thought, gripping the pen to the top of her clipboard so tight it was digging into the palm of her hand.

They walked outside to DonnaMae's car and the instructor circled it, inspecting every detail. He then stood by the passenger door, waiting for her to get in before following suit. He barely spoke, just scribbled on his clipboard before giving instructions.

"Pull out, go to the light, and turn right. At the next light, turn left."

This went on for what felt like forever, each note he jotted down making DonnaMae more nervous.

"So, do you have any plans for the rest of the day?" DonnaMae asked, trying to ease the tension.

"This is not a social event. This is a test. Pull over and park," he said in a cold, calm voice.

DonnaMae followed his instructions, her heart racing as he continued scribbling on his clipboard. *Calm down, it's not a big deal. He's just taking notes. You're doing fine,* she reassured herself.

As they drove on, the instructor's continued silence made her focus too much on his notes and what he might be thinking. Was she doing everything right? Was he satisfied?

"You know, I drive every day with my grandpa. I've been doing it for years."

"Please focus on the road," he said, his eyes fixed straight ahead.

DonnaMae wanted to keep talking, but knew better. She just wanted the test to be over. The only thing left had to be the parallel parking back at the DMV. Almost done.

"Pull into that driveway coming up on your left and park."

Once she parked, DonnaMae glanced over at the instructor as he quickly jotted something down on the side of his paper. Before she could stop herself, the words tumbled out, "How many of these do you do a day?" She didn't mean to keep asking questions.

He let out an annoyed huff. "Back out of the driveway and turn right," he said, his tone clipped.

She couldn't stop thinking that she was constantly making mistakes, feeling like a failure. Why else would he be furiously jotting down so many notes? Her thoughts felt scattered, as if her grandpa's wisdom was swirling around in her mind, causing confusion. Which way was right? *Focus, check all your mirrors and look both ways,* she thought. Everything was reversed, and she felt disoriented, her left and right became jumbled in her mind.

She backed out of the driveway and knew as soon as she drove over the sidewalk and into the street, she had messed up. She didn't stop twice. She did check the road again after she checked the sidewalk. Her face flushed red and she pulled all the way out and turned to drive forward, catching a quick glance of her instructor before looking ahead. He had stopped writing and folded his arms over the clipboard that was in his lap.

"Head back to the DMV, please."

The ride back was filled with silence — no words exchanged, no notes scribbled — only the sound of the tires rolling over the pavement and the distant hum of other cars.

When they pulled into the parking lot, DonnaMae knew something was up when the instructor pointed towards a stall and said "Park right there." They had not done the parallel parking yet, and parking in a stall was surely not part of the test.

She started mulling over the test in her head, parking on a hill, parking by a curb, knowing the proper signals. She knew all of them. This was not one of them.

"We're done. You failed the test. You can reschedule in another week. When we go back inside, just take a number and —"

"WHAT!" DonnaMae was in shock. How did she fail? She knew this test, could do it blind. She must have heard him wrong. "What did you say?"

"Well, before you interrupted me, I was letting you know you can re-take the test again in a week. You failed because you didn't double check when backing into the street and it's an automatic fail. You have to check the sidewalk and the street."

She didn't respond. She knew she'd messed up, but she didn't know it was an automatic fail. The word echoed in her mind, *failed*. How was she going to walk back in and tell her grandpa? Her friends? Her Dad? Her heart sank, and her stomach twisted around it. How could she go home and tell him she failed? That she didn't even get to finish the test?

DonnaMae reached for the door handle but paused, exhaling slowly.

The instructor got out of the car and closed his door.

DonnaMae blinked fast, tilting her head back against the seat.

"How in the hell am I supposed to go inside and tell Grandpa? Then tell Dad? I could really use you right now, Mom. Please help me stay strong. Please don't let me make this worse." She opened the door and stepped out.

Her grandpa stood up as the door opened. He looked so young and fit, like a man half his age. As he walked towards her, DonnaMae burned with shame. She fought back tears.

"I, um... I forgot to double-check when I —" She paused, swallowing hard to keep her emotions in check. "I have to go take a ticket to reschedule another appointment for next week."

His brows furrowed. "Another appointment? You already passed the written test?"

"Yes, sir, but I haven't passed the —" Her voice cracked.

Before she could finish, Grandpa put an arm around her shoulder, pulling her into a comforting side hug. "Well, now you know what to expect for the next test," he said, guiding her to the reception desk to pull a number. "You know, Mae, your mom failed her first driver's test too. It's ok to fail, as long as we learn from it. So, that's what we'll do. We'll find out what went wrong, and we'll practice."

DonnaMae's eyes blurred with tears she was trying so hard to hold back. She grabbed the ticket in front of the little old lady, and she and her grandpa stood there in silence, waiting for the number sixty-five to be called over the intercom.

DonnaMae sighed when her grandpa dropped her off at home. Only Elise's car was in the driveway. *Great*, she thought, her stomach sinking a little. At least she didn't have to face her dad yet.

The smell of fresh laundry hit her as she walked into the living room where Elise was folding clothes. DonnaMae dropped onto the couch without a word.

Without even looking up, Elise said, "You know, the first test is pretty much considered a practice run. Only the second one really counts."

DonnaMae blinked in surprise. "How did you know I failed?"

Elise stopped folding, pushed the laundry aside, and sat down next to DonnaMae, her face soft. "Because I failed my first test, too."

DonnaMae turned towards her, a few bricks falling from her anti-stepmom wall. "You did?"

Elise nodded. "I was a mess about it, but I learned that it wasn't the end of the world. It's frustrating, I know. But we'll figure out what went wrong, and I'll help you however you need. We'll make sure you're ready for the next one."

DonnaMae felt a lump in her throat, but it wasn't from sadness this time. There was something in Elise's voice, a genuine care that DonnaMae hadn't fully let herself hear before. She wanted to let her stepmom in.

"Thanks, Elise," DonnaMae said quietly, glancing down at her hands. "I... I'd appreciate the help."

Elise gave her a small smile, her hand resting briefly on Donna-Mae's shoulder before returning to the laundry. It wasn't much, but DonnaMae could tell. Elise cared. And for the first time, DonnaMae felt ok with it.

The week that followed was packed with practice sessions. Elise started asking DonnaMae to drive whenever they needed to go somewhere, and when it was just the two of them, DonnaMae actually enjoyed it. But whenever they were all together as a family, something shifted. DonnaMae couldn't help but feel out of place, like she didn't quite belong.

Her grandpa made her tackle the highway, and slowly, her fear of the speeding cars around her began to fade. "This isn't a race-track," he reminded her, "but, like racing, if you're a good driver, you'll see the mistakes coming." He always added that sometimes things happen beyond our control — what matters is how we handle it afterward. He made her park in every driveway and alley they could find, drilling the importance of checking all directions when backing out.

Despite all the practice, doubt still lingered. Some nights, DonnaMae would lie in bed, replaying that failed test over and over, wishing she could turn back time, wishing she'd just done it right the first time.

The day of the retest arrived all too quickly. As they pulled into the DMV parking lot, DonnaMae felt a knot of anxiety twist tighter in her stomach. Her grandpa gave her a reassuring pat on the shoulder. "You've got this, Mae. Remember what we practiced."

She nodded, trying to force a smile. They walked into the DMV, signed in, and waited. Sitting in the same spot, with the same lady helping them, it all felt like *déjà vu*.

The same instructor approached her, clipboard in hand, and motioned for her to follow him. This time, she was determined to stay silent and focused. They got into the car, and the test began.

When they reached the point where she had failed last time, her heart rate spiked. She could feel the instructor's eyes on her as she approached the driveway. This time, she took a deep breath, checked the sidewalk and the street multiple times, and backed out slowly, making sure she did everything perfectly.

"Head back to the DMV," the instructor finally said, his voice giving nothing away.

The ride back felt like it lasted forever. They pulled into the parking lot, and the instructor directed her to do the parallel parking. This part was a breeze for DonnaMae, her dad had made her practice countless times with his hot rods on the street. These cones were nothing.

She parked smoothly, shut off the engine, and waited as the instructor scribbled on his clipboard. The seconds dragged on like hours.

Finally, the instructor turned to her. "Congratulations, you passed." His tone was so flat, DonnaMae wasn't sure she heard him correctly.

She stared at him, and blinked. "I'm sorry, did you say... I passed?"

He nodded, handing her the signed form. "You did well. You stayed calm and focused."

DonnaMae's hands shook as she took the form. She stepped out of the car, her legs feeling wobbly. Her grandpa was waiting outside this time, he was smiling from ear to ear, like he had already known she passed. When she held up the form, a smile spread across her face almost as big as his.

"I knew you could do it, Mae," her grandpa said, pulling her into a tight hug. "I'm so proud of you."

His words hit her hard. If he hadn't been holding her, she might have crumpled. *Proud of me?* she thought, blinking back tears. Sure, she passed, but if she'd done it the first time, he wouldn't have had to waste all that time helping her.

As they walked back to the car, the guilt spilled out. "Grandpa, I'm sorry. I should've passed the first time."

He stopped and turned to face her, his eyes soft. "Mae, life isn't about getting everything right the first time. It's about learning and growing." He gently cupped her face like he used to do when she was little. "Failing doesn't mean you're not good at something — it means you're human. And passing today shows more than just that you improved. It shows your drive, your determination to do better."

His eyes glistened with his growing smile. "That's how you're like your mother. You don't give up — you fight to win."

He reached into his pocket, pulling out a set of keys. "And now you've earned the keys to your own car. Use them wisely." He paused. "And always remember, it's not about how many times you get knocked down, it's about how many times you get back up."

August, 2000

DonnaMae closed the door of her car with a soft click and paused. A smile touched the corner of her lips. She loved that this car was hers, and all the memories it held of her childhood with her grandparents made it that much better. The sky was ablaze with hues of pink, purple, and orange as the sun dipped below the ocean's horizon. DonnaMae rejoined her friends at their fire pit on the beach.

The bonfire crackled, its flames dancing along charred logs, casting flickering shadows onto the sandy beach. As darkness settled in, DonnaMae let the fire's warmth soak into her hands and bare toes. The sound of the waves and the scent of saltwater wrapped around her, offering a familiar comfort that calmed her.

There was something magical about the beach at night, especially with a blazing bonfire and her friends gathered around. As a child, DonnaMae had spent countless hours here, building sandcastles and escaping life's worries. The waves washed ashore vivid memories of her mom, even though she'd been gone for ten years. How had ten years passed so quickly?

"MAE! EARTH TO MAE!" Hazel yelled, sitting on a large piece of driftwood a few spots down from DonnaMae.

DonnaMae blinked. "Sorry, I was zoning out on the flames,"

she chuckled softly, trying to mask her embarrassment at having been so lost in her own world.

"I just said I wasn't the only one to get a perfect score on their driving test," Hazel said and winked at her.

"Um, I didn't. I failed my first test. Didn't even get a score," DonnaMae said with a frown.

"But then you aced it," Hazel said

"I passed both of mine on the first go," Izzy said, grabbing another log from the back of Hazel's truck.

"Just barely, because you winged it both times," Hazel said, tossing her arms in the air.

"Just barely passing is still passing!" Izzy laughed as she threw one more log onto the fire.

"That's not gonna work with your SAT test," Hazel said, rolling her eyes.

"Who said I was taking the SATs?" Izzy grinned. "I'm gonna take over my parents' farm. Maybe use them welding skills we learned from DonnaMae's grandpa to fix up the barn and turn a bigger profit."

DonnaMae smiled faintly at Izzy's mention of their recent welding lessons on her uncle's race car. But her stomach churned at the mention of SATs. She hadn't even considered the test, or if she needed to take it.

"You're still going to college, though," Hazel said.

"Good old-fashioned community college is all this girl needs," Izzy cut in, pointing both her thumbs at herself and flashing her white teeth in a full-faced smile.

"Did anyone bring hot chocolate?" Ella asked, turning towards DonnaMae. "We've got two years until college. Let's save that talk for a school night."

The thought of college in two years made DonnaMae feel even more queasy. She had no idea what she wanted to do or where she wanted to go. Working at her grandparents' shop, the Flying A, was the only thing she'd done, and she didn't want to take it over.

"I brought some peppermint schnapps!" Izzy announced cheerfully, jumping up and skipping over to her car.

DonnaMae pushed away her thoughts and replied to Ella's question, "It's in my car. I brought two full thermoses." She felt relieved to step away from the conversation and get the hot chocolate.

The darkness had deepened and stars began to twinkle brightly above. There was a stillness that made DonnaMae pause and stare up at the sky. It was so beautiful, but she couldn't shake the fear of not knowing her future path.

"Mom, what do I do? I know you always had a plan, but I don't," she whispered up towards the stars. A soft breeze swirled around her, making the hairs on her arms stand up. "Mom!" It was like she was six years old again — she could feel her presence. The air was warm and wrapped around her, causing her body to relax. She smiled, gave a small shake that was almost a shiver, and walked the rest of the way to her car.

Grabbing the two thermoses out of the back seat, she noticed the stack of newspapers she had brought for the fire. They were open to the classifieds. DonnaMae laughed. A job? *Thanks, Mom!* she thought, closing the car door with her foot, her hands full of hot chocolate. *Like I could get a real job.*

The thought of not working at the Flying A for her grandparents and actually doing something else gave her a feeling of unease. As she walked back to the fire, she couldn't help but laugh at herself. Maybe it was her mom, maybe it was just a coincidence, but telling your kid to get a job was such a mom thing to do.

In her heart, she wanted to believe it was her mom, still watching over her, guiding her in times of need. But she also knew there was no way she was going job hunting anytime soon. She didn't even know how to make a resume, let alone interview for a job.

DonnaMae settled back down next to Ella, pouring hot chocolate into tin mugs. She handed one to Ella and filled another for herself before passing the thermos to Hazel and Jake.

Izzy returned and added a splash of peppermint schnapps to Ella's drink.

"Mae, ya want some?" Izzy asked, holding out the bottle towards DonnaMae.

"Mae doesn't drink," Ella interjected before DonnaMae could respond.

"This ain't drinking. It's a splash of flavor to our hot chocolate," Izzy said.

"Well, technically, it's alcohol," Ella shrugged.

"We're not drinking to get drunk," Izzy said. "Just spicing things up a bit."

"I might add some later, but right now I just want to taste it as is. I found a new milk chocolate at Calders, and I haven't tried it yet," DonnaMae said, steering the conversation away. It wasn't that she was against drinking. The idea of losing control scared her, and for her, drinking wasn't fun, it symbolized loss and grief.

Izzy plopped down in the sand next to Marie and Hazel, who eagerly extended their mugs, ready for a splash of flavor.

"So, speaking of spicing things up... Mae, any news on Mr. Charming Will?" Izzy gave her a dramatic wink. "I heard he's been dropping hints about asking you out."

DonnaMae's cheeks warmed slightly as she looked down, trying to mask her surprise. "Oh, really? I hadn't heard that." She had tried not to think much about Will after the dance. He was cool, and kind of part of her brother's friend group, which added him to their overall big friend group, but she didn't want to make a big deal of things. So, she did what she was good at: she pushed her feelings aside to keep everyone else happy.

"Yeah," Hazel said, with a side smirk. "He's been practically mooning over you. I think he's planning to make a move soon. Everyone's been talking about it."

"Well, that sounded a little theatrical, but he for sure flirts with you," Ella said, giving Hazel a clear eye roll.

"I'm not sure if that's a good thing or a bad thing," DonnaMae said with a nervous laugh. "He's been... flirty, I guess, but we're just friends."

"Well, he seems to've taken a likin' to ya," Izzy said, bringing her hands up under her chin and resting her elbows on her knees. "So, what's the plan when he finally does ask you out?"

DonnaMae shrugged, trying to play it cool. "We'll see, but I'm pretty sure he's just nice to me because I'm Allan's little sister. But thanks for the heads up."

As the group continued chatting and teasing, DonnaMae tried to ignore the mix of emotions she was feeling about the idea that Will really might like her. Maybe he would ask her out on a date, but would that be ok? It wasn't not like he was a big part of the friend group, but her dad didn't like him, which was the main reason she ignored her feelings.

"Speaking of exciting things," Hazel said, pulling DonnaMae's attention back to the group, "I've been working on this awesome science project!"

DonnaMae was relieved by the change in subject, even if she wasn't sure what they were talking about right before. "Oh, really? What is it?"

Hazel's face lit up as she described her project. "I've got this miniature ecosystem in my backyard. I've got tiny shrimp that are supposed to maintain the balance. It's like having a little piece of the ocean right at home."

"Wait, so you're tellin' me you've got shrimp swimming around in your backyard?" Izzy grinned, the shrimp part finally drawing in her attention.

"Yeah, and I've even got some snails in there to help with cleaning," Hazel replied animatedly.

Ella nearly spit out her hot chocolate laughing. "That sounds like a science experiment I'd rather observe from a safe distance, thanks," she said, waving her free hand in mock protest, "but no thanks!"

DonnaMae smiled, listening to her friends. Her life had changed so much over the past few years. She didn't know what she wanted to be or do yet, but having the Fab Four, her best friends, made her feel grounded. No matter what, they had each other, and that would never change.

Jake leaned back against the driftwood, sharing stories of his latest skateboarding adventures. Soon everyone was swapping their own tales of close calls and daring stunts.

Never one to sit still, Izzy suddenly jumped up, full of energy. "Let's play beach volleyball! Let's see who's got the skills to back up their talk," she teased, running to grab a volleyball from the back of Hazel's truck.

"How the hell are we going to see?" Marie called towards Izzy. "It's pitch black out there."

DonnaMae laughed, "We turn our cars on and point the headlights towards us."

"And if you hit the ball in the ocean, you've gotta go get it!" Hazel said, getting up and pulling out her keys.

"And I'm the scorekeeper," Ella volunteered, pulling her hoodie tight and grinning, "who stays warm by the fire!"

DonnaMae smirked. "Right, scorekeeper and hot chocolate watcher."

"Alright, Marie and Hazel, let's see if you can put some of those dance team moves to work on the volleyball court!" Izzy shouted, spiking the ball towards Marie with a grin.

The group burst into laughter, quickly forming teams and turning the sandy beach into a makeshift court, moving cars around to light the game with their headlights. For the next hour, they dove and spiked, cheered and teased, spilled drinks, and laughed until their stomachs hurt.

After the game, they collapsed onto the sand, breathless and exhausted. Ella passed around a bag of marshmallows, and soon they were toasting them over the dwindling embers of the fire, still laughing about Jake's face plant and Izzy's spin twists and serve moves. "It's time to 'Razzle Dazzle!'" they laughed once more, repeating Izzy's name for the move.

As the night drew to a close, they gathered their belongings and extinguished the fire. Walking to their cars, arms linked and hearts full, DonnaMae couldn't help but smile. The beach had worked its magic once again, helping her escape from all reality, if just for a little while.

But as she sat in her car all alone after, looking out at the ocean one last time, the waves crashing endlessly against the shore, her own wave of uncertainty washed over her. What if the Fab Four went their separate ways because they all ended up in different colleges, or she got left behind because she couldn't figure out what she wanted to do?

She watched the ocean waves push the sand as it rushed the shore. She wondered if she was more like the sand being pushed around by the waves of life rather than the wild, strong, and free ocean her mom had wanted her to be.

Her friends were her anchor, but the thought that their bond might change filled her with an urgent need to figure out her own path. In the end, she was the only person she'd always have, no matter what. Everyone always seemed to leave her — her mom, her sister, her dad, even her brother for his friends. Why would it be any different with her friends?

As she put the car in reverse, she made a promise to herself. She wouldn't be the sand. She needed to figure out how to stand on her own and be more like the ocean. She looked over her shoulder and smiled at the folded-up classified ads in the back seat.

The afternoon sun poured through the rec room window as DonnaMae's friends crowded around her, their excitement feeding off one another. Hazel was carefully applying the final touches of eyeliner on DonnaMae's eyes while Izzy and Ella sorted through a pile of shoes in the middle of the floor, debating which ones would perfectly complement DonnaMae's outfit.

"I think she should just put back on her Carhartts and wear the damn Romeos, be herself," Izzy said, holding up the dark brown pair of work shoes.

"She is being herself. She can also dress like the girl she is," Ella shot back, picking up a pair of plain black sandals. "Just wear these. Your toes are on point and match the dress perfectly."

"You're going to knock his socks off," Hazel said, her voice full of confidence as she stepped back to admire her handiwork.

"Great, then you two can be matching," Izzy said, tossing her head back with a loud laugh.

"Are you sure these earrings are the right choice?" DonnaMae asked, ignoring Izzy, who was already dodging a shoe Ella had tossed at her. Without a full-length mirror in the rec room, DonnaMae couldn't check herself over like she could at home. She knew her dress looked good — it was light yellow with soft blue butterflies and fit her perfectly, snug through the waist before falling into a gentle, flowing skirt. She had a denim jacket to go with it, but the shoes were the final piece. The girls had all met up to help her get ready, and afterward, they planned to share popcorn and hear every detail about the date. It was a ritual they had done with all their first dates, and now it was DonnaMae's turn. She could hardly believe it. She was used to being one of the guys, not dating one. The idea of having a boyfriend was new, especially with someone she had just been friends with for so long. Maybe it could be more. Maybe she'd get to wear his letterman's jacket to the next school assembly.

DonnaMae ran her hand over her earrings and then through her hair. "I love them, but do they go with this dress?" She hadn't thought to check the outfit with the earrings in her mirror at home before she left.

"Absolutely," Ella said, holding up a small mirror from her bag of everything so DonnaMae could see. "They're perfect. They add just the right amount of sparkle without being too much."

"And they're the same ones you wore to the dance. Maybe he'll remember and..." Izzy giggled, lifting her hand to her face and kissing it dramatically.

"Oh my gosh, Izzy!" Ella threw the other shoe at Izzy. "How old are you?"

"Says the one throwing shoes," Izzy said, with an eye roll and another laugh.

DonnaMae smiled, feeling a mix of nerves and excitement swirling inside her. She had been looking forward to this date with Will ever since he asked her out, and her friends really were the best. They had all been talking about this moment for days, making it feel like she was Cinderella going to a ball.

"Ok, shoes on, and you're ready to go!" Hazel said, handing DonnaMae a pair of perfectly white Keds. "Get them dirty, and you'll have to buy me a new pair," she joked.

DonnaMae slipped the shoes on and stood up, feeling a surge of confidence. She twirled in front of her friends, her dress flaring out just enough to make her feel elegant yet comfortable. Her friends applauded, and she couldn't help but laugh as she took a bow.

"You look amazing, DonnaMae," Hazel said, giving her a quick hug. "Will is one lucky guy."

"I still think you would look better in your Carhartt jeans and —" Izzy started, but Hazel elbowed her in the side before she could finish.

As they all headed downstairs, the girls continued to chatter, giving last-minute tips and advice. DonnaMae's heart raced. She was excited about the date, but even more so about the possibility of something real between her and Will.

When she finally arrived at the burger joint, DonnaMae noticed the parking lot was packed. She circled around the front, searching for a spot, but every space was taken. She decided to park around the back, hoping to find an open spot and avoid being late. As she pulled in, her heart nearly stopped.

There, tucked away in a shadowy corner of the lot, was Will's car. And next to it, Will, with his arms wrapped around another girl, their faces pressed together in something more than just a kiss. DonnaMae's breath caught in her throat, a wave of disbelief crashing over her.

"No way... this can't be happening," she whispered to herself, feeling her stomach drop as she watched them, frozen in time, unable to move.

Anger and hurt quickly replaced the disbelief, flooding her body with a hot, prickly sensation, her breathing and heartbeat the only things she could hear. She had been so excited, so hopeful about this date, and now it was all gone, not even a chance, right before her eyes.

Her dad's words — "just a notch on some guy's belt" — hit her like a bolt of lightning. Without thinking, she slammed the car into reverse, tires squealing as she sped out of the parking lot, not caring who might be watching.

Tears blurred her vision, but she didn't slow down. The world around her became a blur as she drove, her hands gripping the steering wheel so tightly that her knuckles turned white. All the excitement, all the ideas of having a real boyfriend — not just a boy who was a friend — had been ripped away in an instant, replaced by a burning sense of betrayal and a rage of anger. Her dad was right — she needed to be the glass doll on the shelf. She was not going to be some girl that Will would just add to his list.

When she finally reached her grandparents' house, she didn't even bother to pull into the driveway. Instead, she parked haphazardly on the street and stormed inside the garage and up the stairs, not bothering to wipe away the few tears that had escaped down her face. She didn't care. She was furious.

DonnaMae burst into the rec room where her friends were still hanging out, waiting for updates on her date. Izzy froze, a handful of popcorn inches from her mouth, while Hazel dropped the magazine she'd been reading on the pool table.

"What happened?" Ella said, her voice sounding so loud in the suddenly silent room.

"That jerk... I caught him with another girl!" DonnaMae said, her voice quiet and shaky. "He was making out with her in the parking lot!"

"That piece of shit!" Izzy yelled, slamming her handful of popcorn down on the table.

"No way! What?" Hazel said, standing up and walking over to DonnaMae to give her a hug. "Are you sure it was him? That doesn't make sense. We all saw him flirt with you every day."

"Oh, it was him and his car!" DonnaMae's tears of anger spilled over, but she wasn't sobbing, she was filled with anger and hurt. How could she have been so dumb, to think a guy would like her for any other reason than to just want to get in her pants? Her dad had warned her, and she didn't listen. "I can't believe I was so stupid... I actually thought he liked me."

"You're not stupid," Ella said, placing a reassuring hand on DonnaMae's shoulder. "He's the one who's a total jerk. You deserve way better."

"Yeah, he is a piece of shit," Izzy said again, standing up.

Hazel suddenly perked up. "You know what we need to do? We need to get back at him. Make sure he knows he messed with the wrong girl."

"Yeah! I'll give him the good old one-two right to the face," Izzy said, throwing a few punches in the air. "And then a good old-fashioned —"

"Not what I was thinking," Hazel said, cutting Izzy off just as she was raising her leg.

A spark lit in DonnaMae's eyes as she wiped away the last of her tears. "You're right. He needs to pay for what he did."

"And I think I have just the idea," Hazel said, waving everyone in towards her.

The girls huddled together and created a plan. By the time they were done, they had everything figured out, all the way down to the date and time. They had a new mission: Operation Revenge, that would let Will know exactly how they felt about his betrayal.

DonnaMae parked her car a few houses down from Will's place, turning off the headlights as they rolled to a stop.

"We probably should have used my brother's truck or something," Izzy whispered.

"Or we just shouldn't be doing this," Ella said in an even softer whisper.

"Why are you guys whispering?" Hazel asked, turning around to face them in the back seat. "We're in the car."

DonnaMae opened her door. "Not for long," she whispered.

The street was eerily quiet, the only sounds coming from the distant hum of crickets and the occasional rustle of leaves in the breeze. Will's house was dark, with no sign of movement inside.

The girls sat silently for a moment, each dressed head-to-toe in black. Izzy was even sporting a ski mask she had dug out from some old winter gear. DonnaMae couldn't help but chuckle as she adjusted her black beanie over her ears, the memory of her brother trying to sneak into the pits on race nights flashing through her mind. She could just picture him, dressed almost exactly like this, trying to be stealthy but always getting caught by their dad. The memory was what gave her the idea — if her brother could pull off stunts like this at ten, so could she. But she wouldn't get caught.

"Alright, let's do this," she whispered, her voice steadying with determination.

One by one, they opened their bags, revealing the tools of their revenge. Ella was the first to pull something out, holding up a jar of olives in one hand and a spray bottle in the other.

"Fancy olives? And… spray butter?" DonnaMae raised an eyebrow, trying to keep a straight face.

Hazel snickered. "What do you plan to do with that, make him a midnight snack?"

Ella shrugged. "What? It's the only thing I could grab without my mom noticing anything was missing. Besides, who even likes these things?"

Izzy snorted, "Pretty sure that is Hazel's favorite two food groups." She pulled out a bright red tube of lipstick. "This, on the other hand, will be perfect for writing 'piece of shit' on the back window of his car." She twisted the tube, revealing the vibrant color that matched the fury burning in DonnaMae's chest. She still couldn't believe he'd been so nice to her while seeing someone else. Why even ask her to go get burgers?

Hazel pulled out a small bag of flour and a jar of peanut butter. "We'll smear this under the handles, on the windows, and then… we make it rain." She held up the five-pound bag of flour. "Or should I say, make a blizzard of revenge?"

DonnaMae let out an evil laugh. "Operation Revenge!" She held up ketchup, mustard, and mayonnaise. "We're turning his car into the world's nastiest hot dog. And…" she lifted up a small jar filled with clear liquid. "I microwaved some bacon grease before we left. Thought he'd appreciate a little extra flavor."

"He'll wake up thinking someone fried breakfast on his car," Izzy laughed.

"When that cools down, it's going to be a nightmare to clean off!" Hazel said, holding her hand up for a high five. "Brilliant thinking."

DonnaMae reached over and their palms connected with a satisfying smack, causing them all to freeze for a moment. They looked around, but the night remained still and silent. "This guy isn't going to know what hit him," DonnaMae whispered. A twinge of sadness tried to creep in, but she quickly pushed it down, replacing it with a determined grin. Will deserved this — hell, this wasn't just for him. This was for all the guys who had been jerks, and really, for anyone who had ever treated her like a joke. She was done being the punchline — it was someone else's turn now.

"He's gonna think his car got into a fight with a rogue food cart, or maybe a tornado of condiments hit it," Ella giggled.

"What?" The girls all burst into quiet laughter.

DonnaMae felt a thrill run through her as they geared up, their laughter fading into focused determination. Oddly enough, she wasn't even nervous.

"All right," DonnaMae said quietly but firmly. "Let's do this. Just remember — nothing that will actually hurt the car, and nothing in the gas tank!" She shot Izzy a side-eye.

"What? I won't!" Izzy said, holding up her hands like she'd already been caught red-handed.

They crept out of the car, making their way towards Will's old, beat-up Chevy Camaro, parked on the street under a dim street-lamp. The car had seen better days — once a deep navy blue, now faded and chipped in places, with rust spots dotting the edges of the doors and fenders. Dents and scratches, souvenirs from careless parking, covered the car. The tires were worn, the hubcaps scuffed, and the interior, visible through grimy windows, was a mess of loose change, old receipts, and fast-food wrappers.

DonnaMae had been in Will's car a few times, usually when they all piled in for a quick lunch, but she'd never really noticed how rundown it was. Now, looking at it in the dark, she realized it was a dirty mess, just like him. And she figured he had probably had plenty of other girls in the back seat of this car. Relief washed over her — she was glad she wasn't going to be another girl in that car, with a guy like Will.

Izzy was already at work, writing "piece of shit" in big, bold letters across the back window with her lipstick. Hazel went straight for the door handles, slathering them with peanut butter. Ella scattered her fancy olives across the hood, even managing to wedge a few into the grille. Armed with a small yellow spray bottle of butter substitute, she spritzed it haphazardly across the tires and side mirrors.

DonnaMae's heart began to race. It was dark, and the street was quiet, but what if someone saw them? What if a dog barked, or —

Hazel ripped open the bag of flour, interrupting DonnaMae's thoughts. "I'll pour the bacon grease. You follow behind with the ketchup and mustard."

DonnaMae squeezed the bottles, squirting the car like it was an actual hot dog. "We might not have time. We should go."

"Oh, hell no!" Izzy walked up, yanking the bag out of Hazel's hands and tossing flour everywhere, including on Ella and DonnaMae.

"HEY!" Ella squealed.

"SHHHH!" DonnaMae quickly glanced around, eyes wide.

"This ass hat is getting what he deserves!" Izzy said, nodding at Hazel. "Let's go!"

Hazel dumped the grease, and Izzy created a tornado of white powder swirling around them. The girls couldn't help but giggle. DonnaMae felt a rush as she quickly ran around, picking up cans and dropping them into a plastic grocery bag.

"All right, we're done!" DonnaMae said, adrenaline pumping through her as Izzy tossed the empty flour bag into her bag.

"Let's get out of here," Hazel said, her voice tense with urgency to leave before they got caught.

Without looking back, they sprinted to DonnaMae's car and sunk into the seats. DonnaMae started the engine, leaving the headlights off as she slowly backed up, taking one last look at their handiwork. Will's car was a disaster — a smile spread across her face as she drove away.

Her heart was still pounding, but laughter soon filled the car as they headed back to the rec room. DonnaMae felt a surge of satisfaction. Will would wake up to a scene of chaos, but nothing that would cause permanent damage — just enough to send a clear message.

"I can't believe we actually pulled that off," DonnaMae said as she drove. With every mile, she felt the weight of her crush on Will lifting away, left behind with the chaos they'd unleashed on his car. *"Operation Revenge was a success!"*

DonnaMae realized that her dad was right. There was something he didn't like about Will and she didn't need guys like Will in her life. She had more important things to focus on, like the application she sent in for a job.

CHAPTER 18

September, 2000

The school bell rang and Ella, Izzy, and Hazel burst through the door to DonnaMae's classroom, their laughter echoing as they hurried to her desk. Their excited chatter filled the room as they gathered around her. DonnaMae kept her head down, focused on packing up her books, trying to steady her racing thoughts about her upcoming job interview.

It had been a few weeks since they pulled off Operation Revenge, and the aftermath had become something of a local legend. Will had been fuming, and everyone in town was buzzing about it. What made it even better was that, on the same night, someone had TP'd a house on his block, creating the perfect cover for their crime. The guys in their friend group had been teasing Will relentlessly, asking which girl he'd pissed off, never suspecting DonnaMae. The girls had sworn to keep Operation Revenge a secret.

When Will confronted DonnaMae about ditching him for burgers, she coolly claimed she'd forgotten because she was out with the girls, who were standing right beside her when he approached. She was proud of Izzy for staying quiet, but it was Ella who surprised her by chiming in with, "Yeah, because we're way cooler to hang out with than you, ya big poop-head," before strutting off, leaving Will speechless and the rest of them fighting back their laughter.

Things had finally calmed down, leaving DonnaMae and her friends with their secret, inside jokes, and a shared sense of victory. Whenever a twinge of sadness about Will crept in, the memory of their prank always brought a smile to DonnaMae's face.

She had stuck to her promise, focusing on her own growth and letting go of her crush on Will. Her thoughts were on the future.

"Are you nervous or scared or —"

"Hazel!" Ella said, cutting her off. "That doesn't help, of course she's nervous."

Izzy leaned in eagerly. "In my interview for Baskin-Robbins, they wanted to know my strengths and weaknesses, like I'm some sort of superhero!"

Ella and Hazel giggled, but DonnaMae felt a knot tighten in her stomach. She knew she'd have to face similar questions soon. With a forced smile, she replied, "That's awesome, Izzy. What did you tell them?" Hoping maybe Izzy's answers would help her.

Izzy shrugged, her grin widening. "Told 'em I'm a master at scooping ice cream, but sometimes I eat too much of it!" Her friends laughed again, but DonnaMae's mind raced. What were her strengths? Would they see through her fake toughness?

Hazel, always the problem solver, nudged DonnaMae gently. "You've got this, Mae. Just be yourself. Remember, they're lucky to have you."

DonnaMae nodded, grateful for her friends' support. She zipped up her bag, trying to appear calm and collected. "Thanks, guys," she said, forcing confidence into her voice. "I've got this." If she could convince her closest friends she wasn't scared, she could convince a stranger.

As they walked out of the classroom together, DonnaMae couldn't shake the butterflies in her stomach. This job interview was more than just a chance for a paycheck, it was a job she wanted and actually found interesting. One she felt like she could relate to and maybe help others.

DonnaMae passed by the large cement sign reading Willows Recreation Center, her nerves kicking in. She was fifteen minutes early, and only a few cars filled the parking lot. A bus was pulling away at the far end, likely having dropped off kids for the after school program.

This was her first real job interview, and she was applying to be a student mentor and after school program aide. She'd volunteered as a counselor at the outdoor school camps, working with sixth-graders, and loved every minute of it. She figured this couldn't be too different. Elise had helped her write her resume, highlighting that experience along with her time at her dad's daycare. Now, all she had to do was make it through the interview.

When Willows called to set up the interview, they told her it would start with a one-on-one meeting, followed by an afternoon spent with the kids to assess her ability to manage and engage them.

Sitting in her car, Tom Petty's "Running Down a Dream" filled the air. The familiar tune helped her calm her nerves. She closed her eyes, counted to three, and tried to center herself. She knew she could do the job if given the chance, but could she convince someone else? Could she make them believe she wouldn't fail them?

As another bus pulled up and kids streamed into the building, DonnaMae wondered how they kept track of program participants versus regular visitors. She decided it was time to go inside and find out.

She checked her teeth in the rearview mirror, ensuring they were free of any remnants from the trail mix she just ate. Then she ran her fingers through her hair one last time before switching off the engine and stepping out of the car. Singing the words of Tom Petty, she took a deep breath and savored the lyrics before mustering up the courage to run down her own dream.

When she stepped through the doors of the recreation center, she was greeted by the lively sounds of laughter and chatter. The brightly painted walls of the room showcased playful murals, each filled with positive words. She walked past the empty front desk, towards an open room filled with tables. A woman in a vibrant windbreaker stood by the entrance, diligently checking kids in with a clipboard in hand. Nearby, another staff member distributed giant pretzels and juice boxes to the children while guiding them towards an empty table. Kids excitedly grabbed their snacks and scrambled to find a seat. As the delicious scent of warm pretzels wafted through the air, her stomach grumbled in anticipation, reminding her of her dad and his after school snack obsession. After school, he had snacks prepared for everyone, but he always made sure to set aside extra for her and her brother. Despite their being in high school, he continued to ask if they had packed a snack for after school, and today she regretfully only had a handful of trail mix on the drive over.

The sound of someone shouting "Charles!" echoed across the room, grabbing DonnaMae's attention.

A short, stocky man emerged from the kitchen, carefully balancing a tray of golden-brown pretzels. Thick-framed glasses perched on his nose, and his movements had the smoothness of an athlete weaving through the crowd. For a moment, DonnaMae thought he had the air of a football player making his way towards the end zone. But as she watched him navigate the room with a calm, authoritative stride, something about him felt more like a chess club president — someone who combined strategy with a quiet confidence. He wore a crisp white button-up shirt, embroidered with *Willows After School Program*, with a small yellow star next to the word "Program."

Halting mid-step, the man caught DonnaMae's eye and flashed a familiar grin. DonnaMae's heart skipped a beat, warmth rising in her cheeks. For a second, she thought the smile must be meant for someone behind her. Glancing over her shoulder, she saw no one.

When she turned back, he was already making his way towards her, the tray of pretzels still in hand.

"DonnaMae, right?" he said as he approached her.

"Hi, yes. How'd you know?"

"Well, it's not often we have good-looking young women walk in here that just want to hang out."

"Umm..." DonnaMae was surprised by his comment and didn't really know what to say, but before she could think of an answer, he was holding out a pretzel to her.

"Pretzel? They're the best. I could eat five, but you know, gotta watch my figure." He raised his eyebrows playfully, running a hand down his body.

DonnaMae wasn't sure if that meant she should take one or if she should not take one because she should watch her figure, but her tummy grumbled at her and she didn't really care about her figure at that moment.

"Yes please," she said, reaching out and taking the pretzel. "Thank you. Should we go eat with the kids?"

"Nah, we'll take ours to go and head to my office to get to know each other first and then I'll have you meet the rest of the team. I already called your teachers and they have had nothing but great things to say about you."

"Oh, well, that's good to hear," DonnaMae said with a forced smile, trying to ignore the uncomfortable sensation slowly rising within her.

Charles turned and signaled a staff member to collect the tray of pretzels resting on the table. He then faced her again. "Alright, shall we?" He grabbed a pretzel, tore off a chunk, and popped it into his mouth while walking.

She wanted to follow his lead and take a bite of her own pretzel — they were warm and soft, and the chunks of salt made her mouth water. But eating felt like the wrong thing to do. What if it got stuck in her teeth? She didn't bring any water, what if her mouth got too dry? Now, she was wondering what to do with this pretzel and wishing she had never taken the damn thing in the first place.

As they entered the small room, a desk greeted them on the right, while a row of tall school-style cabinets lined the left wall. On the other side of the desk, there was a bookshelf filled with a colorful array of books. The room felt surprisingly homey, resembling a small living room with a coffee table in front of the couch. In the back corner, there was an additional table surrounded by chairs. She imagined it was like a small studio apartment.

Without hesitation, Charles walked in and plopped down on the couch, motioning for DonnaMae to join him. "Our goal is to make this space comfortable and welcoming, where kids can relax and feel at ease."

"It's nice, it's cozy," DonnaMae said, sitting down.

"Do you go by DonnaMae or Donna?"

"I actually go by Mae most of the time," she said, angling herself so she could face him. Though the room was inviting, something about it made her uneasy. She brushed the feeling off as nerves and asked, "So, how long have you been doing this? It seems like a lot of work, and you seem fairly young."

Charles laughed awkwardly. "Well, I've been doing this for about two years now. Started right out of college. I've got two older sisters, and they were kinda my inspiration. We were latchkey kids, our parents never home. I saw firsthand how much kids need a safe, fun place after school. So, I put my mind to it and just went for it."

DonnaMae perked up, interested. "How did —"

But Charles didn't let her finish. "I always knew I wanted to do something impactful. I was the one taking care of things at home after my sisters went off to college, and I was left all alone."

All alone. The words tugged at DonnaMae's heart. She knew that feeling well. She opened her mouth to say something, but Charles kept going, barely stopping to breathe. "They're both really successful now, by the way. They work for the school district.

But back then, I felt like I had to make a difference. I remember thinking, 'I can do this, I can help kids in the same situation.' So, I started this program."

As Charles went on, DonnaMae noticed how often he said "I." The program sounded great, but she found herself fixating on how Charles's head seemed too small for his broad frame, his beady eyes behind thick-rimmed glasses staring so intently.

When he finally paused long enough for her to speak, she pulled her focus back. "What does it take to start something like this?" she asked.

"It's a non-profit," Charles said. "We run entirely on grants I write." He paused with a smile and his chest lifted just a little. "It's a lot of work, but it's worth it. I handle everything here, from programming to writing grants. This one's just for middle school kids, but I have big plans. I want to open more. I'm here around lunchtime every day, working on programming and writing grants to fund the program. I'm using this one as a foundation for more."

DonnaMae nodded again, trying her best to keep up with Charles. He was still talking, but her mind kept drifting to her own questions, ones she hadn't had a chance to ask. *How is the program funded just by grants? Are people really out there willing to give money for this kind of thing?* The program sounded incredible, and the more Charles talked, the more DonnaMae wanted to learn about it firsthand. If she could get the job. A knot tightened in her stomach, she needed to impress him.

She glanced down and realized she was still holding the pretzel, untouched. Meanwhile, Charles had set his down on the coffee table, resting it on some kind of notebook. But she didn't have a napkin or anywhere to set hers on. *What do I do with this damn pretzel?* she thought.

"Alright, Miss Mae," Charles said, standing up. "All that's left is for you to meet the team and see if you enjoy working with the kids in the after school program."

DonnaMae blinked. She'd been so distracted, she had no idea

what he'd said before that. Hopefully, she hadn't missed anything important.

Charles picked up his pretzel. "Oh man, we just talked so much our pretzels got cold. Nothing worse than a cold pretzel." He laughed and started towards the door. As DonnaMae stood up, he turned and locked eyes with her. His stare felt intense, almost scary. "Not everyone is cut out for this job, and that's alright."

She watched him walk out the door with a strange feeling in her stomach she couldn't identify.

He called back in an almost flirtatious tone, "Come on, Mae, let's see what you've got, my dear."

She forced a chuckle, shaking off the strange feeling. *So, he's a little strange. He works with junior high kids for a living. Who wouldn't be a little strange, right?* she thought as she pulled her shoulders back, put on her serious smile, and walked out after him.

DonnaMae sprinted down the stairs at home and slid into the kitchen, socks slipping on the hardwood floors. Elise stood at the stove, stirring a pot of something that was boiling. Every ounce of DonnaMae wanted to run up and hug her, but for some reason, she stopped short. "Is my dad in the garage?"

Elise glanced over her shoulder. "I think so. Is everything ok?"

DonnaMae realized she was bouncing on her toes and quickly forced herself to stop.

"Um, yes, I just want to share the good news."

She wanted to tell her dad first. She didn't know why, but she didn't want Elise to be the first person she told. She could run back upstairs and call one of the girls. Heck, with the new three-way calling, she could call all of them. But then, Elise had helped her make her resume, and she was probably more invested in helping DonnaMae get the job than anyone else. DonnaMae wanted to tell her, to hug her and jump up and down, but there was this strange wall. It felt like their relationship had to be professional.

Elise set the spoon down on a folded paper towel on the counter. "What is the good news?" She turned around fully to face DonnaMae.

"Well, the guy from the program called and left me a message on my answering machine." DonnaMae paused to slow down and calm herself. "He said the job is mine if I'm still interested!" She felt like she was about to jump out of her skin.

"Oh my gosh, that is great news, Donna!" Elise clapped her hands together in front of her chest. "I am so excited for you! When do you start?"

"Oh, I don't know. I haven't called him back." DonnaMae wanted to tell her dad first. She wanted him to be proud of her and to give her guidance on what to do next. She figured they would sit down, make a plan, and he would be so proud of her for getting her first real job.

"I'm going to go tell my dad, thanks!" she hollered over her shoulder as she rushed to the garage. She found her dad working on one of his friend's old cars. He was underneath it, completely engrossed in his work. "Daddy?" she said, full of excitement, hoping to get his attention.

Without coming out from under the car, he replied, "What's up, Mae?"

"I got the job!" she exclaimed, unable to contain her excitement any longer.

"That's great, Mae," he said, his voice muffled.

"Daddy!" She fully jumped up and down like she was a little girl again.

"Hold on, this damn bolt is stuck." He grunted.

"What should I do next?" she asked. "He left a message, I was thinking —"

"Call him back and find out," he said, "I can't tell you what to do. I'm not him."

"Well, I was thinking maybe —"

The wrench dropped to the ground with a loud clank. "Ouch – Son of a bitch!"

DonnaMae's heart sank. "Are you ok?"

"Yeah, I just need to come at this from a different angle I think."

DonnaMae nodded, "Right." She paused. "Ok, I'll just go give him a call." She turned to walk out of the garage. "Great talk, thanks," she mumbled as she walked back towards the house.

She heard him muttering about the bolt again and sighed, disappointment filling her. She wanted more of a celebration. She wanted him to be proud of her.

CHAPTER 19

January, 2001

"Do you work today?" Hazel asked DonnaMae as they walked through the front doors of the brand-new YMCA. With its sleek architecture, modern amenities, and expansive windows that allowed natural light to flood the interior spaces, the facility stood out in their small, old-fashioned town. Inside, DonnaMae and Hazel were greeted by a spacious lobby with a high ceiling and the familiar smell of chlorine.

Before DonnaMae could answer Hazel's question, an older lady with short gray hair smiled at them warmly from the front desk as they scanned their badges. "Good morning ladies," she said. "Enjoy your workout."

"Thank you!" DonnaMae and Hazel said together.

The gym's centerpiece was its huge, state-of-the-art swimming pool with multiple lanes for lap swimming, a dedicated section for recreational activities, and a wave pool. The highlight was a towering water slide that spiraled down into a splash pool attached to the wave pool. The swim area was surrounded by comfortable lounge chairs and tables, where people could relax and socialize, almost like a beach. To the left of the lobby was a long hallway that led past the gym to the basketball and then racquetball courts.

DonnaMae and Hazel made their way past all of this to the gym at the end of the hall.

As they stepped into the locker rooms first, Hazel said, "You never answered my question. Do you work today?" She shoved her things into a locker before turning expectantly to face DonnaMae.

"Yes," DonnaMae replied, taking the locker next to Hazel's. "I work every day after school now."

It had been four months since DonnaMae had gotten the job at Willows, and she was loving it. She had originally told them she could only work three days a week, to keep some days open for other activities, but she found herself missing it when she wasn't there. She had even shown up on her off days a few times just to hang out because she had nothing else to do. She loved the kids and missed them when she wasn't at work.

"They must like you," Hazel said. Then, giving DonnaMae a little nudge as they made their way towards the gym, "Or you must like them, if you're working every day instead of just three days a week."

DonnaMae laughed as they entered the gym. The cardio area was first, filled with the latest equipment. Rows of treadmills, stationary bikes, and elliptical machines faced floor-to-ceiling windows, offering a view of the pool. Then the weightlifting section, where DonnaMae and Hazel headed, was equipped with brand-new free weights and resistance machines. The space was brightly lit and organized, with mirrors lining the walls.

DonnaMae sat down on the bench in front of the weight rack and stretched her arms above her head. "I still can't believe we get all this for just sixteen dollars a month," she said, glancing around appreciatively.

"Yeah, it's such a good deal," Hazel agreed, picking up her weights. "And having a place like this to workout is amazing. It's helping me so much with pageant prep."

DonnaMae nodded, starting her set. "I love coming before

school. It's such a great way to start the day. I always feel tired, but then when we're done, I'm so awake."

"You should try a cup of tea before we workout," Hazel said. "It's a great way to wake up." She sat down and pressed the weights above her head.

"That would mean I would have to get up even earlier to make a cup of tea before I picked you up." DonnaMae yawned and stood to select her weights.

"Well, if *you* lived next to the gym, I would pick you up."

"Right!" DonnaMae didn't mind picking Hazel up in the mornings. It was better to drive to the gym together and rock out to music to wake up. It was like their warm-up.

"I'll make you a cup of tea," Hazel said in her best Mike Myers "Coffee Talk" SNL skit impression. "We can have tea talk on the way to the gym."

DonnaMae laughed at the impression as she copied Hazel's weight routine. They didn't really know what they were doing, but they picked a few exercises to do every day from the posters on the walls all over the gym."You know," DonnaMae said, "my boss said he works out here all the time. We could ask him for some lifting advice."

"Maybe." Hazel shrugged, switching from her overhead press to a bicep curl just like the guy on the poster.

Later that day, warm sunrays offered a brief reprieve from the chilly January breeze as DonnaMae and Hazel left school and crossed the street to meet the other girls at The Grubin' Hub for lunch. DonnaMae pulled her Carhartt jacket tighter around her. "Brr," she shivered. "You sure you still want to hit the gym in the morning?" She loved their early workouts, but the temperature was dropping, and tomorrow morning was bound to be even colder.

"Yes, I'm fine," Hazel said. "The workout keeps me sane, and I'm gonna need it this week." She zipped up her coat and crossed her arms over her chest. "It does feel like it's getting colder."

Izzy skipped over and playfully pressed down on DonnaMae's shoulders. "What keeps you sane?" she asked with a grin.

"Hello, Izzy!" DonnaMae laughed, turning to face her. "Wait, why are you in your cheer uniform? Aren't you freezing your ass off?"

"Cause there's a match tonight, and Varsity has to wear uniforms for all events, even if we don't cheer." Izzy twirled. "If you'd tried out with me again, you would have known." She bounced in place like she was cheering for the football team right there.

"Um, I loved, cheering," DonnaMae said, raising her arms in surrender, "don't get me wrong. But I'm not sure all the cheer routines were my thing. I mean, I'd be going left while you guys were going right, or I'd have my hands up when everyone else had theirs down."

Izzy grinned, nudging her gently. "So, you get a little mixed up now and then. You still had more spirit and energy than the whole squad, and definitely more heart."

"Like I said, I loved it, especially getting everyone to cheer for our football team. Being on your shoulders and yelling at the stands to get louder? That was the best part! But honestly, Izzy, it's fine. I have other things I want to try. We only get four years in high school, and I've got so much I want to do!" DonnaMae reached out to Ella as she approached.

"Are we getting burgers for lunch?" Ella asked, meeting DonnaMae in a hug. "It's freezing out here, let's go inside."

"After you tell us all about your new crush in math class!" DonnaMae said, tossing the end of Ella's scarf around her neck.

"Oh my gosh, stop it." Ella blushed as she turned to face the rest of the group.

"OHHH!" Izzy said, dancing around Ella.

"Seriously, it's nothing. He's just cute. Now let's go get lunch. I'm starving." Ella elbowed DonnaMae in her side as she walked past her towards The Grubin' Hub. "I can't wait to have a BLT. And Hazel, let me guess, a veggie burger?"

"I actually need to run over to the music room and meet Maria. She's letting me borrow her shoes for tonight's pageant practice."

"The pageant is in just a few weeks," Ella said, stopping and turning back to Hazel. "Are you excited? Or are you nervous?"

"Or are you just ready for this shit to be over with?" Izzy offered.

"Oh gosh, be nice!" Ella said, hushing Izzy and giving Hazel an apologetic smile.

"It's ok, it's not her thing, but I'm actually loving the pageant and all it offers. I'm learning so much and hopefully I can walk away with a few scholarships for college." Hazel gave Izzy a smirk that took hers down a notch.

"You know, Izzy, I think you should do this next year."

"Fuck off!"

Ella threw her hands up, ready to scold Izzy, but before she could get a word out, DonnaMae was right back in Izzy's face. "Yeah well, I double-dog dare you to do it next year."

This was one thing about Izzy that DonnaMae knew to be true: She would never back down from a dare.

"Ohhhhhoho! You think so, Mae? You think just because you dare me to do something, I'm going to do it?"

Everyone stood there silently. No one moved. Ella went to speak and DonnaMae stopped her, knowing the pressure was on and the longer they all stood there staring at Izzy, the more likely she was to cave.

"Fine," Izzy said. "I'll do it if you do it!" She laughed, clearly expecting to get off the hook.

"If you're doing it then I'm in," DonnaMae said, crossing her arms.

"Right," Izzy laughed. "What is your ass going to do for a talent anyway? Bowling?"

"Yep, and yours can be bailing, hay!" DonnaMae snapped back with a smile.

Everyone burst into laugher.

"Ok Izzy, I'm holding you to this," Hazel said with a roll of her eyes. "Both of you, actually. Next year you are both doing this." With that, she waved and bounded off.

"Oh yeah, we are so doing this." DonnaMae said. "Now, let's go get some food. I'm starving."

DonnaMae walked into the recreation center, her footsteps echoing off the polished floors. It was the calm before the storm, and today was going to be a storm. Well, she hoped it would be a controlled storm. As she entered the office, a heavy silence hung in the air, and darkness filled the room. Charles had informed her that he would be late, because he was going to be at training with two of the other employees. He'd asked her to be early to run things. She was always early to set everything up, but today she would be doing it alone.

Charles was kind of an odd guy, but he seemed to know what he was doing, and he had accomplished so much at such a young age. DonnaMae admired him for his determination and desire to always improve. She wanted to ask him if she could learn to help write one of the grants. He had a collection of books on grant writing in the office that always caught her attention and she wanted to learn more. Today was the ideal opportunity for her to show him that she could confidently take charge and venture beyond her comfort zone. Knowing he would be absent for the first half of the day, she was determined to seize the opportunity with everything she had.

Thoughts of messing things up or forgetting things crept into her mind as she hit print on the sign-in sheet, but she pushed them aside. She had done this a hundred times by now and she knew she could do it again today. With the sign-in sheet printed, she carefully reviewed today's menu for snacks. Next, she retrieved two carts — one brimming with games and crafts, and the other loaded with mouth-watering snacks. She had carefully prepared for this a week in advance by making a detailed checklist, which she printed and laminated for easy reference by everyone.

"Shoot, the station cards," she said out loud. "I knew I was forgetting something." She snatched up the station cards and began making her way out the door, struggling to manage both carts, when the shrill sound of the phone ringing startled her. The carts had formed a blockade, preventing her from entering the office. Before she could reach the phone, the answering machine picked up and her coworker Seth's voice filled the room. He was out sick for the day.

A wave of panic washed over DonnaMae. "Oh no!" she exclaimed. They were already short-staffed, and now it would only be her and Jake, who was always late.

As she made her way back to the office, her heart raced. She urgently grabbed the phone to call Charles, but hesitated with her finger hovering over the dial pad. She punched in the first half of his number, then quickly changed her mind and hung up. The thought of calling Charles made her cringe.

Her mind whirled with conflicting emotions. She knew she could do this, that she had the skills and knowledge to handle the situation. But what if she messed everything up? What if she failed spectacularly? The fear of losing her job gnawed at her, yet a stubborn need to do this herself pushed back. She was determined to prove herself, to show that she could manage without running to Charles for help.

She considered calling her dad, but remembered he was at work. The fear of failure made her heart pound. What if everything went wrong? What if she got fired? Then she would fail her dad and Charles. She closed her eyes, took a deep breath, and steadied herself. She had faced challenges before, and she could prove to both her dad and Charles she was awesome. She could do this. She had to do this.

With renewed determination, she pondered who she knew who was cleared to work with kids. "Hazel," she said. She dialed Hazel's number and then immediately remembered that Hazel had rehearsal tonight.

DonnaMae was about to hang up when Hazel's voice came through the line. "Hello?"

"Oh, my gosh, Hazel!"

"Yes, Mae?"

"Oh, my gosh, Hazel!"

"Mae? Is everything ok?"

"Yes — I mean no — but I forgot you have rehearsals, so never mind, sorry I —"

"No, they canceled it tonight. There was some kind of electrical problem and they had to call the fire department."

"No way, that's great! I mean I'm sorry. Umm... are you free?"

"Yes, what's up, Mae?"

"Well, you know how we have to get hours for volunteering? And, umm... I have an idea — You know what? Forget that." DonnaMae cut herself off. She didn't have time to sugar coat this into being some grand idea to get her way. She needed her friend. "I need you. I have no staff and I'm about to have fifty kids here, and I'm not sure I can do this by myself, and Charles is trusting me to be the lead while he's gone for the first half of the day, and I —"

"Breathe, Mae, I got you. I'll be there in fifteen."

"Oh my gosh! Seriously?"

Hazel laughed. "Yes, I need the volunteering hours, anyway."

"Thank you so much!" DonnaMae hung up the phone, feeling like Hazel had just lifted a bag of bricks off of her.

She had set everything up and was bringing the second tray of Cheez Its and apples out of the kitchen when Hazel walked through the front doors. Hazel and some girl with shoulder-length curly brown hair.

"Over here," DonnaMae called, taking one hand off the snack tray and waving it at them. As she glanced at her watch, she couldn't believe that only three minutes remained until the kids would begin streaming through the door. And just as she thought that, Jake walked in right behind them. Late as usual.

Hazel made her way to DonnaMae. "I brought backup. LeAnn, this is Mae. Mae, meet LeAnn. She's in the pageant with me and she had nothing to do tonight as well. She'd already driven to my house, so I figured, why not bring her along?"

"Wow," DonnaMae said, "that's great because he is my only other help." She pointed at Jake, who just walked by, grabbed a snack, and sat down by the sign that said "Gym."

"Ok, well, how can we help?" Hazel asked, laughing.

"I can check kids in if you both want to help me hand out the snack to them after they check-in," DonnaMae suggested. "Check-in is a great way to learn the kids' names. As they check in, I will make a point of using their names, and when I hand them a snack later, you can do the same. They will break off into groups by the signs, like Jake did." She laughed with a head nod in his direction. "This is the activity they will do after they eat their snack." DonnaMae surveyed the room. "However, since there are only three of us, I set up just three tables. Now that there are four of us, we can break up the games and craft table into two groups. And one of us can go to the library for reading and homework."

"Wow, ok Mae, you got this on lockdown," Hazel said. "Sounds good, let's go."

The day went better than DonnaMae could have ever imagined. "Have a great rest of your night, girls," she said as she checked out two of the girls who walked home. Looking up from her clipboard, she spotted Charles walking through the door. Her heart pounded. She was so afraid of what he would say. Would he be upset with her for not calling him?

She cut off her fearful thoughts and glanced around the room, smiling with pride. The kids hadn't skipped a beat. They'd thrown themselves into the activities with enthusiasm and no questions. The day ran like a normal day. DonnaMae laughed as Charles approached, watching LeAnn grab her fake microphone they had made out of a rolled-up piece of paper. They had used poster paper to write up the words to their favorite Disney songs, and LeAnn had brought in a Disney CD from her car. The music filled the room, and the kids were singing and dancing together. Even a few of the boys who had been playing basketball in the gym had come in to join the fun.

Charles paused a few steps away from DonnaMae, taking in the scene. His eyes widened in surprise, and then a slow smile spread across his face.

"Well, this is impressive," he said, walking the rest of the way to meet her. "I didn't expect to see this." His eyes landed on Hazel, who was cleaning up the pearler beads with three other kids. "And who is that?" He looked her over one more time and then switched to LeAnn. "And that?"

DonnaMae felt a blush creep up her cheeks. She knew he was commenting on how beautiful her friends were, but she just ignored it like she was learning to do with most of his side comments. "Oh, that's LeAnn and Hazel. Seth called out sick, and I knew we were already short-staffed, so I called them to help out."

Charles raised an eyebrow. "You called in reinforcements? Smart move." His gaze drifted back and forth between Hazel and LeAnn. "It looks like they're doing a great job, and they look great doing it."

Sometimes, DonnaMae found Charles's random, out-of-place comments confusing. They didn't seem to fit with the smart and successful young man who had created and run this entire program. Maybe it was just a quirk of his, like he didn't always know how to read the room, or he had spent too much time alone growing up. Whatever the reason, DonnaMae had decided it was best to just let those comments of his go. Charles was kind, after all, and his heart always seemed to be in the right place.

"Hazel is the one I was telling you about," she said, "who I workout with in the mornings."

"Ahh, well, I can always show you a thing or two. Nothing like a five AM workout to start your day!"

"That's funny, I was actually going to ask you if you could stop by and give us some lifting tips."

"Well, for you, anything, Miss Mae!"

DonnaMae rolled her eyes and changed the subject. "We've actually had a really great day." She glanced back at him. "What happened to you?"

"There was a crash on the bridge and we got stuck for an hour. I called the office line, but it sounds like you were busy."

"Oh!" She hadn't even thought about checking the office phone. She'd been out with the kids the whole time. "Yeah, honestly, I haven't even gone back to the office at all. Sorry I —"

"Mae, it's ok, this is amazing!"

DonnaMae and Charles watched as LeAnn led a group of kids in a spirited rendition of a song from *The Little Mermaid*. DonnaMae felt a twinge of emotion as she listened to the familiar lyrics. Some days, she wanted to hate Disney and Mickey, because they had always been her mom's thing — something that was forced on DonnaMae. But today, she couldn't help but love it.

Charles turned to her and raised an eyebrow. "You really stepped up, DonnaMae. It's not easy keeping this many kids entertained, especially on short notice. And you called in extra help without me having to ask. That shows initiative."

DonnaMae swallowed hard, feeling a mix of relief and pride. "Thanks, Charles. I just wanted to make sure the kids had fun and everything ran smoothly."

"And you did," Charles said, his smile returning. "You should be proud of yourself. You managed the situation perfectly."

"Wow, really? Thanks!"

"Now, do your friends need jobs? 'Cause it looks like they would fit in here in more than one way." He winked at her and walked off.

She felt a now-or-never sense of urgency wash over her. "Hey, Charles!"

He stopped and turned around. "Yes, Miss Mae?"

"I was wondering, can I borrow a few of your books on grant writing? And..." She paused, for what felt like forever.

Charles just stood there, staring back at her. "And?"

"Well, I was thinking, maybe for the next grant you write, I could help with it? Or learn more about how you do it. I, um, well, it looks really interesting, and I was thinking it might be fun. But I totally understand if you say no and have your own way of doing things. I —"

"Mae, I think that would be a great idea, and I would love to do that with you." A soft smile crossed his face. "And Mae, you don't have to ask to borrow anything in my office. *Mi casa, tu casa.*"

As he walked away to check on another group of kids, DonnaMae allowed herself a moment to savor the praise. She had been so worried about failing, about not being able to handle things on her own. But she had done it. She had pulled it off. The kids were happy, Charles was impressed, and she would get to learn more about grant writing. Right now she felt like she could fly.

The next morning, DonnaMae pulled up to Hazel's house at five AM. Frost lingered on the corner of her windshield. Although tired from the long day yesterday, she was still ready to hit the gym.

She still couldn't wrap her head around the fact that she and

Hazel and LeAnn had pulled yesterday off. They not only success-fully pulled it off, but by the end of the day, Charles had extended job offers to both LeAnn and Hazel. Despite being busy at the moment, they both confirmed their availability in a few weeks after the pageant ended and accepted.

A soft glow illuminated Hazel's front porch, indicating that Hazel was about to make her appearance.

The treetops still glistened with frost, and the puddles in Hazel's driveway were frozen over.

"Burrr!" DonnaMae instinctively turned up the heat in her car. She patted the dashboard like it was a dog. "You are such a good girl," she said to the beloved old car. "Sorry it's so cold out."

Hazel walked out with two steaming mugs in her hands. The familiar aroma of tea mingled with the crisp morning air as she opened the car door and climbed in.

"Mmm, tea, thank you," DonnaMae said as she took the car out of park, put her foot on the brake, and glanced over her left shoulder, away from Hazel. When she lifted her foot off the brake and turned to her right to check behind her before backing out, she lifted her arm to put it over the seat. At that very moment, Hazel went to hand DonnaMae a hot mug of tea. DonnaMae knocked the mug out of Hazel's hand and into her lap.

"Oh, SHIT, that's HOT!" DonnaMae screamed, accidentally slamming the gas pedal instead of the brake. Her car smashed into the telephone pole behind them with a loud crunch. Hazel and DonnaMae were flung forward, the cups of tea spilling all over them and the car.

"AHHHHH!" they both yelled as the hot liquid soaked into their clothes. They swung the car doors open and jumped out.

"My car!" DonnaMae yelled, fighting back the urge to burst into tears. The trunk now resembled a hungry Pac-Man, as if someone had wedged a telephone pole into its gaping mouth to prevent it from devouring the small white dots.

Her grandpa was going to kill her.

"Well, shit!" DonnaMae looked at Hazel, who was rubbing the back of her neck. "Should we still go to the gym?"

Hazel scrunched her face in confusion. "What?"

"I didn't get up this early to just back into a pole and then give up for the day."

Hazel laughed. "Only you would suggest we still go to the gym."

"I mean, we're already drenched in tea, so let's call it our warm-up and go add some sweat to the mix." DonnaMae shrugged.

"Well, my heart rate is up, that's for sure," Hazel laughed.

"For real though," DonnaMae said, placing her hand on her chest with a huff.

As they walked into the gym, DonnaMae noticed Hazel was favoring her right shoulder. "How's your neck? We can leave if you need to."

With a grimace, Hazel touched her neck. "It's fine. Let's do weights, maybe just legs today."

"Sounds good to me."

DonnaMae could see the pain and annoyance brewing in Hazel, and she didn't want to upset her. But at the same time, DonnaMae was trying not to freak out about her own problems. Her car was destroyed. If they just did a quick lift at the gym, then she would be home before her brother left for school and maybe he would know what to do. He was always breaking shit and fixing it. Her dad was great at fixing things, but honestly, she hoped he wouldn't be home. Maybe her brother could help make the car look not as bad before she had to tell her dad. Her stomach twisted — she had to tell her grandparents.

"How does that sound?" Hazel asked, holding a weighted ball out for DonnaMae.

"Sorry, what?" DonnaMae asked.

"Did you hit your head this morning?" Hazel laughed. "I was saying you can do the one with the ball above your head and I'll do the squats with no weights."

"Oh yeah, you probably shouldn't have any weights."

"Why would you go to the gym if you're not going to use any weights?" a familiar voice asked.

DonnaMae jumped and almost dropped the weighted ball. "Charles, what are you doing here?"

Charles smirked. "You said you need some lifting advice. I'm here to help!"

"Oh, um, we're ok for this morning, bu—"

"First things first," Charles interrupted, "you should always do cardio before you lift, so let's move over to cardio." Charles turned to face the cardio equipment and Hazel rolled her eyes at DonnaMae in the mirror. "Looks like you two can do the treads, and there's an elliptical open for me."

DonnaMae's stomach twisted even more. She wanted to please her boss, but she could also see Hazel's mounting frustration, along with the slew of other emotions that were written all over her face.

"Charles," Hazel said, "we've already started lifting. Thanks, though." She nodded in the mirror for DonnaMae to join her in a set of squats.

Charles turned back to them.

DonnaMae tightened her grip on her med ball. Her friend was squatting and her boss was staring at her with a questionable look on his face. She had asked him to join them, but she didn't think it would be the next day. She lifted the ball above her head. "Maybe you can come join us after you do your cardio." She started to squat with Hazel, keeping her eyes on Charles' reflection in the mirror.

"Well, if you want my help with the squat form, then you should probably listen to the expert and come warm up first." Charles crossed his arms. He almost looked like Adeline when she didn't get what she wanted at home.

Hazel sighed and stopped squatting. "My neck is actually worse. I'm done. Maybe some heat in the sauna will help." She grabbed her water bottle off the bench. "Come get me when you're done with your workout and we can leave." She walked off.

"Ready for some cardio?" Charles asked, tilting his head to the side with a grin growing like he had just won. "Always gotta warm up before hitting the weights!"

DonnaMae forced a smile, her exhaustion barely concealed. She really wanted to lift weights. She felt like she needed it, to release this tension that was growing inside her. But now she was stuck between pleasing her boss or her friend. "Actually, Charles," she said, "I'm not feeling too great. Got a bit of a headache. We've had a rough start to our day."

"But we had plans to lift together. Cardio first is all I'm saying?" His grin turned quickly into a frown.

"I know, I'm sorry. Trust me, I need the workout." *Or to punch something*, she thought as her hands curled into fists by her side. "Maybe another time?"

Charles sighed. "Fine, see you this afternoon." Irritation filled his voice. He turned and walked off towards the cardio equipment.

DonnaMae joined Hazel in the sauna. The warm air wrapped around her as she sank onto a bench, closing her eyes without a word.

"Mae, your boss is so strange. He just showed up to workout with us?"

DonnaMae kept her eyes closed to try and maintain her emotions. "I asked him to give us some advice. It's not like we're lifting experts, and it was probably good advice to warm up first." She let out a slow breath. "If you hadn't —" She stopped herself. She knew pointing fingers would only make things worse. "If our morning had been normal, it would have been nice to have some advice." She paused and then laughed, "He'll be your boss soon, too."

Hazel laughed along. "Sorry for being bitchy," she sighed. "I'm just in pain, and with the pageant around the corner I need all the workouts I can get in before I —"

DonnaMae opened her eyes and looked right at Hazel. "Hazel, you are perfect. You look amazing in your swimsuit and you are beautiful." She swallowed the knot in her stomach as it tried to work its way up her throat. "I'm also sorry for being bitchy. I'm just worried about my car."

"Yeah, I get that," Hazel said.

"Let's just chill for a few minutes, get out of here, and try to make it a better day." DonnaMae closed her eyes, feeling relieved that she would for sure be home in time to have her brother help her.

———

DonnaMae's heart raced when she pulled into the driveway at home. All the cars were there except Elise's, which meant Elise had taken Adeline to school today and their dad had a late start. Hopefully, he was down at the corner having coffee with his buddies and not —

Before she could even finish her thought, her brother came running out the back door to her car. "What the hell happened, Mae?"

DonnaMae hadn't even stepped out of the car before Allan started circling the back, inspecting the damage. She wanted to scream or cry, but for some reason, she found herself laughing. Her brother looked so ridiculous, running his hand over the back of her car, his face as if he had seen a ghost.

"Mae, why are you laughing? This is crazy! Did you hit a tree?"

"I — I wanted to have a Pac-Manmobile, so I —" She couldn't even finish the sentence, she was laughing so hard.

"Sis, you're hysterical! Did you get hurt? Are you ok? Your car is totaled!"

Letting out a long, slow exhale to try and regain her composure, DonnaMae walked over to her brother. "Can you fix it? I backed into a pole."

"You mean you smashed into a pole. Is the pole still standing?"

She scrunched her face. "Yes, it was the telephone pole across from Hazel's driveway. How would it not be standing?"

"Ummm, because, have you looked at this?" her brother asked, pulling on the hood and trying to open it. "This is fucked!"

"Can you make it less fucked before Dad sees it?" she pleaded, eyes wide and hands together like she was praying.

"I can try, but first tell me what happened. How the hell does one hit a pole this hard?"

DonnaMae recounted everything while her brother went to find a mallet and some other tools. He got to work, trying to open the trunk and hammer out the dent. He managed to get the hood open and mostly straightened out, but the back, where the latch lined up with the hood, was a different story.

"Phew," he said when he was done, "I'm going to need another shower. And now I'm going to be late for school. So are you. I think this is as good as —"

"What the hell are you doing to your sister's car?" Their dad practically jogged over to them.

"He's helping me, Dad," DonnaMae interjected, stepping between her brother and her father. Her fear for herself vanished as her need to protect her brother took over. "I backed into a pole and asked him to help me fix it!"

Their dad tried to step around her. "And he suddenly has a degree in car rebuilding?" DonnaMae moved in front of Allan again. They always seemed to fight about everything, and she hated it. "You ever think maybe you just made it worse?" her dad asked Allan. "Or that maybe you should have asked me before using my tools?"

"DAD!" DonnaMae cried, blocking him again. "I asked him to fix it. He's helping me."

"Your brother has control of his own actions, Mae, and I'm not talking to you."

"Hello! I'm the one who backed into a pole!" she exclaimed, throwing her hands into the air.

"Forget it, Mae." Allan dropped the hammer at her feet. "You're on your own. I have to go to school anyway. I'll be sure to ask if they have any classes in auto body repair so I can help you next time you back into a pole." He gave their dad a hard stare. "At least I was here to help her!" Then he walked back into the house.

"Dad, why did you get mad at him for helping me? Now he's never going to help me. You never care if we use your tools."

"Your brother never puts them back. Example A!" her dad said, gesturing to the tools on the ground.

"Well, yeah, but I'll put them away. They were to help me fix my car!"

Her dad picked up the hammer and crowbar and walked towards the garage. "We just got into it last night over him not putting tools back and using my tools without asking."

"Dad, um, I backed into a pole at Hazel's house this morning. I'm fine, but Hazel has a sore neck."

"How's the pole?" he laughed.

"Seriously? Dad, I —"

"Looks like you better go talk to your grandparents. They gave you the car."

She tried to ignore the knot reforming in her stomach and the anger brewing inside her. Her dad walked back out to the car with a roll of duct tape and taped the hood down. "Not sure who did the better number on the car, your brother or you."

She wasn't sure if he was mad at her or her brother at this point. But as he said, it wasn't his car, so the only thing he would be disappointed about was her not being more careful.

"Well, I was backing out of Hazel's driveway, and I slammed the gas instead of the brakes when Hazel —"

"I'll call the school and excuse you from your first class. You'd better head straight to the shop and talk to your grandparents. The duct tape will hold — just drive slow." He paused and looked her in the eyes. "And drive carefully, DonnaMae. Pay attention."

She could have screamed — she was so annoyed with how this interaction with her dad turned out. She would have been happier if he'd just yelled at her and grounded her or something, at least let her tell him the whole story of what happened. Her anger gave way to defeat and she hung her head. "Yes, Daddy. Sorry."

She headed into the house to get ready for school. She would go to the shop before school to break the news to her grandparents — more likely to break their hearts that she was such a bad driver. How was she supposed to do that? How could she bear to see their faces when she told them she had wrecked the car they had given her with so much love and trust?

CHAPTER 20

January, 2001

DonnaMae sat in her car, staring at the Flying A. The building's bright yellow and blue stood out under the dull gray sky, its bold "Flying A" sign stretching across the top. The large garage doors had yet to be opened. Massive windows framed the customer entrance, revealing the shadowy interior that would soon be lit up and full of customers. The stone-textured siding between the windows added a rugged, unpolished charm, reminding her of how long this place had been here, steady and familiar. Yet today it felt more imposing than ever. The weight of her mistake pressed heavily on her chest. Her list of people she was letting down today kept growing. Hazel, Charles, her brother, her dad, and now she had to add her grandparents to the list — the two people who supported her the most in the world. Her stomach twisted. She felt sick, dreading the disappointment she would soon see in their eyes. Hands trembling, she reached for the door handle. The knot in her stomach tightened. She swallowed hard, fighting the urge to vomit right there in the parking lot.

She knew she had no choice — soon they would come out and see her sitting in her car. She would rather tell them herself than have them discover the duct tape and her brother's handiwork before she could explain.

It might have been easier if her dad had flipped out on her — then she could go cry to her grandparents about how mad he was. But he wasn't mad, just disappointed, and she knew her grandparents would be, too. "UGH!" She let out a ragged breath, opened the door, and walked into the shop. She suddenly wished Elise had been there this morning. Maybe she would have stepped in, or maybe DonnaMae could have gone to her for advice instead of her brother.

The familiar scent of fresh coffee and baked goods wafted through the shop. Usually she found these scents comforting, but now they made her feel worse. She heard the clinking of dishes and the low hum of conversation from the back room. She knew her grandparents would be in the back, getting ready to start their day and open the shop.

"Good morning, sweetheart!" Her grandmother's cheerful voice filled the room as DonnaMae entered the kitchen area. "You're here early! Is it a late start today? Want a pastry before school?"

DonnaMae managed a weak smile. "Hi, Grandma. Actually, I need to talk to you and Grandpa."

Her grandpa looked up from his papers, his glasses perched on the end of his nose. "Everything alright, Mae?"

The lump in her throat grew as tears welled in her eyes. "Not really. I... I had an accident this morning. I —" Her voice cracked, and she had to clear her throat to steady herself.

Concern washed over her grandparents' faces. "Are you hurt?" her grandmother asked as she rushed to DonnaMae.

"No, I'm fine. But the car... it's not. I, um, I backed into a pole." The words tumbled out, DonnaMae's shoulders sagged, and she looked down at her shoes, no longer able to hold their gaze. "I'm so sorry. I am so, so sorry."

To her surprise, her grandpa let out a hearty laugh. "Ahh, well, shit happens, kid. I've done worse than that." He set the papers aside with a relaxed gesture. "Let's go take a look at the damage."

Her grandmother wrapped her in a tight hug. "Oh, Mae, don't scare us like that. A car is just a car. We're just so glad you're ok!"

Unable to hold back any longer, DonnaMae's tears spilled over. She reached up to wipe them away, her hands trembling.

"Oh, Mae, it's ok. If I had a nickel for all the things your grandpa and the boys have hit with cars, I'd be rich."

The unexpected humor made DonnaMae chuckle through her tears. "I feel so bad. I am so sorry."

"And that, my dear, is what makes you a good human: You care." Her grandma stepped back from the hug, brushing away a blonde strand from DonnaMae's face with a tender touch. "Now, tell us what happened while I finish fixin' your grandpa's coffee." She smiled. "Would you like a cup of tea, my dear?"

"Yes, please. I never actually got one this morning." Donna-Mae's voice was barely above a whisper.

They walked outside together, and DonnaMae felt like each step was a mile. When they reached the car, her grandparents inspected the damage, her grandmother shaking her head and her grandfather frowning as he examined the duct-taped hood.

"Your brother did this?" her grandfather asked, his tone unreadable.

"Yes. He tried to help me fix it before Dad saw. I'm really sorry. I know how much this car means, and I let you down."

Her grandpa put a hand on her shoulder. "We'll get it fixed, DonnaMae. It's just a car. You'll be without a car for a few days, but that's it."

Her grandmother nodded, "Accidents happen, sweetie. We're just glad you're safe. Now, let's get you some pastries. And I will take you to school and work today."

As they walked back into the shop, DonnaMae expected to feel relieved, but instead, she felt more guilty than ever. They weren't mad at all, despite her having completely wrecked the car they gave her. It was almost funny to them. She couldn't help but wonder if this was the universe's way of paying her back for what she and her friends had done to Will's car. If it was, she hoped the universe was also serving Will some justice for being such a jerk. But probably not, because he was a guy, and guys seemed to get away with anything.

***

"Thank you, Grandma, for the ride to work. Love you."

"Do you need a ride home?" DonnaMae's grandma asked as DonnaMae got out of the car.

"No, thank you, I can just walk home. Love you." DonnaMae closed the door to her grandma's car and turned to face the recreation center. Arriving early gave her a much-needed break from the day's drama. School had been exhausting as she played the "fake it till you make it" game, maintaining a smile so forced it practically made her face ache. Her day had continued to spiral downwards — she dropped her fries at lunch, then in a clumsy attempt to catch them, knocked over her Snapple, shattering the glass. Scrambling for help to clean up had made her late to her next class.

As she walked through the doors of the recreation center, a genuine smile crept onto her face for the first time all day. It was quiet as she walked down the hall to the office. When she went to insert the key, she found the door was already unlocked. A soft glow spilled out from inside as the door eased open.

Charles was sitting at the desk, his brow furrowed.

DonnaMae stopped in her tracks, not sure if she should walk back out or walk the rest of the way in. "Oh! Hi, I didn't know you were here yet, sorry."

"You're early," he said, not taking his focus off the computer. "Come on in."

She hesitated, searching for the right words. Today, she didn't have the energy to recount her story again, and she felt guilty for using a headache as an excuse to skip her morning workout. "I just came straight here from school today," she finally said.

"Glad to hear you're feeling better. Come here so I can show you this," he said.

DonnaMae carefully placed her backpack on the floor next to Charles's desk and went to stand behind him to silently observe.

Charles tilted his head to the side and massaged his neck, emitting a low groan of discomfort.

DonnaMae just ignored him and stared at the screen. "What's this?"

"Ahh, well, this is me having a kink in my neck because my lifting partner bailed on me this morning and I had to do upper body day without a spotter."

DonnaMae rolled her eyes and sighed. "I meant, what'd you want to show me?"

"Well, I would show you if I could stop rubbing my neck, but I need my hands to show you so..." he turned his head just enough to give her a smirk and turned his palm up, offering her his neck.

With a teasing tone, she remarked, "You are such a drama queen," as she brushed his hand away and started massaging the side of his neck. She felt guilty that his pain was because she'd canceled on him, and now two people had neck injuries, both incidents directly linked to her actions. At least she could help with his. She was far from being a skilled masseuse. In fact, this was the first time she had ever touched anybody in this way. "Ok," she said, "now, what are you going to show me?"

"Well, there is this new grant, and I was thinking maybe you could apply for it. I will gladly assist you with it, but I believe you have the ability to write it yourself. You did such a great job the other day, making sure things were covered when everyone bailed for work, and your leadership around here has been outstanding. Your passion for these kids really shows. You have connected with each of them and they all love you."

DonnaMae stopped rubbing Charles's neck and clapped her

hands. "YES! Oh my gosh! Yes, this would be so awesome! Thank you so much!"

"Uuuuhhhhmmm…" He cleared his throat and pointed to his neck and shoulders. "Both sides are sore, actually, and I'm not done showing you everything." He pulled a packet of paper off the printer. "Here's the application. Take it home and read it over and know it forwards and backwards so you can really think about how you want to apply for it. Why does the after school program matter to kids?"

"Are you kidding me? The program is so important. Look at all the —"

"Don't tell me. I know all the reasons. You don't need to sell me on the idea." He shook the packet at her. "You have to sell them."

DonnaMae wanted to grab the packet and start reading, but she didn't want to get yelled at for stopping rubbing his shoulders.

The door swung open and Charles jumped up and turned to face DonnaMae, almost knocking her backwards.

"Ahh! What the heck!" DonnaMae said, stumbling backwards to regain her balance.

DonnaMae's coworker Katie stood in the doorway. "Hey guys, sorry, did I intrude on something?" Katie asked, backing out of the room.

"No!" Charles said. "I was just getting excited about the grant that Mae is going to be applying for to get us more funding for our program." He held up the packet of paper, giving it a good shake before handing it to DonnaMae.

Taking the packet in both hands, DonnaMae was so excited she brushed off the uneasiness she'd felt when Charles jumped at Katie's arrival, as if he'd done something wrong.

Charles stood. "She'll have to put in a few late nights working on it, and maybe even some weekends, but I know she can handle it!" He strutted up next to DonnaMae and wrapped his arm around her shoulders.

Charles believed in her. It made DonnaMae feel like she was soaring through the sky, her heart filled with joy in that moment. She was grateful for his arm resting on her shoulders, grounding her — otherwise, she might have floated up to the ceiling.

DonnaMae left before closing time, eager to get home and start on the reading.

As she stepped outside, the chill of the night air bit into DonnaMae's skin. She pulled her gloves from her coat pocket, slipped them on, and zipped up her coat tight before pulling her hood over her head. The fabric rustled softly against her ears, muffling the distant sounds of traffic. The streetlights cast a dim, golden glow on the sidewalk, and her breath formed small clouds in the air. She quickened her pace, her boots crunching against the frosty ground. The cold was sharp and bracing, but her excitement kept her warm. The thought of telling her dad the good news made her heart race. She could barely feel the freezing air nipping at her cheeks.

Charles had reminded her to inform her dad that she'd be working late a few nights next week and he would order them takeout.

As DonnaMae approached her house, the familiar scent of wood smoke from the nearby chimneys filled her nostrils, mixing with the crisp, clean smell of winter. She saw the soft light spilling out from under the garage door and knew her dad was in there working on his latest project. She couldn't wait to tell him the news. She was sure he would be so excited! She let her imagination wander as she walked the rest of the way to the garage. She imagined her dad wrapping her in his arms, telling her how proud he was of her and how excited he was. She would jump up and down with excitement. Maybe he'd even offer to take her to the library. They could go together, like she used to go with her mom when she was little. He could help her find a few books. Maybe they would even find him some cool ones on old cars.

Sure enough, her dad was in the garage, bent over the hood of her favorite truck: A flatbed 1957 Ford, painted sparkly forest green. They had used the truck for their float in her freshman class Homecoming parade. Everyone dressed in vintage clothes and danced on the back as DonnaMae's dad and his best friend drove them slowly around the track, blaring music from the speakers. They had cut out cardboard props of famous landmarks from their town and hung a banner from the side of the flatbed that read, "Class of 2002." The next year, her dad's friend, who owned a wrecking yard, offered up his flatbed, which was much bigger and could fit more kids on the back. But his truck was not nearly as pretty.

DonnaMae's smile widened as she watched her dad work. She moved towards the heater, feeling its warmth, and caught her dad's attention. He straightened up, wiping his hands on a rag, and smiled at her. "You're home early from work," he said.

"I have some exciting news!" DonnaMae said.

"Well, I hope it's not as exciting as your news from this morning," he chuckled, turning to his toolbox and rummaging around in it.

She dropped her backpack and unzipped it, pulling out the packet of paper. "Charles asked me to help — no, he said I could write — or, I mean *apply* for the next grant for the after school program."

"Do you know anything about grants?" her dad asked without stopping what he was doing.

"No. But this will be how I learn. He said he would teach me. I'll have to work late a few nights and —"

"Make sure you let Elise know when you won't be home for dinner."

DonnaMae felt like her heart sank to the bottom of her stomach, pulling her excitement down with it.

"Oh. Ok." DonnaMae returned the packet to her backpack, pulled the pack over her shoulders, and slowly ushered herself out of the garage. Maybe her dad had more to say, or maybe he was excited for her. Who knew? But once again, his attention was on anything but her. She decided leaving before she became more disappointed was the better choice.

As DonnaMae strolled into the kitchen, Elise said, "Hey Donna , you're home early. Dinner will be done soon!" She seemed to always be in the kitchen cooking.

"Ok thanks. Want to hear my news? I just told dad, and he was so excited for me. He thinks it will be an amazing opportunity for me."

Elise stopped stirring the pan on the stove and turned to give DonnaMae her full attention. "Yes, what is it?"

"MAE!!!" Adeline screamed, running into the kitchen.

"It's just a project for work, not that big of a deal," DonnaMae said, scooping up her little sister and turning her around in circles. They twirled through the house and crash landed on the couch, where DonnaMae tickled Adeline until they were both laughing so hard, they had to stop to catch their breath.

DonnaMae lay there panting like a puppy dog, wondering why she'd just lied about her dad's reaction. Why didn't she just tell her stepmom, who was ready to pay attention to her? Elise could probably even help DonnaMae with the grant writing. She was so smart, and she was always reading something.

No, DonnaMae thought, jumping up and dashing up the stairs to her room and closing the door behind her. *I have to do this on my own. I'll get the grant, and my dad will be so proud of me for doing this on my own. Charles thinks I can do this. He's done lots of them. If he believes in me, that means I must have shown him something to make him think I can pull this off.*

She pulled the packet out of her bag and dropped back to her bed. Some of the words were familiar, but the majority of them all seemed to be scrambled all over the page. She knew this wasn't going to be an easy task and she wished she could just have someone read this to her. Why didn't she just ask Elise for help? She hated reading. How was she going to figure out what any of these words were? She didn't want Charles to think she was stupid.

There was no room to feel sorry for herself; there was only room to figure it out, and that was what she did for the rest of the night.

CHAPTER 21

February, 2001

Sweat clung to DonnaMae's skin as she walked through her bedroom door, fresh from the gym. Her muscles were pleasantly sore, the kind of ache she craved. She loved pushing herself harder, feeling the burn as she reached failure. There was something deeply satisfying about the gym, where failure was a good thing, unlike the rest of her life.

Today, DonnaMae had worked out alone since Hazel was busy preparing for her big day in the pageant. DonnaMae had headed straight home after her session instead of hitting the sauna. Not that it mattered — she had worked out so hard her shirt felt like she'd already been in one.

DonnaMae tugged off her sweaty tank top. As she pulled on one of her dad's oversized crewneck sweatshirts, Allan whistled from the doorway. "Damn, is it rainin' outside?" he asked, nodding at the drenched shirt she had just dropped on the ground.

"Oh my gosh, Brother, stop!"

Allan leaned against her door frame. "What time ya showing up to the rec room tonight?"

"Who's asking?" DonnaMae asked, adding some extra sass to her tone.

"The person hosting the party of the year," Allan shot back with a large grin and raised eyebrows.

"You say that about all your parties!" She rolled her eyes. "Besides, I'm not going to your party in the rec room with your Naked Juice tonight." She crossed her arms over her chest. "The Miss Howard Pageant is tonight, and I'm going with The Fab Four to support Hazel."

"First, and most important: You know the Beatles?!"

"NO!" DonnaMae groaned. "You say that every time."

"Well, maybe it's time for a new name?" Allan shrugged. "Ok, but seriously, it's called Skip-And-Go-Naked," he said, mimicking her sassy tone and body language. "And second, who's gonna collect all the money for keg cups?" He threw his arm up dramatically.

"Third, it's perfect! You and your —" Allan paused as he scanned her room until his gaze landed on a pile of clothes on the floor "— your Hick Chicks can all come to the party after the pageant and bring the rest of the pageant girls."m

"Hick Chicks?" DonnaMae furrowed her brows, following his gaze to the messy pile.

"Yeah, it fits. Matches those dumb Romeo shoes and Carhartts you all wear." He snickered. "It's got a nice ring to it. I like it. I'm callin' y'all the Hick Chicks."

DonnaMae rolled her eyes again, but before she could respond, Allan was already back to talking.

"Ohhh, and bring the new Miss Howard. I'm sure she will want some of this," Allan struck a ridiculous side pose, flaunting his body like a model.

"Ew, get out of here!" DonnaMae groaned, grabbing a white angel bear Beanie Baby. "I'm pretty sure they're all taken and don't want *any* of that!" She tossed the Beanie Baby at him, hitting him square on the hip.

"Ouch! You should probably be careful with those. They might be worth money someday," Allan said, bending down to pick up the Beanie Baby before tossing it onto her bed. "And don't be jealous that all your friends like me," he added with an evil smirk and a wink. "It's fine, we can share."

"Gross! Brother, get out of here!" DonnaMae moaned. "Ever since you got your braces off, it's like you gained some weird level of confidence with that new smile!" She chucked another Beanie Baby at him, smacking the wall just inches from his head.

"Hey, I got you that one," he said, his smile fading. "And yes, my smile —" he gave a cheesy grin "— is fantastic. Thanks for noticing." He placed his hand under his chin to showcase his smile. "Ok, but for real, just come up to the rec room after the pageant. We'll just be getting started, aaaaand ... you had a great idea last time, charging five dollars a cup at the door. We made enough money to pay for the keg and go bigger this time."

"But what if I wanted to get drunk on your Go Get Naked Juice and not be in charge of all the money? What if I wanted to party this time?"

Allan started laughing. "Skip-And-Go-Naked, Sis. It's called Skip-And-Go-Naked," he corrected with a head shake. "Although, Go Get Naked could be a possibility ... I mean with the pageant girls and all..."

"Oh god! Just stop!" DonnaMae said, throwing her hands up.

Allan's brow furrowed slightly. "Wait, do you *want* to drink? If so, that's cool, I support it. But you party harder than all of us, and you're probably the only sober person in the room." He paused, scratching his head. "Actually, now that I think about it, you being the only one who remembers everything might not be such a great idea." He laughed. "It does explain why you always have the stories the next morning. The ones the rest of us can't remember... or don't want to." He hmphed, as if piecing it all together. Then, turning his focus back to her, "So, do you want to drink?"

DonnaMae fiddled with the last Beanie Baby on the window ledge, her mind elsewhere. She never really felt like she was missing out, even though she didn't drink. She always had a good time partying with everyone. While her brother was the life of the party, she was the planner, making sure every detail was perfect. The funny part? She'd unintentionally become the bouncer, standing at the door, making sure everyone bought a cup before coming in.

It was comical: The smallest person in the group, a little blonde girl, was the one controlling the crowd. But it worked. If there was any sign of trouble, DonnaMae had no problem showing people the door. There was something about being in charge that gave her a natural confidence, and she didn't fear confrontation. She'd take guys twice her size by the arm and tell them it was time to leave, no hesitation.

DonnaMae knew she wouldn't be able to handle things the same way if she was drinking. It helped that if anyone did push back a little, Allan's friend Clifford was always nearby for backup. He looked like he could toss someone out a window with ease, though DonnaMae was more likely to do that than he was. Clifford was actually the nicest guy you'd ever meet. But just having him step up behind DonnaMae got people to shut up and listen. Allan and DonnaMae rarely had any issues with the parties Allan threw in the rec room. No one wanted to risk getting kicked out or blacklisted from their parties. But if DonnaMae and Clifford were both drunk, it wouldn't work.

"Hello, Mae? Do you want to drink?" Allan asked again, snapping her out of her thoughts.

DonnaMae didn't look up. "No, I, umm..."

"So? What's up, Mae?" Allan asked, his tone softening. "I thought you'd be excited about another party." He chuckled, "Remember last time? You had money spilling out of every pocket and even your bra. And that group you wouldn't let in until they paid? That was badass. They finally left, got cash, and came back, and then you refused to give them their change."

"Yeah." DonnaMae set the little brown dog Beanie Baby back on the window ledge, keeping her back to Allan. "It would just be nice to not always be 'Allan's little sister,' to not get made fun of, and maybe, just once, be as cool as you." She paused, waiting for him to jump in like he always did, to tease or reassure her so she wouldn't have to keep talking. But this time, he stayed quiet.

DonnaMae turned around and met his gaze. "I don't like drinking because... I don't want to lose control. I need to be in charge — of me, of everything. What if something goes wrong? If I'm drunk, who's going to be there to make sure everything's ok? Who's going to..." She swallowed hard, trying to keep her emotions at bay. Fear pulled at her heart. "You're all I've got left, Brother. I can't lose you. And if something happens, I need to be in control to make sure you're ok."

Allan's face softened as he walked over and sat on her bed. "Mae..." He paused as she sat down next to him. "You're still figuring out who you are, and you've come a long way from the days when we couldn't get you out of your bedroom." He smiled, giving her a nudge. "You're a good kid, and that's cool. You don't need to be like me." He guffawed. "I think it's cool that you don't drink. I literally just called you a badass at the last party. And I love that you make us money. Seriously, who cares if you drink or not?"

"Everyone. Everyone cares, and the peer pressure to drink —" she stopped short, unable to explain, and he wouldn't understand.

"Mae, that just shows how much of a badass you are. You don't cave to peer pressure. You know what you want and don't let others change it."

"Yeah, right." She laughed, but it was more at the idea that he thought she knew what she wanted and didn't care about what people thought. That was Allan. He didn't care what anyone thought. But she wasn't him, and she knew he wouldn't get it. Everyone adored him, but she was just *Allan's little sister*. The only time people paid her any attention was to make fun of her.

She stood up, forcing a smile, the one she wore to mask her true feelings. "Guess I'll just have to get used to being in my big brother's shadow."

Allan stood and placed a hand on her shoulder. "Mae, you are what you make yourself." His voice was sincere, but she was tired of the conversation and tired of the lecture. Right now, all she wanted was to be done with it.

Just as she expected, Allan had no idea what she was really talking about. He put on his cheesy grin and said, "So, see you and The Hick Chicks later tonight," brushing off the deeper conversation as if it never happened. The moment was over, either because he'd picked up on her fake smile that he probably knew all too well, or because he was done with the heart-to-heart. It wasn't really their thing, unless he was half-wasted on whatever new drink or drug he and his friends had tried that night. Then he'd come into her room late at night, wake her up, and talk about everything and anything until she fell back asleep or made him go to bed.

DonnaMae actually liked those moments. They let her know he was home safe, and she didn't have to worry. He always told her where he was going, and most of what he was up to, and the nights he didn't come in, she woke up in a panic, running to his room to make sure he was ok.

"Hick Chicks," DonnaMae laughed, wondering what the girls would think of the new nickname. She glanced out the window just as Allan's friend Paul's white station wagon pulled up in front of the house. "Paul's here!" she called, turning back towards her brother, but he was already bolting out the door.

Skip-and-Go-Naked was a concoction made from a thirty-pack of beer, five frozen lemonades, and half a gallon of vodka, and Paul's car was about to be loaded with all the ingredients, a garbage can to mix it in, and some red Solo cups. The last garbage can they'd used for mixing the drink had broken when someone tried to roll down the rec room stairs inside it. They were lucky that the only thing that broke was the garbage can.

After the last party, the guys had talked about their goal of filling the garbage can completely with the drink, and DonnaMae had no doubt they were going to try again. Her brother had plenty of older friends to make sure they got all the supplies. In a small town, they weren't hard to come by, and with it being her brother's senior year, every party had to be a big one.

Guilt tugged at DonnaMae. She didn't have much going on today until the pageant and she could easily help set up the rec room before heading over to support Hazel. After a moment of hesitation, she picked up her phone and made a quick call.

"Remember the time your sister thought getting T-Bagged was with an actual tea —" Paul stopped and then started laughing. "Nope, never mind, it was you that received it. So no, you wouldn't remember! She was pissed. In fact, you're lucky she was there, or you would have looked like Luka with —"

"— Permanent marker all over your face, Brother," DonnaMae said, jumping up behind Paul and using his shoulders to boost herself higher into the air. "I've also saved your ass a time or two, Paul." She gave him a side hug. "You're welcome."

"What's up, Mae?" Paul hugged her back.

He was DonnaMae's favorite out of all her brother's friends. He was like having an extra big brother around. He seemed to have a heart, unlike most of them, and he was actually a pretty nice guy.

"First off, boys are immature and gross. Girls would never do that shit," DonnaMae said with a gagging sound before laughing. "And second, I made a quick call. The girls and I will head up to the rec room to help set up, but then we have to haul ass to the pageant."

Allan burst out laughing.

"What's so funny?" DonnaMae asked, placing her hands on her hips. "Wait, never mind. I don't want to know!"

"You really don't want to know?" Allan gasped, still trying to catch his breath.

"I kinda do," Paul said, raising an eyebrow at Allan.

"I was just picturing a girl 'T-bag,'" Allan said, making air quotes with his fingers.

DonnaMae palmed her forehead. "Ugh — you're so gross!" She gave Paul another quick hug, "Good luck with him."

Paul laughed, "I'm not sure how the hell the two of you are related. I think maybe your brother was adopted."

"Pretty sure I was the one who was adopted," DonnaMae smiled, glancing at Paul.

Sometimes she wished Allan was more like Paul. Maybe then he'd understand her better. But she knew Paul could be just as dumb and crazy as the rest of them. Still, he seemed to be the most mature one of the group.

"Ok, well, I'm going to go get ready and then I'll pick up the girls and head that way," DonnaMae said, nodding towards her car. "But remember, I can't put anything in my trunk, so you'll have to pack it all in Paul's." Her grandparents had fixed her trunk, but if she opened it again, it might not close. The replacement trunk was a lighter color than the rest of the car, but it worked fine. She was saving up for a truck. For now, her car was just motivation to save every penny she made.

Allan dropped to his knees, laughing so hard he could barely speak. "You're on a roll today! You can't make this shit up. Don't worry, Paul loves putting things in his trunk!"

Paul kicked Allan as DonnaMae walked away to get ready. Allan had once told her that when she got older, she'd finally understand his jokes and laugh along with him. She was still waiting for that day. *Boys are so immature*, she thought.

"YUCK, it smells like ass in here," DonnaMae said, walking through the rec room door with Ella right behind her.

"Yeah," Paul said, brushing his hands together like he was brushing off the smell. "We left the bucket of mop water out last time. But I just flushed all the water down the toilet and all the windows are open, so we should be good."

"That's why it's so cold in here," Ella said with a shiver.

Allan burst through the door, clutching a thirty-pack of Keystone Ice. "Run down and get the last case of beer out of the car. You'll warm right up."

"Why are you so outta breath?" Paul teased. "I thought you were running in the mornings. So much for you getting into shape."

Allan lifted his shirt and flashed his six-pack while juggling the case of beer in his other arm. "What are you talking about? I'm in better shape than you are."

"Hold on and I'll bust mine out and we can see who's better," Luka said, walking through the rec room door.

"Oh gosh, please don't!" Izzy said, walking in behind Luka and shielding her eyes with one of her hands. "I don't know what you all are talking about and I'm pretty sure I don't want to see it."

"Yeah, no one wants to see your scrawny ass, Luka," Allan said, setting the beer down on a table.

"Ella, your Strawberry Boone's is in the car still," Izzy said, bumping past DonnaMae and Luka with a case of Zima's and a bag of jolly ranchers lifted in the air. "And it smells like ass in here."

"Quit bitching and let's get started," Allan said, opening a can of beer.

Paul and Luka ran down to get more supplies and soon they were mixing the ingredients all together. Allan had bought a new mop for the rec room and he was using it upside down to stir the drink.

"How do you plan on serving the drinks?" DonnaMae asked, walking over to the bar.

"Let's push it behind the bar so no one can just get into it," Allan said, grabbing the handle as Paul and Luka helped him drag the full garbage can behind the bar.

"Oh yeah! I can stay behind the bar, and everyone can pay for their cup and get their drink at the same time," DonnaMae said, excited at the idea of playing bartender. "And for refills, I'll know who paid and who didn't! No freebies for friends."

She glanced around, thinking it through. "But... how?"

"Just dip one cup in and pour it into the others," Izzy suggested, grabbing two cups to demonstrate. "Less sticky mess to clean up after."

"I guess that'll work," DonnaMae agreed, nodding as she set up the bar exactly how she wanted it for the party later that night.

"I have an idea." Allan walked behind the bar and found a spoon. With a knife he made a small slit in the side of the cup, fed the spoon in backwards through the hole, and then bent the top of the spoon into a hook so it would hang off the garbage can handle. "It's a keg-cup-ladle!"

"Damn, that was good thinking," Izzy said.

"Too bad we don't have a way to just pump it into the cup," DonnaMae said. "This is going to be messy!"

"Let's save that invention for another day," her brother said with a smile.

"Shit," Izzy said, looking down at her watch. "We've gotta go, we're going to be late!"

"You only need to see the end, right? It's fine!" Luka said

"Don't forget to bring the pageant ladies back with you!" Allan called after them as they ran out the door.

DonnaMae thought she heard her brother call her name and she stopped on the top step. Allan poked his head through the door. "Mae, I got you a container of pink lemonade. It's in the fridge."

"Um, thanks?" She gave him a puzzled look.

"It's for tonight," Allan said, glancing over his shoulder before lowering his voice. He looked down at the girls gathered at the bottom of the stairs. "Just pour some in a cup and drink it. No one will know it's not the naked juice," he added with a chuckle. "Everyone will leave you alone."

DonnaMae's heart swelled, nearly ready to burst. He had actually listened. "Thanks, Brother," she said, her voice soft with gratitude. With a huge smile, she practically skipped down the stairs to join the girls.

The rec room was packed shoulder to shoulder with bodies swaying to the beat of Def Leppard's "Pour Some Sugar On Me," blaring from the stereo. A few were dancing in the middle of the room, others played pool, while groups huddled into cliques, shouting over the music to talk. DonnaMae stood behind the bar, slinging cups of her brother's sugary, lemony concoction, when she spotted Hazel and LeAnn walking through the door.

"Hey, come grab your congratulatory drink!" DonnaMae called, waving both hands in the air.

Hazel and LeAnn had killed it tonight at the pageant, with their stunning voices and stage presence. LeAnn had been the runner-up for Miss Howard, and Hazel had won best platform, both of them walking away with multiple scholarships. Throughout the show, DonnaMae had wondered what it would be like to stand on that stage and win something, but she wasn't like Hazel or LeAnn. They were effortlessly girly, good with makeup and heels, and, most of all, talented.

"Is congr-ul-tary even a word?" Ella whispered, leaning over the bar.

"That's not exactly what I said," DonnaMae laughed, handing Ella a glass of water. "But if it's not a word, I just made it one."

"Ohhh, look at you, sexy bartender," LeAnn said, giving DonnaMae a flirty wink while blowing her a kiss.

"Thanks. Can I get you ladies a drink?" DonnaMae lowered her voice and leaned over the bar. "On me."

"Oh yes, we'll take two," LeAnn said, obnoxiously loud, before leaning in with a grin. "Is there a tip jar?"

As DonnaMae stood up to pour them drinks, she noticed Izzy shouldering her way through a group dancing with drinks sloshing out of their cups as they raised them in the air. Just as Izzy reached the bar, someone bumped her, sending her drink flying all over DonnaMae.

DonnaMae screamed, jumping back, but it was too late. She looked down at her soaked shirt, then at Izzy, who was doubled over, laughing and apologizing between giggles.

Without missing a beat, DonnaMae jumped up onto the bar, and cupped her hands around her mouth as the chorus of the song hit. "Pour some sugar on me!"

Izzy and LeAnn quickly climbed onto the bar stools, joining in. Before long, the entire room erupted into song, stomping and singing along so loudly that DonnaMae half-expected the floor to collapse, sending them all down into the garage below. The song ended with a roar of laughter and cheers.

"You were off cue," Ella slurred, pointing at DonnaMae. "I think you've had two... few three... too many, singin' and dancin' on the bar."

They all burst into laughter at Ella, knowing full well she was the one who needed to be cut off.

"I'm not sure that even made sense, Ella," DonnaMae chuckled, refilling her glass with water.

"I knoooooow," Ella groaned, throwing an arm around Hazel with a stumble.

As the night went on and the room began to empty, the girls claimed the couch and some sleeping pads from under the pool table, which already had a few people passed out on top of it.

Izzy laid her head in DonnaMae's lap. "Are we really doing the Miss Howard County Pageant next year?"

DonnaMae ran her fingers through Izzy's long red curls. "Yes, Izzy, we are. And you'll probably win."

LeAnn hiccupped loudly. "Actually," she paused, hiccupping again, "I'll be winning next year."

"Don't you mean this year?" Ella mumbled, curling up next to DonnaMae on the other side of the couch and pulling a blanket over herself.

"How are you still awake?" Hazel asked, tilting her head back towards Ella.

"'Cause I don't want an icky on my face," Ella muttered, her words barely coherent, but the girls understood. They all laughed, recalling the poor guy who'd passed out earlier and gotten a Sharpie makeover.

DonnaMae glanced around the rec room. The fake drink idea from her brother had worked; not one person had bugged her tonight about not drinking, and she'd had fun and was sober. She could take the girls home, but crashing here for the night felt right. The real fun would be waking up the next morning, watching everyone struggle while DonnaMae made coffee, water, or, as Luka always requested, another beer. Then they'd all walk to The Bee-Hive for breakfast, where buttery, mouthwatering cinnamon rolls or butterhorns awaited.

Scanning the room one last time, it looked like someone had tossed in sleeping gas, causing people to collapse wherever they stood. With a smile on her face, DonnaMae leaned into Ella and closed her eyes, already dreaming of the giant cinnamon roll she'd devour in the morning.

CHAPTER 22
May, 2001

The sweet aroma of cinnamon and sugar swirled through the air at Willows Recreation Center as DonnaMae stood amid the chatter and laughter of kids eagerly devouring their snacks before going outside to enjoy the spring weather. Today's treat was one of DonnaMae's all-time favorites: big, soft, warm pretzels. There were two types, one filled with sweet cinnamon cream cheese, and the other plain, sprinkled with large salt crystals. DonnaMae couldn't get enough of the cream cheese ones. It was like someone had combined a cinnamon roll and cheesecake, then stuffed it into a pretzel.

She double-checked her sign-in sheet and picked up the last pretzel dusted with cinnamon and ripped off a piece. The creamy filling oozed out of the soft dough, and just as DonnaMae was about to toss the bite into her mouth, Charles walked up.

"Can I help you?" she asked with a smile, and then tossed the bite into her mouth.

"You know those are filled with a ton of calories, right?" he said, taking the rest of the pretzel from her hand and setting it down on the tray.

"Um, ok?" DonnaMae said, her shoulders slumping as guilt

crept in. She shifted uncomfortably, glancing down at the pretzel and then back at Charles, her smile fading.

"Let's go pick up the new equipment for karaoke," Charles said, a grin spreading across his face.

"Really?" DonnaMae jumped. She had been trying to convince him for weeks that adding a weekly karaoke would be perfect to mix things up, especially on rainy days.

"Yes, we have extra staff here today. Let's drive up to Olympia and pick it up."

"Ok, let me get my coat and call my dad to let him know we're heading out of town."

"If we leave now, we'll be back before your shift is over. No one will even know we're gone," Charles said with a wink.

DonnaMae hesitated. She didn't like the idea of not telling her dad. What if something happened to him? How would anyone reach her if her phone ran out of minutes? She'd meant to buy a new phone card last week, but kept forgetting to stop at the store.

"I'm not sure..." she started, glancing around the room, but Charles was already on his way out the door, not even giving her a chance to respond.

Frustrated, DonnaMae realized she had no choice but to chase after him if she wanted the equipment before he changed his mind. She still wanted to call her dad, but there wasn't time. A knot formed in her stomach as she grabbed her coat and hurried after Charles.

"Wait up, I'm coming!" she called out, breathless by the time she reached his truck just as he cranked the engine.

The loud beats of "OPP" by Naughty By Nature blasted through the speakers. DonnaMae shook her head at Charles's taste in music before climbing into his jet-black four-door truck.

"You down with OPP, Mae?" Charles asked with a smirk.

"Oh yeah, you know me!" DonnaMae replied, quoting the lyrics, then added with genuine curiosity, "Is OPP some kind of drug or something?"

Charles burst out laughing as he backed out of the parking spot. "Seriously, how did you make it this far through high school?"

"Well, it wasn't by doing drugs!" DonnaMae shot him a sharp look.

"Or by your book smarts."

DonnaMae felt his words hit her like a punch to the stomach. "Right, I'm so dumb, that's why you hired me," she muttered, turning to gaze out the window to hide the sting in her eyes. She knew she should be used to comments like that by now, but they always seemed to cut deeper than they should. *Water off a duck's back, water off a duck's back*, she repeated to herself, hearing her brother's voice in her head. She let out a slow, deep breath, trying to calm herself down.

Then, without warning, she felt a warm hand rest on her thigh. All the hairs on her arm stood up. She didn't move.

"That wasn't nice. I'm sorry," Charles said, his fingers gently gliding back and forth on her thigh.

An unsettling feeling crept over DonnaMae. She hadn't even noticed the music had been turned down. How long had she been staring out the window? And why was Charles's hand on her leg?

"Mae, come on. You know I think you're smart, talented, and beautiful," Charles said softly, his words only increasing her discomfort as she shifted her attention towards him.

Before she could respond, he continued, "This is supposed to be a fun trip! We're celebrating! We're getting new equipment with the grant you helped write."

"WHAT?!" she practically shouted, her seatbelt the only thing keeping her from jumping out of her seat. "You didn't tell me my grant was approved!" she said, her smile stretching from ear to ear.

"Now there's my pretty girl and that beautiful smile of hers," Charles said, flashing her a grin as he gave her leg a quick squeeze, his touch now feeling affectionate and reassuring.

"Did we get the whole thirty grand?" DonnaMae asked, beaming with excitement.

"Yes!" Charles said, keeping his eyes on the road.

"WOOOZERS! That is something to celebrate for sure!" she cheered.

DonnaMae was so caught up in her excitement that she didn't notice they had left the freeway until they were already turning onto a quiet backstreet.

"Where are we going? I thought the music store was down-town," she said, her brows furrowing.

"It is," Charles said casually. "I'm just making a quick stop to pick up something for my girlfriend."

The road felt like it stretched for miles, eventually leading to a strip mall filled with various shops and restaurants. The farther they drove, the more isolated and abandoned the area became, giving DonnaMae an eerie feeling compared to the liveliness they had originally pulled into.

They pulled into a parking lot with only a few other cars. She couldn't imagine what Charles would be getting for his girlfriend here, and she didn't care. When he opened his door, she leaned her seat back and closed her eyes. "Have fun."

"Um, no. I need your help. Come on."

"You need my help to what? Fight off any zombies that might walk out of that building?"

Charles stood there glaring at her. It was like she could read his mind: *Come on, Mae, how old are you?*

"UGH!" she huffed with an eye roll. DonnaMae pulled her seat back up and stepped out of the truck to follow him. "Where are we, anyway?"

Charles walked up to a storefront that looked like a café, though the windows were completely blacked out. The small building was attached to a larger structure that might have once been a cinema, but now seemed out of business, with faded signage and chipped paint.

"This place gives me the heebeegeebees," DonnaMae said in a low whisper as she stepped up next to Charles.

"Don't be so immature," Charles said, holding the door open for her to walk through.

DonnaMae straightened her posture. *I'm not immature*, she thought defensively, though she couldn't shake the weird feeling that lingered as she stepped inside. As she passed Charles, she half expected zombies to pop out. The thought almost made her laugh, but she held it in.

DonnaMae's feet sank into a vibrant red carpet, the color matching the red embroidered flowers on black silk curtains lining the walls. In the middle of the room stood two large circular racks, overflowing with colors and textures. As she got closer, it became clear that the racks were filled with bras and underwear in all shapes and styles.

Oh, he's getting his girlfriend a bra, she thought, her cheeks flushing. *Oops, that's kinda awkward.* Guilt tugged at her for feeling irritated earlier when he called her immature, so she turned away, giving him privacy to do his shopping, figuring it must be strange for him to shop for something so intimate with her tagging along.

The room smelled faintly of incense, though DonnaMae couldn't spot its source. It was small, no bigger than the office at the after school program, with a short hallway leading to a back area made of curtains. To the right was a glass counter where an older woman sat, completely engrossed in her book, oblivious to everything around her as though she were curled up on a couch at home.

DonnaMae wandered back to the racks, her fingers grazing the luxurious fabrics. She pulled out a bright purple set, its sheer lace more delicate and intricate than anything she'd ever seen. The fabric was nearly transparent, except for the area around the nipples, and the boy short underwear followed the same design, completely sheer except for the crotch.

"That one is perfect."

DonnaMae about jumped out of her skin as Charles grabbed the piece out of her hand.

"Oh, glad I could be of some help," DonnaMae said, stepping back.

"Do you think it will fit Tina?" he asked, holding it up to DonnaMae. "She's about your size."

"Um, I guess." DonnaMae stepped back again

"I have to be sure. They don't let you return things here."

DonnaMae stopped stepping backward. That made sense. She looked at the purple bra a little closer. "Yeah, it looks like my size, should be fine."

"Perfect!" he said, handing it to her. "Can you try it on really fast? The dressing room is right there." Charles pointed to the little hallway with the room made of curtains.

Uncomfortable, DonnaMae fidgeted and let out a hesitant, "Umm..." as she tried to find the right words.

"It will only take you a second, then we can go get the equipment."

DonnaMae still felt bad for being rude earlier, so she figured this was the least she could do. With a quiet sigh, she walked towards the back, sliding a curtain aside to reveal a chair, side table, and tall mirror leaning against the wall. She closed the curtain and stared at her reflection.

Bra shopping with Dad and Grandma at JCPenney was awkward, she thought, *but this...* The bras here were nothing like what she was used to. Her old, frayed tan bra had become her favorite simply because it was comfortable. These lace pieces were made to be seen, to make a statement.

DonnaMae stood barefoot on the floor, examining the vibrant purple fabric in her hands. She wasn't sure if she was supposed to try it on over her bra or wear it like a regular bra. There wasn't much to it, clearly more decorative than practical. Avoiding her reflection for a moment, she decided to go for it, unclasping her bra and putting on the lace one.

Once she clasped it in the back, she froze, staring at herself in the mirror. It fit perfectly. For a second, she felt like one of those glamorous Victoria's Secret models. A smile spread across her face as she placed a hand on her hip and struck a playful pose. *Maybe I could've been a model,* she thought with a laugh.

She picked up the matching underwear and slid them on over her own, noticing how comfortably they fit. The delicate lace felt soft against her skin, and despite the little bits of her own underwear poking through, they were barely noticeable. She was pleasantly surprised by how good the lingerie looked and felt on her.

"Does it fit?" Charles's voice sounded so close. DonnaMae's arms immediately wrapped around her chest, her eyes darting around to make sure he wasn't in the room.

"Yes. It does," she said, her voice tight.

"Perfect, come on out."

"Yes, sorry. I just have to put my clothes back on."

"Nah, step out here so I can see. Gotta make sure it fits right and looks good."

DonnaMae froze, her eyes locked on her reflection in the mirror, her arm tight against her chest. She didn't want to go out there, and she *definitely* didn't want her boss to see her like this. But he was her boss. She knew she'd never hear the end of it if she refused. Wrapping her arms tighter around her chest, she glanced down at the underwear. The front seemed to cover enough, and her own underwear underneath took care of the back.

With a deep breath, she reluctantly walked towards the curtain, pulling it open just enough to take a small step out. She kept her head down, avoiding eye contact, her arms still crossed over herself.

"What's wrong? Don't you like it? Should I get her something else?" Charles asked, his tone light, as if he were talking about a pair of shoes.

"No, it's fine," DonnaMae mumbled, stepping back towards the curtain, eager to escape back inside.

"Well then, let me see you. Turn around."

DonnaMae stood frozen, squeezing her legs and arms tightly together.

"Mae, it's the same as a swimsuit. It's not a big deal. My god, don't be so immature, you're acting like a child."

His words cut through the air, sharp and belittling.

DonnaMae's arms fell to her sides, and she stood up straighter. *I am not a child*, she thought.

"See, you look perfect. Turn around. Let me see all of you," he said, his tone still casual, as if it were nothing at all.

As DonnaMae obediently followed his instructions, static echoed in her ears, leaving her feeling like a puppet under his control. His voice was the strings pulling her body in any direction he desired her to go. With fluid movements, she turned and spread her arms out to the side, bending over to touch the floor. Turning again, moving forward and backward until she was given permission to go change. Back behind the curtains, the bright purple lingerie fell from her body to the floor, along with her confidence and her youth.

DonnaMae found herself back in the truck, arriving at the rec center, but she couldn't remember the specifics of how they got there or what the newly-purchased equipment looked like, or if they even had a conversation on the way back. Despite this, she still wore a smile, and would continue to do so until she was home safe and could take a shower to wash away the day. *Tomorrow will be a new day. Tomorrow this will all be forgotten.* "Water off a duck's back," she whispered to herself as she opened the door and got out of the truck.

"Mae," Charles said, stopping her in her tracks. "Remember, today stays between us. We don't want anyone to ruin my surprise for Tina."

"Right." She nodded in agreement before walking into the

comforting sounds of the recreation center, shutting out the negativity and leaving only a forced smile.

—

When DonnaMae got home, she pulled into the driveway next to a white Chevy two-door truck that looked just like her dad's, but shorter and stockier, with a blue line along the bottom. She got out of her car and circled the truck. It was a nice-looking truck, an '88, but it looked brand new. Even the tires were polished. She wanted to ask who the truck belonged to, but she honestly didn't want to see her dad, or anyone. She just wanted to go inside and take a shower.

When she looked up, her dad and step-mom were staring at her through the house window. *UGH*, she thought, *so much for avoiding everyone.*

Then little Adeline came darting out of the house. "SUR-PRISE!" she screamed at the top of her lungs, jumping towards DonnaMae to pick her up.

DonnaMae did, and wrapped her arms tightly around her little sister. For some reason, this made her have to fight back the urge to cry. "Surprise to you too, my little ladybug."

"Wait, you have a surprise for me?"

DonnaMae laughed. "No, silly, I was just saying it back to you because you were surprising me with a big hug."

"That was not your surprise. That was just a hug." Adeline wiggled free. "That is your surprise!" she said, pointing behind DonnaMae.

"What?" DonnaMae turned around, looking for something to pop out at her. "What is?"

"This is," Adeline said, running up to the truck and crawling into the bed. "I helped Dad wash it up for you!"

"Wait, what?" DonnaMae took a step towards the truck. "That's for me?"

"Sure is!" her dad said, walking up behind her. "Happy early-birthday."

"Seriously? Noooo." She turned around and threw her arms around her dad, and this time she could not fight the tears.

"We thought it might bring you good luck for your test tomorrow if you got it early."

"You have been working so hard," Elise said, a soft smile forming on her lips to match her gentle voice.

"This is seriously all mine?" DonnaMae asked, pulling back from her dad and wiping tears from her eyes.

"Well, I don't think she likes it," Adeline said. "She's crying. I knew we should have got a pink car."

They all laughed and DonnaMae couldn't stop the tears from falling. She loved the truck, and she loved her parents for getting it for her, but she felt like she didn't deserve it, especially after today. She felt like she was nothing but a liar, and if they only knew what she really was, they would not be buying her a brand-new truck.

CHAPTER 23

...

DonnaMae couldn't shake the shame gnawing at her insides as she sat at the breakfast table. It felt as if she had committed a crime and received a reward for it.

"You're quiet this morning, Mae," her dad said, his voice cutting through the silence. He placed a perfectly-cooked piece of French toast on her plate, the warm, buttery aroma filling the room. "You don't seem too thrilled about breakfast," he said, tilting his head to one side. "Did you dream about driving your new truck?" he added with a big, cheesy grin.

DonnaMae wanted to be happy, wanted to feel excited and grateful. They had taken the truck for a drive last night, and she *loved* it. The navy blue upholstery matched her dad's truck, and he'd even installed a new stereo system. It was perfect, just like his. She *should* be excited, but something didn't feel right.

Her dad's French toast was her favorite, topped with peanut butter, strawberries, and a spray of Cool Whip, but she didn't feel like she deserved to enjoy it. In fact, she didn't feel like she deserved to enjoy anything at all.

"I'm just..." DonnaMae started, but her voice trailed off. She wanted to tell her dad everything, to hear him say it was ok, that none of it was her fault, and that he would have done the same thing. Well, maybe not *exactly* the same. The image of her dad trying on a lace bra suddenly popped into her mind, and she couldn't help but laugh inwardly, remembering him dressed up as Mimi for Halloween.

"Well, look at that, a smile!" her dad said, spraying a dab of Cool Whip on top of her French toast, pulling her from her thoughts. "Must be the sight of this piece of perfection I just made."

It was perfect. He had pulled out all the stops this morning, even buying fresh strawberries just for her. She picked up a strawberry that had slid to the side of her plate and placed it into her mouth. The sweetness spread across her tongue, a real smile forming on her lips as she reached for another slice of strawberry.

"Thanks, Daddy, it *is* perfect," she said, savoring the taste, but the weight of the secret still hung heavy on her mind. How could she ever tell him? It would break his heart, let him down completely. He had taught her to be tough, to stand up for herself, to fight back. She had already let herself down. She couldn't bear the thought of disappointing him, too.

A thought of her own reflection in that tight purple lace crept in and made her shudder.

"Did you not get any sleep? Did you stay up late studying again?" her dad asked, setting a mug of tea down next to her plate.

DonnaMae sat up a little taller, trying to refocus. "No, sorry, Dad. I didn't sleep well and... um..." At least that was the truth, she thought. "I'm nervous. What if I fail the test again? That'll be three times. I don't think I can handle that."

She had nearly forgotten all about the test retake. That was the reason he was making her favorite breakfast, and why they'd given her the truck early. Today would be her third attempt at passing the test for the Running Start Program at the college. Hazel had already successfully enrolled for junior year, but DonnaMae hadn't made the cut because of the reading section.

The problem was, the bigger, unfamiliar words weren't ones she could guess from memory like she usually did when reading. The pressure of the timed test only made it worse, and she struggled to make sense of the words. She wished it was something she could study for, but no amount of preparation seemed to help untangle the letters when she sat down in front of that exam.

Her stepmom had gotten her a few books on improving vocabulary, and DonnaMae was trying to work through them. She felt thankful that Elise was so smart. Having someone who cared enough to help without making her feel dumb meant more to DonnaMae than she could express. Even though she pretended it was because the kitchen had better lighting from the big bay windows, DonnaMae always set up her study sessions at the kitchen table while Elise cooked. The truth was, she liked having her stepmom close by.

Elise never judged or made fun of her when she struggled with a word. If DonnaMae stumbled over something, Elise would walk over, quietly read the word aloud for her, and then go back to what she was doing, never making a big deal out of it. It was such a small thing, but it made a world of difference to DonnaMae, knowing she had someone who understood and supported her, no matter how slow her progress felt.

At least this time, DonnaMae had the math part figured out. The first time she took the test, she had failed both sections. She hated taking tests. Hazel had offered to help her study, encouraging her to retake the test so they could both be in the program together. After failing the first retake, DonnaMae knew she needed more than just a few weeks of studying. She was determined to get into this program to prove to herself that she could do this, and to prove to everyone else that she wasn't dumb.

"Mae, you know, you don't have to do the running start program," her dad said as he sat down at the table next to her. "Maybe just enjoy your last year of high school and don't worry about it."

Emotions swirled like a storm inside DonnaMae. "So, you think I'm not smart enough to go to college while I'm in high school?" DonnaMae blinked back tears.

"Mae, that's not what I said. You —"

"Dad, I'm going to do this program. If you don't believe in me, fine, just stand in line. There are plenty of other people in front of you. I'm the dumb girl that can't read. The dumb girl in the dumb English classes. Don't worry, I already know all of this."

Her high school had placed her in the lowest level English class, Room 101, the bottom of the barrel. It was filled with kids who messed around, barely paying attention, who didn't seem to care about learning. But DonnaMae did care, and she *wanted* to learn. She couldn't wait for the day when she'd walk into that office and tell them to skip rocks, because she would be taking college-level English now. She had gone to the administration plenty of times, telling them she didn't belong in that class and that she wanted to learn. But instead, they'd suggested testing her for dyslexia. When they started the process, they called her dad, saying she needed to be placed in a class with kids who had disabilities. Her dad shut that down, calling the school to stop the testing.

That's when DonnaMae found out about the Running Start program, which would allow her to take college courses while still in high school. She made up her mind right then that she was going to do it.

"I never called you dumb," her dad said. "I am your biggest fan, and I —"

"I'm suddenly not hungry!" DonnaMae pushed her chair back, jumped up from the table, and sprinted out of the room, racing against her tears to make it to her room before they fell.

It was a little after one in the afternoon when DonnaMae left the college testing center and pulled up to the Flying A. The distinct smell of car oil greeting her as she turned off her truck and jumped out. Keeping her head held high and a smile painted on her face, she walked into the shop. She was grateful no one was manning the front desk when she arrived, because it gave her a few more moments before facing her grandpa. But by the time she reached the back room, her smile had faded.

"Well, hello, Miss Mae! What a surprise to see you!" her grandma said, welcoming her with open arms.

"Shouldn't you be in school?" her grandpa added, barely glancing up from his plate as he took a bite of his baked potato.

"Hi, Grandpa. Nice to see you too," DonnaMae said, folding into her grandma's hug, savoring the warmth of the embrace.

Her grandpa finally looked up, his eyes meeting hers, and in that moment, she knew he could see her pain. They had a connection that was unlike anything she had with anyone else. She was his little girl, and he had a way of reading her without her having to say a word. He was her anchor, the constant reminder to stay true to herself.

"Well, what's going on?" he asked, softer now as he stood up, dragging a chair to the counter. "A girl's got to eat. Grab yourself a plate and have some of this meatloaf I made last night."

Her grandpa had been a cook in the Korean War, and his food was always amazing. He took pride in every dish he made, and no one could whip up comfort food like him. His baked potato with all the fixings — including real bacon bits, not the store-bought kind — was one of her favorites. The counter, which doubled as a cutting board and dining table, was where they gathered daily for lunch.

"I'm not really hungry, I —"

"Nonsense," her grandpa interrupted, his voice firm but caring. "Joyce, fix her a potato. Mae, sit down."

DonnaMae stepped back from her grandmother's embrace, feeling the weight of her emotions. "I had my test again today, for the college program, and... " She trailed off, fighting the tears that threatened to fall. She didn't know whether to cry or scream, she was so overwhelmed with everything. She let out a shaky breath, lowering her voice. "And I..." she cleared her throat, "failed... again... for the third time." She sighed and dropped her head.

"Aahhh, phewy," her grandpa said, waving his hand dismissively. "So what? You'll just take it again."

"How come Mom was so smart and I'm so —" DonnaMae's words stopped dead in her throat as her grandpa's expression shifted. His look alone silenced her, warning her not to finish that thought.

The room became eerily quiet. No one moved, no one spoke. It was always like this when DonnaMae mentioned her mom. Other people could talk about her, could say things like, *you're just like your mom*, but the moment DonnaMae brought her up, everything changed. Faces would fall into that familiar *poor little girl without a mom* expression, and suddenly, there was nothing more to say.

"You're so smart," Grandma Joyce said, quick to shower DonnaMae with praise and shift any uncomfortable conversation to something lighter, as she always did. It was her way of making everyone feel happy and loved. "We couldn't survive without your help. You're our little shining star, our singing girl. Don't you have a choir concert this week?"

DonnaMae went along. "I don't have a concert this week, but I do have pageant stuff." She didn't mind the topic change, it was actually a relief. She had been meaning to talk to them about the pageant anyway. She wanted to practice the interview questions with her grandma and see if they could go shopping for an interview suit. She also needed to figure out a talent for the show, and, unfortunately, a swimsuit.

But right now, the idea of trying on a swimsuit, or anything resembling a bra or underwear, made her stomach churn. The last thing she wanted was to see herself in the mirror without clothes on.

Later that day, DonnaMae sat in her truck outside Willows Recreation Center, staring at the large windows of the empty gym. Soon, kids would fill the space, playing basketball or four square, following the schedule she'd carefully planned for the month. But one thing remained unplanned: whether or not Charles would be in. His truck wasn't there, but he could have parked in the back or caught a ride.

DonnaMae had arrived early, wanting to be fully prepared for the bookfair she had scheduled. The book fair featured gently-used books that children could choose from for free. She had worked with the local library to set this up, had poured her heart into it. But despite her excitement for the event, she couldn't seem to shake the fear at the thought of seeing Charles.

"Let the fear fuel you," her brother had told her once when she'd tried out his invention, the "Skeen-Board." She had ridden it on her knees down a steep hill, gripping the handles, shaking so badly she thought she'd throw up. But by the end, she had fun and came out of it alive.

This, though, wasn't a board with wheels. She couldn't just close her eyes and hope to make it safely down the hill. In fact, when she closed her eyes, the memories replayed in her mind, making everything worse.

How could she let this fear fuel her? How was she supposed to walk inside with her head held high, knowing that every time Charles looked at her, he'd see all the flaws she tried so hard to hide? She could feel herself becoming his next joke, just like every other time she'd tried to prove herself to anyone else. She had wanted him to be proud of her, but instead, she'd failed. And now she was exactly what everyone had always made her out to be: A joke. She had worked so hard to be something different here, to create a DonnaMae that people respected, one Charles respected.

No matter how hard she worked, she always ended up being the one people laughed at.

DonnaMae let out a defeated sigh. The rush of cool air hit her when she opened the car door. She was in charge here. Everyone turned to her with their questions. Some days, Charles didn't even bother showing up, leaving her to run everything. As long as no one knew the truth, she could keep up the illusion that nothing was wrong. She had mastered that skill better than anyone.

Stepping out of the truck, DonnaMae whispered to herself, "Let my fear fuel me," closed the door, and walked towards the center. She could do this.

"Mae. Mae, wait up!"

DonnaMae froze at the door, her fingers gripping the handle. "Oh, hey, Charles," she said, keeping her eyes on the door as she pulled it open, hoping he wouldn't notice the fear in her voice.

Charles jogged up behind her, his breath heavy. "I literally parked right next to you," he laughed, out of breath. "You looked like you were deep in thought when I pulled in."

"Oh yeah, I've just got a lot on my mind today, exams and the book fair." DonnaMae walked briskly past the front desk, her thoughts racing as she tried to think of anything to keep from heading into the office alone with him. She stopped at one of the tables, scanning the room for a distraction. "Do you think we should put the books —"

"DonnaMae!"

The sharp use of her full name stopped her in her tracks. Nobody called her that, not even her stepmom. Irritation flared as she turned to face Charles. "What!"

"Whoa, ok. I know you've got a lot going on today, but you don't have to be so bitchy! I just want to talk to you for a min—"

"I am not being bitchy, Charles," she said, her tone curt. "I just don't have time to talk. I need to move the tables, and the girls from the library will be here soon."

"They'll be here in two hours, Mae. Sit down, please." Charles pulled out a chair and sat down. "I want to talk to you for a second," he said, pulling out the chair next to him.

Talk. The word echoed in her head. What did he want to talk about? Everything in her screamed to run, to bolt out the door and not look back. Her heart raced, and for a moment, she considered leaving. But her feet wouldn't move. She couldn't just walk away. This job wasn't about him, it was about the kids. She loved this job. If she left, she'd have to explain why, and that was not an option.

Charles tapped the chair next to him, his face blank, his usual smirk nowhere in sight. It was as if he had carefully wiped away all emotion. "I've been thinking about this for a while. You do so much around here, Mae."

She sat down reluctantly, her mind spinning. Was he going to fire her, or was this some kind of compliment? She clenched her fists at her sides, trying to steady herself.

Charles reached into his pocket and pulled out a small box. "You're a key part of why this place runs so smoothly," he said, setting it on the table in front of her.

DonnaMae was glad she was sitting down, because if she'd been standing, she might have run. *What the hell is that?* she thought, her eyes glued to the small black box in front of her.

"Open it," Charles said, nudging the box with his stubby fingers. His hands were big, but his fingers were short, almost like they belonged to a chunky baby.

Her mind whirled. What could be inside? It was too small for more lingerie. And he had a girlfriend, he wasn't about to give her a ring... *right?* But the creeping unease in her gut told her that whatever was in that box, it couldn't be good.

Stop being ridiculous, she scolded herself. With a deep breath, she reached forward and opened the box. Inside was a shiny silver name badge, gleaming under the fluorescent overhead lights.

"So... what do you say?"

DonnaMae blinked, unsure how to respond. She lifted the name badge from the box. Her name was engraved on it, and directly under her name, "Assistant Director."

"What? No way! Seriously? Me? Why? Are you sure?" she

asked, mashing all the words together so fast it came out sounding like one long word.

Charles chuckled, standing up and looking down at her. "Yes, Mae, of course, you. You've earned this. You do so much around here; more than you probably realize. Your work with the kids, organizing events like today's book fair — it makes a real impact. These kids get the chance to experience something they wouldn't have otherwise, and that's because of you. You've gone above and beyond, and it's time you're recognized for it."

Every other emotion disappeared as excitement surged through DonnaMae. She jumped up, gave Charles a quick hug, and stepped back with a wide smile. "Thank you so much! I'm so excited. I can't wait to tell my dad!" Charles was treating her with the respect she'd been hoping for. Maybe she'd just been overthinking everything. He believed in her, and now she had to show him she was a mature professional, ready for the role of Assistant Director.

Charles snickered, his smile slightly crooked. "Alright, but you know, you don't have to tell your dad *everything*."

"Oh, he will want to hear about this, are you kidding? I can't wait to tell him."

"Right, well, what are you standing around for, Assistant Director? We have a big day ahead of us!"

DonnaMae clapped her hands together, lightly bouncing on her toes. "Yes! Right, let's go!" She hurried towards the office, reaching the door faster than she ever had before. As her hand gripped the doorknob, a smile spread across her face and she paused. This was the first time she would walk through this door as the Assistant Director. If she could handle this, she could definitely pass her test and get into college early. She just needed to believe in herself the way Charles did.

CHAPTER 24

July, 2001

DonnaMae stood at the door of the college registration area, staring through the window at the familiar sight. Kathy, the receptionist, sat at her desk, her silver hair pulled tightly into a bun, glasses dangling from a beaded string around her neck. She was focused on the bulky computer in front of her, clicking the mouse repeatedly. DonnaMae knew what would happen next: Kathy would look up, smile that same sad, empathetic smile, and greet her like she always did.

"Hello, DonnaMae, back again? Did you bring your extra paper and pencil, my dear?" That smile said everything, the unspoken message that DonnaMae knew too well: *Here comes the poor girl who keeps failing.*

It was as if she were back in grade school, waiting her turn to read out loud. Her stomach used to twist into knots as she counted the paragraphs, trying to predict when her turn would come, so consumed by fear that she couldn't even hear what others were reading. Her finger would touch each word, desperately trying to unscramble the letters, like the bouncing ball in sing-along videos. But time always felt too short, and the pressure unbearable. She knew the teasing would come, the stifled laughs, the whispers, and she silently wished someone else would struggle more, just to take the heat off her.

The memory was so vivid, it felt like DonnaMae was right there again, trapped in that moment, her palms growing sweaty as her turn approached. But this time it wasn't just to read, it was to take a test that could change her future.

"NO!" DonnaMae said to herself. "Not today. I can do this." Her new Assistant Director title flashed in her mind like a neon sign.

Straightening her posture, she lifted her chin, taking a deep breath. "I can do this," she whispered again. This day was going to be different. She had worked hard, and now it was time to believe in herself just as much as Charles believed in her. She stepped inside with a smile on her face and a heart full of determination.

"Hello, Miss Kathy! I love that sweater you are wearing. That purple looks so good on you!"

Kathy stopped clicking her mouse, glanced down at her sweater, and patted it with her left hand. "Oh, this old thing. Thank you, my dear."

"Is that mouse giving you trouble again today? You would think they would get a new one by now. Gosh, it's only been what...? Six months?" DonnaMae laughed at her own joke about how long she had been coming in.

Kathy laughed and gave her a genuine smile.

"I got my paper and pencil today," DonnaMae said, holding them out in front of her. "I'm ready to pass this test."

"Well then, my dear, let's get you started. I have computer station number four reserved for you back through those doors, and the proctor will be walking —" She stopped and gave DonnaMae a smile, "Oh you know the drill. Go on in, my dear, and kick butt."

When DonnaMae reached her station, a little white piece of paper caught her eye:

"Today is your day, DonnaMae - xx Kathy."

She smiled. DonnaMae wasn't the only one shaking things up today. Plopping down with a grin, she felt ready. *Relax, read the words, and take your time*, she heard her stepmom say.

The screen lit up. It was time. She settled into her chair and set the note aside.

Six freaking times. If you fail, this will be failure number six. Old doubts resurfaced, telling DonnaMae the words would look scrambled, there was nothing she could do about it.

She closed her eyes and blocked them out. "Ok mom, I know you are here somewhere. Everyone says you are a part of me. I need you today more than ever. Please be here with me today, help me pass this test." Her voice was below a whisper. She let out a slow breath and opened her eyes, lifted her chin proudly. "I won't quit, I can and I will do this."

Just as DonnaMae finished her mental pep talk, the buzzer on the screen pierced the silence. Her heart jumped, letters on the screen looked like a scattered Scrabble board. "Focus," she said to herself, grabbing a sheet of paper, and holding it up to the screen, blocking everything except one line at a time, just like using her finger to follow along in a book.

It worked. Even though she had to reread each line several times, the words started making sense. With her heart rate slowing, her focus sharpened, and before she knew it, she was halfway through the test.

DonnaMae clicked the finish button on the test with three minutes to spare. She was done.

She sat back in her chair, unsure how she felt. She knew she would be ok if she failed. She would just come back and take it again. But she felt different this time, she felt like she knew what she was reading and she felt good about her answers. She pushed back in her chair and stood up.

"DonnaMae," Kathy said in a hushed tone, walking towards her, "you passed." She held the printout with a smile that lit up her entire face.

"What?" DonnaMae blinked in disbelief. She had to have heard that wrong. "I'm sorry, what did you say?"

Kathy's grin widened. "You passed, DonnaMae. You did it."

DonnaMae stepped forward, her voice low and shaky. "I passed?" The words felt unreal coming out of her mouth.

"I printed your results as soon as you hit submit. DonnaMae, you passed."

DonnaMae almost knocked Kathy backwards as she flung her arms around her. "I passed!"

DonnaMae didn't wait to hear what came next. She let go of Kathy and headed straight for the doors. But before stepping out, she turned back, smiling with her whole face. "Thank you, Kathy."

Kathy walked over, "I'm proud of you, kid," she said, her voice soft and warm. "In all my years, I've never seen anyone with as much determination as you. You will go far in life."

DonnaMae felt a lump rise in her throat. "Thank you," she managed to whisper before dashing out the door. She skipped towards her truck, her heart racing with excitement, eager to share the news with everyone.

Strangely, her first thought was to tell her stepmom. They weren't particularly close, but through this challenge, she felt like Elise had been in her corner the whole time. Any time DonnaMae had struggled with a word or concept, Elise was right there, patient and encouraging. "Read the real word," she'd remind her, helping DonnaMae realize that she'd been guessing or rushing through words without truly taking the time to read and understand them.

It struck DonnaMae that while she had silently asked for her mom to be there with her today, in reality, Elise had been there all along. She could hear Elise's voice in her head, reminding her to slow down and to give the words another try instead of skipping over them just because they were unfamiliar. Maybe having two moms wasn't such a bad thing after all. DonnaMae kind of liked having Elise around, and honestly, she wasn't sure she could have done this without her.

She drove past her house to see if her dad was home, and when his truck wasn't in the driveway, she decided to stop by her step-mom's work to tell her the good news. It was on the way to her grandparents' shop if she took the back roads.

Elise was the office manager at a local law firm. Whenever DonnaMae stopped by, she always felt out of place. It was so quiet there, and she was far from quiet. The only thing she liked about the office was that it was in an old 1920s building with big windows that let in lots of light.

When DonnaMae walked through the front door, the sound of the tiny door bell echoed through the whole place. Elise was standing at the front reception desk, talking to the new girl with long black hair. DonnaMae knew they had hired a new reception-ist, and that Elise was training her. She suddenly felt like she shouldn't have come, like she was interrupting her at work.

"Oh, I'm sorry, I didn't mean to bother you," DonnaMae said, turning back towards the door. "I can come back later, or I can —"

"Donna, it's ok. What do you need? Is everything alright?" Elise took a step towards her.

"Oh yes, I'm fine, but it can wait. Sorry to bother you at work." DonnaMae pushed the door, the bell ringing again, its sound feeling like a punch to her chest. Why had she come here? Why did she think Elise wanted to be her mom?

"Mae, it's not a big deal," Elise said, her voice calm and reassur-ing. "Nancy was just showing me pictures of her new baby niece. You're not interrupting anything."

DonnaMae froze, her hand still on the door. Maybe Elise did want to be her mom, after all. She turned back, no longer able to contain her excitement. "I passed! I passed my test, and —" She stopped to calm herself. "I wanted to tell you first... and to say thank you for all your help." Her voice softened to a whisper.

Elise flung her arms around DonnaMae, pulling her into a big hug. "Oh DonnaMae, I am so proud of you! You worked so hard! You name it, whatever you want for dinner, I'll make it!"

DonnaMae stepped back, "Really? Steak, mashed potatoes, and my dad's gravy!"

Elise laughed. "I can't make his gravy, but I know when you tell him, he'll be thrilled to make it for you!" She adjusted her glasses on her face. "But I can make your favorite caramel popcorn for dessert!"

DonnaMae jumped up and clapped her hands, instantly regretting it as the quiet office amplified the sound. "That would be awesome, thank you!" she whispered, giving Elise another quick hug. "I need to tell my grandparents and call Dad from the shop."

Without waiting for a reply, she dashed out the door. Usually, Elise felt more like a friend, but in that moment, DonnaMae realized something had shifted. For the first time, Elise felt like her family, and it felt surprisingly nice.

When DonnaMae stepped into the Flying A, the warm scent of apple pie mingling with a hint of fried chicken and car oil wrapped around her like a familiar hug. She couldn't help but smile as she made her way towards the kitchen.

"Grandma, Grandpa, it smells amazing! I could smell it all the way from the front of the..." Her words trailed off as she froze in the doorway.

Her grandparents were standing at the kitchen sink, each holding a coffee cup and staring across the room with concerned expressions.

"Wait... what's wrong?" DonnaMae followed their stares and saw her Uncle Jay standing, arms tightly crossed against his chest, his face etched with worry.

"Oh, hi Uncle Jay," DonnaMae said. "I didn't see you there. What's up?"

Uncle Jay sighed, uncrossing his arms as he glanced at her grandparents. He shifted his weight uncomfortably before meeting DonnaMae's gaze. "Mae, something happened this morning..."

Her heart dropped. The excitement she'd felt a moment ago about passing her test evaporated, replaced with cold dread.

"Your brother was in an accident," her grandma said, like it was a game of charades and she needed to get her answer out first before Jay could finish.

DonnaMae's breath caught in her throat. "Is... is he ok?"

"Oh, Joyce, now you got her all worried!" her grandpa said, like nothing was actually wrong. "Your brother got hurt on his street luging trip this morning and it sounds like he broke his wrist or arm or something and —"

Her grandmother abruptly cut in, "I knew he shouldn't have gone on this trip. I hate this whole street skateboard thing he is doing."

Her grandpa responded and DonnaMae desperately tried to follow the conversation, but was too lost in her own thoughts. Her brother was hurt, and she didn't know how badly. She couldn't bear the thought of losing him, and she regretted not going with him.

"Allan will be fine," Jay cut in to the conversation and Donna-Mae's thoughts. "He just won't be able to finish out the racing season. He was supposed to be home in time to race this weekend, and it sounds like it's not just this weekend we need to be worried about."

"How did you guys find out?" DonnaMae finally exploded, letting the words fly out of her mouth faster than she could think about what she was saying. "What happened? Are we sure he's ok? When will he be home?"

"Everything is fine. Let's eat lunch," her grandpa said, turning towards the cutting board and pulling up a chair. "Mae, here, grab a plate, we have apple pie for dessert."

Her uncle Jay took a step forward. "Dad, we should probably talk about this and —"

"Ahhhwwfff," her grandpa huffed. "It will work out." He waved dismissively and then looked up at DonnaMae and gave her a wink. "We have plenty of extra drivers around here, and Allan is fine. He's tough."

DonnaMae was still worried about her brother, while everyone else seemed to only care about racing. Looking at her grandpa, she noticed him grinning at her as he stirred his food. It felt like he was trying to tell her something.

Suddenly, it clicked. *Racing.*

This could be her chance.

She had gone to every race, knew the ins and outs of the pits, and could drive stick. Her heart started pounding with excitement as the idea formed in her mind.

"I'll do it!" she blurted out, louder than she intended.

"What are you going to do, Mae?" Grandma Joyce turned to DonnaMae, eyebrows raised

"I can race for my brother this weekend!"

"Oh, honey, that's a boy's —" Joyce began.

"You sure you're ready for it?" Jay asked, his arms crossed over his chest again.

DonnaMae's eyes darted to her grandpa, who gave her a nod of approval.

"Hell yeah, I can!"

Her grandma gasped, "DonnaMae!"

"Sorry, I mean yes. I can go early and get some practice in beforehand," DonnaMae said, her voice more calm and controlled, but she was buzzing with energy.

"I don't think this is a good —" Grandma Joyce tried again, but DonnaMae cut her off this time.

She turned to her grandma and grabbed one of her hands. "Grandma, I can do this, it's not just for boys, and I'm just like you: Strong and brave. And I know you don't think so, but you have broken all the rules of what women are supposed to be. You went to college, you have an accounting degree, you played basketball, you worked at the shop while raising kids. I'm your daughter's daughter and I am a part of you. Please let me do this and show everyone who thinks I can't or shouldn't that I can, just like you!"

A slight smile appeared in Grandma Joyce's eyes. "You sure are your mother's daughter. Go show this world what women can do. Just don't forget —" she locked eyes with DonnaMae, "— you are a girl doing boy things, not one of the boys."

DonnaMae threw her arms around her grandma's waist and squeezed her so tight her arms hurt. She understood what her grandma was telling her, and she was ready to be a girl that did boy things.

"Ok," Uncle Jay said, also smiling, "I'll see if I can find you a fire suit. And we should probably order you a helmet. But for this weekend, I think you can just wear your brother's stuff." He walked out of the kitchen.

...

CHAPTER 25

Sweat trickled down DonnaMae's back as she walked through the pits in her brother's fire suit, the midday sun beating down mercilessly. Uncle Delmar Jr. and Uncle Jay walked on either side of her, making their way to check the lineup for her upcoming heat race. The air was thick with scents of gasoline, dirt, grilled burgers, and exhaust: things DonnaMae normally loved, but today with the heat it was almost overwhelming.

Her fire suit felt like a sauna, trapping the heat between its layers. First, there was the fireproof base layer — tight and itchy against her skin, designed to withstand extreme heat in case of a fire. Over that, she wore the thick, quilted suit itself, which covered her from neck to ankles like a one-piece jumpsuit. She had unzipped the upper half and tied it around her waist, leaving the sleeves dangling at her sides. The heavy material, built to protect against flames, made it nearly impossible to cool down.

She tugged at the knotted waist, longing for relief. For a moment, she considered taking off the next layer, leaving her in just her sports bra, but she quickly dismissed the idea. *I'm already standing out as the only one out here with boobs, she thought, glancing around.* She remembered her grandma's advice: "Don't forget, you're a girl doing boy things," and thought *well, that is very apparent right now.*

As they approached the giant Howard Raceway pegboard where the lineup sheets were freshly pinned, DonnaMae's heart raced. Her eyes darted across the papers, searching for her number, forty. It was her uncle's number, then her brother's, and now it was about to be hers. The lineup for each heat was determined randomly, with the fastest racers in the heats moving on to the A race, and those who didn't make the cut starting in the B race. The winners of the B race would then have the chance to join the A race from the back of the pack.

She finally spotted her name next to the number forty, and her stomach flipped. Her palms grew slick. She wiped them nervously on the knotted waist of her fire suit. This wasn't just any number — it was a symbol of her family's racing legacy. Howard Raceway had been a staple in her family since the early 1950s, starting with her great-grandfather. Now, it was her turn to carry on the tradition.

She wished her dad could be in the stands tonight. After the push truck accident that wrecked his sprint car, he'd had a falling out with the track owner, who'd refused to take any responsibility for the accident. Now, her dad's prized car was scrap metal, and he hadn't been back since. She desperately wanted him in the pits with her. He'd named her after a famous race car driver, and now she was about to do what he'd always wanted her to do, but he wouldn't be there to see it.

Anger towards her dad shot through DonnaMae. "Looks like I'm in the back of the pack. Let's go."

"No, Mae, you're not," her uncle said. "You're actually in the front. Your brother was crushing this season before he got hurt."

"Wait, what?" Fear pulled up beside the anger in DonnaMae as she spun around to where her uncle was pointing. "SHIT!" Her anger was replaced by a knot of nerves twisting in her stomach.

Her brother was a great driver — she'd been to every race.

What was I thinking? I'm not a race car driver, she thought, feeling lightheaded. "Be right back," she called, forcing a cheery tone, before jogging towards the bathrooms. She heard a few chuckles behind her and was certain they were laughing at her: just a peppy blonde girl in a fire suit, completely out of place. What a joke. She was a joke.

Through the heavy cement walls of the restroom, the noise of the track dimmed. DonnaMae's heart pounded in her chest. Her hands trembled as she gripped the edge of the sink, staring at her reflection she could barely make out in the dirty cracked mirror. What was she thinking? She wasn't her brother or her dad. She wasn't anything like them.

DonnaMae splashed cold water on her face as her mind wandered to all the times she'd watched her brother dominate the track, with her dad standing by, beaming with pride. She wanted so badly for them to be proud of her. But right now, she felt like she was drowning. Clenching her fists, her nails dug into her palms as she fought to steady her breath, trying to push down the rising panic.

"Why did I agree to this?" she whispered to herself, her voice shaky. "I'm not like them."

A guy walked in the door. "Fixing your makeup before the race?"

She stood up tall, quickly applied a smile, and turned around, "Oh, sorry I —"

It was Mike, the family friend who owned the wrecking yard where they always went to scavenge parts for their cars. He also raced, and had known DonnaMae her whole life, watching her grow up at the track. "You alright?" he asked, laughing as he placed a hand on her shoulder. "Saw you sprint to the bathroom and figured I better check on ya. Make sure none of these meatheads are giving you a hard time."

DonnaMae swallowed the lump rising in her throat, forcing

herself to stay calm. "No, I'm fine. Just got a little hot, needed to splash some cold water on my face."

Mike gave her a reassuring smile. "Mae, your family's been racing on this track for years. You've earned your place here, just like the rest of 'em. Don't let anyone get in your head."

DonnaMae gave Mike a hug and said "thank you" before stepping back. She noticed him nodding towards something behind her and she turned around. Her gaze landed on the urinals lined against the walls, and she felt her face flush. "Also," Mike added with a chuckle, "this is the guy's bathroom. The women's is on the other side. Thought you might want to know for next time." She'd been down in the pits a dozen times this year, but her thoughts had distracted her so much that she'd run into the wrong restroom.

Letting out a small laugh, she mumbled, "Uhh, thanks. I just got confused." With that, she quickly walked out of the bathroom. Tears welled up in her eyes, but she bit her lip, determined not to let them fall.

When she got back to the truck, her Uncle Jay handed her his small black cell phone. "Here, this is for you."

"Hello!" she said into the phone.

"Mae!" a crackly voice came through on the other end.

DonnaMae raised an eyebrow at her uncle, who mouthed "Allan."

A wide grin instantly spread across her face. "Brother! Oh my gosh, I'm so glad to hear your voice. I'm at the front of the pack in the heat race, and... " she hesitated.

"Of course you're at the front. You're driving for me."

She rolled her eyes, even though he couldn't see her. "Well, I'm not you! What if I crash or —"

"Mae, stop," Allan interrupted, his voice sharp even through the crackling line. "You got this. I only have a few minutes, so shut up and listen."

She let out a laugh. "Some pep talk."

"It's ok to be scared. It means you're alive and human, like Dad always says. Mae, use that fear. Don't let it hold you back. Let it light your fire. You've done it before and had fun, remember?" His voice crackled and cut in and out.

"Allan?" she asked, trying to catch him through the static.

He came back through, barely clear. "Look at the crazy stuff I'm doing out here. You think I'm not scared? Of course I am. But that fear fuels me. Now go have fun, Mae. You've got this." More crackling drowned out his words.

"But Brother, I'm not you. I'm not as good or as cool as —"

"I gotta go, Mae," Allan cut in again. "Shut up and drive. Kick ass. Let the fear fuel you. You can do this. I love you! And for fuck's sake, have fun and stop freaking out."

"I love you too, Brother, I —" The line cut out, and her brother was gone.

She handed the phone back to her Uncle Jay with a deep breath. "Thank you."

For the first time all night, DonnaMae felt ok. Allan was right, he was out there making mistakes, and he was still fine. She could do this.

It was time for the drivers' meeting. DonnaMae joined the group as everyone gathered to listen to the night's rules. A few drivers who knew her family offered good luck wishes or encouraging words, while others gave her disapproving glances or ignored her completely. She tried not to let it get to her, but part of her wished she already had her helmet on. With that on, no one would even know she was a girl.

The longer DonnaMae stood there, listening to the track manager talk, the more out of place she felt. It became harder to focus on what was being said as the reality of what she was about to do fully set in. This wasn't just a race, it was her stepping into a man's world, trying to prove she belonged.

DonnaMae slid her helmet over her head and climbed into the driver's seat. She buckled her harnesses.

Her uncle leaned into the car to check the belt latches.

Lifting the helmet visor, DonnaMae blurted out, "Shit, I have to pee."

Jay chuckled, giving her belts a final tug. "Well, you better drive fast, because you're up, kid. Time to start your engine."

FUCK, she thought, the need to pee intensified. Her foot pressing down on the clutch, she flipped the metal switch and the engine roared to life. Vibrations pulsed through her body as she shifted into reverse. Her uncles guided her as she backed out. Her gloved hands trembled as she gripped the wheel. The sun glared directly into her eyes.

"Shit! Wait! My sunglasses," she screamed and frantically waved her hands out the window to get her uncles' attention.

Jay jogged back over.

"I forgot my glasses! They're on the seat of the truck. Can you grab them, please?"

With a quick nod, he sprinted back and returned with the glasses. "Just drive," he said, handing them over. "You'll be fine. After the first few laps with the pace truck, the nerves will settle, and you'll have a blast." He leaned in, rubbing the top of her helmet. "It's in your blood, kid! You'll be a natural." He gave her head a playful shake.

"Thanks," DonnaMae said, slipping on her sunglasses. *Just another thing to live up to.* She flipped down her visor and pulled off to go line up.

"Ok, we got this. Just you and me," she said, tapping the dash of the car as she sat waiting for her turn to pull onto the track. She closed her eyes, inhaling slowly while tilting her head back. "Alright, Mom. This one's for you. Time to kick ass and take some names... like a girl."

Opening her eyes, she watched the cars ahead start to roll forward. She let out a nervous laugh. "Ok, maybe we just get through this first race... Then we'll kick ass and take names once I figure out what the heck I'm doing."

The cars followed each other one after the other like a row of baby ducklings following the mama duck: the pace truck.

"Ok, ok, I got this. It's not so bad," she said, feeling out the track and the car, checking her viewpoints. She relaxed her grip on the wheel just a little.

One lap, two laps, three laps, and the pace truck pulled off the track. Two more corners to go, and the green flag would drop.

The engines roared louder, drivers revved up, and the pace picked up.

She was four cars back from the front. Her brother was a damn good driver. She had big shoes to fill, and she knew it. Her heart pounded like a jackhammer in her chest. "It's go time," she said as they rounded the last corner.

She eased onto the throttle, just like her dad had taught her. *Pretend there's an egg under your foot. Stomp, and it breaks — press slowly, and you gain speed without losing control.*

"Remember the egg... Don't break the egg... Screw the egg, let's gooooo!" she yelled, slamming the pedal down and blasting through the green flag, leaving the guy waving the flag in her dust.

Mud splattered across DonnaMae's visor, blinding her as she rounded the first corner. Panic tightened her grip when the car beside her edged closer, trying to pass. She floored it on the straight stretch, adrenaline pumping, but with one hand on the wheel and the other fumbling for the tearaway on her visor so she could see again, the car wobbled beneath her and the next corner rushed towards her.

Backing off the throttle, DonnaMae let the guy pass, opting for control over a risky spinout. Gritting her teeth, she cleared her vision and hit the next corner, drifting high to hold her spot, hoping to regain her position and maybe pass him back.

She pulled out of the corner but cut down too low, and the driver behind her clipped her back end. Her car spun in a half-circle, and images of her dad flipping down the track flashed through her mind. Her chest tightened, as if the air had been sucked from her lungs. She tried to shift into reverse, but she killed the engine. She was a sitting duck, trapped in the middle of the track with cars barreling towards her like a pack of hungry wolves.

DonnaMae flipped the switch to start the engine — nothing. Cars were closing in fast. In her panic, she had forgotten the clutch. Slamming it down, she flipped the switch again, and the engine roared to life. Just as she was about to throw it into reverse, the yellow flag snapped through the air. A safety official was already at her window. She barely processed his words, catching only, "You're going to be at the back of the pack."

The cars circled around her as she sat in the infield, realizing how far off track she had spun. Letting out a slow, shaky breath, she tried to calm herself.

"You ok?" the official asked, holding up his thumb in reassurance.

DonnaMae managed a thumbs-up in return. She was ok — no damage, just a spinout.

The official waved his hands, yelling instructions over the roar of engines, pointing out where she should pull in to turn around and get back into the race.

DonnaMae was in last place. "So much for holding my line. New goal: Don't finish in last place." She let out a laugh, "Or maybe just finish the damn race alive."

Her uncle was right, by lap three she settled in, and was feeling pretty good. She even passed a few cars. She wasn't in fourth place, but she wasn't in last when she drove through the checkered flag.

After the race, her uncles sat her down in the dirt, like they had when she was a little kid, and used a stick to draw out the track. They found a few rocks and used them as cars, explaining how to go in high on the corners and come out low. With each race, they showed her something new, teaching her the little tricks of the trade. All they did was build her up, letting her know how well she was doing. Despite a few lingering nerves, her fear slowly gave way to excitement.

The final race was about to begin. DonnaMae adjusted her helmet and climbed into the car. Her uncle gave her a thumbs-up as she revved the engine, feeling the familiar vibrations.

"Alright, let's do this," her grip firm on the wheel. She followed the other cars onto the track, focused and determined to do better this time.

The green flag dropped and DonnaMae shot forward, weaving through the pack with confidence. She could feel eyes on her, knowing she was the only girl out there, and it gave her drive. Lap after lap, she pushed harder, her focus sharpening with every turn.

The race was intense, but she was passing cars and holding her position with each pass. When the checkered flag waved, signaling the end, she crossed the finish line in fourth place, right where she had started the night. She was smiling so wide her face started to hurt. She wished her brother had been there to see it and silently hoped her dad had changed his mind and shown up after all. She was living up to her name he gave her, like he had always wanted, and he was missing it.

Back in the pits, DonnaMae pulled off her helmet, letting her long blonde hair fall loose as she wiped the sweat from her brow. Adrenaline still pumped through her veins, making it hard to focus. People were streaming in from the stands, stopping by their favorite racers for autographs or a quick word. Standing on her toes, she scanned the growing crowd for her dad, hoping he had shown up after all.

Before she could spot him, Ella, Izzy, and Hazel came running up to her.

"You were incredible!" Ella practically screamed, wrapping her in a tight hug.

"Like, total badass," Izzy grinned, slapping her on the back. "Only girl out there, and you so rocked it."

Hazel gave her a high-five, "So proud of you, speed racer!"

Maria and LeAnn walked over next, with Charles and some of the crew from work trailing behind, all cheering and laughing.

Some even asked for her autograph, making her laugh. She smiled and signed whatever they handed her, but she kept glancing around. Still no sign of her dad.

As the crowd around her thinned out, DonnaMae's grandpa approached, his eyes glossy. "You made us all proud today," he said, pulling her into a hug. "Your mom would be proud." He paused, his voice catching slightly. "Your mom is proud of you."

DonnaMae swallowed hard, fighting to keep her tears in check. "Thanks, Grandpa. That means a lot."

She smiled, knowing she had the whole summer to improve and, if things went well, maybe next summer too. The thought filled her with excitement. She already had her pit crew in mind, and by the end of the night, she was planning custom shirts for everyone.

"It's not just a good driver that wins races. It's a good crew," her grandpa's voice echoed in her mind as she planned. And just maybe, if she was good enough, if they were all good enough, her dad would come and watch her race.

CHAPTER 26

October, 2001

DonnaMae's summer of racing rolled right into the start of her senior year. It felt surreal telling people she couldn't hang out because she was busy racing over the weekend, and her uncle was already talking about plans for her next season on the track. Even though her dad still hadn't come to watch her race, the fact that he always seemed to know how she did gave her a flicker of hope that maybe, just maybe, he'd show up next year.

As the long summer days faded into crisp fall mornings, her focus shifted to her packed schedule. Senior year was shaping up to be the busiest yet. At work, she loved the energy of being the Assistant Director, guiding the kids through new projects and programs as the older ones helped the younger ones settle in. She was running the show, allowing Charles to be focused on the next location he wanted to open.

Then, of course, there was the upcoming Miss Howard Pageant. Her grandma was her biggest cheerleader, making her walk in heels every time she visited. On top of it all, her college courses had started. After everything she went through to pass the admissions test, DonnaMae was determined to do well.

Racing season ended, and while DonnaMae didn't finish at the top, she hadn't landed at the bottom either — a promising start for next year. Between high school, college, her job, choir, and weekend bowling, she'd learned to juggle it all.

With Halloween around the corner, DonnaMae was loving fall — the crisp air, the changing leaves, and the seasonal drinks. Wednesdays quickly became her favorite day of the week. Her mornings started with Greek Mythology class, where stories of gods and legends captivated her. What made Wednesdays even better was the freedom to stop by her favorite tea shop before heading back to high school.

DonnaMae parked her car in front of an off-white and blueish-gray building with matching wooden shutters that added a charming touch to the shop. There were flower pots neatly arranged underneath each window, and an old wood sign gently swaying over the entrance that read "Cadlers" in bold letters. A few wrought-iron tables and chairs sat under the awning of the build-ing, inviting customers to sit outside and enjoy their tea in the fresh air.

DonnaMae could smell the aroma of fresh-baked cookies before she even opened the door. The bells on the door jingled as she walked in, letting Fran and Chuck know she was there. They were the cutest couple she had ever met. They lived in the loft above the shop and were the owners.

The cozy atmosphere embraced DonnaMae as soon as she stepped fully inside, the door closing behind her, shutting out the crisp fall air. It was as if this place had a magical ability to make her feel relaxed and at home, especially during this time of year when the leaves were turning golden and there was nothing better than a fresh cup of hot tea. She had always loved tea, but this place opened her eyes to a new array of tea varieties, far beyond the limited world of commercial teas she had known. To her right, rows of shelves were lined with jars of loose-leaf teas, their aromas mingling with the scents of the freshly-baked pumpkin cookies and spiced apple scones that filled the glass showcase. Twinkling fairy lights intertwined with garlands of orange and brown leaves created a soft glow around the small pumpkins on the counter. Behind the counter, a chalkboard decorated with little white ghosts and purple bats displayed the day's tea offerings. The House Blend was DonnaMae's favorite, brewed and ready daily with a hint of cinnamon that made it perfect for the season.

Fran, with her bright red curly hair, was wearing her usual apron as she bustled around behind the counter, cheerfully rearranging the cookies. Her plump frame and rosy cheeks added to her warm, inviting presence. "Hello, dear. I saved you a fresh-baked Monster Cookie," she said, her blue eyes sparkling. She pulled out a golden-brown cookie, speckled with oatmeal and colorful bursts of M&M candies, butterscotch, and chocolate chips.

"Oh, no thank you," DonnaMae said, that's ok I —"

Fran snapped the cookie in half, crumbs scattering onto the napkin beneath it. "I accidentally broke this one, so it's on the house. When a cookie is broken, all the calories fall out," she winked. She carefully tucked the pieces into a small white paper pouch and nudged it gently towards DonnaMae across the counter.

This was one of DonnaMae's new favorite places to visit. Fran always made her feel so welcome, treating her like she was her own daughter. The day DonnaMae had first walked into the shop, they had instantly connected, chatting for over an hour about life. Fran had lost her mom at a young age, too, and this shared experience had bonded them in ways few others could understand.

"Any idea what we'll be sippin' on today?" Fran asked, turning towards the board behind her. "Want the usual House Blend, or are we feelin' fall-ish again today? I have a new spiced chai brewing."

DonnaMae smiled. "I think I'll stick to my usual today."

As Fran prepared the drink, she glanced back at DonnaMae with a curious look. "So, how's the job going, DonnaMae? You seem to light up whenever you talk about it."

DonnaMae's eyes brightened. "I love it, Fran. Actually, I feel like it lights me up."

"Oh, really? Tell me more!" Fran said, her eyebrow raised.

DonnaMae hesitated for a moment. This was the first time she had shared this with anyone. Maybe it was because Fran felt like a safe place, a judgment-free zone. DonnaMae took a deep breath. "Working with latchkey kids — I feel good helping them, but it feels like they are helping me more than I'm helping them. These kids are so amazing," she said, her excitement bubbling over as she spoke about the program and the kids. "I see them and hear them for who they are, and I love them and all their daily accomplishments. They love me for mine." DonnaMae's smile grew as she paused, thinking about what she had just said. "It's crazy how much someone can grow when they feel loved and supported, and I get to give that to them." She let out a little laugh and popped a small piece of the cookie into her mouth. "Wow, these are really good today!" she said, covering her mouth with her hand.

"Well, thank you," Fran nodded approvingly. "That sounds wonderful, dear. I think this job is perfect for you. I'm glad you found your calling."

DonnaMae blushed slightly at the praise. "Thanks, Fran." She thought about her job and how much she loved working with the kids, helping them navigate their lives and find their strengths. "I wish we had a program for just girls, to help them figure out the crazy transition into womanhood." The idea of focusing on girls, giving them the support she wished she'd had, was something she thought about often.

Fran handed DonnaMae her tea with a warm smile. "I have no doubt you'll figure it out, sweetheart," she said with another wink. "Be careful, it's extra hot, I double-cupped it."

DonnaMae wrapped her hands around the cup, feeling the warmth seep into her fingers.

As she drove to school, Fran's words, "found your calling," kept coming back to her thoughts. Was this really her calling? She had always thought of it as just a job she happened to enjoy, but now it felt like more. She didn't just like working with the kids, she genuinely cared about them. She'd do it for free if she had to. Maybe this was her thing. Maybe she was meant to do more than just be an assistant director.

DonnaMae was running fifteen minutes late for her favorite class: history with Mr. P. He had a way of making history come alive, turning lessons into experiences rather than just facts. His interactive approach always made her eager to learn. Some days she would show up late only to find the classroom empty because he'd taken the class somewhere in town for a lesson, or decided to teach outside. Just last week, she'd walked in to find him standing on a desk, passionately talking about the Cold War and the intense rivalry between the US and the Soviet Union. Every day with him was a surprise, she never knew what she was going to walk into. She wished more teachers were like him.

DonnaMae pulled into a prime parking spot, right in the front. All she had to do was cross the street and head to her classroom on the third floor. *This never happens, she thought. Must be my lucky day.*

She turned off the truck, grabbed her keys, and reached for her tea cup nestled between her legs. Just as she lifted it up by the lid, the lid popped off, sending scalding tea spilling into her lap.

A sharp pain shot through DonnaMae's legs as the hot liquid seeped into her brown corduroy pants. Without thinking, she bolted out of the truck, kicking off her shoes and frantically stripping off her soaked pants. She hopped around the lot like a crazed animal, fighting to get the burning fabric off her skin.

Finally free of the pants, she felt instant relief as cool air hit her legs. But then reality sank in. She was standing, pantsless, in nothing but her little boy SpongeBob SquarePants underwear.

The moment of relief vanished. DonnaMae slowly turned towards the school, dread taking over. *Please don't let anyone be outside*, she prayed, scanning the yard. Seeing no one, her shoulders relaxed, and as she exhaled, her gaze drifted up to the third-floor window, the very room she was supposed to be in. Her heart dropped. There, in the big bay window of her classroom, her entire class stood gathered, pointing and laughing at her.

"SHIT!"

DonnaMae dove back into her truck, slamming the door shut. "OUCH!" Her thighs, still on fire, pressed against the seat. Her skin burned, matching the bright red flush she felt spreading across her face.

Peering out the window, DonnaMae muttered, "Shit." Her eyes fixed on the pile of discarded pants and shoes lying in the parking lot. She glanced down at her keys, still clutched in her hand. How they managed to stay in her hand she had no idea, but she was grateful. She started up her truck and backed it out, maneuvering it sideways to shield herself from the school's view.

In one swift motion, she opened the door, hopped out, and snatched her pants and shoes from the ground, tossing them into the truck. Her heart raced as she slammed the door shut and sped off, the heat from the spill still burning her legs.

Grabbing her phone, DonnaMae prayed she still had enough minutes left to call her dad.

"Daddy, are you home?" she asked, her voice trembling as she fought back tears.

"No, Mae, what's going on?" She could hear the worry in his voice and felt bad.

"I'm..." Her voice cracked. "I'm on my way ho —" The call cut off, her minutes gone.

"Shit!" she screamed, slamming her phone onto the seat beside her and pounding the steering wheel with the palm of her hand. *So much for my lucky day!*

Her legs felt like they were on fire, and each time her raw thighs brushed together, it knocked the air from her lungs. Gritting her teeth, DonnaMae forced her focus onto the speedometer, making sure she wasn't speeding. "I am fine," she repeated under her breath, hoping that if she could convince her mind, her body might follow.

When she finally pulled into the driveway, the pain was almost unbearable. Her thighs were a deep, angry pink, like someone had dusted them with blush powder, and blisters had begun to form. Her skin was tender, and even the lightest touch sent a stabbing pain through her nerves.

Climbing out of the truck was agony, trying to keep her legs apart. She winced as her burned thighs accidentally touched. She braced herself against the door, biting her lip to keep from crying out. Just as she steadied herself, she noticed her dad's vehicle pulling in behind her.

"DonnaMae, where the hell are your pants?" he hollered with his head half out his window.

She pointed wearily to the truck. "In there... with my shoes."

He pulled in and parked, "Why in the hell are your pants —" He stopped as he walked closer to her.

"Daddy," DonnaMae said, her voice breaking as she flung her arms around him. Silent tears streaked down her face, and for the first time all day, she let them fall.

"Let's get you inside and you can tell me what happened," her dad suggested, his eyes darting around the neighborhood for any lurking spectators.

"I burned my legs so bad," she said, stepping back so he could see the big red splotches and blisters on her inner thighs.

"Oh yeah, you did, let's go get some ice." He wrapped his arm around her shoulder as she wide-leg waddled towards the house.

DonnaMae settled on the couch with towels and ice packs on her legs. Her dad brought her a cup of tea and set it on the coffee table next to her. "I figured you never got to drink your tea, and this one isn't scalding."

"Thanks, Daddy." A smile touched her lips.

"Ok, tell me what happened," he said, taking a seat on the couch.

DonnaMae took a deep breath and recounted everything to her dad. She could see the corners of his mouth twitching as he fought back the urge to laugh. "So there I was, in front of the school, down to nothing but my underwear..."

Her dad managed to keep a straight face. "Wait, let me get this straight. You were doing a striptease in front of the entire school?"

DonnaMae groaned, burying her face in her hands. "Not exactly a striptease, Dad. It was more like an emergency wardrobe malfunction, not to mention my skin was melting off."

A chuckle escaped him. "Did you at least make some tips?"

DonnaMae glared at him, "Not funny. No, no tips. Everyone was inside staring at me from the window, how would I make any tips? Also, once I realized I was in my underwear in front of the school, I didn't stick around."

He shook his head. "Well, I'm going to call Cadlers and have a word with Fran about how dangerously hot their tea is. Maybe suggest they include a 'Warning: may cause impromptu strip shows' on their cups."

DonnaMae laughed, "You better not. Fran would be mortified."

Her dad leaned back, crossing his arms. "Don't worry, I'll be discreet. I'll just tell her about the tea spill and leave out the part where my daughter took all her clothes off."

DonnaMae rolled her eyes, but she was grateful that no one else was home. It was just the two of them. It was nice having her dad take care of her, even if he was teasing her

"Just glad you're ok," he said with a smile. "And that your dignity is only slightly bruised."

"Dad, how did you know what you wanted to be when you were younger?" DonnaMae asked, changing the subject.

"First, I'm still young, and second, if this is your way of telling me you want to be a stripper when you grow up, I'm not sure I'm ready for this conversation."

DonnaMae threw a pillow at him, laughing. "You're impossible!" She shifted on the couch, "No, Dad, I am being serious."

"I still don't know what I want to be when I grow up." He tilted his head, "Why?"

His tone had shifted, and she hoped he was really going to give her some advice. "Did you have anything you were passionate about and you knew that was what you wanted to do?" she asked.

"I'm passionate about everything I do."

She crossed her arms over her chest. "Ugh, Dad... you are not helping!"

"Your mom always knew that she —"

"I know, I know, she always knew she wanted to be a teacher," DonnaMae sighed, her voice softening. "I just... I know I really love my job, but I keep wondering, how do you know when you've found your calling?"

Her dad gave a knowing smile. "Your mom knew she wanted to be a teacher before she even knew what a teacher was."

It was comforting to hear him talk about her mom, even if it was the same stories she'd heard before: How her mom had taught her brothers, her friends, and even her stuffed animals. DonnaMae nodded along, but it wasn't the answer she was searching for. In truth, she wasn't entirely sure what answer she was looking for. She couldn't shake the thought of how much she loved what she was doing now. Did that mean something?

Her dad stayed with her the rest of the day, and they watched some boxing together, chatting casually about his latest projects. When he left to work on them, he kept popping back in to check on her.

By the time everyone else got home, DonnaMae had begun to see the humor in the day's events. As she recounted the story, the absurdity of it all became clearer, and she found herself laughing along with her family. Allan, as usual, chimed in with the same stripper jokes her dad had made earlier, which made her laugh even more at how alike the two of them were.

Elise, on the other hand, looked completely mortified, her wide eyes and horrified expression matching exactly how DonnaMae had felt in the moment.

Then her dad shifted the conversation. "Can you believe DonnaMae has been drinking tea since she was six?"

Adeline, her little sister, scrunched up her face in mock disgust. "What six year old drinks tea?" she asked, sticking out her tongue dramatically.

The room burst into laughter, the lightheartedness of the moment wrapping around them all like a warm blanket. For the first time, they all sat in the living room laughing together on a random weeknight like a family, all five of them.

That night, DonnaMae's thighs still throbbed with pain as she lay in bed, despite the burn medicine and ice packs. She tried to get comfortable, hoping sleep would finally bring her some relief. Just as she started drifting off, her phone rang.

She jumped and then winced in pain.

Her dad had recently bought her one of those new cordless phones. He'd ordered a few for the daycare and gotten an extra one just for her. She loved it, but always forgot to put it back on the charger. Tonight it was sitting right next to her head, ringing.

"Hello?" DonnaMae said, her voice heavy with exhaustion.

"Hey, were you sleeping?" Ella asked. "I was just calling to see how you were holding up."

DonnaMae let out a short laugh. "From the burns on my legs from the tea, or the ones on my ego from my entire history class seeing me half naked in the parking lot?"

"Umm... maybe both," Ella said, stifling a cough to cover her laughter. "But hey, you could think of it as practice for the Miss Howard County Pageant. You know you have to wear a swimsuit on stage, right?"

There was a pause, and DonnaMae could practically feel Ella grinning through the phone.

"I mean, there's not much difference, right? Underwear... swimsuit bottoms," Ella said, a few giggles escaping her.

"I think there's a big difference between being on stage in a swimsuit and standing in front of the school in little boy briefs with SpongeBob SquarePants blowing bubbles on them," DonnaMae said, half laughing.

"Well, you can thank Hazel for making us watch *Charlie's Angels* and you all deciding to wear little boys' underwear like Cameron Diaz," Ella shot back, laughing.

"Hey, they're comfy!" DonnaMae giggled, shrugging. "And it's ok, Ella, you can laugh. It is funny — except for the burns. According to my dad, I won't be wearing pants for a few days."

"Wait, what? How are you going to school then?" Ella asked, sounding extremely concerned.

"I'll just have to wear skirts and wrap my legs with this gauze stuff," DonnaMae sighed.

"Ohhh!" Ella burst into laughter this time. "I was thinking, like, *no pants* at all, and I was like, um, how's that going to work?"

"Not that it would matter. Everyone already knows what it looks like," DonnaMae said, rolling her eyes. "I'm just glad no one was carrying a camera. That would've sucked, and probably ended up in the yearbook."

"The kids in photography class carry around cameras, though," Ella said. "You never know, one of them might've been lurking around a corner."

"Oh my gosh, *thanks*, Ella! Great nightmare-inducing thoughts!" DonnaMae laughed, shaking her head. Then she paused for a moment before asking, "Ella? When did you decide that you wanted to be a teacher?"

"In sixth grade, we got to go to the younger kids' classes and help them and it was my favorite thing to do." She paused for a moment, like she was remembering it. "We only got to do it a few times, but I volunteered to do it almost every day."

"How do you know you'll still like it now?"

"I don't know, I just do." Ella laughed, "What's with all the questions?"

"I'm just working on my interview questions for the pageant," DonnaMae said. She didn't know why she didn't want to talk to her friend about her real thoughts, but right now she just wanted to keep them to herself.

"Ok well, let me know if there's anything else I can help with."

"Ok, thanks. Goodnight." DonnaMae clicked the off button.

She considered getting up to hang up her phone, but decided she could deal with it in the morning. It would charge all day while she was at school, anyway.

Her mind flipped with thoughts. For the first time, she knew what she wanted to do when she grew up: She wanted to be like Charles.

She could use this idea as her platform for the Miss Howard County Pageant. She and Izzy had both filled out all the forms and were starting training next week, but she had left the platform and talent sections blank, unsure of what she wanted to focus on. Now, she knew.

DonnaMae realized how full her plate was about to get — with the pageant, work, college classes, and her senior year of high school, it was going to be intense. She made a mental note to get a new planner and stay organized.

I should probably stop eating so much Baskin-Robbins ice cream and Monster Cookies, she thought, smiling to herself. *And maybe talk to Charles about what he went to school for.*

Her mental to do list grew as she drifted off to sleep.

CHAPTER 27

January, 2002

It was the first week of January. The air was cold and crisp, DonnaMae's breath forming soft clouds as she exhaled. Salt scattered across the ground crunched under her feet as she made her way into work. Her planner was tucked under her arm, with every page perfectly filled out until the end of the year, except the few days off she needed to get approval for, for the pageant.

With the pageant just a few months away, and graduation right around the corner, DonnaMae had her plate full but organized; pageant training sessions, school finals, and college application submissions all laid out in her planner. Now that she knew she wanted to run after school programs for girls, she had everything mapped out. After graduation, she planned to roll right into summer classes at the college that would give her a head start. But first, she needed to negotiate a new schedule that would allow her to leave work early or start late, and have a few full days off each week.

DonnaMae stood by Charles's desk, adding her days off on the calendar and circling the day of the pageant.

"Yikes!" she said, stepping back from the calendar. She surveyed all the pencil marks she had made.

"Why are we 'yikesing?'" Charles asked, suddenly standing behind her.

DonnaMae jumped and whirled around, using the planner she had in her hand to deliver a swift strike to his shoulder. "Ahhh!" she cried out. "What the hell! When did you come in?"

"Just now. You just seemed really focused," he said, rubbing his shoulder where she had hit him. "Ouch! I didn't realize you were armed and dangerous, otherwise I would've given you a heads up."

DonnaMae smiled and stepped back out of his reach. *He's in a good mood today, that's good,* she thought, turning back to the board. "Well! Let that be a warning for next time," she said with a short laugh. "But in all seriousness, I'm worried about the pageant, my work schedule, and... " DonnaMae paused, her shoulders dropping. "Maybe this was a bad idea. Maybe I shouldn't run. What I was thinking? The scholarships would be great for college, and if I'm going to a four-year school, it's not going to be cheap." She took a quick breath and kept going. "But I don't even have a talent, and have you seen me try to walk in heels? Let alone dance on stage with everyone else."

She didn't turn around. She could feel Charles's eyes on her, and she was certain they would be full of disappointment. Her stomach tightened. She heard him sigh, and she stepped closer to the wall, wishing she could run through it. Why had she said that all out loud to him?

She cleared her throat and straightened up. "LeAnn needs the same days and times off," scribbling both their names onto the same dates on the calendar. She stood there, waiting for a response, already bracing herself for a lecture.

"Maybe I —"

"Mae, stop," Charles said softly, pulling her arm lightly and guiding her to turn towards him. "Come on," he motioned for her to follow him to the couch.

DonnaMae hesitated before she followed him and sat down.

He gave her a playful nudge with his elbow. "You are so

amazing at such a young age," he said, "you're miles ahead of other kids your age. Balancing college, a job —" he paused, putting his arms out, showcasing the room, smiling at her "— where you're the Assistant Director, running things around here, and you're still in high school!"

DonnaMae shifted, a small smile tugging at her lips despite herself.

"You're involved in more activities than I can count," Charles continued, ticking them off on his fingers. "FBLA, DECA, choir, musicals, outdoor school, bowling teams, and driving race cars in your spare time." He raised his eyebrows at her. "And you get up every morning to workout. Honestly, Mae, I have no idea how you do it."

Charles's words eased the tightness in her chest, and she realized maybe she wasn't giving herself enough credit, and maybe saying all the things she had been thinking out loud was a good thing.

"It's really not that much I —"

Charles cut her off, his tone more serious now. "I'm not done yet." He put his hand on her leg. "The pageant? It's just another challenge. You've faced and overcome way harder things. We'll figure out the work schedule. Don't even worry about that." He shrugged, "we can hire another person. I'm going to have to get ready for you to go off to college, anyway."

"That's not for another year. I'm staying here for a year, remember?" she cut in quickly, not wanting to be replaced. Maybe she shouldn't have said anything.

Charles ignored her comment and continued. "And you're using us as your platform. Why would I not support you? I'm proud of you, Mae, and I believe in you." His voice softened with sincerity. "I wish you knew how truly impressive you really are."

He paused, his hand gently squeezing her thigh before standing up and walking over to the calendar on the wall.

DonnaMae sank back into the couch, feeling as if she could

melt into its cushions. His words played on a loop in her mind. *I am proud of you. I believe in you. She couldn't stop thinking about it. I am proud of you.*

DonnaMae was glad she had talked to him. It felt good to have someone she trusted who truly saw her for who she was — someone who listened because they genuinely cared. Now she was more determined than ever to kick ass and prove how important after school programs could be, especially the kind she envisioned — programs that could change the lives of young girls.

She suddenly wanted to share her newfound career goal with Charles. This was her path. She wanted to go to school for it, come back, and help expand the programs they had dreamed about. Starting all-girls after school programs in different cities was no longer just a dream. It felt possible, especially with Charles by her side.

"Mae!" Charles stood by the calendar, waving his hands above his head. "Hello? Earth to Mae, can you hear me?"

"Huh? What!" So consumed by her thoughts, she was completely oblivious to what he had said.

"I said, I gave it the green light. Your new schedule?" Charles chuckled. "I'll advertise the job opening today so we can start interviewing someone to cover your absence this week."

"Thank you!" DonnaMae practically leaped up from the couch. "I can also ask around. Maybe some of the guys from the Outdoor School program would want to work here."

Charles laughed, shaking his head. "Right, I forgot to add *all* those outdoor programs to your endless list of shit you do."

He looked at his watch. "Come on, I need a coffee. Let's go get drinks before the kids get here."

They got into Charles's truck and cruised down the quiet streets, the late afternoon sun casting long shadows over the town. DonnaMae loved the rugged charm of her hometown, its downtown still holding onto the remnants of its old logging days. DonnaMae leaned back in her seat, taking it all in.

The streets were quiet, only a few cars parked along the curb, and the old Star movie theater advertised a double feature of *Spider-Man* and *The Lord of the Rings: The Fellowship of the Ring*. The town always felt frozen in time, stuck somewhere between its industrial past and the changes of the future.

Charles turned on the radio and "The Humpty Dance" by Digital Underground filled the truck. He started rapping along, grinning as he bobbed his head and threw in a few wild hand gestures for effect.

DonnaMae laughed and shook her head.

"So, what's your strategy for the pageant interviews?" Charles asked as the music faded out.

Mae was caught off guard and had to think for a moment. "I guess my strategy is to stay true to myself. I want to highlight the importance of after school programs and how they can change lives. I've seen it firsthand, and I think my passion will come through."

Charles nodded approvingly. "That's a solid plan. Authenticity always wins. Plus, you've got the experience and the drive. Just remember to have fun with it too." He winked at her. "You're known to be a little too serious at times."

"What?! I am not, I —" She stopped as they pulled up to the coffee stand.

The smell of freshly brewed coffee drifted into the truck as Charles leaned out the window to place their order. "One large caramel frappuccino, extra whip, please, and... " He paused, glancing over at DonnaMae expectantly. "What about you?"

"The same, please," she said, still thinking about if she was too serious. She had thought she was the fun one. She was always dancing around and being silly. She actually figured she was annoying most of the time, but the kids loved it.

"Actually, Mae, why not try something sugar-free? You know... the pageant." He turned to the barista. "Just one caramel frappuccino macchiato."

Mae blinked, slightly taken back, but not wanting to show it. "I'll just have an iced tea, no sugar, please."

The barista, a cheerful young woman — her name tag read Sarah — smiled and nodded. "Coming right up! How's your afternoon going?"

Mae grinned. "Busy, as usual. But it's about to get better with this tea."

She laughed. "I hear you. It's always a good day when it starts with a good drink. Here you go." She handed over their drinks with a bright smile.

Charles took his drink, and as he handed DonnaMae hers, he whispered, "Wow, those boobs are huge. I mean, they could serve as floatation devices!"

Mae's eyes widened in shock, and she quickly shifted the conversation. "So, Charles, I've been thinking a lot about what I want to do after this." She figured now was as good a time as any, and the last thing she wanted to do was talk about this girl's boobs. "The pageant is just the beginning. I really want to focus on expanding after school programs, maybe even start all-girl programs in different cities, like you talked about."

Charles' eyes lit up with excitement. "That's a fantastic idea, Mae. You have the passion and the vision. And you've already got a great start with everything you've done here."

DonnaMae felt a rush of pride. "Thanks, Charles. That means a lot."

Charles reached across the console and squeezed her hand. "You are amazing, Mae."

DonnaMae pulled her hand back out of his grip and gave him a slight push on the shoulder. "Stop, you're going to make me blush. You are just full of compliments today." She let out a loud laugh. "Ok, but seriously, do you have any college suggestions?"

DonnaMae was at Cadler's with her three best friends. It was the first Saturday morning in over a month that all four girls didn't have something going on.

Hazel walked up to the counter and ordered four scones, three teas, and one hot chocolate.

"Um, I'll take a cookie instead of a scorn, please," Ella said, walking up behind Hazel.

"I think you mean scone," DonnaMae corrected Ella with a laugh.

"Nope, I meant scorn, because that's what it will do to me if I don't have a cookie."

"What?" DonnaMae said with a shake of her head.

"So, have you figured out your talent yet?" Izzy asked Donna-Mae, scooting in her chair.

DonnaMae collapsed onto the table like she had just passed out. 'UGH! No," she sighed dramatically. "They want me to sing Nora Jones. I don't even know who that is, and I don't want to sing. They said something about our voices sounding a lot alike."

"Why don't you want to sing?" Ella asked, pulling out the chair next to DonnaMae and sitting down with a giant cookie.

"Because I will scorn everyone's ears." DonnaMae cast a side glare at Ella, then smiled. "And I sound like a dying cow," she said in a slow, croaky voice as she laid on the table like she was dying.

"What?" Ella said, putting her hands on her hips, "You sing all the time. You're in, like, three choirs, and you just did a duet, or double duet thing, with Marie at Cabaret last year."

"It's called a quartet," DonnaMae said, "and it was more of a comedy singing and dancing thing. Marie and I dressed up like guys and the guys dressed like girls. It was supposed to be funny, and I wasn't singing on stage alone, and people were supposed to laugh at us. That was the point."

"Ok, fine," Ella rolled her eyes, "do something funny." She gestured towards Izzy. "Like Izzy, she's reading a poem!"

Izzy snapped her head to Ella, "Hey, a poem is not funny."

"It's funny that you are doing a serious poem," Ella laughed.

"Hey that was good Ella, nice one!" Hazel said, raising her hand up for a high five. "You're kinda on a roll this morning."

"That was good," Ella laughed, high-fiving Hazel. "I'm proud of that one." Then to DonnaMae, "Ok, but seriously, what are you going to do?"

"Too bad you couldn't drive a race car on stage," Izzy said. "Then you would win the whole pageant for being the most badass." Izzy paused. "Hey, speaking of racing, are we still painting the car next Wednesday night? I have to get time off work."

"Yes," said DonnaMae. "But we can't paint until after the shop closes. I don't think you'll need to ask for time off, 'cause who eats ice cream that late at night, anyway?"

Everyone turned towards DonnaMae, no words, just raised eyebrows from each of them.

"What?" DonnaMae asked, shrugging her shoulders.

"YOU!" they all said at the same time.

"Not at ten PM," DonnaMae said in shock. "That's just crazy talk."

Her friends rolled their eyes at her.

"Anyway," DonnaMae went on, "speaking of painting the race car, my brother made all my sponsor stickers and my pit crew stickers." She pulled a rolled-up sheet of paper from her handbag and laid it out on the table.

"Aww, we're all on it!" Izzy said with a smile, turning towards Ella.

"Window washer?" Ella said, her eyes on the paper, confusion consuming her face. "I don't wash your windows. I don't do anything. I'm just there for support and conversation."

"That's the point," said Izzy.

"There are no windows on race cars," Hazel and DonnaMae said together before Izzy could finish.

"Yes, there are," Ella countered with an evil stare. "How else does she see while she drives?"

"Ella, there's no glass on the windows to wash them," DonnaMae said, laughing so hard she thought she might pee her pants.

"Well, duh!" Ella said and then it was like a light bulb went on and she started to laugh, "Ohhhhh!"

Hazel picked up a decal. "I love how the after school program logo turned out!" She flipped it around so everyone could see. "Is Charles sponsoring you?" Hazel raised an eyebrow.

DonnaMae shook her head, her smile broadening. "No, I just wanted to put it on my car. I love it, and well, I feel like this is me sponsoring the program." She glanced down at the pile of decals on the table, her smile growing wider. "I've decided this is what I want to do. This is it."

"You figured out your talent!" Izzy said, practically jumping out of her chair.

DonnaMae shook her head again. "No, I know what I want to go to school for." She paused, glancing around at her friends. "You all have always had a plan and knew what you wanted to be, but I've never really known."

Her friends started rattling off things they thought she wanted to be: a singer, an actress, a teacher, a race car driver, an undercover detective, and a bunch of other things she had mentioned over the years. DonnaMae laughed at their enthusiasm. "I loved trying all those things, but I didn't love them." She met each of their gazes. "But I love the after school program. I love helping latchkey kids have a place to feel at home." She paused, clearing the lump forming in her throat. "I want to start programs for girls, and I want them to feel like they have a safe place to go to ask questions, or to talk to someone, or just to have a friend when they need one."

Ella clapped her hands. "WOW! You should say that on stage for the pageant, too! I almost wanted to cry!"

"That's awesome," Hazel said, beaming. "I knew you loved it there, and honestly, you do such an amazing job running the program. We all know you're in charge, not Charles."

"Damn!" Izzy huffed, dropping her head into her hand, propped up by her elbow on the table. "That means you'll be going off to college with these two hooligans."

They all laughed.

"No, seriously!" Izzy continued. "You're all going off to school, and I'll be the only one left here."

DonnaMae reached over and patted Izzy's hand. "No, I'm going to finish up at the community college first, and take a year to learn more at work, and then... " She paused, taking a deep breath. "I'm looking at the University of Washington. Paul and I have talked about moving to Seattle together."

"Mae and Paul sitting in a tree, K I S S I—" Izzy stopped singing with the thud of DonnaMae's elbow almost knocking her off her chair.

"That's gross! He's like my second brother," DonnaMae said, making a gagging sound.

"And we all know he's, like, on and off with her cousin and that one bigger girl — her name starts with a J, I think?" Hazel said, rolling her eyes.

Izzy's eyes grew wide. "Oh yeah, she is a real piece of —"

"Anyway," DonnaMae cut Izzy off again "I'm going to get my business degree, and then, I'm not sure. Charles is going to help me figure it out."

Ella's smile faded. "He gives me the creeps."

"Who? Paul?" Hazel asked.

"Charles." Ella hugged herself, rubbing her arms.

He could be kind of inappropriate at times, but was he creepy? *Nah*, DonnaMae thought, *he's just awkward*. He wasn't much different from any other guy she knew. DonnaMae laughed, "You think everyone is creepy, Ella!"

"Stranger Danger," Izzy said, just as Fran brought over their order.

"I hope I'm not a stranger," Fran chuckled. "However, these scones are so good they might be dangerous."

"And that's why I got a cookie!" Ella said, causing all the girls to burst into laughter.

———

DonnaMae sat on a stool in the garage beside a milk chocolate-colored two-door 1936 Chevy sedan with no wheels that was suspended off the cement floor by jack stands. Her dad was under the car. All she could see of him were his legs in his usual gray coveralls sticking out from the side of the car a few feet from her.

Allan was at the counter tinkering with a metal part for his street loose board. He had what looked to be a wheel axle clamped between the jaws of the vice, and he seemed to be trying to break it.

Tom Petty and the Heartbreakers played "Free Falling" in the background, and the familiar garage smells of burnt metal and motor oil infused the air. The garage was a special place for DonnaMae — a spot where she and her brother and her dad used to spend a lot of time together. But those days were becoming increasingly rare. As kids, it felt like she and Allan were always in the garage together, surrounded by the smell of motor oil and the sound of tools clinking. If their dad didn't have a project for them to work on, he always came up with some sort of game for them to solve.

DonnaMae suddenly snickered. "Dad, do you remember when you used to duct tape Brother and me together and then time us to see how fast we could get out of it?"

Her dad rolled out from under the car on his creeper, just barely missing his head on the car's underbelly as he sat up with a laugh. "You guys got too good at getting out. It used to entertain you for almost an hour."

DonnaMae winced and closed her eyes. Her dad was always hitting his head on everything. She fixed her eyes on her brother. "Want to try it again now?"

Allan didn't turn around. "Maybe that can be your talent. We can duct tape you to a chair in a prom dress and you can get out in under three minutes."

"Hey, that's an idea," her dad said, turning to DonnaMae with a shrug.

"This morning, Izzy said it would be cool if I could race a car on stage."

"If you were good enough for it to be your talent, maybe," Allan smirked over his shoulder and then went right back to work.

"Hey, say three nice —"

"What if you changed tires on a fake car on stage in under three minutes?" her dad suggested, cutting DonnaMae off.

DonnaMae liked the way her dad was thinking. What if she did something with working on cars? She had been around them her whole life. She surveyed the garage, taking in the toolboxes, the posters of all the race cars. Her eyes stopped on the old yellow metal Pennzoil sign. "OIL!" she cried, practically knocking her stool over as she jumped off. "What if I changed oil on stage? Dad, can you make me a motor out of cardboard?"

"There is nothing your dad can't do," he said, now back under the car.

"Why would you bother making a motor?" Allan asked, finally turning around and strolling towards the back of the garage. "We already have a real motor right here."

"How in the hell are you going to get that motor on stage?" their dad asked, rolling out from underneath the car again to look at Allan and the 350 Chevy small block hanging from the motor rack.

"Dad, if they get thousand-pound pianos on stage, I'm sure they can figure out how to get this motor on stage."

"I think there is a girl playing the piano this year," DonnaMae said.

"I can clean it up for you and paint parts of it pink," Allan suggested. "I'm sure I can get a few parts from the wrecking yard that we can also paint pink, like a fan."

"I can wear a pink dress to match, and long white gloves."

"How are you going to change oil in three minutes?" Dad asked, standing up and walking over to Allan by the motor.

"Dad, it will work!" Allan said with a tinge of frustration in his voice.

"Son, I'm not saying it won't work. I'm asking how."

"She'll only use half-filled oil jugs."

"What about draining the oil?"

DonnaMae stood there watching her dad and brother go back and forth about how she would do her talent, and whether it would work or not. Tuning them out, she started to think about how she could do this and make it into a production.

"Mae, can you do that?" Allan's voice cut through her train of thought.

"Can I do what?"

"You said you have rehearsal starting next week. Can you practice with just a chair or something to get down your routine until Dad and I can get the motor ready for you and over to the theater?"

"Yes, but I should probably do a run through here a few times so I know what I'm doing. I'm going to do it to Shania Twain's "Man! I Feel Like a Woman," and I'll put all my tools in a purse. And no, Dad, we don't need to go shopping. I have a white one from a dance I can use."

By the end of the night, they had made a routine and had the time down to under three minutes and DonnaMae's dad had even bought and polished up a chrome plated oil cap so she could pause and use it as her mirror to put on lipstick during the whole thing. Her purse would carry more than makeup.

CHAPTER 28

February, 2002

The weeks flew by in a whirlwind of preparation, and before DonnaMae knew it, it was February twenty-second, the day of the pageant.

It felt like just moments ago she was practicing her walk and rehearsing her interview answers. Now, standing under bright stage lights, she faced a panel of judges for the on-stage questions.

Her hands shook as she held her microphone, and she took a steadying breath. The first question was about her platform: Why she believed after school programs were so important? DonnaMae smiled, confidence growing as she spoke passionately about helping kids find their purpose and giving them a safe, fun place to spend their time.

Then came the second question: How did she manage stress and deal with the urge to give up? She chuckled, drawing laughter from the audience. "Sometimes, there's not much you can do but recognize it and just keep on trucking," she said, her natural humor shining through. As she spoke, her nerves melted away, replaced by a sense of joy at connecting with the audience.

Next up was the swimsuit competition. Walking across the stage, DonnaMae focused on her posture and kept a bright smile on her face. She had found the perfect athletic-style two-piece while shopping with her brother in Olympia. Dark blue with two red stripes down the side, it made her feel sporty rather than exposed. It reminded her of beach volleyball, and she loved how it showed off the muscles she'd built from working out.

Now, it was time for the talent portion. Izzy and DonnaMae stood off to the side of the stage to watch LeAnn sing "Journey to the Past" by Liz Callaway from the movie Anastasia.

"Damn, she is good!" Izzy whispered.

"Yeah, she for sure has us all beaten in the talent section," DonnaMae said, unable to pull her attention away from LeAnn. "This whole place will be in tears by the time she's done. She dominates the whole stage."

"What?" Izzy said. "No! You have the talent in the bag. You joking me? When has anyone ever changed oil on stage in a beauty pageant?"

"Right, but the motor just got here today. I've never even practiced on it. This will be one hundred percent all by the seat of my pants." DonnaMae felt her nerves kick in; her stomach grew queasy.

"You've been changing oil since you were, like, five," Izzy said, placing a hand on DonnaMae's shoulder. "I think you'll be just fine."

The audience started to clap and Izzy stared wide-eyed at DonnaMae. "Shit, I'm next."

DonnaMae squeezed her best friend's hand, "You got this. Remember, everyone is naked, and after this I never have to hear you say this damn poem again. Now go kick some ass!"

DonnaMae blew her a kiss as Izzy walked out on stage and LeAnn walked off the other side.

DonnaMae was up next and she was too nervous to watch Izzy. *Oil pan, pull the plug, oil filter change, plug, add oil, check makeup, add more oil.* She repeated the steps over and over in her head. She lived by the seat of her pants. It was better if she didn't have a plan.

She didn't have to focus on how to do it right, and Izzy was right: She knew how to change oil.

"Mae," one of the guys from the stage crew approached her, "do you want the motor on the stage before you walk out, or do you want us to push it out after?"

"I want it on stage before I walk out," DonnaMae said firmly. "And please make sure it's covered with the silver sheet."

She had spent hours making that sheet, large enough to cover the entire motor. A wooden dowel was sewn onto each end to hold it in place, ensuring the audience wouldn't see what was underneath until she made her grand entrance and revealed the motor with dramatic flair.

She walked back behind the curtain. The crowd was clapping and cheering for Izzy. "Oh Shit! Here we go." DonnaMae closed her eyes and tilted her head back towards the ceiling, "Ok mom, you ready for this? Let's show them what girls can do, even in heels." She swallowed back a wave of sadness. "Damn, I wish you were here for real tonight."

The main curtain closed and the stage guys rolled out her motor and set her props down behind it in a Pennzoil box. Allan had made the motor perfect. It was painted a solid gray with pink headers and a pink fan on the front to add flare. The pink was rich and bold, the exact color as DonnaMae's dress. DonnaMae's white satin gloves ran up past her elbows, matching the color of the purse that she clutched tightly in her left hand.

"You ready?" the stage director asked her, waiting on her to pull the curtains open and start the music.

"Yes, I'll go out when the music starts, just like we practiced without the motor." She kept her focus trained on the motor.

The curtains opened, revealing a stage with nothing but a tall object covered by a sparkling silver sheet. A hush fell over the auditorium. DonnaMae could feel the audience's confusion, and it was exactly what she wanted. The crowd probably thought she was about to do a magic show. In her mind, that's exactly what she was about to do — just with a little more grease and horsepower.

Right on cue, her brother's voice rang out through the silence, breaking the tension and making her smile even bigger, "LET'S GOOO, MAE!"

And then, Shania Twain's "Man! I Feel Like a Woman" blared through the auditorium, lighting the fuse of DonnaMae's stage presence. She counted to three, then strutted out in her bright white stilettos, twirling her purse, singing along, and giving the audience all the flair she had.

As DonnaMae whipped away the sheet to reveal the motor, the crowd erupted with cheers and laughter, hoots, and hollers. With a playful twirl, DonnaMae kicked things up a notch, adding a little dance as she pulled out her props. All nerves vanished. She was in her element, in pure bliss. The audience was eating out of the palm of her hand, and she was loving every second of it, owning the stage like she'd been born for this moment.

She displayed the oil pan like Vanna White on the *Wheel of Fortune*, pulled the plug, drained the oil, strutted back to grab the filter wrench, and twirled it for effect. Then, with a flourish, she added oil while showing off the Pennzoil box like it was a prize. Quick touch-up with her makeup, a playful glance in the oil cap "mirror," and the grand finish, all right on beat.

Then, just as she hit her final move — the walk off and glove removal — DonnaMae's right heel hit a patch of oil and she slid forward. *Shit, shit, shit,* she thought, scrambling to find her balance. She leaned back instinctively like she was behind the wheel of her race car, arms flying up as she fought for control.

She caught herself. Instead of face-planting, she turned the slip into part of the act. Throwing her gloves over her shoulder without a backward glance, her eyes locked on the audience, a sly smirk plastered on her face.

With a firm stomp of her left foot, she planted herself, steady and confident. Wiping her hands together in a final touch as the song ended, she struck a pose as if the whole thing had been planned. Then she disappeared offstage.

The crowd went wild. The cheers were deafening, louder than anything she'd ever heard before. Her heart pounded and she gasped for a breath like she'd just crossed the finish line of a race.

Nailed it.

"Go on back out there, you've got a standing ovation," the stagehand said, waving her towards the stage.

Still catching her breath, DonnaMae looked up at him in disbelief. "What? No!" she gasped. But the roar of the crowd hadn't died down — they were still going wild.

DonnaMae hesitated for only a second before stepping back out onto the stage. She was met with an overwhelming wave of cheers. The entire room was standing, clapping, and screaming. Not a single person was sitting down.

Her heart swelled as she soaked it all in. "Do you hear them, Mom? That's for me. That's for us," she whispered to herself, her smile stretching wider than she thought possible. She took a deep, grateful bow, then another, as the crowd continued to roar. Someone threw a flower onto the stage. She laughed and picked it up as the curtain closed in front of her, but the sound of applause followed her as DonnaMae stepped off the stage.

"Where are we going?" DonnaMae asked, turning to Ella as she drove the girls away from the aftermath of the pageant. Izzy and DonnaMae had changed into tank tops and sweatpants, their hair and makeup still in full perfection.

"Where do you think we're going? Your brother put together an after-party in your honor in the rec room."

"Of course he has!" DonnaMae laughed. Tonight, they'd crowned her Miss Congeniality. Not winning Miss Howard County didn't bother DonnaMae at all. She had won the talent portion, and she had won by rebelling against the norm. She had won by being herself. She had finally figured out who that was, and nothing could keep her from the path she had chosen. She was on top of the world.

The next morning, DonnaMae stretched her arms over her head as she got out of bed, feeling the lingering post-pageant haze. "I need a hot cup of tea," she mumbled to herself, "and then I'll get this day going."

She barely made it to her bedroom door before her little sister Adeline appeared. "Did you say tea party?"

"I did not say tea party. You don't even like tea. We've tried this before." DonnaMae giggled at the memory of setting out every mug in the house and filling them each with a different type of tea in hopes that her sister would try one she liked, but nothing worked. Adeline hated them all.

"But I like hot chocolate, and the cookies from Cadlers," Adeline said, giving DonnaMae her big puppy eyes.

"You want to go with me to Cadlers? I suppose we can make that happen. Go get dressed. And we have to go ask your mom."

"I already did. She said yes."

"Try again, little one. I'll go ask your mom. Go on, go get dressed." DonnaMae led Adeline out the door.

DonnaMae loved her little sister, and she realized she'd miss that little girl the most when the time finally came to leave for school. She was going to need to make sure she spent lots of extra time with Adeline this next year.

DonnaMae shuffled among her notebook, planner, and random pieces of paper on the coffee table in front of her. It had become a disorganized maze of paperwork. She thought life would slow down after the pageant, instead it had only gotten busier with college scholarship application deadlines, finals, and the new employees they had hired for the after school program. She'd just finished filling out her schedule and was now working on her to-do list for the staff retreat she was planning when Charles walked into the office.

"Hi," she said, not looking up from her pad of paper.

Charles walked over and set something down on the table next to her. "Chai tea latte for my number one girl."

"Thanks," she said, scribbling down a note before checking her calendar.

Charles dropped onto the couch beside her. "You sure you wanna be in charge of this?" he asked, taking a sip of his own drink.

Ignoring his comment, DonnaMae tossed her planner aside, searching for the notebook where she'd written down the date. Rummaging through her scattered mess of papers, she almost knocked over the chai tea he had just brought her. "Shit," she said under her breath, grabbing the cup just in time and finding the notebook.

"You've got graduation in two weeks, finals for your college classes, and —"

DonnaMae held up her hand, not looking up from the paper she was scribbling on. "Shhhh, you're distracting me."

Charles sighed, "All I'm trying to say is —"

"Are you saying you don't want me planning the training retreat?" DonnaMae's pen clattered to her paper as she made direct eye contact with him. "I just finished running in a beauty pageant, while doing a heck of a lot more than finals and graduating, and you know I can do this, or you wouldn't have asked me to plan and organize it. So Charles, if you don't want me to do it, just say the words and it's all yours. I will gladly go off gallivanting around town acting crazy with the rest of my class, if that's what you think I should do."

Charles broke her stare with a smile, "Ahhh, look at my spicy little Mae, coming out to play. No, no, please proceed. Is there anything you need from me?"

"Yes, actually. Do we have any of those soft pretzels in the freezer? I'm starving and I would kill for one of those." She swallowed. Just the thought of a warm, soft pretzel covered in salt made her salivate.

"Well, someone is off her pageant diet," Charles chuckled as he stood from the couch.

"Diet? Gross, why would I ever diet? If you don't like what you see, look the other way," DonnaMae said, full of sass. He was right, she was on one today. But his comment made her mad. She never went on a diet she didn't need to. Did she? Maybe if she had gone on a diet she would have won. Maybe. *Nope,* she stopped her own self-destruction, *it is what it is, and I don't need to be on a diet.*

"Damn, where did my little Mae go? Who is this woman you replaced her with? You turn eighteen and it's all just —"

DonnaMae shushed Charles before he could finish, waving her hand to shoo him out the door. "On with you! I have work to do. Please go."

She really was excited to be graduating, and to be moving forward with her dreams of running her own programs. Graduation meant she would be one step closer, and then she would be heading off to college, which was also why she really wanted to plan this retreat. She wanted the new team to be trained and perfect for when she was away.

CHAPTER 29

June, 2002

The sun peeked through the clouds, shining directly into her eyes as DonnaMae turned off the main road. Flipping down her visor, a picture from graduation fluttered onto her lap. She picked it up, smiling as she placed it on the seat beside her. This was one she'd treasure forever — a snapshot of her and her friends standing outside the gym in their caps and gowns. DonnaMae grinned at the memory, still fresh from last week. It perfectly summed up the rollercoaster that high school had been for the "Hick Chicks." Hazel, Izzy, and DonnaMae had all sat through the ceremony naked beneath their robes, while Ella had refused, trying to talk them out of the idea entirely. These three girls were DonnaMae's world, and even though they were about to head in different directions, DonnaMae knew deep down that nothing — not even the miles between them — could break their bond.

DonnaMae pulled onto the gravel driveway of the beach house she'd booked for the Willows staff retreat. While everyone else would be carpooling, she had driven alone to arrive early and prepare. She'd spent endless hours organizing every detail, determined to make it an unforgettable weekend for everyone, and to impress Charles. This was his idea, and when he had asked her to help plan it, she said she wanted to do the whole thing. She wanted to be able to use the experience for her job applications while at college.

DonnaMae opened her truck door, breathing in the salty ocean air. The house she'd rented sat right on the beach, with its back door facing a front-row view of the ocean. Reviews had suggested leaving the windows open to hear the waves all night long. DonnaMae could hear them from her car.

She stepped out of her truck and walked around the house. One of her favorite things about beach houses was their quirky, laid-back beach life charm. This one was no exception. Colorful blown glass balls and intricately-carved wooden animals lined the walkway. The Crayola-red front door looked freshly painted and slightly out of place against the weathered wood shingle exterior. A slightly overgrown cobblestone path ran alongside the house, leading to a large wooden deck in the back that looked worn from years of use. A few flower pots and two wooden benches served as a kind of railing around the porch with the benches facing the ocean, and in the center, a firepit beckoned for people to gather around. A collection of rickety folding chairs with faded colors and rusty frames leaned against the side of the house.

DonnaMae stepped onto the deck and sat on one of the benches. The ocean stretched out endlessly before her, waves rolling in, their white crests curling and crashing onto the shore. This was why she had picked this place. Someday she would own a house just like this. Well, not just like this, but with a similar view right on the beach. She could sit here and listen to the ocean all day and night and not have a care in the world.

A strong breeze tossed DonnaMae's hair around her face as the sun worked to burn away the morning clouds. She hoped the sky would clear up in time for the team-bonding activities she had planned. Peering down the beach in each direction, she made a mental note of the best hiding spots. She still needed to stash the scavenger hunt items before everyone showed up. She had already divided everyone into two teams, and the list of things for them to find was ready to go.

DonnaMae reached into her pocket and pulled out a bag of sand dollars and seashells she had stopped and picked up along the way to put out on the beach. One of her favorite things was strolling along the shoreline, searching for shells. She knew they weren't always easy to come by, and she wanted to make sure everyone got one.

"I enjoy cocktails and long strolls along the beach..." a voice murmured behind her.

DonnaMae leaped from the bench as Charles placed his hand on the small of her back. "OH SHIT!" She'd been so lost in her thoughts, she hadn't heard him approaching.

"Well, that's not the reaction I was hoping to get," Charles said with a smirk. "Most girls jump at the chance to take walks on the beach with me, not jump away from me."

"Most girls?" DonnaMae asked, tilting her head. "You mean your girlfriend?"

Charles puffed out his chest. "You can't tame a wild stallion." He placed his hands on his hips while turning his head to the side like he was Gaston from *Beauty and the Beast*.

And just like Belle would have done, DonnaMae rolled her eyes. "Ugh, you're the worst." She walked away towards the beach to put out her shells.

Charles stood there for a moment, holding his pose, and then dashed after her. "I knew you loved long strolls along the beach."

The ocean roared louder as DonnaMae got closer, but not loud enough to drown Charles out, and as tempting as it was, she didn't want to be too close to the ocean to drop her shells.

Charles was an odd duck, but DonnaMae looked up to him. She was grateful for all the new things he was teaching her. Not very many eighteen year olds could say they'd written a grant and actually received the funding for it, but thanks to Charles, DonnaMae had. The responsibility of being his Assistant

Director thrilled her, knowing that he trusted her to be in charge.

"I like long walks on the beach by myself," DonnaMae said as Charles followed her. "You can only join me if we go over the plan for the weekend."

"You're always so serious! Do you ever have any fun?" Charles asked, turning and jogging backwards in front of her.

DonnaMae stopped and pulled a few of the shells from her pocket. "I am fun. This is fun," she said, sprinkling them along the beach.

"Wait... what are you doing?" Charles stopped. "Why are you putting seashells on the beach? Most people walk the beach to find them."

"It's part of the scavenger hunt. I wanted everyone to come home with some good shells, not just broken ones. And if we don't pick them up, someone else will and it will make them smile." She smiled and kept walking.

Charles caught up to her. "And this is why you are such a special person. This is your idea of fun: making sure other people are happy."

"Yeah." She stopped, looking out over the ocean. "It makes me happy to know others are happy." She nodded to herself, feeling good about her statement.

DonnaMae started walking again. "So, everyone should be here in an hour. I have the agenda printed out in my truck. I just want to walk the other way and put some more of these out and then we can head back in and get set up."

By the time she got back to her truck, her hands were freezing and she could not wait to get inside to warm them. Charles was already inside unpacking the food. She was grateful that he was in charge of food, because that wasn't something she was good at. That was more her stepmom's thing. She unloaded her truck and headed inside.

Inside, the fireplace divided the house, with the living room on one side and the kitchen on the other. Charles stood in the middle, leaning over the glowing fire. The living room welcomed DonnaMae with its cozy brown shag carpet, instantly transporting her back to cherished memories of her grandparents' house.

"Kinda colder than I thought it would be out here," Charles said, pulling DonnaMae from her thoughts. "Thought it would be a nice idea to have a fire going for everyone when they walked in. Kinda makes the place feel extra cozy."

"Yes, it does!" DonnaMae agreed. "I love that the fireplace is the centerpiece of the house." She set her stuff down on the coffee table behind him and walked over to warm her hands. "Have you gone upstairs yet?"

"Yes, it's just a big open loft with four beds."

"Four beds?! Oh no, that's not enough! I thought it said eight beds?" DonnaMae quickly glanced around the room like she might find the missing beds lying around the house.

"There are eight beds in total. The main bedroom has a bed, and there is a guest room with bunk beds."

"Umm, that's still only seven beds."

Charles turned around to face her and pointed to the sofa behind her. "And that is a Hide-a-Bed."

A shiver ran down DonnaMae's spine at the word. "Yuck, I hate those things," she said, shaking it off.

"What? That's the best bed in the whole house! It's right in front of the fire and the TV."

"No thanks, my mom died on one of those things. It's all yours. I'll take the main bedroom." DonnaMae grabbed her bag and wandered off towards the main bedroom.

"Damn, Mae," Charles said to her retreating back, "way to be a buzzkill."

"It's not a buzzkill," DonnaMae called over her shoulder, "it's just the truth." She walked down the hall into what seemed like the main bedroom, simply because it didn't have bunk beds. The entire room was shades of brown. Dark brown walls, a milk chocolate bedspread and pillows, even the lampshade was a golden brown. It was kinda creepy. She crossed the room to the offwhite curtains with deep brown embroidered flowers and pulled them open, letting sunlight flood in. Tiny specks of dust floated in the air, catching the light. "That's better," she said, cracking the window just enough to hear the ocean. "Now that's perfect." *The sound of the waves always makes everything better.*

As she walked back to the bed, she noticed that the same brown shag carpet from the living room covered the floor. "Nope, not even the ocean can save this room. It needs professional help."

"You need professional help," someone said from the doorway, "in here talking to yourself."

DonnaMae spun around. "LeAnn!" She skipped to the door and pulled her friend into a big hug. "You're early!"

LeAnn stepped back with a grin. "You really think I'd let you do all the setup by yourself?"

"I'm so excited you're here!" DonnaMae said, clapping her hands together like she was about to break into a cheer.

LeAnn had become one of DonnaMae's favorite parts of going to work. Running in the pageant together had grown their friendship, but working together had brought them even closer. LeAnn had the best sense of humor and could always make DonnaMae laugh. She also had the voice of an angel, and the kids at karaoke night never failed to get her to sing. DonnaMae's favorite was when LeAnn belted out "Part of Your World" from *The Little Mermaid.*

"Ok, so where's the agenda? We all know you've got one, and I'm sure it's planned down to the minute," LeAnn said, one hand on her hip and the other extended, waiting for DonnaMae to place something in it.

DonnaMae slapped LeAnn's hand like a high five. "It's out on the coffee table," she laughed. "Oh, and have you seen the back deck? It's perfect!"

"It's a house on the beach. How can it not be perfect?" LeAnn asked, throwing an arm around DonnaMae's shoulders.

They both laughed and hugged again before heading into the living room. The fire had warmed the space nicely, and Charles was right: it felt extra cozy. There was just one thing missing. DonnaMae grabbed a paper sack and pulled out a small sandwich bag filled with tea bags. "But first, let's make a cup of tea, then we can go over everything."

LeAnn grinned. "Of course you brought tea!"

CHAPTER 30

...

Everything was going according to plan, even if they were running an hour behind. DonnaMae bounced with excitement as she watched her coworkers connect during the activities she had planned. The atmosphere in the beach house was alive with laughter and energy, and she could see new friendships forming before her eyes. With this team, she was confident the summer program was going to be the best one yet.

She jumped up onto a chair in the living room to get everyone's attention. "Alright, everyone! Last event of the day, and this one's going to be a blast!"

As the chatter died down, one of the new hires, Sami, laughed. "Good, because I was starting to get bored," she said sarcastically.

"Yeah, Mae," LeAnn joined in, "cause nothing we have been doing has been fun." She shot DonnaMae an approving smile.

"I mean, Jason and I were having fun until our water balloon broke," said another new hire, Matt. His hoodie had dried, but he pulled it away from his body as if it was still soaking wet.

"Don't be a crybaby," LeAnn said with a quick glance at Matt. "At least you didn't fall in the sand like Charles." She pointed at Charles, who'd had to change his sweatshirt.

"Let's be real," Jason said before Charles could chime in. "Charles and Katie walked way too far towards the ocean. Totally his fault he ended up in it."

"Ok! Ok! Anyway," DonnaMae hopped down from her chair, "follow me, it's time for the last activity." She walked to the sliding glass door that led out to the back deck. "You might want to grab more than a sweatshirt. It's getting chilly out there."

A rush of cold air greeted DonnaMae as she stepped onto the deck. Two sand pails waited on the beach below, one a bright blue and the other a flamingo pink.

Once everyone had joined her on the deck, DonnaMae strode onto the sand, grabbed the pink bucket, and shouted, "LeAnn, Sami, and Katie, you three are a team!" Then, lifting the blue bucket, she added, "Matt, Jason, and Seth, team two!"

Even though DonnaMae had a naturally loud voice, it was no match for the crashing waves and the buzz of everyone talking. Without missing a beat, she dashed back to the deck and jumped onto a bench. "EVERYONE FREEZE!" she shouted, like she was playing a game of freeze tag with the kids from the program.

Once she had their attention, DonnaMae motioned for everyone to gather around. As they did, Seth called out from the back, "I win! Everyone moved, and we were supposed to be frozen."

"Yeah, no," LeAnn shouted over her shoulder, "we're not playing Simon Says. You lose. Get your ass up here."

DonnaMae grinned and held up the buckets. "Each team gets a flashlight, a marker, and an envelope," she explained. "Inside the envelope is a list of items your team has to find. The team that finds the most in an hour wins."

Charles cleared his throat, "I know we're running an hour late and you're all getting hungry, so while you're off playing in the sand, Mae and I will make dinner."

Everyone turned to look at him.

"What are you looking at me for?" he asked, checking his watch. "GO! The clock's ticking. Fifty-eight minutes left."

"Girls against boys," LeAnn laughed "I like this! Let's go, beaches, we've got some shells to find!" Linking arms, the girls dashed off the porch, leaving the guys behind.

"It's an envelope, Seth, just rip it open," Matt said, tugging at their team's envelope.

"Yeah, and it has paper inside that we —"

Before Seth could finish his sentence, Matt tore the paper in his rush to yank it from the envelope.

"Right, that's what I was trying not to do!" Seth huffed.

"Did you put tape in the bucket?" Jason asked, flashing DonnaMae a hopeful smile.

"Nope, sorry!" she said, holding back her laughter.

"Come on, let's go!" Seth urged, already heading off the deck. "The girls are probably already finding stuff."

"Well, they seem like they're off to a great start," Charles said sarcastically as he shrugged and turned to head back inside.

DonnaMae beamed as she lingered, watching everyone walk along the beach with their buckets and flashlights. "So far, today has been a success, don't you think?" She turned around to find Charles standing at the door, gazing at her. "What?"

"Nothing, I'm just so proud of the woman you've become."

"Thanks, I think... Don't you mean the Assistant Director I've become?"

"Yes, I guess I mean that, too."

DonnaMae was so delighted with how everything was falling into place that she brushed off Charles' comment without a second thought. She was proud of herself. She was only eighteen, and she'd spearheaded this event. *Look out world,* she thought, *I plan to be unstoppable one day!*

"Let's get the salmon in the oven," Charles said, waving her inside. "Maybe have a glass of wine."

"You know I don't drink."

"Ahh yes, I always forget, you are such a goodie two shoes."

DonnaMae rolled her eyes and shook her head. *I'm not about to take the bait on that one,* she thought as she joined Charles inside.

An hour later, the delightful aroma of tangy lemon and garlic filled the kitchen as salmon sizzled in the oven. A dish of mixed brown and wild rice sat on the counter, covered with a dish towel. Charles brushed some corn on the cob with a homemade buttery mixture while DonnaMae set a stack of paper plates on the counter.

"Table is set and ready," DonnaMae said. "Paper plates were such a good idea. I was dreading hand washing all the dishes after dinner."

"Just the dishes from cooking," Charles said, pointing at the kitchen sink, which was half-filled with dirty pots and bowls.

DonnaMae sighed. She hated washing dishes.

Charles glanced at her and laughed. "We cooked," he said with a grin. "I think the team can handle the cleanup. Afterward, we can relax by the fire with a drink before watching the movie."

DonnaMae perked up, relieved she wouldn't have to tackle the dishes. "I brought some peppermint tea."

"I'm going to make you a drink you'll love," Charles said, turning back to his cooking.

"Charles, I don't drink," DonnaMae repeated, starting to feel annoyed.

"I know," he said. "It's non-alcoholic, just sparkling water, cranberry juice, and a dash of lemon. It's refreshing, and I'll add a little —"

"Oh, that does sound good," DonnaMae interrupted. "Can you make it now?"

"It's an after-dinner cocktail," Charles said.

Before DonnaMae could say any more, the sliding glass door opened and the joyful sound of laughter filled the room, halting their conversation.

With the rice dish in her hands, DonnaMae stepped into the

dining room, greeted by a salty breeze from the open sliding glass door as everyone returned from the beach. The dining room, which also served as the entryway from the beach, felt incredibly spacious. A large, rustic wood table dominated the center, surrounded by a mix of mismatched chairs. Against the wall near the sliding door was a long wooden bench with a rug underneath to catch any sand as people slipped off their shoes. Large windows lined the room, offering breathtaking ocean views from every angle.

"It smells amazing in here!" LeAnn said, kicking off her shoes by the door.

DonnaMae placed the rice in the middle of the table. "Dinner is ready. Leave your buckets by the door, and after you wash up, come join us at the table. There is one rule: you have to sit by at least one person who was not on your team from the scavenger hunt."

"I hope it tastes as good as it smells," said Seth. "Charles's cooking sounds dangerous." He peaked around the walkway into the kitchen, clearly waiting for a response from Charles.

DonnaMae smiled, "Well, he put mayonnaise on the salmon, so it might be good and it might just taste like a school lunch."

"My grandma does that," Katie said. "Looks and sounds gross, but you don't taste it at all. Says it keeps the fish moist."

Matt burst out laughing. "She said, 'keeps the fish moist!'"

"Oh, grow up," Katie said, flipping Matt off and walking away.

Charles walked into the room with a large tray in his arms. "This extra-mayo, moist salmon is done and ready to be enjoyed by all."

"Saved by the salmon," said Jason.

The room burst into laughter.

The dining chairs quickly filled, and conversation flooded the table. DonnaMae smiled, pleased to hear that everyone had found the seashells she'd hidden and enjoyed the scavenger hunt. Sitting around the table, sharing a meal, it felt as though they had all known each other for years. The ease, the laughter, it was like they were family.

DonnaMae thought the salmon turned out pretty good, but she liked the way her stepmom made it better. At least the mayo wasn't gross, like she thought it would be. Charles had caved and made her the after-dinner cocktail to go with her dinner. It was delicious, and she would for sure accept the second one he'd promised to make for her when they were done with cleaning.

As dinner wrapped up and everyone started pitching in to clean, DonnaMae ran back to her room to change into her sweats and baggy t-shirt. When she returned, it was just LeAnn finishing up in the kitchen. DonnaMae took a long drink from her glass, picked up a dish towel, and started drying off the counters. As she went, it was as if all the day's work caught up to her and she felt her movements grow sluggish, as if she was wading through thick mud.

"You ok?" LeAnn asked, placing a hand on DonnaMae's shoulder at the kitchen counter where she was putting the last glass back in the cabinet. "Or did you spike that drink of yours?"

"Someone spiked it with extra lemon," DonnaMae said, scrunching her face as she took another sip. "This one's a lot more tart." She laughed lightly but could feel the exhaustion setting in. The weight of the day's events had left her drained, though still content. At least all the events were complete. All that remained was to relax and enjoy the movie.

DonnaMae had never seen *The Breakfast Club*, but she'd heard it was a must-watch classic. She wasn't sure she'd make it through the whole thing, but she'd at least join the group and give it a try.

"The guys got the movie set up," LeAnn told her. "Katie pulled out the Hide-a-Bed. Maybe you should just call it a night and join her. We're pretty much done in here."

DonnaMae didn't protest. She walked into the living room and stared at the Hide-a-Bed. *Yuck*, she thought as unease washed over her. Her family no longer owned the one her mom had died on, but for most of DonnaMae's life, it had been there. They just never pulled out the bed part. The last time she'd seen one pulled out was the day she said goodbye to her mom. The image of her mom lying lifeless flashed in her memory, and she shook her head to banish the haunting image.

DonnaMae's memories of her mom's death were mostly hazy and detached, but now and then, something would trigger a flood of painful memories. She had learned to push them away. It usually worked. But tonight, the emotions felt heavier, gripping her harder than usual, refusing to loosen their hold.

With one more mental pep talk, DonnaMae tried to shake it off. She crawled onto the bed, curled up in the corner by the arm of the couch, and pulled a throw blanket around her.

The movie had just started, but DonnaMae was already struggling to keep her eyes open. Her body felt impossibly heavy, as if her limbs were sinking into the couch, weighed down by an invisible force. Everything around her was slightly out of focus, like she was peering through a foggy lens. It wasn't just exhaustion; it was different, like she was trapped between being awake and in a deep sleep, caught in a strange, dreamlike state where nothing felt real. The room tilted and her eyelids fluttered shut, but the sound of laughter jolted her awake. She forced a chuckle, trying to seem alert, but her mind was sluggish, slipping further away from reality.

"Look out, I'm coming in," Charles yelled as he dove onto the Hide-a-Bed, landing between DonnaMae and Katie.

"What are you doing?" DonnaMae's voice came out sounding more like a grumbly moan than a question.

"If you remember, I called this bed," Charles said, pulling a blanket up around him and fluffing a pillow behind his head.

"Ugh," she grumbled and turned her back to him, still curled up in her little corner. She thought about going to bed, but she was too tired to get up and walk to her room. Besides, she didn't want to be the first to go to bed. She could at least wait until the end of the movie.

Only half the room was actually watching it. Jason and LeAnn were talking to Seth about the hotel across the street that was said to be haunted, telling him that some people claimed to see ghosts on the top floor when the moonlight shined on the windows. Tomorrow's plans included eating breakfast at that hotel to learn about the building's history.

"They say the attic room is left alone," said Jason, "and no one ever stays in it so the ghost doesn't bother the other guests."

DonnaMae felt like she was a ghost, floating around the room, listening to parts of everyone's conversations, occasionally drifting back to the fog. She wasn't a light and flowy ghost, she was a heavy, slow one. She felt like she was floating, yet anchored down so she couldn't move.

Allison Reynolds was yelling, "You do everything everyone tells you to, and that is the problem." This made DonnaMae laugh inwardly. It was like the actress was yelling right at DonnaMae. *You say jump, I say how high. Welcome to my world,* she thought. Her dad would tell her she was a people pleaser like her mom, and that it used to drive him crazy. He used to tell DonnaMae she didn't have to please everyone, and it was ok to do what she wanted to do. *Funny thing,* she thought as she drifted back to her body curled up on the couch. *You have no clue you are the person I am always trying to please.* The sound of the ocean roared through the window with a breeze that sent a chill down her legs. She reached for an extra blanket. At least, she thought she did, but her arm didn't move. Her lids fluttered while she tried to keep her eyes open, eyeing the blanket at her feet and willing herself to...

Darkness took over.

The ocean sounded louder, almost like someone was holding a seashell to her ear, and she could feel the wind on her neck. Her body, previously cold, suddenly felt enveloped by heat. It was as if someone had wrapped a heavy, heated blanket around her back. It was nice. A smile creased her lips. She felt her body melt into the warmth as she let the sound of the ocean lull her back to sleep.

Minutes later, her eyes fluttered open at the feeling of something warm stroking her leg, something touching her skin. How was something touching her through her sweatpants? Her heart raced. For a moment, fear crept up into her chest. The warm thing felt like a hand. But the touch was gentle and warm; soothing, like when her dad used to rub her back at bedtime when she was little. DonnaMae's thoughts drifted back to the pink walls of her childhood bedroom, being tucked in tight and safe in her little bed. The pink walls dimmed in her mind until she slipped into nothingness again.

A strange sensation pulled DonnaMae awake. A warm, ticklish sensation between her legs. It almost felt good, but no, it felt wrong. Something was wrong. And then it hurt. There was too much pressure. A hand cupping her where no one had ever touched her before. She became aware of a warm body pressed against her back, someone pulling her in, holding her tight. His breathing was fast and hot on her neck. She could feel him, all of him, pressing into her.

She opened her mouth to scream at the top of her lungs, "STOP!" but no sound came out. She tried to move, tried to pull away, but nothing. His hand slipped out of her underwear and found its way along her stomach and up her shirt.

DonnaMae tried to see in the dark, to figure out where she was and who was touching her, but her thoughts and questions faded with the darkness that took her again.

She drifted in and out of consciousness, oscillating between dark oblivion and a dreadful awareness of unwelcome fingers tracing paths of sensation along her skin. *STOP! STOP! PLEASE!* The words echoed in her mind, her screams lodged in her throat, unable to escape. An eerie silence settled around her, heavy and suffocating.

Summoning all her willpower, DonnaMae fought to tear herself free from the man's grasp. This time, she managed the smallest movement.

His arm froze on her.

For a moment, nothing happened. Then, through the dark, a haunting whisper sent shivers down DonnaMae's spine. "My beautiful Mae."

She recognized his voice with a sickening turn of her stomach. Was this all just a nightmare? Was she still asleep?

The muted thunder of waves outside was the only sound for a few still heartbeats. Then, with a forceful tug, he pulled her body to his and DonnaMae knew she wasn't asleep. His hand roamed without restraint, touching places she desperately wished it wouldn't. He pressed her into him firmly. His groping grew more urgent, more forceful with each pull.

DonnaMae's heart raced with fear and panic. Why couldn't she scream? Why couldn't she move? Her body was like a weighted sack cast into the sea, and she was trapped inside, screaming to get out as it sank. As his lips brushed against her neck with a humid exhale, the subdued crashing of the breakers filled DonnaMae's ears. She let the sound fill her mind, chasing away all thought and feeling like water chases air from a sinking ship.

A strange darkness enveloped her, bringing an unwanted sense of calm. Letting the sound of the waves swallow her whole, DonnaMae faded to the bottom of the dark ocean, lost in its nothingness. Just her and the sound of her ocean.

Loud chatter and the stomping of running feet snapped DonnaMae back to awareness. Her predator released his grip, retreating with fear from the sound that had startled him.

"We're going to go check out the hotel ghost," a voice called through the house. "Want to join us?"

A second voice whispered harshly in response, "Shh! Everyone else is sleeping. Get your shoes, let's go."

When the voices and the stomping, shuffling feet were gone, an empty darkness settled over DonnaMae. Still anchored to the couch by the heaviness that had overtaken her, she shivered in the dark. There was no longer a warm body pressed into hers. There was nothing touching her. The others had scared him away. Or was she dreaming? Was any of this real?

The ocean grew louder, pulling her back into its darkness once more.

CHAPTER 31

…

DonnaMae blinked. Tears clouded her vision, turning the darkness into a blur of shadows. The cold tile beneath her made her shiver as she curled her knees to her chest, rubbing her legs.

"Where am I?" Her voice cracked, barely audible, drowned out by the relentless pounding of her heart in her head. The room seemed to be slowly spinning. Her stomach churned as a rancid, sour stench filled her senses. *Vomit.* She pulled her shirt up over her nose, gagging at the smell.

Her breath was short and shaky, fear curling her into a tighter ball as her mind raced, unable to piece together how she had ended up here, still unsure where she was. The slow creak of the door opening made her blood run cold as she froze in place.

"Mae?" a voice called, familiar yet distant.

DonnaMae's panic grew. She didn't move.

Light seeped into the room, making DonnaMae's eyes burn as if they were on fire. *How long have I been in here?* She squeezed her eyes shut, trying to block out the painful brightness.

"Mae, are you in here?" LeAnn's voice echoed through the room. "DonnaMae, what are you — OH MY —" LeAnn gasped.

DonnaMae slowly opened her eyes as LeAnn stepped fully

into the room, the door slamming shut behind her, sending a throbbing pain through DonnaMae's skull. Reaching out, she touched LeAnn's leg to make sure she wasn't trapped in a dream. Her head swam with confusion, the line between reality and a dream blurred.

LeAnn flicked on the light and squatted down in front of DonnaMae, her face etched with concern.

DonnaMae wiped her face, trying to clear the fresh stream of tears. She swallowed hard, forcing back a sob that threatened to break free. LeAnn, without saying a word, reached over and flushed the toilet, then spun off a handful of toilet paper from the roll and handed it to DonnaMae.

"I'm in a bathroom?" DonnaMae asked as a hiccup escaped. She quickly covered her mouth, fighting back the urge to be sick.

LeAnn squeezed herself next to DonnaMae, wrapping an arm around her trembling shoulders. "Are you ok?" she asked, her voice soft. "What happened?"

"Honestly…" DonnaMae paused. "I'm not really sure. I didn't even know where I was until just now. Well, actually, I still don't know where I am."

"Damn, maybe this place really is haunted," LeAnn said with a short laugh, though the worry in her voice was loud and clear.

Crying wasn't something DonnaMae did in front of people. The last thing DonnaMae needed was for LeAnn to start freaking out. She needed to figure things out and piece together what had happened. The sour smell and the liquid her fingers had slipped in on the floor made it clear she'd gotten sick, but everything else was still a blur.

"I must have food poisoning. My stomach is really upset and, well…" She nodded towards the toilet.

LeAnn just sat there, staring at DonnaMae as if she were her favorite toy broken beyond repair. She stood up and wet some paper towels under the sink. "I knew that fish Charles made was no good. Glad I didn't eat it. I mean, who puts —"

"Charles!" DonnaMae pressed herself against the wall, pulling her knees tighter to her chest, as if she could vanish into the wall behind her. "Where?" Her eyes darted to the door, and her entire body started to tremble. "Where is he? Is he with you?"

It was all coming back faster than she could handle. The pieces were falling into place. His hands on her, caressing her. She shivered at the thought of his breath running down her neck. *My beautiful Mae.* The room felt like it was spinning faster and DonnaMae couldn't breathe. She gasped for air.

"MAE!"

LeAnn reached her just in time, pulling DonnaMae's hair back as she retched into the toilet. Only clear liquid came up, her body heaving with nothing left to give.

"Mae, I don't think you have anything left to throw up." LeAnn handed her a wet paper towel and used the other one to wipe up the small splatter of vomit on the floor, then tossed them into the trash. She sat back down on the floor in front of DonnaMae.

"Mae, what happened?"

DonnaMae leaned against the wall behind her, pressing the cold paper towel against her lips. "Honestly, LeAnn, I don't really know. I'm still trying to figure it out. I don't even know how I got here."

"Well, we all walked over here for breakfast and I thought you had gone ahead of us to make sure we had a table."

DonnaMae sat quietly before responding, not sure if she should really let LeAnn know how much she didn't know. "Where is 'here?'" she asked in a low, quiet voice, dropping her eyes to the floor.

"Seriously? Mae, we're at the hotel across the way from the beach house."

DonnaMae stood in the shower, turning the water hotter until it scalded her skin, letting it cascade down her face. Soon she was sobbing again, her body trembling. Her arms were raw, like the rest of her, scrubbed over and over as if she could somehow cleanse herself of everything. She leaned against the shower wall and slowly slid down, resting her head in her hands, elbows on her knees. The water washed away her tears, but it couldn't touch the pain or the deep sense of filth that clung to her.

It was Sunday, and her family was out to brunch and the markets. They'd be back soon, and she'd have to face them. She needed to scrub everything away so she could just be herself again. She needed to feel normal.

She reached up for more soap and didn't bother with the loofah. The scent of cucumber melon mixed with the steam. She needed to feel every inch of her skin covered in soap. Every spot he had touched had to be washed clean. The lingering smell of him made her stomach churn, but this time she swallowed the nausea down, pouring out more soap and breathing in the scent of it.

DonnaMae had tried to piece everything together, but nothing made sense. Only fragments of memories came together, leaving gaping holes in the bigger picture. It was like trying to solve a puzzle with too many missing pieces. She vaguely remembered LeAnn mentioning that Charles had given her his credit card, saying he had to leave for a golf tournament. She recalled taking a short walk to get some fresh air, and LeAnn making her eat some bread. After that, the next thing she remembered was parking in her driveway.

She couldn't remember packing her truck, talking to her team, how clean they left the beach house, or if everyone left when she did. The details were lost.

Pain throbbed behind her eyes as she tried to remember something, anything. *What all happened?* Ice-cold water showered her skin. How long had she been sitting there? When had the water turned cold? Shivering, she turned it off and stepped out.

Wrapping a heavy, deep purple towel around herself, she felt nothing. She stood there, unsure of what to do next, when the sound of the front door opening and slamming shut jolted her. *They're home.*

The pitter-patter of little feet rushed up the stairs, making DonnaMae's heart jump. Instinctively, she reached out and locked the door.

"Mae, you're home!" The doorknob jiggled. "Want to play dollhouse with me? Or dress-up?" Their secret knock followed, a playful rhythm, *dun dadda dun dun.* Adeline was waiting for her to finish.

DonnaMae stared at the mirror that was so fogged over she couldn't see herself. She was missing — she was truly seeing what she felt, a girl who had just become nothing. How was she supposed to tell her eight-year-old little sister that she was gone? That her big sister was broken and could not play?

"Mae...? Hello, Mae... Earth to Mae!" Adeline tried the knock again.

DonnaMae cleared her throat. "I'm not feeling good."

"Oh no, you sick? Should I go get Mommy? She can make it better."

Mommy. Her mommy was dead, and no one could make that better. The pain would never go away, no matter how many years passed. A child grieved forever for the parent they would always long for, and DonnaMae would always be that child. Something flickered inside her, a sadness, anger, or just the desperate yearning for her mother to hold her and tell her everything was going to be ok.

But no, she had a dad — a dad who she could never tell what had happened. Not only because she didn't want to let him down, but because she knew he would be so angry he'd do something reckless and end up in jail. Her dad was all she had left, and this — what she had allowed to happen — would break him. She couldn't lose him too.

"Mae, you ok?"

"Go away!" The flicker inside DonnaMae erupted into flames, and she didn't have time to think before the words flew out of her mouth, sharp and burning through the door.

"Sorry," came a small whisper, fragile and hurt, barely audible over the storm of DonnaMae's swirling thoughts.

But DonnaMae was too broken to respond, too shattered to do anything. Moments later, she found herself on her knees, holding her own hair back as the little she had left in her stomach came up into the toilet again.

A louder knock on the door stirred DonnaMae awake. She realized she was lying on the bath mat with her towel still wrapped around her. She must have fallen asleep.

"Donna?" Elise's voice followed the knocks. "Are you ok?"

DonnaMae coughed, her throat dry. "I think I got…" Her voice cracked. She sat up slowly, clearing her throat and trying again. "I think I got food poisoning at the beach."

"Do you need anything?"

DonnaMae hesitated. She needed so much, but none of it was anything Elise could give. "No, thank you," she finally managed.

"Ok, well, if you feel like it, I made you a cup of peppermint tea to settle your stomach, and a glass of cold water." The sound of glasses clinking came through the door. "They're right by the door."

"And so am I, just in case," her little sister's voice chimed in. DonnaMae could hear Elise trying to coax Adeline downstairs, but Adeline stubbornly refused, insisting she needed to stay close in case her big sister needed her.

With a deep breath, DonnaMae pulled herself to her feet, gripping the sink to steady herself. She avoided the mirror, not wanting to see her reflection. Splashing cold water onto her face, she felt the room level out. It was freezing now, all the steam from her shower long gone. *How long was I passed out?* Time felt slippery, lost among the missing pieces in her mind. She wrapped her damp hair into a messy knot on top of her head, pulled on one of her dad's old shirts, and brushed her teeth, desperate to get rid of the awful taste in her mouth.

Cracking open the door, she found Adeline sitting cross-legged with her blanket and her newest stuffed animal — a fuzzy green turtle — clutched in her arms.

Adeline looked up at DonnaMae with wide eyes and a frown. "Mae, are you going to die?"

Adeline had been asking a lot of questions about death lately, ever since her pet hamster S'mores had passed away. Even though DonnaMae felt like she'd already died inside, that was the last thing she wanted her little sister to worry about.

Forcing a smile, DonnaMae sat down beside Adeline on the floor. One thing she'd learned from working with kids was to always be on their level when talking to them — it made them feel heard. "No, Ladybug, I'm not going to die. And I'm sorry I yelled at you."

Adeline snuggled in close, her small body warm against DonnaMae's. "Love you, Mae."

And with that, DonnaMae felt her tension melt.

She took a sip of the hot peppermint tea, letting the warmth soothe her throat. "Love you too, Ladybug."

She didn't have a mom, and she couldn't tell anyone what had really happened to her. But she had this, she had them. She had things to live for. She just wasn't sure how to keep going.

CHAPTER 32

...

DonnaMae stared at the clock as she lay in bed, watching the minutes tick by — 12:01, 12:02.

She still smelled of oil and dirt from the racetrack. She'd placed second tonight, and her pit crew had been amazing. But her mind kept replaying the moment she'd lost control, drifting too high on the far back corner of the track. The dirt, piled up from the season, had risen almost as high as the guardrail, and before she knew it, she was over the guardrail and splashing into the duck pond behind the track. Somehow, with her foot on the throttle, she never stopped. She powered through, muddy water flying every-where, circled around the back of the track, and pulled into the pits. Her crew had been waiting for her, ready to spring into action. She'd wanted to drive right back onto the track, but they'd chased her down and stopped her at the entrance. Right there, on the spot, her entire crew crawled under and around her car, making sure it was ready to race again. Izzy slammed her hand on the hood of the car and yelled, "Go give 'em hell!" while Paul and Ken gave her a thumbs up, letting her know she could go. Despite starting at the back of the pack, she'd rejoined the race, which was still under the yellow flag that she had caused.

By the end of the night, she'd crossed the finish line in second place. She hadn't won, but she'd worked her way back to the front.

DonnaMae rolled onto her back and adjusted her pillow. Racing had become her only escape. When she was on the track, nothing else mattered, she could let it all go. And after, she felt safe enough to celebrate with her friends. She felt like herself.

Until tonight.

He had shown up. With her staff, no less. He'd stood next to her in the photo, his arm draped over her shoulders, whispering, "Don't forget to smile." His presence had shattered the one place where DonnaMae felt normal, the one thing that let her escape everything.

Now she lay there, wide awake, too exhausted to shower, too anxious to sleep. Her mind raced, not with thoughts of her victory, but with dread about what Monday at work would bring.

DonnaMae loved her job, working with the kids, leading her amazing team... but the mere thought of seeing *him* at work filled her with hate. In his presence, she'd become cold, mechanical. She did only what was required and never stayed late or came in early like she used to. She arrived on time, or a few minutes late, always ensuring someone else was there before her. Every day, she kept her distance from him, responding with short, one-word answers, avoiding eye contact, and always placing a desk, a chair, or something else between them.

It was clear he wasn't a fan of her new behavior. The tension between them thickened each day, and fear gnawed at her constantly. She couldn't stop worrying about when he might try something again.

Eventually, sleep crept in and took over, pulling DonnaMae into a brief, restless slumber.

She snapped awake again, her whole body trembling as she tried to shake away the memory of his hands pulling at her thighs, pressing his body into hers as he hugged her too tightly. She leaped out of bed and headed straight for the shower to wash him away.

He haunted her dreams. That's when she found her missing pieces, though never enough to finish her puzzle.

DonnaMae jumped into her truck and slammed the door shut, desperate to escape her thoughts, even if just for a few minutes. She wished she could be out on the dirt track right now, driving her race car at full speed. The feeling of freedom, of letting everything go, was what she craved.

She backed out of the driveway and headed towards the bridge. As she rolled down her window, the early morning sun began to rise, casting a soft golden glow across the quiet streets. The sky was painted with hues of pink and orange, blending into the soft blue of the morning. The light danced across the water below the bridge in shimmering reflections. DonnaMae pressed her foot a little harder on the gas pedal and felt the engine rumble beneath her.

Wind rushed through the cab and through her hair. DonnaMae tightened her grip on the steering wheel as her truck picked up speed, the speedometer quickly climbing past seventy, despite the speed limit sign outside that read thirty-five. She was in control, and no one could slow her down, nothing could stop her. The exhilarating sensation of pushing past limits coursed through her veins, and she pressed harder on the throttle, the roar of the exhaust echoing through the empty streets.

Alanis Morissette's "Ironic" bled through the speakers, and DonnaMae leaned forward to turn it up. A small smile tugged at the corners of her lips as she thought, *If I could play music in my race car, I'd win every race.* Her foot pressed deeper into the floor, and for a moment, everything felt right. Just her, the music, and the open road.

Just as she let her smile fill in her face, she noticed red and blue lights flashing behind her. Her smile faded and her freedom turned to fear. *Isn't it ironic,* she thought, and couldn't help but laugh at herself.

She was still laughing as she pulled off to the side of the road. She had to try to breathe, to control herself. She'd never been pulled over before. What was she supposed to do? She fought hard to tuck her smile and laughter away while a man in a blue police uniform walked up to her window.

"Morning," the officer said in a surprisingly kind voice. "I noticed you were going a little fast. Where are you headed in such a hurry this early?"

"Oh, I was?" DonnaMae asked, her mind scrambling. "Sorry. No, I'm just heading..." She paused, realizing she didn't have an answer ready. "I couldn't sleep, so I was going to workout," she finally managed.

"Well, you were going thirty over the speed limit, Ma'am. The limit on the bridge is thirty-five, and I clocked you at seventy-five."

"Oh!" DonnaMae's stomach sank. She knew she'd been driving fast, but wasn't sure what to say next. *Yes, sorry, it felt good to drive fast? I know someone else who's committed a bigger crime — want me to drive you to him? I'm running away from him, isn't it your job to catch the bad guys? Instead, you're here with me, and he's a fan favorite, living right under your nose. Hell, you probably go golfing with him.*

Her thoughts spiraled, anger brewing inside her. She tried to reel it back in, "I'm sorry, I've never, um —"

"Can I see your license and registration, please?" the officer interrupted, his tone polite but firm, giving her no time to collect her words.

A sinking feeling took over. DonnaMae was about to get her first speeding ticket.

DonnaMae walked into work thirty minutes late, her second speeding ticket in just two weeks crumpled in her hand. After the first ticket, she'd felt defeated — embarrassed by the mark against her attempts to hold everything together. Now, she couldn't even muster the energy to care. The familiar scents of morning snacks greeted her: cinnamon rolls, apple slices, and milk. The kids were scattered about, some eating snacks, others already playing board games or waiting for their walk to the library.

"You're late!"

His voice stopped her cold. Her heart skipped as she quickly pivoted, making sure he wasn't close enough to touch her.

"Yep," she said, locking eyes with his beady stare.

"Yep? That's your response to being half an hour late? I had to —"

"Oh, sorry, you actually had to come out of your office and work?" DonnaMae cut him off sharply.

"Maybe you should just take the rest of the day off!?" Charles snapped, crossing his arms in the way that was becoming his usual stance these days.

DonnaMae felt the anger brew inside her. She wanted to scream at him. He was the reason for everything wrong in her life. She hated him. But he held all the power. He was her boss, and he could take everything from her. She needed his letter of recommendation for her college campus job, and she had to keep this job until she left for school. She knew she had to play nice.

"Sorry," she said, holding up the crumpled ticket in her hand. "I got another speeding ticket on my way here." She blinked back tears, forcing herself to swallow her anger.

"Oh man, Mae, I'm sorry," he said, stepping closer and slipping his arm around her shoulders.

The touch made her stomach turn, and she knew he'd spotted her vulnerability. He always did. This time, she was catching on. She froze, not even a breath escaping her lips.

"Do you want to go grab a coffee? We can talk about it," he said, gently guiding her towards the hallway, towards the office.

DonnaMae moved stiffly, like a Barbie doll controlled by someone else. Panic simmered, but she knew that she had to stay calm, be smart, and think fast.

"I'm already late and I'm in charge of the craft today, so I kinda want to stay here, thank you." She stopped walking and turned from under his arm. She forced a smile, hoping he didn't see through it. "But if you go," she turned on her charming childish voice, "I would love one of those chai tea things you get me. They're my favorite." She could only hope he would leave and never come back.

She took a few steps back, just enough to be out of his reach but still make it seem like she wanted to be near him. She tried to think of other things she could get him to pick up while he was out to keep him away longer. "We're running low on glue, and after today's lanterns, we'll definitely be out. And I'm sure the kids would love a new CD for karaoke this week."

"And you said I never work," Charles teased, his voice dripping with fake charm. "I guess I can do that for my favorite girl. I'm sorry you got a ticket, Mae, but it's nice to have my girl back."

Bile rose in her throat. His words made her stomach churn. She turned quickly to avoid puking on his shoes. Without another word, she hurried down the hall, desperate to escape. Relief washed over her as she finally reached the craft table, practically collapsing into the chair. But the nausea lingered, twisting in her gut.

How much longer can I keep this up? she wondered, the weight of it all pressing down on her.

As the days went by, DonnaMae perfected the art of avoiding him at every turn. When he asked her questions, her answers were short but now carefully sweet, always accompanied by a forced smile. Each time, it was becoming harder to summon that smile, while the numbness that had settled over her grew more comfortable, more familiar.

DonnaMae had figured out how to isolate herself, how to disconnect from her emotions and the world around her. The less she saw everyone, the less she needed to find the effort to put on a show. Her friends were embarking on their own journeys, getting ready to move away or start a new job, and she would do the same if she could make it.

The days blurred together, not just at work, but at home and in her summer night classes at college. Half the time, she didn't even register what was being said or what was going on around her.

The sound of her own scream echoed in DonnaMae's ears as she was startled awake by yet another nightmare. His hands were on her again, the overwhelming feeling of helplessness suffocating her. She sat up, heart pounding, the darkness of her room closing in like a weight on her chest.

She couldn't take it anymore. She had to do something. *But what?*

Quietly, she slipped out of bed, careful not to wake anyone. The house was still, the silence broken only by the sound of her shaky breathing. She tiptoed down the creaky stairs, each step echoing loudly in the quiet night.

The old computer sat in the corner of the living room, hopefully holding answers. Holding her breath, DonnaMae powered it on, praying the noise wouldn't wake anyone. She flinched as the dial-up modem beeped and screeched, the sound sharp and jarring in the stillness. Finally, the connection was established. She opened the web browser, her fingers trembling as she searched for something — anything — that could help her escape this nightmare.

The internet was a scary thing. DonnaMae hated using it for

school research, let alone for something like this. She didn't even know what she was looking for, or how to start. Yahoo's homepage was cluttered with links, news articles, and flashing advertisements. There was no simple way to just ask a question and get a direct answer.

She stared at the search bar, her mind racing as she tried to figure out the right words to type. Fingers trembling, she slowly typed: "What to do if your boss hurts you."

She paused, backspaced, and typed again.

"How to report someone at work who is —" She backspaced and typed again.

"Rape."

The word stared back at her. Her heart pounded faster as she hovered over the search button. She had no idea if this would lead her to help, or get her into more trouble.

Click.

The computer whined and made more noises as the search results loaded, and links filled the screen. Many were confusing, unrelated. Blinking banners, pop-ups, and scrolling text made it hard to focus. DonnaMae clicked on one link, but it was a dead end, full of legal jargon that made her head spin.

Frustrated, she tried again. The page took forever to load, each second feeling like an eternity. She glanced over her shoulder, making sure no one was around. Finally, the page opened to a thread of anonymous posts. Some people shared their stories, while others offered advice.

One post stood out. It was from a girl who described the police process, how she'd needed evidence, how her case had been dismissed because she didn't have enough proof. DonnaMae's heart sank as she read. She didn't have evidence either.

She clicked on another link that led to an article on a legal advice site. It outlined the steps to reporting sexual assault: preserving evidence, seeking medical attention, taking immediate action. The more she read, the more hopeless she felt. She had waited too long. She didn't have any of the evidence they said she needed. Her memories were fragmented at best, and she couldn't even piece together a full story to tell anyone.

Tears welled in her eyes as the crushing reality set in. She fought back the urge to break down, her head aching as exhaustion took over. She wanted nothing more than to sleep, to escape it all.

She closed the browser, shut down the computer, and crept back up the stairs, feeling more defeated than ever, the weight of her secret suffocating her even more.

As she lay back in bed, staring blankly at the ceiling, her thoughts raced. *Who would believe me anyway? And even if they did, it's probably my fault.* She'd let him think it was ok. She didn't fight back, didn't get up, didn't say no. A chill wrapped around her and she pulled the covers tighter.

Why didn't I move? What's wrong with me?

CHAPTER 33

July, 2002

DonnaMae stepped through the front door of her home, eager to escape the heat of the day, only to be greeted by the sharp edge of her dad's raised voice.

"What is wrong with you? Why are you acting like this?"

The temptation to turn around and escape back outside was overwhelming, but a glance at the mail slips clutched in her dad's hand stopped her. *Speeding ticket number three.*

"DonnaMae!" Her dad's voice cut through the air, sharper now as he waved the ticket in the air.

Honestly, she didn't even fully grasp her own behavior anymore. The only thing she knew for certain was that her world was falling apart. Not in the way a building might collapse in a single, violent crash, but slowly, like a cookie crumbling in her hands. Piece by piece, her life was disintegrating in a slow, messy way, with no way of putting it back together. The worst part was, she didn't really care.

DonnaMae didn't turn to face her dad — she didn't want to see his face. She stared straight ahead on the stairs, mentally detaching from the conversation. She could feel her dad's gaze burning into her back.

"Another speeding ticket, DonnaMae? And this attitude, like you just don't give a damn?" Something in his tone shifted, "What is going on, Mae? Talk to me."

Ugh, this is just going to be another fight, DonnaMae thought. *What's the point? Why stay and fight? He doesn't understand. No one does, and no one ever will.*

She was too tired, too drained to muster the energy for another argument. But lacking the strength to push back, she gave in and spit out the only truth she could bear to share with him. "I don't know," she said, her voice barely above a whisper.

"That is not an answer," her dad's voice tightened at her response.

DonnaMae could feel the pressure building inside her, the urge to cry working its way up. She couldn't take it anymore. The constant battle, the loneliness that swallowed her.

"I hate my boss. I hate my job! You wouldn't get it, and you wouldn't care." A single tear slipped down her cheek as she glanced at him.

His face fell.

He didn't have time to respond before she bolted up the stairs, her legs carrying her as fast as they could go, straight to her room.

DonnaMae had to get ready for work — the job she used to love, but now the very thought of going there filled her with anxiety.

DonnaMae had grown into her role as Assistant Director — something she'd thought she'd earned through hard work and dedication. She had trusted him — he was her mentor, her friend, her boss. She'd actually believed he respected her.

She dropped onto her bed, burying her face in pillows. *What did I do wrong? How did I let this happen? I ruined everything, and now I have to pull it together again, pretend like nothing happened?*

The door creaked open. "Mae," her dad said gently, walking over and sitting down beside her. "If you hate your job, then leave it. You should never do something you don't love. It's just a job."

"It's not that simple," she sobbed, finally lifting her head to look at him. "I don't want to leave. It's not my job that's the problem."

Her dad frowned, "Then what is it?"

Her chest tightened, the words she'd been holding back wanting to escape. *How do I tell him? He'll be so angry. I messed up.* She wanted to tell him everything, but she knew it would crush him.

She sat up on her bed, "It's my boss, he..." She stopped speaking, becoming lost in a memory from a few days ago.

Down the hall, she'd seen his beady eyes peering at her over his glasses, sending an uneasy chill down her spine. "We need to talk," he had said, his voice dripping with malevolence.

She'd been walking towards him to grab more craft supplies, and there he was, standing in front of the dark, closed library, unlocking the door.

Shit! she thought. No, not him, not here. I don't want to talk to him — especially not in there, alone. Not after what had happened. But he swung the door open and gestured for her to step inside, his body blocking her path, leaving her with only one option: a dark, dungeon-like room filled with books, and him, the Dragon.

Reluctantly, she stepped in, placing the table between them as he sat down. She couldn't focus on his words. She didn't care what he was saying. All she wanted was to get out of there. Her mind raced, scanning the room for an exit strategy. What if I tipped over the table and ran? she thought, her hands sliding under the table, her fingers brushing the underside as she mentally prepared for a quick escape.

And then it came. His fiery words snapped her back to the moment.

Without realizing it, DonnaMae yelled the Dragon's words aloud to her dad. "One of us isn't going to make it here, and I can promise you, it's not going to be me."

"What?" Her dad pulled back, his face crinkled. "Make it where? Who?"

DonnaMae came out of her thoughts and realized she had to tell her dad something. "That's what he said to me. He told me I needed to change, that I have a bad attitude."

She paused, biting back the urge to spill the whole truth. "Dad, he says things about the other girls at work. About their butts and boobs. He thinks it's funny, and I tell him it's not!" She wasn't ready to tell her dad the full truth, but at least she was giving him something. And it felt good.

"Dad! He thinks he's funny. He's the one in charge, and he let me know it when I tried to tell him I don't think it's ok. He took me into the library and threatened my job."

She could feel the anger fuel her words as she continued. "How do I go back to work with that? But I love the kids and the team. I love them all, I can't leave them." DonnaMae stood up now, filled with fire. "I hate him, Dad. I hate him."

The Dragon's fiery words played like a soft broken record in the background of her thoughts. She didn't remember what else he had told her in that dungeon that day, but she had heard him loud and clear before she stood up and walked out. She didn't need to tip the table over. She didn't need to run. She just knew she was done. She knew he was right: only one of them was going to stay and it wasn't going to be her. Charles knew how much she loved her job, and he thought this would make her be a good girl again. Make her do what she was told, be his little puppet.

"DONNAMAE!" Her dad said, pulling her back to the conversation. "You need to go to Willows and quit your job right now."

"I can't, I'm scared. I'm scared of him." As the words fell out, DonnaMae was no longer eighteen. She was her daddy's little girl, and she was broken.

He stood up and wrapped her in his arms.

Folding into him, DonnaMae's tears marked his light blue t-shirt with dark stains.

"It's going to be ok," her dad whispered. "We got this."

'We.' He said 'we.' She was not alone. She could do this if she was not alone, could finally fight back. All she needed was someone in her corner.

DonnaMae stepped back to dry her face. "Dad —"

He stopped her. "Go to the rec center's main office and ask to talk to the manager. Have him call your boss down and tell the manager everything, and then tell them today will be your last day, due to feeling uncomfortable working with this man." He spoke slow and steady, placing his hand on her shoulder.

DonnaMae liked the manager. He was nice, but he was also friends with her boss, and he was gone just as often as Charles was. She would be lucky to catch him there. It was mostly just the receptionist who was there.

Charles knew how to schmooze everyone. If he wanted something, he knew how to get it. He was great at talking people into things, or making them think they knew what they wanted.

"I can't," DonnaMae said. "He's friends with my boss. No one will believe me."

"They will. No one there will see this coming. They all know how much you love and support the program. To leave it all with no notice will be a statement in itself."

He was right. DonnaMae knew everyone in that place. She ran the activities and organized all the events more than Charles did. The question was, what statement was she trying to make?

"Dad, I'll just look like I was the one that quit. I'll look like the bad guy, leaving the program with no notice. The program I helped build."

"Mae, it doesn't matter what other people think! *You* will know the truth, and you are doing what is best for you. Those kinds of people are not the ones you want in your life anyway. You'll have lots of people come and go in life." Her dad paused and stepped back, creating some distance between them. "DonnaMae, do you want to work for this man anymore?"

The word "No!" jumped out of her mouth quicker than she expected, almost like someone else answered for her. "No, I don't," she said again, this time with confidence.

"Then you know what you have to do." He turned towards the door. "Clean up and get ready like you are going into work, go to the manager's office and ask if he has a minute. Tell him you would like him to please be in the room because you are going to quit and you do not want to do it alone. Let him know you would like to be done on the spot because this man makes you feel uncomfortable." Her dad walked to the door, "I'll be in the garage." He left her to do her thing.

Like a coach before a game, he just gave her the play-by-play and now she needed to get ready to go execute it. Except this was no game. This was her life, and she was about to turn her crumbling cookie into a building collapsing down all around her, fast and hard.

Dressed and physically ready, DonnaMae walked down the stairs and out the door to find her dad in the garage.

"Dad, can you come with me?"

He walked up and gave her a hug. "No, I can't go with you. This is something you need to do on your own." Breaking from the hug, he placed his hand on her shoulder. "Mae, tell them everything. Don't let him push you around. You got this. You are stronger than you think and braver than you know. I know this, because you are my daughter and you are just like your mother."

DonnaMae managed a smile. "I know. I'll be ok." She knew that was her pre-game pep talk, and that meant it was go time. She knew the plan.

"Ok, Mae, I'll be right here when you're done."

DonnaMae got into her truck and drove away. She knew she was going to be late and the kids would already be on their way to their activities of choice.

CHAPTER 34

...

DonnaMae pulled into the parking lot behind the recreation center and parked, her hands gripping the steering wheel longer than necessary. Normally, she parked in the front, but the back lot was closer to the manager's office. It gave her the best chance of walking in unnoticed. She sat there for what felt like an eternity, trying to convince herself this was the right decision. Finally, she climbed down from her truck.

Her steps were slow, but her heart threatened to outrun the rest of her body. Keeping her head down to avoid any interaction with others, she made a beeline for the manager's office.

Jason's office door was open. DonnaMae knocked gently on the door frame, then poked her head in. "Hello, can I bug you for a minute?" she asked, her voice barely steady.

Jason looked up with a warm smile. He was a larger man, the kind who radiated friendliness and good humor, yet there was something about him that commanded respect. He carried an air of authority that made even DonnaMae want to be on her best behavior around him.

"Yes, of course, come in. What can I help you with?" he asked, his tone cheerful and inviting.

DonnaMae sat down at the desk in front of Jason, and suddenly the office felt much smaller than before. Her palms were clammy, but she kept her voice steady. "I need to ask you to do me a favor."

Jason tilted his head, raising one eyebrow. "Yes? What's that, Miss Mae?"

She took a breath. "Can you please call my boss down so I can quit? I need you to be my witness."

Jason straightened in his chair, concern washing over his face. "Is everything ok?"

"No, it's not," DonnaMae said firmly, her heart racing, but she had no choice but to keep going now. "I no longer feel comfortable working for, with, or around this man, and I'd like to be done working here today."

She sat up straighter, pulling her shoulders back. *Stick to the plan. Stay strong,* she reminded herself. "Can you please call Charles down here?" she asked again.

Without another word, Jason picked up the phone and dialed, calling Charles to his office. The tension in the air was thick, and DonnaMae could feel her pulse in her ears.

"It's nice outside today, right?" she said suddenly, shifting towards the window, trying to keep the conversation light and avoid any further probing.

Jason glanced up from the phone and nodded. "Yes, it is."

DonnaMae could tell he wanted to know more. Just as he parted his lips to ask, there was a knock on the door frame.

There he stood, the dragon, the one she was about to slay.

"What's this about?" Charles asked in an overly pleasant voice with a slimy smile slithering across his face.

"That's what I would like to know," Jason said, turning his gaze to DonnaMae.

DonnaMae glanced down at the chair between her and her dragon. *SHIT!* she thought. She was about to be trapped. She didn't think to not sit by the window. She didn't think to make sure she had a plan to escape.

"Please, take a seat and close the door," Jason said to Charles, pointing to the chair next to DonnaMae.

As Charles sat down next to DonnaMae, bile curled in her throat at the smell of him and she quickly stood from her chair. Suddenly he looked so small, almost childlike, sitting in that chair below her, like a little boy in the Principal's office, about to get in trouble.

She gave them both a quick once over, landing her focus on the now-baby dragon. "I quit!" She pushed her chair in. "I no longer feel comfortable working around you or with you as my boss."

Charles said nothing. His lips formed a hard line, and he did his typical cool guy head nod, like he was agreeing with her.

He's probably trying to think of a way to turn this around on me, she thought.

"Would you like to tell me why and what happened?" Jason asked, sounding just as shocked and confused as when she'd told him the first time.

"He knows exactly why and what happened," DonnaMae said, and quickly realized she'd said it with too much sass. *Stick to the plan.* "Please, take this as my verbal notice, I am done as of today," she said, turning to face Jason before turning back to face Charles and the door. "I asked Jason to be my witness for my verbal notice. Thank you, Jason."

"Is there something you would like to talk about?" Charles asked, acting clueless.

But she knew she had the upper hand on this one. "I don't think so, unless you would like me to talk about it."

"Well, that's too bad," he said, pushing back in the chair, suggesting he had nothing else to say.

DonnaMae wanted out of the room first. The feeling became so strong she walked towards the door. Before walking out, she

turned and faced them both. "Ok then, I think we are done here."
She walked out of the room.

Down the hall towards the back exit, DonnaMae came to a
sudden stop. She could hear the chatter of her kids in the center.
Shit! It hit her like a wave, the sounds of laughter, the joy in the
kids as they relaxed and enjoyed the activities planned for them, the
team and program she had helped create, and was about to walk
out on forever.

"DonnaMae, can you come help me with —"

DonnaMae tuned out everything around her and kept her eyes
fixed ahead. She couldn't turn around, couldn't face them. All she
could do was run towards the door. Her chest tightened, the walls
seemed to close in on her, and the air felt thick, suffocating. She
could barely catch a full breath, her mind repeating one desperate
thought: *Get to the door. Get out before anyone sees you. Before he
sees you.*

She burst through the double doors that led to the parking lot,
where her truck awaited her. The rush of fresh air hit her like a
brick wall, forcing her to stumble backward. She bent over, hands
on her knees, gasping for air.

Out of the corner of her eye, she noticed a white truck. It
looked like her dad's. She stood up, trying to get a better look, but
the world spun around her. Her body felt weightless, and as she
tried to move forward, it was as if the ground was slipping out
from under her. Everything went blurry around the edges.

Before she hit the ground, her dad's strong arms caught her,
pulling her into safety.

"Hold on, Mae, I got you," he said softly, steadying her as he
stood her up and walked her towards the truck. "It's ok. I'm here,
and you're ok. I've got you."

His voice grounded her, and she clung to him, feeling a small
sense of relief.

DonnaMae leaned her head against the truck window as her
dad drove. Tears silently streamed down her face as she watched

the world pass by, the world she thought she knew so well. But now, everything felt different. Nothing would ever be the same.

"Where are we going?" she asked, her voice soft as she watched the blur of trees outside her window.

"Nowhere," her dad said, glancing at her with a soft smile. "Sometimes you just need to go for a drive."

Why can't I talk to this man? Why can't I let him in? Why could I not share with him and let him help me carry this heavy load?

"Dad, why did you come?"

"I had a feeling you needed me, that I needed to be there. We can drive as long as you need."

"Dad," DonnaMae said, her voice trembling as dried tears clung to her cheeks. She turned in her seat to face him, searching for the right words. "Dad, he did things to me. He put his hands on me, he —"

"Just now?" he asked half-slamming on the brakes, his eyes widening in alarm.

"No!" DonnaMae said quickly. "No, it was on the staff retreat. At the beach house." As the road wound and the trees continued to blur past, she told him what she could remember from that night. Her words came in fragments, but she shared what she could — how she'd felt off, like she wasn't herself, how things had gone blurry and she couldn't remember everything, couldn't move. But she left out the harsh details, the ones that haunted her dreams. Those memories were too raw, too painful to talk about. She was too embarrassed, too ashamed to admit the stuff before the beach house.

As DonnaMae spoke, her dad's grip tightened on the steering wheel, his knuckles white. His jaw was clenched, she could see the pain in his eyes. It was a look she recognized, the same one from the day her mom died. It haunted her, and now, she felt like she had broken him all over again. She had no words to fix it, no distractions to offer, no way to ease the hurt she saw, the hurt she had just caused.

The truck was heavy with silence when she finished talking, her words still hanging in the air as she waited to feel relief for finally telling her secret. They came to a stop at a red light. She turned back to the window.

"Why —" her dad's voice broke the silence. He paused, taking a breath before trying again. "Why didn't you tell me sooner? Why did you wait to tell me this? Why didn't you come to me?" His voice was hollow, as if someone had drained all the emotion from him.

"I didn't tell anyone," she said.

Fear flashed over DonnaMae as they got closer to home, the reality setting in that she couldn't avoid going back to the rec center to get her truck. She turned to her dad, trying to form the words.

"I'm sorry, Mae," her dad said, shaking his head, his eyes fixed on the road ahead. "I'm so sorry."

Fear consumed her. She had no response, her mind fixated on the rec center. "My truck, I have to get my truck. How do I get my truck? I don't want to go back there."

He glanced over at her. "We'll get your truck later. Right now, we're going to the police station."

DonnaMae trembled. "No! We can't, Dad. I have nothing to tell them. Nothing. They'll laugh at me." Memories from her childhood flooded back, of being made fun of, of being laughed at. "No, please!"

Her dad reached over and squeezed her hand, but she barely felt it.

DonnaMae told him everything she had learned online, how she believed going to the police would be a waste of time, how the lack of clear memories left her feeling powerless. She explained the night she thought she'd gotten food poisoning from the fish, how LeAnn had found her sick in the bathroom.

Her dad, usually so strong and sure, seemed at a loss for words. His broad shoulders, once a symbol of protection, now sagged as he processed her words.

He sighed deeply, and for a moment just silence sat between them.

Taking a deep breath, DonnaMae re-asked her original question, her voice barely above a whisper. "I need to get my truck, but I don't want to go back there."

"It will be ok, Mae. I'll be here with you. We'll get your truck and I'll follow you home." His strong, reassuring dad voice was back.

Driving into the Willows parking lot, her dad pulled up right next to DonnaMae's truck, giving her a nod that said it all. It was time. She took a deep breath and stepped out of his truck.

"Mae."

His voice stopped her, and she turned to face him.

"He's not going to get away with this," her dad said, his voice firm but gentle. "One way or another, he'll get what's coming to him."

DonnaMae blinked back the fresh tears that stung her eyes and opened her mouth to speak, but the words wouldn't come. She didn't know what to say, and if she tried, she feared she would break right there in the parking lot.

She couldn't break, not now. She needed to get to her truck, she needed to get out of this parking lot.

"Mae," her dad's voice broke through her thoughts. "Don't let this destroy you. Don't let him win. Go to your truck, and let's go home. I'll be right here with you the whole way."

His words gave her the strength she needed. DonnaMae pulled her shoulders back, took a deep breath, and kept her head held high as she walked towards her truck. She was not going to let him win.

CHAPTER 35

August, 2002

Hours turned into days, and days turned into weeks. Soon it had been almost a month since DonnaMae had quit her job. She'd thought telling her dad would be the saving grace, that justice would be served. They didn't go to the police, and she was grateful for that, but it also felt like they were getting nowhere. At night, DonnaMae often found herself sitting like a child at the top of the stairs, tucked around the corner where no one could see her, listening to her parents talk about what to do. She overheard her stepmom confirming what she had found on the internet during her late-night surfing: There wasn't much they could do. Elise's boss had warned them to be ready to face a storm if they tried to fight this, and the storm would most likely not end with a rainbow, but with flooded roads and broken homes.

Tonight, after tucking her little sister into bed and singing "Wee Baby Moon" by Kathy Reid-Naiman, DonnaMae could hear her parents' conversation floating to the top of the stairs. She slid down the wall into her normal spot and pulled her knees into her chest, hoping to hear an update.

"Well, they want us to come in and have her tell her story on record," Elise said.

Her parents had decided to get a lawyer and go to the school board to stop the schools from allowing kids to go to the program. But the school board didn't want to make a scene, and everything was being kept quiet. In all honesty, DonnaMae was ok with it being quiet at this point. She already felt defeated and had shut the world out. Charles knew too many people and had too many higher-up connections, and she was just a teenager who people thought was looking for attention.

In the kitchen, her dad grunted. "The story where she supposedly was drugged and molested by her boss."

DonnaMae could hear her dad's eye roll as the words fell out of his mouth. Her heart broke hearing him say "supposedly." She expected others to think she was crazy or not believe her, but her dad was supposed to be the one person who did.

Elise had suggested DonnaMae see a therapist. In therapy, DonnaMae learned she had been groomed and likely drugged, which explained the memory loss and inability to respond or escape.

The therapist explained how attackers often prey on girls who feel weak or seek love, repeatedly bringing up DonnaMae's mom's death as a contributing factor. After that, DonnaMae stopped talking during the sessions. Instead, the therapist spoke, insisting that none of this was her fault. Her boss had manipulated her, building trust only to break it. Yet, all DonnaMae heard was her own failure, the shame of not seeing it sooner. The words that were meant to comfort only made her feel worse.

Everything her boss had said, about her hard work, her achievements, now it all felt like lies. She questioned everything. Had she really earned the grant? Or the position of Assistant Director? Had she truly been running the program, or was it all an illusion he'd created to manipulate her? She felt foolish for not seeing the manipulation, for letting her guard down when she should've been protecting herself.

DonnaMae shut down emotionally, and her dad finally

decided that therapy wasn't helping, so they stopped going. She gave up the fight and let her parents take the reins, distancing herself from friends by claiming she was busy, masking her pain with a forced smile. Most people didn't even know she was no longer working at the after school program. It was easier to let them believe nothing had changed.

"Dale!" Elise said in the kitchen. Her voice held a sharpness that made DonnaMae flinch.

She could sense the argument brewing between her parents. A tear slid down her cheek and dripped onto her hand, but she didn't move to wipe it away. Another tear followed as she tucked her head against her knees, feeling the weight of the problems she had caused pulling her deeper.

She wished her brother was there. She wished she had told him everything. He didn't even live that far away, but he wasn't with her now. More than anything, she longed for someone to be in her corner, to fight for her. But that fight felt over, and as she sat there, she knew she was done trying.

DonnaMae pushed herself up from the floor, feeling annoyed by it all. People always seemed to show up when they thought she needed them, offering comfort, but when the real need came, when it truly mattered, she always felt the most alone. She wanted to be seen as the strong girl she knew she was, the one who was kicking ass at life despite everything. But instead, people only saw the sadness, the story they whispered about in sympathy.

This would just be another chapter in the narrative of "that poor girl." People would either pity her, or worse, think she was crazy or pathetic. It made her sick to think about it.

Sighing, DonnaMae crawled into bed, not even bothering to change out of her sweats. She figured she'd probably wear them to the gym in the morning anyway.

When DonnaMae had told her brother she wasn't working out anymore since Hazel had moved away, he invited her to join him at his gym. It was a small, hole-in-the-wall place where he worked out with some buff guys from his new job.

DonnaMae had started going with him in the early mornings. They never talked about their struggles or lives — they just lifted weights. Her brother, who had gone from a lanky kid to a solid, stocky guy, amazed her. He and his crew motivated her to lift heavier and push herself even harder.

Even though she felt weak and defeated in other areas of her life, building physical strength was something she could control, and it gave her a reason to get up each morning.

There was a soft knock on her door.

"Mae?" Her dad's voice followed as the door creaked open.

She rolled over, pulling the blanket up to her face to wipe her tears. "I'm sleeping," she mumbled.

"Ahh, sleep talking?" he said with a gentle laugh.

She stayed silent. He was the last person she wanted to talk to right now. She didn't want to talk to anyone. All she wanted was to sleep and hope the nightmares wouldn't come. But her dad walked over and sat on the edge of her bed.

"I have some updates," he said, clearing his throat. "The school board is willing to hear your story, but they want you to come in and tell it. They'll need to record it."

DonnaMae didn't respond, but he pressed on. "The lawyer said if you know of anyone who worked with you or heard him say inappropriate things, it could help your case."

This made her slowly sit up. "What do you mean, help my case?"

"Well, we might not be able to go after him for, um —" He cleared his throat again, but this time he paused for a minute.

She wanted to scream, *for my 'supposed' incident, because no one believes me.*

"Well, we are going to do everything we can to prove he should not be able to run the after school programs. Your story will be one, but if we can just get other people to talk about what he says that is inappropriate, it will help."

"Ok... Ok..." She said it a few times until he cut her off.

"Our appointment is next week."

"Ok," she said one more time as her dad stood up and kissed the top of her head.

"I love you, Mae," he said, turning to leave. "Good night."

DonnaMae spent the week calling people she could trust and telling them she left Willows because she had heard enough of the way Charles talked about women. She went to the coffee stand and got the barista to write a statement, found out he'd said things to her all the time and hit on her every time he went there. He actually made her very uncomfortable, but was a good tipper. LeAnn and Hazel both wrote letters, and before she knew it, DonnaMae had five statements and was feeling like she was finally doing something.

The day of the hearing arrived, and she dressed in the suit her grandmother had bought her for the pageant. She had her letters in hand and was ready to go. Both her parents were waiting in the car when she got outside. The drive there was silent.

When they arrived, she walked into a conference room. The walls were bare, the fluorescent lights harsh. There was a long table in the center of the room with a recording device placed conspicuously in the middle. Chairs lined both sides of the table, but the room was empty except for the people there to question her.

DonnaMae started out strong, recounting her story clearly and confidently. But when the school board lawyer started questioning her, she began to doubt herself.

"What were you wearing to work that day, DonnaMae?"

She hesitated, feeling the weight of the question. "I... I was wearing my usual work clothes."

"Was that tight pants? Did you wear tank tops? Were you showing skin?"

DonnaMae stumbled at these questions. Why did it matter what she wore to work?, "I, um, I was wearing the same thing everyone was wearing?"

"The same thing these girls were wearing?" he waved his hand over the stack of letters she had collected. "Did you tell the girls to write these statements?"

"No, they —"

"Then why are they just now coming forward with this information? Did you influence them in any way?"

"No, I —"

"Are you sure, DonnaMae? It seems very convenient that all these statements are coming out now, just when you need them."

Her confidence wavered. Her dad's voice saying "supposedly" echoed in her mind, making her feel small and unsure. She wanted to look away, to look to her parents for support, but she didn't want to look weak, so she held eye contact with the attorney.

"I needed them because I wanted to —"

"Did you ever feel uncomfortable around him before this alleged incident?"

"Yes, but —"

"Then why didn't you report it earlier?"

"I... I didn't think anyone would believe me."

"Why is that?"

Her voice shook. "Because he's been there longer, and people like him."

"So, you're saying it's a popularity contest?"

"No, that's not what I meant."

"Then what did you mean?"

The questions kept coming, each one chipping away at DonnaMae's confidence until she felt like she couldn't breathe. Tears welled up in her eyes and she found herself shutting down, unable to answer anymore.

The school board lawyer's eyes were cold, judging, and disbelieving.

"I can't do this," DonnaMae said, breaking eye contact to turn and face her parents. Her own lawyer had spoken up a few times during the meeting, but not enough to make a difference, not enough to help. The room felt suffocatingly quiet. It seemed as if no one was fighting for her, and she didn't have the strength to fight anymore. She was tired of taking hits, tired of having nothing left to throw back. She had been knocked down and this time she didn't want to get back up.

The school board's lawyer leaned back, a smug smirk spreading across his face. "No further questions," he said.

DonnaMae stood up and walked out of the room. Behind her, voices clashed—her dad yelling, her lawyer shouting over him, and then her stepmom's voice, softer but no less urgent. She kept walking, tears blurring her vision, hating the heels on her feet, hating that they slowed her down.

"I'm walking home," she called over her shoulder, her voice breaking as she pushed through the heavy doors and into the open air. The brick walls had felt like they were closing in on her. She needed to breathe. She needed to run.

Without thinking, she bent down, yanked off the ridiculous heels, and let them drop onto the pavement. The cool concrete bit into her bare feet, but the pain was nothing — nothing compared to the ache in her chest, the weight pressing her down. And then, she ran.

She ran until the wind dried the tears on her face, until the pounding of her feet numbed everything else. The sting of the ground, the burn in her lungs — it was a relief. It was real. It was less than the pain that had taken over, less than the guilt that clawed at her insides.

She had done this.

It was all her fault.

DonnaMae had always loved the small town where she had grown up, with its tight-knit community and familiar faces. But now it felt smothering, and she yearned for escape. She needed to go somewhere where no one knew who she was. She needed a fresh start, and the only way to achieve that was by escaping all these people who knew her backstory, and who knew *him.*

DonnaMae pulled up to the crowded college parking lot. She didn't think it would be this busy today. She was hoping no one would be here and she would go unseen. Being invisible had become her new superpower. It made things so much easier than putting on a show. Some days were harder than others and she just couldn't seem to put on a smile, and on those days she found herself up at her mom's headstone, or at her grandpa's shop, finding something to fix on her race car.

DonnaMae climbed out of her truck and headed towards the administration building, but a glimpse of a dark blue truck pulling into a spot a few cars away caught her eye. A chilling sensation traveled down her spine, freezing her in place. She knew that truck — it was his.

The truck backed out and idled. DonnaMae couldn't see the driver, and maybe, just maybe, he couldn't see her either. *MOVE YOUR FEET!* She yelled at herself, but her body wouldn't respond. The truck rumbled as it straightened out and eased back into the parking spot.

Every fiber of her being screamed for her to run, but she stood frozen, as if standing still could somehow protect her from being noticed. Then the truck's engine cut off, and the sudden silence made her heart hammer in her chest.

MOVE!

Fear surged through her, and she sprinted back to her truck, her breath ragged and her hands shaking. Her fingers fumbled with the keys, panic rising as she fought the urge to turn around and see if he was coming for her. Did he know? Did he know she'd been talking to other girls, urging them to come forward?

Her keys slipped from her hands. *Shit, shit, shit!* frantically scooping them up. The one she needed was right on top. "Thank you," she said under her breath, opening the door.

She could feel him behind her, his breath on her neck. She wiped her neck, shaking, and jammed the key into the ignition. The engine roared to life. Without a second thought, she slammed the truck into reverse, tires screeching as she sped out of the parking space.

Shifting into drive, she floored the gas pedal, leaving a trail of tire marks and fear behind her.

She didn't need to see him, she could feel him. She knew it was him. Beads of sweat formed on her forehead as her chest tightened, each breath more shallow than the last. She pulled into the driveway and slammed on the brakes, launching forward in her seat.

By the time she climbed out of the truck, her dad and stepmom were already sprinting towards her from the house. She was home. She was safe. But she couldn't breathe, her heart pounded so fast and loud it drowned out everything else, the drumming growing louder, a soft ringing filling her ears.

DonnaMae dropped to her knees, gasping, "He's following me!"

Her parents were beside her in an instant. Her dad rubbed her back while Elise crouched close, whispering soothingly. "Breathe, Donna, just breathe. Slow and steady, honey. Breathe."

Elise always called her Donna. She was the only one who did. And right now, it was comforting. Right now, she wasn't Mae or DonnaMae, she was Donna. And Donna could breathe. Donna was safe with her stepmom by her side.

Rocking herself back and forth on her knees, DonnaMae wrapped her arms tightly around herself, trying to steady her breath.

Her dad counted slowly. "Breathe and count to three. Focus on the counting."

She tried to breathe in sync with each number, holding onto her dad's voice.

———

DonnaMae sat on the couch, her focus on the steaming cup of chamomile tea her stepmom had brought her. She'd always hated the taste and smell of chamomile, but right now, its warmth brought a sense of calm, her breathing and heartbeat finally settling back into a normal rhythm.

"I'm sorry," she said softly. "I don't know..." She couldn't finish, unsure of what to say, or how to explain. She lived in a constant state of trying to hide her fear. Today, she'd lost control, and shame filled her.

She couldn't hide behind a fake smile, couldn't run to her mom's headstone for comfort.

"I always think I see him. I always get scared, but today..." she paused. "Today I saw him. I *knew* it was him." The words poured out of her. "And honestly, I think it's him every time I go anywhere around here. He's just waiting for me to slip up so he can grab me."

Her voice trembled as she spoke. "All these secrets, trying to get the other girls who've spoken up before to come forward, trying to get him fired. I'm his biggest problem, and he's going to do whatever he can to eliminate me. Just like he always told me: eliminate your biggest problem and then you can move forward."

Tears threatened to fall. DonnaMae wrapped her hands tightly around the mug, swallowing them back. "I..." she cleared her throat, trying to steady herself. "I'll go back tomorrow to register for my classes. I'm sorry. I'm fine. I just —" She paused, struggling to hold it together, trying to convince herself that tomorrow, everything would be different. But deep down, she knew that was a lie.

DonnaMae stopped talking. She didn't want to go back to school, she didn't want to go off to college, and she certainly didn't want to run after school programs. She never wanted to step foot in an after school program ever again. She suddenly felt the urge to go for a run or lift something heavy.

An idea hit her. "Dad, do you remember the school you went to look at with Brother last year in Seattle?"

"Yes, Lake Washington Tech College," her dad said, tilting his head to the side.

"Do you still have the brochures and pamphlets you brought home?"

Her dad got up and walked over to the computer cabinet, pulled out a handful of different pamphlets and books. He set them down on the coffee table. "I saved them all just in case you wanted to look at them, and then I guess I just forgot about them until now."

DonnaMae set her cup down and spread the materials out on the table, searching until she found the booklet she was looking for, the one with "LWTC" in big bold letters across the top. She flipped it open and thumbed through the pages until she found what she was looking for. She dropped the book open on the coffee table. "Exercise Science. I knew I had seen it here. I want to go here and get my degree in Exercise Science."

Her dad looked at her and raised an eyebrow. "Exercise Science, huh? That seems —"

"Yeah!" DonnaMae cut in, feeling a sense of clarity she hadn't felt in a long time. "I think it's exactly what I need right now."

"Mae," her dad said, glancing between Elise and her, "I don't know if they can get you in on such short notice. It's kind of a process to apply to colleges."

"I don't think she has to apply to this one," Elise said, picking up the book. "I think she can just enroll."

"What about Paul? And all your friends? And all your credits at the college, and —"

DonnaMae cut her dad off, "Dad, stop! Paul was only waiting for me. He's ready to move now. He told us that just last week."

"And her credits will transfer," Elise said.

DonnaMae knew her stepmom had felt just as defeated as she did about everything. She didn't talk to Elise about it, but she knew. She could feel it in Elise's words and in her touch. "This isn't right. This isn't fair," she had heard her stepmom say to her dad one night as they walked away. Her dad would never understand the way Elise would.

In addition to feeling anger towards herself, DonnaMae also harbored resentment knowing that she wasn't the only girl who had experienced this, and that it would continue to happen, leaving her feeling helpless. There was nothing she could do, there was nothing any woman could do, up against a man who held the power.

"Do you think this is a good idea?" DonnaMae asked, turning her gaze only to her stepmom.

"I think it's what you might need to move on," Elise said in her soft voice, but there was something in her tone that felt grounded, matter of fact.

Knowing there truly was no other option, DonnaMae stood and faced her dad. "I'll call Paul and start packing. The sooner I'm out of here, the better." Her words were firm, but inside, she felt a hint of sadness and loss. This was what she'd told herself she wanted, what she knew she *needed,* but it didn't stop the ache that came with it.

Once again, she was the one being punished, the one hurting, the one sacrificing to make things ok. And this time, leaving meant saying goodbye to the things she loved most — her grandparents, her uncles, racing, and her mom.

As she walked towards her room, DonnaMae stretched herself tall, trying to push away the sense of defeat. *What I would give to finally win,* she thought.

CHAPTER 36

September, 2002

In just a few weeks time, DonnaMae had spoken to Paul about moving early, driven up with her dad to visit and register at her new school, found an off-campus apartment, packed up her bedroom, and even bought a few new things for the move, including some new adidas jogger outfits.

Telling her grandparents about the change was harder for her than it was for them. They were thrilled she was heading off to college, and when she explained that she wanted to get a jump start on her education, they accepted it without question. She didn't tell them the full truth, about why she was really leaving or what had happened. She just said she'd been accepted to a different school that allowed her to start early, and they fully supported her decision. She decided the conversation about her change in career plans would have to wait for another time.

Her grandmother, excited for this new chapter, took her garage sale shopping for two weekends in a row, helping her find everything she needed to furnish her new apartment.

Telling her friends about the move had been easy. They were all preoccupied with their own transitions, and excited for DonnaMae to be part of their same journey. Izzy, however, was the only one who seemed genuinely bummed. They'd had plans to paint the race car and tackle a few other projects, but with DonnaMae cutting her racing season short, those plans had to be put on hold. Izzy understood, or at least she said she did. She mentioned she had a new boyfriend and was busy with her own life changes, including moving in with him. But DonnaMae could see Izzy's disappointment. Even though she felt bad, DonnaMae knew there was no other choice.

Being surrounded by family and having all these things to focus on made it easier for DonnaMae to push everything else away, burying her fears deep inside. Though the nightmares still haunted her at night, during the day she found ways to keep her mind occupied.

DonnaMae was surprised by how easy it was to walk away from everything. The last person she told was her brother. She only shared part of the truth about what had happened, and the thought of leaving him and their early morning gym workouts was hard. He thought it was cool that she was changing her focus and going to school for exercise science. He even joked that he'd be calling her for advice on building bigger muscles, which she thought to be funny because he was doing fine on his own.

The drive to her new town was only three hours away from Howard. DonnaMae followed behind her dad's and Paul's trucks. Whenever one truck changed lanes, the others followed suit. Her stepmom had printed out MapQuest directions for each of them before they left, but they still stayed in a perfect line, each truck packed to the brim and secured with bright orange tie-down straps.

As DonnaMae turned off the freeway and headed towards Redmond, Washington, her nerves fluttered, causing her to grip the steering wheel tighter. Her truck hummed steadily as it cruised down the narrow two-lane road. She glanced at the crate of CDs stacked on the bench seat beside her just as a bump in the road sent them bouncing, and she quickly reached out to steady them.

She drove past a large campus of sleek, modern buildings, the word "Microsoft" stretched across the front of one. This was a big difference from the brick and wood structures she had grown up around in her hometown. Turning onto another road, she passed the town center. A trendy café caught her eye, with a line out the door and the aroma of freshly brewed coffee wafting through her window as she rolled it down. "Tully's Coffee," she noted. This wasn't anything like Cadlers back home. This place was sleek and modern. A chalkboard sign advertised the drink of the day: a vanilla soy latte. *Yuck, soy?* she thought, wrinkling her nose as she drove past.

At a stoplight, DonnaMae pulled up behind Paul. The main street was a delightful mix of old and new, with older storefronts that looked freshly painted. The light turned green, and DonnaMae continued forward, spotting the big apartment complex that would be her new home. *The start of a new chapter,* she thought as she pulled into the parking lot and located apartment G147. It all felt so big and different. She hoped she could make this new town feel like home and escape the pain of her old one.

"That's everything," Paul said, dropping a cardboard box in the middle of the apartment. "Well, that was a workout." He wiped his forehead with the back of his tan arm. A small curl of his dark brown hair stuck to his forehead as he glanced around the room.

DonnaMae loved that Paul was here with her. He wasn't her brother, but he was the next best thing. His laidback and fun personality would make him easy to live with, she hoped. She was glad to have a friend with her. She had no interest in making new friends and she felt safe with him around. This was her new chapter to her new life, but she didn't really know what she wanted out of it, other than to escape her old life.

"Almost everything," her dad said, walking past Paul with his arms full of grocery bags.

"Where did all that come from?" DonnaMae asked, brows raised.

"The grocery store. Well, the cab of my truck, but I bought them at the store when we all went to get lunch. You guys are going to need some food to get started," he replied with a smile.

Every counter was covered with boxes, and so was the table they had brought up earlier. "Maybe just set them on the floor," DonnaMae said as she watched her dad scan the room.

He walked over to the fridge. "They don't all belong in the fridge, but at least for now the things that need to stay cold will." He slid the bags off his arms and into the fridge.

"Did you get milk?" Paul asked with a laugh.

When they were kids, DonnaMae's dad used to get so mad at Allan for drinking all the milk after school, when it was actually Paul who did it. A few months back, Paul bought a few jugs of milk and came clean to her dad. It was one of the funniest things DonnaMae had ever seen.

"Yes, I even bought milk!" her dad said, walking over to DonnaMae. He wrapped his arms around her. "Fresh start, Mae. This will be good for you," he whispered just to her. "I love you, and I will be back in just a few weeks for the parent orientation thing."

DonnaMae had forgotten he was coming back for that. "Oh yeah!" she said, standing up straight and pulling back from the hug. "Will Elise and Adeline come with you?" she asked, her sadness fading as excitement took over. Who would have thought that she would ever be excited to see her stepmom?

"I'm sure they will want to," he replied. "And maybe they'll have a place to sit down by then." He waved his hand over the mess as he walked towards the door.

"Probably not," Paul said with a laugh. "Have you seen how much stuff this girl brought?"

"I left some cash in the drawer by the fridge," DonnaMae's dad said. "You guys go out and get to know your new town, buy some soy lattes." He made a gross face. "Check out the movie theater. Your brother said he's coming up tomorrow. Make him take you to lunch." He opened the door and paused for a moment before turning around. "And Paul, look out for my little girl, would ya?"

"Yes, sir," Paul said, giving a playful salute.

Her dad laughed and walked out, closing the door behind him. DonnaMae stood in the middle of the room, staring at the closed door, her heart sinking. How could she hold so much anger and love for one person? She wanted to hate him for not believing her. Why wasn't he fighting for her, fighting to make this right? But at the same time, he was her daddy, and he was all she had left of her parents, and it wasn't really his fault.

As DonnaMae tightened her shoelaces with a firm double knot, a refreshing breeze brushed against her skin, momentarily masking the heat of the day. Just thirty minutes ago, she'd thought a midday run would be a great way to take a break from her studies, which had consumed her life. It was mid-September; it was supposed to be cooler, but the heat was relentless.

Only a few weeks into her first quarter of college, DonnaMae had signed up for twenty-five credits, knowing it wasn't the best idea, but unable to stop herself. She had become a shell of herself, burying every part of her in school to avoid life. Charles had taken everything from her, leaving her hollow. She ate, slept, studied, and attended class and nothing more.

Paul had been checking in on her, urging her to slow down, warning her she was going to burn out. He'd suggested going to the mall, getting out more, but she couldn't escape the fear that Charles was still out there, watching her, waiting. Her dad had bought her mace, which stayed in her truck or her backpack, though she hadn't really needed it. She barely went anywhere besides the store, and only when Paul was with her.

Sweat already beaded on her brow, and for a moment, DonnaMae hesitated. But the need for a mental break and some physical exercise pushed her forward. Working out had always been her escape, and she knew she needed it.

DonnaMae shook out her arms and did a little jog in place to warm up her legs, even though they felt warm enough with the heat from the sun. With a quick adjustment to her cap to keep the sun off her face, she was off with a brisk walk to start.

School was fine. She enjoyed what she was learning, and it was nice that no one knew her and nothing was expected of her. She could smile when she wanted to and didn't have to when she didn't feel like it. She just wished she had more reasons to smile, to feel something real. Hoping a run would help, she picked up her pace.

It was a quiet Tuesday afternoon with no signs of human activity or passing cars. The apartment complex stood in eerie silence. *Everyone must be at work*, she thought, glancing around the parking lot as she walked over to the path that led along the water. She ran her thumb over the safety lock on her mace and exhaled a deep breath to slow her racing heart.

Everywhere she looked, she saw him. Every guy with glasses made her do a double-take to make sure it wasn't him. Fear prickled her skin as she stepped onto the path and started to jog, the can of mace clutched between her fingers. Soon, her feet matched the pace of her heart.

She had seen the trail out the window of her apartment and was intrigued by the sight of people running, walking, and biking on it, laughing and having fun. So she'd researched the trail and discovered it was called the Sammamish River Trail. It was 10.1 miles long and ran along the Sammamish River from Marymoor Park in Redmond to Bothell. The path was a well-maintained, paved area that would be perfect for her to begin her training, it was not secluded but also not on the streets.

Her heart pounded as she jogged, she could hear her brother's voice in her head, encouraging her to live a little, to not let fear control her life and to let fear fuel her. But fear was her constant companion now; it was no longer a fuel, it was a straight jacket.

She had to keep running, if only to outrun the shadows of her past that threatened to consume her, to show herself she was ok here. This was a new town. She was safe, she knew it, she just needed to believe it.

Her feet pounded the pavement and she couldn't help but wonder how she had ever liked doing this with her brother.

She realized she was pushing herself too fast, too hard, and too soon. The air was hot and thick, urging her to slow down and walk. She spotted a mile marker on the trail and chose that to be her slowing point. She directed all her attention towards the marker, running faster and faster. Her lungs were on fire, but she refused to let that stop her, pushing herself to keep going. The tips of her fingers brushed over the marker, just as her lungs felt like they could take no more and might erupt out of her chest in flames. She then slowed to almost a complete stop, barely walking, as she sucked air into her lungs. The details from her anatomy class came to life in her mind as she imagined her hardworking lungs. Inhaling deeply, she could feel the rush of air entering her lungs, supplying her bloodstream with much-needed essential oxygen and then exhaling and releasing carbon dioxide. "Talk about hands....on ....learning," she gasped with a laugh.

After taking a few more deep breaths, she started to jog again, this time slower. Her head spun with thoughts of how out of shape she was. What would she do if she was attacked? Her fingers tightened around her can of mace, and she couldn't help but laugh at herself. What was this little can going to do to save her if she couldn't even run to get away after spraying it? Up ahead, DonnaMae spotted a large clearing of grass, and she decided it would be her stopping point for a breather. But instead of speeding up she kept her pace slow and steady. Approaching the grass, she felt unexpectedly energized and decided not to stop after all. She slowed just enough to take in the lush green that seemed out of place in the middle of this nature trail.

A huge banner with a shadowy figure in gloves delivering a high kick caught her eye. The banner, hanging on the back of a large brick building at the edge of a strip mall, read "KICKBOX-ING" in bold, black letters. Intrigued, DonnaMae was drawn towards it, reading the words repeatedly as if to imprint them in her memory. She circled around to the front of the building, confirming it was part of a strip mall but filled with gyms instead of the usual shops. The first, Sidekicks Gym, was still closed. The hours on the door showed it opened from three PM to ten PM, with a phone number listed below: 425.321.5425 (KICK).

That's a number I can remember, she thought as she cupped her hands around her eyes and pressed her face against the glass to peer in. This was not a Taebo gym like the classes she had tried at the YMCA back home — this was the real deal. It looked like there was a real boxing ring inside.

As DonnaMae stepped away from the glass, a thrill ran through her. It felt like she was supposed to find this place. She wanted — no, she *needed* — to gain the ability to fight for herself and protect herself.

Several doors down, she could hear the thump of loud music and the heavy clang of weights being dropped. Curious, she wandered towards the sound. An extremely tan and buff guy stepped out of a propped-open door and leaned against the frame. He looked to be in his forties, with short-cropped hair speckled with gray. His face, aged with lines that hinted at years of hard work, carried a kind expression. There was a softness in his eyes and a welcoming demeanor about him that contrasted with his chiseled physique. "Hey," he said in a deep voice that matched his body. "You here to check out the gym?"

"I was just out for a run and thought I'd check this place out. I just moved here and my roommate would love —" DonnaMae stopped herself before she overshared. She didn't know this guy. Fear kicked her heart rate up. "My roommate, Paul he's actually out running an extra mile while I stop by. The gym at our apartment is pretty basic, and we — he, um —" She coughed and cleared her throat, and her mind. "I would love to check it out."

The guy chuckled. "Most apartment gyms are pretty basic. Welcome to Ironside," he said, gesturing broadly. "I'm Mike. We offer memberships for twenty bucks a month, or one-twenty if you pay upfront for the year." He pointed to a chalkboard sign near the door.

"Thanks," DonnaMae replied, thinking that the sign might be more useful outside the door. As she walked into the gym, she was greeted by old-school cardio machines, stair steppers and rowing machines that looked to be from the 1950s, along with some newer treadmills and ellipticals.

She moved past the cardio area to the weights. Rows of dumbbells, squat racks, and various machines filled the space. This place felt like a proper lifting gym. She was impressed. *This is perfect,* she thought, already excited to tell her brother about it. She knew he'd approve.

DonnaMae headed back to Mike, who was still holding up the door.

As she approached, he straightened in the doorway.

"I'm going to be late to meet my roommate." She paused, peering towards the path as if Paul might be waiting for her. "He'll love this place, and we'll both most likely get memberships."

"Sounds good, kid. You training for anything?"

"No, not right now. I'm just going to school, but I'm studying exercise science."

"Why didn't you mention it sooner? We offer college discounts. The whole year is only ninety-six bucks."

"Seriously? That's an amazing deal." DonnaMae thought of

the cash in her savings jar at home, meant for fun expenses. Her grandmother Joyce had helped her set up a bank account when she was twelve, and DonnaMae had been diligently saving for college ever since. But her cash jar, filled from lawn mowing jobs, car washing, and babysitting gigs, was her fun money. Thanks to generous graduation gifts and extra cash from both sets of grandparents, she had plenty to afford a membership here. "Thank you, I'll definitely be back," she said, waving goodbye to the large man by the door as she headed back to the trail.

Her mind buzzed with thoughts. Though she was usually reluctant to commit to anything, the gym struck a different chord, making DonnaMae feel good, like it was something she needed back in her life. Memories of Hazel's laughter during their treadmill races, and workouts with her brother, who had encouraged her to lift heavy weights, came flooding back. The gym had become a place that motivated her to keep moving forward when she wanted to give up on life altogether, after everything she had lost to Charles. The mere thought of him still sent a shiver down her spine. She shook his image away, refusing to let the darkness he brought into her life steal the one thing that had made her feel something today.

"With the right help, everything can burn," she remembered her grandpa saying after the rain would put out their campfire, "no matter the rainstorm that passes." He'd pour some gas on the fire and toss a match, and they would all watch as the flames burst back to life. Could boxing and the hole-in-the-wall gym be the lighter fluid DonnaMae needed to reignite her inner fire?

Her grandpa would think it was so cool if she started boxing. She would have to write him a letter when she got home, after she told Paul everything.

A shadow of doubt crept over her excitement. What would her dad think? Would he view this as a distraction from her studies, or would he approve? Or, would it just be one more thing for her to want him to be proud of, only to be left disappointed? Maybe she just wouldn't tell him about it yet.

———

DonnaMae burst through the door of her apartment and buckled over, out of breath from her final sprint home.

Paul stood in the middle of the living room with his backpack over one shoulder.

"Where — are — you — " DonnaMae asked between pants as she straightened up, "going?" She exhaled and closed the door behind her.

"I think the real question is where did you go? You left the house, and —"

"I have so much to tell you," she cut Paul off. "First, I passed my test this morning." She raised her right hand in the air and gave herself a high-five with her left. "Comparing the human body to the way a transmission in a car works really helped me remember all the things for my test." She walked past Paul and dropped onto the couch. "Oh, and it was written, not multiple choice with those damn fill in the circle things that I get mixed up, so that helped too."

"Wow, Mae, that's grea—"

She cut him off again. "And second thing, I went for a run." She paused and rolled her eyes at him. "Yeah, yeah, I know, you told me so. Anyway, I found a gym and it was not just a normal gym — well, wait, I found one of those too — well, kinda. It was a bodybuilding gym, but it was only ninety-six dollars for a whole year up front and I have that in my cash jar —"

"Wooooow, Mae, slow down. What has gotten into you? Did you run to a coffee shop or something? I haven't heard you talk this much since we moved." Paul laughed and dropped his book bag to the floor. "Maybe you should try breathing for a second."

"So, where are you going?" DonnaMae asked, her eyes dropping to his bag.

"I'm just getting back from the library." He paused and pulled in his chin, "And did you just high-five yourself?"

She realized that she had high-fived herself because she was feeling good. Maybe it was the run, or maybe it was remembering that a part of her still liked being alive, and running, and feeling something — even if it was her lungs burning and her legs feeling like they were going to fall off. But she dismissed Paul's question with a quick shrug. "Ok, so, this gym," she started over.

"The not-so-normal one, or the bodybuilding one?"

"So you did understand what I was saying," DonnaMae said with an annoyed sigh.

"I think I'm starting to learn fast-forward mode," Paul laughed.

After telling Paul everything, DonnaMae ended up driving back down to the Ironside Gym with him, and she was right, Paul loved it. He agreed that Allan would, too. They both signed up for memberships before going to check out the boxing place, but it was still not open.

On the drive home, Paul agreed that DonnaMae's dad would probably think boxing was a distraction from her studies, and a waste of money to have two gym memberships.

DonnaMae tried to talk Paul into trying a boxing class with her that night, but he said he didn't need two gym memberships, and honestly had no interest in learning to box.

She was on her own for this adventure, and it scared the shit out of her.

By the time four PM rolled around, DonnaMae had convinced herself that this boxing was a good idea because this was what she was going to school for: exercise. She had already come up with a plan to make it all work. She could go to Ironside Gym a few days a week in the morning with Paul on her way to classes, and then on the other nights she could go to boxing classes. The boxing gym didn't open until three PM, and classes were even later, which would give her time to study beforehand, and give her a break before studying after. She had also already checked her account and figured out a budget for the boxing gym. She had no idea how much it was going to cost, so she made three budgets, figuring one of them had to work. Now all she had to do was get the nerve to go take a class, by herself, in a place that was most likely going to be all men.

"Last chance to join me," she told Paul before heading out, "come now or forever hold your — eww, I think you might need to do some laundry." DonnaMae pinched her nose dramatically, pointing at the pile of dirty clothes that had formed a small mountain in front of Paul's bedroom door.

Paul glanced over his shoulder, raising an eyebrow. "Yep, that's another reason I'm not going with you. Thanks, Mae." He faced her, momentarily abandoning the stack of textbooks on his desk. "And unlike you, I don't have cocaine running through my veins. I need sleep, so I have to study at normal hours of the day." He flashed her a smug grin before turning back to his books.

DonnaMae rolled her eyes and stepped back from his door. "I'm not on drugs, I'm just a hard worker." She looked at his clothes, "And I like clean clothes. Have fun with your books and dirty socks." She laughed and walked away.

"Always do," he called after her, his voice already fading as he refocused on his studies.

She walked down the hallway, her newfound confidence fading as she neared the front door. An all-too-familiar knot tightened in her stomach. The idea of going to the boxing class alone had seemed bold and empowering just moments ago, but now it felt like a bad idea. Her steps slowed as she reached the door. She hesitated, her hand hovering above the doorknob, the weight of fear pressing down on her chest. What if she couldn't do it? What if she walked in and everyone stared, judging her? What if there were guys there who looked like *him*? The thought made her skin prickle. She took a deep breath, trying to steady herself, but the fear only grew. She was alone in this. It was just her, standing on the edge of something that felt too big to handle. Her mind started to spin with excuses, reasons to stay home, to avoid the risk. Maybe she wasn't ready. Maybe this wasn't the right time.

DonnaMae turned to head back to her room just as Paul stepped out of his room with his arms full of dirty laundry. "I thought you were leaving?" He gave her a quick once over. "Ahh, your chickening out?"

"No!" With a shaky hand, DonnaMae reached for the front doorknob and gripped it tightly as if it were a lifeline. The fear was still there, gnawing at her resolve, but she forced herself to turn the knob, to open the door. "Bye!" she yelled back as she closed the door behind her.

Warm evening air hit her face. Her heart thrummed. *One step at a time,* she reminded herself. *Just take it one step at a time.*

She started walking, her feet heavy but moving forward. She was no chicken — she needed to do this. She could do this.

CHAPTER 37

...

DonnaMae tapped the steering wheel with her fingertips as she sat in her truck, staring at the boxing gym through the windshield. Tightness coiled in her stomach. The idea of starting the engine and driving away felt far more appealing than stepping inside for her first class.

She had imagined this would feel like the first day of school: not a big deal. But it wasn't. On the first day of school, everyone was new — nobody stood out. This was different. She was the only new person, and possibly the only girl. What if she failed and everyone laughed? All eyes would be on her. What if this was all pointless? What if this broken, hollow version of herself was who she was now? Maybe she just needed to accept that there was no going back, no getting herself back. Maybe this was her now, and she should just turn around and go home.

"What if?" Her grandpa's voice came to her mind so clearly that it made her look over her shoulder, half expecting to see him standing next to her truck. His words echoed in her mind. "What if you never try and miss out on something amazing?"

"Alright, Mae, you got this," she said to herself, struggling to recall the three positive things she had once held dear. It had been so long since she'd thought of anything positive, especially about herself. "You're strong, you are..." She closed her eyes to focus. "You are... come on, Mae... I AM!" But her thoughts remained dark. *I am not strong*, she thought. *If I were, I wouldn't be here, sitting in this parking lot, wanting to drive back home.*

She tilted her head back, staring at the ceiling of her truck. "Ok, Mom, now what? How do I be as tough as you?" DonnaMae let out a flustered laugh. "Great, now I'm not just talking to myself, I'm asking my dead mom for answers." She shook her head.

As she sat forward, a tall man with a dark complexion and a bald head swung open the glass door of the gym and propped it open with a doorstop. DonnaMae sighed. "Well, I guess that was my cue. Time to rip the bandaid off." She flung the truck door open and climbed out as the man disappeared back inside.

Inside the gym, the air was heavy with the scent of Pine-Sol, bleach, and musty old sweaty socks. A woman with short blonde hair sat in one of the three gray chairs by the door, flipping through a magazine. In the room to DonnaMae's right, a group of kids dressed in white Karate uniforms and colorful belts were energetically shouting "HAH" in unison, following the lead of a tall man with gray hair wearing a black belt. A tall, unattended reception desk stood to DonnaMae's left, with a teak-hut-like structure behind it that seemed strangely out of place. Mexican music spilled through two large glass doors in front of her, one propped open, letting the lively tunes fill the space.

In the distance, DonnaMae spotted the tall bald man who had opened the door earlier. He was now mopping the expansive boxing ring at the back of the room, singing to himself. His voice wasn't perfect, but it was oddly comforting, reminding her of the times her dad used to sing and make up silly songs while working around the house. Curious, DonnaMae stepped through the open doors onto the hardwood floors and was surprised by the slight spring in them. She watched the man intently as she approached the ring. He wore a red t-shirt with the sleeves cut off, revealing a tapestry of tattoos on his muscular arms. Each stroke of the mop made his muscles flex, and she noticed how the tattoos shifted and stretched with the movement. He wasn't shredded like the guys she usually saw at the gym, but he had a solid, strong build.

As she drew closer, a wave of self-doubt crept in. Maybe she should turn around and walk back out.

Before DonnaMae could turn around, the man caught her staring. A big smile spread across his face as he leaned the mop against the ropes of the ring. He placed one foot on the bottom rope and smoothly ducked under the top, stepping out to meet her.

"*¡Hola señora, bienvenida a mi casa!*" he said, his voice far friendlier than she had expected. "I'm Che. How can I help you?"

"Oh, um, *hola!*" DonnaMae extended her hand to him, trying to recall any Spanish from her freshman year but drawing a blank. She quickly abandoned the idea, not wanting to make a fool of herself. "I'm DonnaMae, but you can call me Mae," she said, making sure her handshake was brief but firm. Her dad had always told her that there was nothing worse than a weak handshake, and she could already tell this man wouldn't appreciate one either.

"*Hola*, Mae," he replied with a warm smile. "That's a good grip you've got there."

DonnaMae smiled and glanced around the gym. "Wow, is all of this yours?" she asked, feeling a bit of the tension melt away as she admired the space. She had never seen anything like it. Her grandpa had told her stories once about boxing in the military, but this was a real boxing gym.

"*Si*, I just bought it a few months ago," Che said, his smile growing wider and his chest lifting. "So, I can't take all the credit. But I've been coming here for years, so I'm proud to be the new owner."

DonnaMae felt a strange sensation settle in. There was something about this place that felt like home, similar to the comfort she got walking into her grandparents' shop. But beneath that feeling was an underlying rush, like what she felt before a race or before stepping onto a stage. It wasn't just nerves; it was more than that. It was that little rush she craved and wanted more of every-time it passed.

"Let me give you the grand tour," Che said, motioning for DonnaMae to follow as he led her around the gym, explaining its layout. Behind the boxing ring, the weight area sprawled out, filled with mismatched dumbbells and old workout machines. The floor dipped slightly and was covered with black rubber tiles. The place had a gritty charm that made her feel like this was a world all its own.

Off to the side towards the back was another room with a large garage door open to the air. The room was filled with heavy bags of various sizes and shapes. There were long bags, short bags, and a few bags hung sideways. One, in particular, caught DonnaMae's attention: a small bag suspended between two rubber bands from the floor and ceiling.

"That's called a double-end bag," Che said, following her gaze.

She nodded, unsure what the bag was used for, but decided not to interrupt and ask.

By the time they returned to the lobby, a few people had walked in, all greeting Che as "Coach" and exchanging friendly hellos as they headed into the gym.

Che walked behind the front desk and pulled out a piece of paper, two black boxing gloves, and two rolls of cloth — one green, one yellow. He placed them on the counter and looked up at DonnaMae with a grin. "Class starts in twenty minutes. I just need you to sign this waiver, and then we'll get your hands wrapped. I'll show you the basics before it starts," he said, sliding the paper towards her.

DonnaMae raised an eyebrow, tilting her head to the side. "How did you know I wanted to try the class?"

Che chuckled, leaning against the desk with his arms crossed. "Well," he said, gesturing towards her outfit, "you're dressed to workout, and all you've got with you are your keys and a water bottle. What else would you be here for?"

DonnaMae glanced down at herself, then back up at him, a small smile creeping onto her face. "Oh, yeah, duh," she said, feeling her cheeks warm. She grabbed a pen from the cup on the desk. "The schedule you've got taped in the window said tonight was Boxing 101. Is that a good class to start with?" She let out a nervous laugh. "I mean, I could always come back if the class is too full."

Che shook his head with a reassuring smile. "Oh no, you're already here. This is the perfect class for beginners." He paused, glancing at the carpeted room behind her. "Unless you were here to try karate, then you'd want to talk to Sensei Hussin."

DonnaMae laughed, shaking her head. "Oh no, I want to learn to box. Maybe kickbox too; I don't really know. But I *definitely* want to try boxing first..." She trailed off, realizing she was talking too much. She quickly signed the paper and turned back to Che, who had already moved from behind the desk to stand next to her.

He unraveled the long green wrap, part of it spilling onto the floor. "Hold your hand out flat," he instructed, demonstrating with his own hand. "I'll wrap your hands, and then we can head into the gym."

DonnaMae did as he asked, watching as Che carefully wrapped the cloth around her hands. His movements were smooth and practiced, completely natural to him, but entirely new to her. As the wraps tightened around her fingers and knuckles, her hand felt like it was holding his masterpiece, each layer snug and perfect.

Both hands securely wrapped, one in green and one in yellow, DonnaMae felt amazing. She hadn't even put the gloves on yet, and she already felt like a fighter.

Once they walked back into the workout room, Che set the gloves down on the floor in front of the wall covered from floor to ceiling in mirrors. The repetitive thuds of boxing gloves striking punching bags and the occasional grunts of exertion from the guys already working out filled the room. DonnaMae scanned the room through the mirrors. Once again, she was the only girl. But what else had she expected? It was a boxing gym.

She pushed back the fear creeping up inside her, reminding herself that this shouldn't be intimidating. She'd been the only girl in plenty of places before. But still, the urge to turn around and walk back out the door tugged at her.

"You want to keep your hands locked at the sides of your face," Che said, demonstrating with his fists, drawing her attention back to him in the mirror.

Focus, Mae, you're fine. Breathe and focus. This is why I'm here, she thought to herself, pulling her hands into tight fists beside her chin.

"Good, now let's start with your fight stance," Che said as he directed her to stand with her feet hip-width apart, then to drag her right foot back so its toes lined up with the heels of her left foot. He proceeded to lead her through a series of punches, from a jab with her left hand to a cross with her right, known as punches one and two, all the way to punch number six, an uppercut with her right hand. It was a lot of information, but as he helped her put her gloves on and instructed her to practice throwing punches for the next five minutes until class started, she became completely engrossed and excited to continue practicing.

A few moments later, Che burst back into the room, urging everyone to grab a rope. He walked over and flicked a switch on a box mounted above the wall where the ropes hung. The box had three lights — green, yellow, and red — and as the bell rang, the green one lit up, signaling the start of class. DonnaMae swiftly peeled off her gloves and approached Che, snagging a rope from the wall hook. She'd been so caught up in perfecting her punches that she hadn't noticed the gym filling up until nearly everyone was bouncing around with jump ropes. It was like a blast from the past, reminding her of her grade school days, which was probably the last time she had jumped rope. Standing at the back of the class, she watched everyone skip rope effortlessly, as if it were as routine as brushing teeth. Gripping the rope tightly, she felt a pang of fear as she swung it over her head. With a thud, the overly long rope smacked the ground in front of her as she jumped and twirled it again, this time smacking herself instead of the floor. "Ouch," she yelped, drawing a few glances from nearby classmates.

"Your rope is too long," Che remarked, handing her another one. "Put both feet on the center of the rope, and the handles should reach your armpits." He showed with her old rope, which was a perfect fit for his tall frame. At five feet two inches on a good day, it was no wonder DonnaMae struggled with the old rope. Testing the new one, she found it to be a perfect match. She tried again, managing three jumps before whipping herself again, but this time she bit back her outcry.

When the bell rang and the yellow light illuminated, signaling the end of the two-minute, thirty-second interval, Che exclaimed, "Burn out!" Everyone began jumping with high knees or double unders, until the bell rang again and the light turned red.

"Thirty seconds of rest!" Che called out, his voice cutting through the labored breathing that filled the room.

By the end of three rounds, DonnaMae's legs felt like jelly, her calves burned, and her arms were covered with angry red welts. She wondered how she'd survive the remainder of the class when it had only been ten minutes.

Che directed everyone to complete three rounds of shadow boxing. As they punched the air and moved around the floor, he walked the room, giving advice and adjusting form and footwork. DonnaMae found herself stealing glances at a few guys ahead of her. Their movements were so fluid, as if they were battling opponents in a ring. She thought back to watching fights with her dad as a little girl. Her favorites were watching Muhammad Ali's old matches, and Manny Pacquiao was her favorite now. While these guys were not Ali or Pacquiao, their focused intensity was just as impressive as they bobbed, weaved, and threw punches in their imaginary fights.

Glancing at her own reflection, DonnaMae chuckled. Her movements were clumsy, like a drunk person swatting at a fly.

"Protect yourself at all times," Che said, walking up to her and demonstrating proper hand positioning with his fist next to his cheeks. "Every punch you throw should come back to your face."

"Yes, sir," DonnaMae replied with a nod and tapped her chin after each punch, her arms growing heavy with the need to rest them. She pushed through throwing punches as Che observed.

"Good, keep moving, but plant your stance before punching," he advised before moving on.

Throwing a jab and a cross, DonnaMae took a couple steps before throwing again, this time stumbling, her feet tangling. She dropped to one knee with a thud but quickly jumped up, resuming her punches. She could feel the eyes of her classmates on her, but she blocked them and the few chuckles around her out, focusing on her movements and punches.

When the bell rang and the light turned red again, Che's voice shifted, commanding the group to line up against the glass. DonnaMae noticed three other women in the class. She wasn't sure if it comforted or intimidated her. She wasn't the only female, but she certainly felt like the only one desperate for water and a nap.

Che went down the line, pairing people up and assigning one person mitts and one person gloves.

A tall older woman with short bold hair approached Che.

Che glanced between her and DonnaMae. "Kris, meet Mae," he said. "It's her first class. Show her the ropes, and after class I'll hold mitts for you for a few rounds."

Kris gave a low grunt, rolled her eyes, and promptly declared, "I'll hold mitts first," before Che could assign jobs to either of them.

DonnaMae knew the pressure of being the only girl in a male-dominated space. Having another woman there made her feel the need to prove herself, not just to the men, but almost more so to the other women who were there first and knew what they were doing. She didn't want to let them down.

DonnaMae slid her gloves on as Che laid out the class instructions. It was all about combinations — he'd call out numbers, creating sequences, and the holders would signal when to throw. They each moved at their own pace, but the three-minute timer controlled them all. When the bell hit yellow, it was time to "Burn It Out" with a flurry of jabs and crosses.

As the bell rang with the green light, Che barked, "One, one, two!"

DonnaMae focused on the red pads with white dots held by Kris. *Jab, jab, cross — left, left, right,* she reminded herself.

"Are you gonna hit the mitts or just stare at 'em?" Kris's tone was sharp, yanking DonnaMae back to reality.

"Oh, I thought I waited for you to say punch?"

"I did. So punch!" Kris snapped. "Let's try again. Punch!"

DonnaMae reached out, but her jab fell short, her arm locked out awkwardly. She tried again, this time stepping forward, and her jab landed but just barely on the side of the mitt. She followed-up with a cross and barely missed Kris's face, sending DonnaMae into an apologetic frenzy.

"No apologies in boxing," Che intervened, stepping in front of Kris and facing DonnaMae, but glancing back over his shoulder at Kris. "Let's focus on bringing the mitts to her and remember, we are all beginners at some point."

Che brought his bare hands up like he was surrendering. "Punch."

"Um, you —"

"Punch!" he barked again.

DonnaMae took a deep breath and threw her punches — jab, jab, cross — perfectly this time, guided by Che's hands.

"Again," he demanded, and she repeated the sequence, landing each punch over and over. "Good work! Now, with Kris," Che directed, moving on to the next pair without a backward glance.

DonnaMae eyed the timer, feeling like these were the longest three minutes of her life. She pulled her gloves back to her face, ready to go again.

Kris yelled, "Punch!" and DonnaMae unleashed the combination once more, landing every punch with newfound force.

CHAPTER 38

···

Beep. Beep. Beep.

DonnaMae groaned, rolling over and blindly slapping her hand down on the snooze bar of her alarm clock. Every muscle in her arm ached as she slid it off the nightstand and burrowed deeper under her cozy down comforter. The red numbers on her clock glared back at her: four-thirty AM.

She didn't even know it was possible to feel this tired. *Why did I agree to workout with Paul before school?* she thought, pulling the blankets up around her chin.

After last night's boxing class, DonnaMae had signed up for a membership on the spot. The class had been tough, but she felt a strength building inside her, one she thought she'd lost; the same feeling she only found when she was lifting with her brother or tearing around the racetrack. She had stayed late, working on her punches and trying out the heavy bags in the back room while watching the advanced boxing class. She'd lingered for nearly another hour, determined not to look like a fool in her next session, which was supposed to be tonight. If she could find the energy to drag herself out of bed.

The snooze time ran out and her alarm blared again.

DonnaMae groaned, throwing the covers back and dragging herself into a seated position. She felt muscles in her upper body she didn't even know she had. "Ok, if I can just get my ass moving," she muttered, stretching her arms over her head and letting out a long yawn, paired with a groan as she rolled her stiff neck and shoulders.

"If I make it through today's workout, school, and another boxing class, I'll reward myself with a nice, hot bubble bath after," she promised herself, trying to muster up some motivation. A smile spread across her face as she thought of the bath and body store she'd seen in the town center. She had a break between classes today, and it was only a five-minute drive from campus.

She hadn't ventured out into town yet, but maybe today she'd try. There was a bookstore there, something Howard didn't have. She'd just gotten into reading for pleasure over the summer, after Elise had given her *Jemima J* by Jane Green. DonnaMae was hooked, unable to put it down. The story had pulled her in, making her eager to see what happened next, despite her usual struggles with reading.

Books on CD had also become a favorite of DonnaMae's, though they were more expensive. Recently, she'd dropped her Discman, and the resulting scratch on the CD made it skip during chapter thirty-two. To make matters worse, she'd discovered one of the CDs was missing. Now she was stuck not knowing what happened next, unless she could figure out which CD case her sister had mistakenly stored it in, assuming it wasn't still back in her old room at home.

DonnaMae pulled open her closet. Even her armpits hurt. She hadn't known that was possible. "Maybe a new book and a bubble bath," she said, grateful she wouldn't need to change throughout the day as she grabbed her usual workout clothes. The best thing about studying exercise science and anatomy was that everyone wore workout gear to class, making her life that much easier.

Her school was modern, with wide glass windows and open

spaces that felt more like a cutting-edge business than a traditional school. The building had a fresh new smell, and the polished floors gleamed under the bright lights. DonnaMae walked quickly through the crowded halls, avoiding eye contact, her headphones on. She liked to keep to herself, avoiding opportunities for people to talk to her.

When she arrived at her classroom, she slipped into her usual seat in the second row. It was the perfect spot to feel tucked in and still up close enough to learn and stay focused. From here, she could take detailed notes and record the lecture without the distractions of her classmates. She didn't talk or participate, preferring to blend into the background while still soaking up the material. Joining in discussions would draw too much attention to her, so she kept her head down and focused on her studies.

The door swung open and in walked Mrs. Adler, DonnaMae's favorite teacher. Her gray hair was pulled into a long French braid and the bright blue and green swirls on her shirt made her green eyes seem even more vibrant. Though she was probably in her early fifties, she moved with the energy of someone much younger. Her loud, booming voice commanded attention the moment she stepped into the room, but it was her sense of humor that made her unforgettable. She had a knack for turning even the dullest topics into something interesting, often cracking jokes that had the whole class laughing.

"Good morning, everyone!" Mrs. Adler said, her voice echoing through the room. "Hope you're all ready to get your hands dirty today, because we're diving into some practical anatomy!"

DonnaMae set up her notebook and recording device, ready for class. Mrs. Adler had a gift for bringing the subject matter to life, and in those moments, DonnaMae felt truly connected to what she was learning.

In her other classes, it was a different story. DonnaMae struggled to tune out the constant chatter of classmates who were more interested in the weekend's party than in the lessons. The guy behind her was always flirting with the brunette next to him, his voice cutting through her concentration like nails on a chalkboard. The cold classrooms were a blessing, though — they gave her the perfect excuse to stay bundled up, helping her maintain a low profile as she focused on getting through each day.

As the day wore on, DonnaMae's muscles ached with every step. She kept telling herself that all the soreness would be worth it in the end, but right now, all she could think about was a hot bath. As she walked down the hallway towards the back parking lot, she checked her watch. She had an hour and a half break before her next class, and for once, the idea of going out to buy a new bubble bath didn't fill her with the usual dread of being out in town alone. It was almost enough to make her forget her fears, if only for a little while.

As she neared the exit, a girl walking in front of her stopped and held the door open. "Thank you," DonnaMae said, keeping her head down as she walked past.

"It's Donna, right?" the girl asked, almost jogging to catch up.

"DonnaMae," she said, slowing down and finally glancing over. The girl looked about her age, with long straight blonde hair parted down the middle.

"I'm Cassie. I sit next to you in class."

DonnaMae hesitated, unsure of how to respond. "Oh, hi." She glanced down at her watch again. "Um, I've got to go," she said, quickly.

Cassie's friendly smile faltered slightly. "Oh, ok. Well, maybe we can catch up later?"

"Maybe," DonnaMae said, already starting to walk towards her car. She felt a little bad for brushing Cassie off so abruptly.

As soon as she got into her truck, DonnaMae locked the doors and took a deep breath. She used to know everyone around her, always friendly, always connected. But here, she preferred staying under the radar. The fewer people who knew her, the fewer she could disappoint.

She started the engine and pulled out of the parking lot, trying to push the encounter with Cassie out of her mind. She didn't have time for friends — not when she was still struggling just to keep herself together. She already had three amazing friends, and she couldn't even keep up with them. Guilt pinched at her for not writing or calling them back, but she knew they were off having the time of their lives, making new friends — ones worthy of their friendship.

After kickboxing class that night, DonnaMae felt exhausted and ready for bed by the time she stepped into her apartment. The class had been intense. Jeff, a fiery-haired instructor with a military background, had pushed them to their limits with his drill-style coaching. He was fit, clearly strong, and every kick he demonstrated had a sharpness to it that showed exactly how hard he expected them to work.

The class had begun at a bar along the wall of mirrors that looked like it belonged in a ballet studio. DonnaMae and the other students had lined up along the bar and practiced every kick DonnaMae could imagine: sidekick, back kick, front kick, roundhouse kick, jab kick, high kick, and low kick. Each move was drilled into them, over and over, until their legs burned.

Kicking off her shoes and dropping her gym bag by the door, DonnaMae felt the satisfying ache in her muscles — a reminder of her hard work. The thought of sinking into a hot bath with her new lavender bubble bath was tempting, but so was collapsing onto her bed. She stood for a moment, torn between the two.

The apartment felt strangely quiet.

"Paul?" DonnaMae called out before poking her head into his room.

Empty. He was probably buried in his studies at the library or somewhere on campus. Their differences in study habits always amused DonnaMae. She preferred the comfort of home, while he claimed home was too distracting and he needed a different environment. She always laughed at that because, for her, every environment was distracting. At least at home, she could be in her pajamas and be alone.

DonnaMae made her way to her bedroom, feeling the exhaustion settle in. She needed to study, but she was too tired even to think about dinner. The new book and bubble bath she'd been looking forward to would have to wait. All she had the energy for tonight was a quick hot shower and the warmth of her bed, and hopefully a peaceful night's sleep.

CHAPTER 39

...

Che, busy on the phone, gave DonnaMae a quick nod as she walked past the front desk.

She wave at him, then grimaced from the soreness that had settled in after a week of workouts.

In less than a week, this place had started to feel like a second home to DonnaMae. The spring-loaded floor gave a subtle bounce under her feet. It was her favorite part of the gym, the way it made her feel light even when her legs felt like they weighed a ton.

The gym was quiet today compared to earlier in the week. "Break Stuff" by Limp Bizkit played at half volume through the overhead speakers. There were only a few guys in the gym, one jumping rope while another concentrated on a speed bag. A tall, thin man was shadow boxing in a corner of the ring. Across the gym, a guy in the weights area wearing a paint-splattered white tank top and work pants seemed equally focused on the mirrors as on his workout. DonnaMae wasn't sure if he was fixing the weights or working out with them. She headed for the women's locker room.

She dropped her gym bag onto a long bench in front of the lockers and pulled out her black hand wraps and new boxing gloves she'd gotten with her membership. She tossed her keys into her bag before shoving it into a locker without a lock. Maybe it was pointless to use a locker without a lock, but she did it anyway. She was likely to be the only woman there, anyway.

Tonight was open gym and fight night, a chance for the more advanced boxers to spar. DonnaMae knew she wasn't anywhere near that level, but she was excited to watch and learn. A small laugh escaped her. *Me fighting, could you imagine?* Shaking her head, she grabbed her water bottle and headed out of the locker room.

In the corner of the gym, an older gentleman pedaled slowly on a stationary bike, his eyes scanning the room as he observed the action around him. The guy who had been jumping rope earlier was now shadowboxing with small weights in his hands that looked like mini dumbbells. DonnaMae kept finding herself glancing at the man on the bike. There was something familiar about his face, though she couldn't quite place where she had seen him before.

The bell rang, signaling the end of a round, and the gym fell quiet except for the sound of Fort Minor's "Remember the Name" playing in the background. DonnaMae smiled to herself. She knew all the lyrics by heart. It felt oddly fitting to hear the song in an actual fight gym.

Grabbing a jump rope from the rack, she stood near the man on the bike and hesitated. "Are you a professor?" she asked him, backing up to prepare to jump.

"I'm a teacher of sorts, but not a professor," he said with a friendly chuckle.

"Oh! Where do you teach?" she asked, tilting her head as the bell rang again, signaling the start to a new round.

"Engaging in cardio while conversing is a great way to enhance your breathing," the man said. "Also, green means go." With a smirk, he nodded at the timer on the wall.

"Oh, right," DonnaMae starting her jump rope routine. She

wasn't a pro at it, but she had made progress since her first attempts, learning to keep her hooded sweatshirt on until she finished jumping. It seemed to be a trend among the guys in the gym. Some even sported hoodies with the sleeves cut off, keeping the hoods up during their workouts, which she found odd.

"So, what do you teach?" she asked, glancing at him between jumps.

"I'm Sensei H. I teach karate," he replied with a warm smile. "But in this setting, you can just call me Coach Joe."

"Ah, right! You teach in that room with the Buddha decor and carpet floor —"

SNAP!

The jump rope lashed against DonnaMae's arm. She bit back a yelp and gritted her teeth, swallowing the pain, then straightened the rope before continuing. "Is there no —" she cleared her throat, trying to keep her cool. "No karate tonight?"

"No karate tonight," Coach Joe chuckled softly. "It's important to mix things up in training, keep the body guessing, you know? That's why I'm here on this bike. Gotta keep the heart pumping in different ways."

DonnaMae nodded, still jumping rope, her feet starting to find a rhythm. "Yeah, that makes sense. Mixing it up keeps things interesting."

"Exactly," Coach Joe said. "Besides, it's beneficial for fight training."

"Oh, so you're also into boxing?" DonnaMae asked, running out of breath.

"You bet. I dabble in boxing and kickboxing, and lend a hand with the fighters here and there." Joe raised an eyebrow. "What brings you here?"

"Oh, I'm just here to workout and learn a thing or two," DonnaMae said, feeling her cheeks flush. Why would he think it was a good idea for a girl to learn to fight?

As if he'd read her mind, Coach Joe said with a reassuring smile, "Every girl should know how to defend herself."

There was something about the way Coach Joe spoke that put DonnaMae at ease. He was knowledgeable and passionate about being here, and as they continued talking, she noticed herself letting her guard down. He talked just as much as she did, if not more, which was a relief. It gave her a chance to catch her breath. She learned that he had nine black belts and was originally from Florida. He also had a full-time job working with big cranes and tech. She enjoyed the conversation so much that she ended up jumping four rounds instead of her usual three.

After the last bell on the fourth round, DonnaMae hung up her rope. "Are you going to do some shadow boxing?" she asked, turning towards Coach Joe as he got off the bike.

"Yes," Joe said, walking to a white bucket against the mirrored wall. He pulled four of the small dumbbell-like weights from the bucket, the same ones DonnaMae had seen the other guy using earlier, and walked back to her.

"Um, what are those for?" DonnaMae asked, eyeing the weights like he was offering her moldy cheese.

"These are hand weights," Joe said, holding out two for her. "Just one pound to start for you." He shifted the other two larger weights in his hands. "These are three pounds, for me." He held the weights up by his face, curling his fists around them tightly as he turned to the mirror but kept his focus on DonnaMae. "We'll do the first round with weights to practice form, then drop them for the second round to work on speed and —" The bell rang green, cutting him off mid-sentence.

DonnaMae pulled her weighted hands into tight fists, bringing them up to her face, mimicking Joe's stance. The weights felt heavier than she expected, but she clenched her fists and focused, following his lead.

"Good, now work on breathing with your punches, and relax

your shoulders," he said with a quick head nod and a smile between his punches.

DonnaMae dropped her shoulders away from her ears and moved around the gym, throwing punches and ducking imaginary blows. She focused on her form, her breath in sync with each movement. It felt like only seconds had passed when the bell rang yellow, signaling it was time to burn it out with jab-cross combinations. She threw punches as fast as she could, the ends of the weights occasionally clanking together as her fists flew past each other. Her arms started burning. Thirty seconds began to feel like an eternity. When the bell rang red, her arms were dead and ready for a break.

Joe turned to face her, dropping his weights to the floor. "Drop your weights."

Gladly, she thought, but then Joe started punching.

"Skip the rest on the red bell and go straight into punching," he said, turning to focus on his own form. "Work on speed and feel how light and fast your hands are. Let them go."

DonnaMae did as instructed. Her hands felt lighter and she could throw faster, but her arms were screaming for that break. She tried to focus on her speed, blocking out everything else, but the burn in her shoulders made it hard to stay in the zone. All the noises in the gym kept pulling her attention; the music, the steady thud of the heavy bags, a guy jumping rope behind her.

"Keep your hands up," Joe called to her, pulling her focus back to the mirror. "Stay focused. This is not about form, it's about speed training. Punch faster!" he barked at her in a voice that made her feel like her grandfather was scolding her.

She quickly pulled her fist back to her face and pushed through the burn in her shoulders, throwing every punch she could think of without stopping. It was a four-minute burn out, and when the bell rang yellow, even though her arms felt like they were going to drop to the floor, she held them up and punched over and over until the bell rang red.

"Good job," Joe said, dropping his arms by his side. "Shake out your arms, grab some water, and we'll do it again."

A small smile crept onto DonnaMae's lips. She had done it. She hadn't given up. It was a small win, but it was a win. Suddenly, her arms didn't feel so heavy. After a quick drink of water, she felt ready for another round. She knew she could do it, and this time, she would do it better.

With Coach Joe's advice, she worked on her strikes and foot-work, feeling the burn in her muscles as she pushed herself harder. In the mirror, she liked what she saw: a girl who could fight back, a girl she hadn't met before. That image fueled her to keep going, determined to work even harder. She was ready to get to know this girl.

Sweat trickled down DonnaMae's arm as she pulled off her gloves.

"Good job today," Joe said, pulling his own gloves off.

They had done three rounds of shadow boxing and then Joe had her practice throwing punches without her gloves on, learning how to punch correctly before doing some mitt work. Then they did six rounds of heavy bag together and before DonnaMae knew it, two hours of training had gone by.

Che was standing in the corner of the boxing ring, where two guys fought each other.

Joe tapped DonnaMae's arm. "You should watch some of the sparring and do some stretching." He pointed towards the ring. "Watching to learn and stretching are just as important as the working out part of training."

DonnaMae was happy to sit down, and she actually really enjoyed watching boxing, but right now, she was starving and exhausted. "I can stay for a little while but I still have homework to do tonight, and —" She paused and glanced around the room, "I'm not really training to fight, but thanks for the advice."

Joe was already stretching out his legs, which DonnaMae found strange because they hadn't even trained their legs. But she figured she had better just join in for a few minutes before she headed out. He did just spend his whole workout teaching her, she probably shouldn't just walk away now.

CHAPTER 40

November, 2002

DonnaMae felt trapped in a suffocating fog, the air itself turned against her. His hot breath clung to her neck, his body heavy and pinning her down. She tried to scream, but her voice failed her. She tried again, but still no sound came. The urge to fight was slipping away, her strength fading as his grip tightened. She tried to punch and kick, but nothing would move.

The roar of the ocean grew louder, each crashing wave pulling her closer. The cold air wrapped around her, making her shiver as moisture from the sea clung to her skin. Desperate, she wrapped her arms around herself, digging her heels into the wet sand. *He is going to drown us.*

"My beautiful Mae," his voice whispered in her ear, and she screamed.

"Stop. Please, stop!" DonnaMae's scream ripped through the silence, yanking her from the nightmare's grip. She shot upright in bed, her body drenched in sweat, heart hammering against her chest like a caged bird. Her trembling hands fumbled for the light switch and light flooded the room, chasing away the shadows. Even though it had only been a dream, the feeling of his touch lingered, burning against her skin. Frantically, she rubbed at her hip, desperate to erase the ghostly imprint he'd left behind.

He was there, in her bed, taking the fresh start she had worked so hard to create. He had won again. Just when she had dared to believe that she was moving on, that the nightmares were fading into the past, he had returned. It was a cruel reminder that she was pathetic, weak and easy to break.

The move to a new town, the month of relentless boxing classes, all her effort, it was all to outrun him. Reality hit her like a heavy blow to the gut: every time she got back up he was going to be right there to knock her back down.

Shivering, DonnaMae looked around her room one more time just to make sure she was alone as she shuffled towards her bathroom. She paused, listening for any sounds in the apartment, grateful that she hadn't woken Paul.

She turned on the shower. As she peeled off her sweaty t-shirt, she caught a glimpse of her reflection in the builder-grade mirror above the sink. Tear streaks stained her face, helplessness knotted in her stomach. Steam and the sound of running water filled the room as she fixated on her reflection, filled with rage. Why had she let this happen to her? How could she be so weak?

"Why are you so pathetic?" she said, yelling at herself through gritted teeth. Her fists clenched at her sides. "You are so —" Before she could finish another insult, her rage exploded and without even thinking, she spun to the right and slammed her fist into the wall. A smirk twisted her lips. A perfect punch.

It was a move she'd been practicing with Joe. He'd said if she wanted to nail the punch, she had to do it bare-knuckled first. He'd told her a story of how he used to punch some kind of mucky waterboard thing made of solid wood. When he told her about it, she thought he was nuts. Why would anyone punch wood bare-knuckled? But now she understood why. It hurt to punch the wall, but it was oddly satisfying. And she landed it perfectly and pulled her fist right back to her face. Without even thinking about it, she did it again and then again. The skin ripped open on her knuckles and blood spots stained the wall, but with each punch, her pain and anger disappeared as her satisfaction grew.

Bang! Bang!

A loud pounding on the door stopped her mid-punch.

"DonnaMae?" Paul's voice called through the door. "Mae, are you ok?"

"Shit," she grabbed a towel off the rack and wrapped it around herself quickly. "Yes, sorry I was just practicing my punches and —"

"At two AM you're practicing punching?" Paul asked through the door. "In the shower? What are you punching?"

She hadn't even thought about what time it was, or that she was making any noise. She was just so angry, and it felt so good to feel something other than helplessness. "Um, yeah sorry about that," she said, her eyes widening at the sight of blood smeared across her hand when she reached for the doorknob. She opened her hand and closed it a few times, feeling the slight ache in her fingers. "Ohh," she whispered with a wince, but a smile re-traced her lips as she watched a droplet of blood trickle down her hand.

"Mae, are you sure you're ok?" Paul asked again.

DonnaMae opened the door just a crack and steam seeped out. "Yeah, sorry, I had one of my bad dreams and then I went to take a shower and, I don't know, I just decided to practice my punching." She paused and let out a little laugh. "Yeah, I know it sounds crazy, bad idea. Sorry, I didn't think about the time or the noise. Go back to bed. I'm going to take a shower and make some tea and get some studying in before we go to the gym."

"Were you punching the wall?"

Silence hung in the air. She didn't know if she should answer.

"Mae, you are crazy. Do you ever sleep? One of these days it's going to catch up with you. You can't just go, go, go all the time, it's not normal."

"We all know I'm not normal," DonnaMae shrugged, tired of

hearing everyone tell her she was doing too much. The constant lectures on burnout were getting old. "Goodnight, Paul," she said, pulling the door closed with a smile she hoped was reassuring enough for him to leave her alone.

Paul could be a real butthead, especially when it came to DonnaMae's Disney movies, or whenever they played Monopoly and he was ruthless. But in his own way, he was family, the only real family she had out here. And she appreciated him for that. Since she'd moved, her own brother barely called, always busy with his life. Between his new job and new girlfriend, she never heard from him. Keeping her distance from people, even family, felt easier anyway. It was simpler to hide her pain, and to keep her secret tucked away. With Paul, it was different. They talked, but never dove into anything deep. He looked out for her, but never pushed to know more than she was willing to share. It was honestly nice.

DonnaMae let the towel fall in a puddle by her feet on the floor and stepped into the cascading water of the hot shower. Her focus remained on her hand as the water washed away the smears of blood, revealing raw knuckles where her punches had landed. As the sting in her hand eased, a strange comfort lingered. Pain wasn't foreign, it had been there her whole life: the loss of her mom, the teasing, the constant feeling of never being good enough. And then, when Charles shattered her, it left her feeling weaker than ever. But now, in a twisted way, the ache grounded her, making her feel almost stronger. She welcomed it, let it fuel her, reminding her she was still here and pushing forward. If she could, she'd go straight to the gym, but that wasn't an option tonight.

Instead, she'd throw herself into studying for her kinesiology vocab test, writing out terms to tape to her mirror and shadow-boxing her way through each one. It was time for her to start working on herself, rebuilding who she was.

After drying off, DonnaMae dug through her bathroom

drawer and found a tube of antiseptic cream and spread it over her knuckles. She knew she had a first aid kit in her car that had an ace bandage and gauze in it, but she was not going out to her car at this hour. She went over to her dresser, pulled out a long sock, wrapped it around her hand, and tied it at the top. "I knew I kept these damn cheer socks for a reason" she said out loud with a laugh, admiring her handiwork.

Pulling her books and index cards out of her backpack, she sprawled out on her bedroom floor and got to work.

<hr>

DonnaMae pulled into the parking lot of Sidekicks Gym. She was an hour early for class, but needed a break from studying and didn't want to go home. As she parked, a jaw-cracking yawn escaped her and the need to just close her eyes and take a power nap was almost overwhelming, but she wanted to learn the speed bag today before class.

DonnaMae had been training at the boxing gym for just over a month, and each punch, each kick made her feel more alive. Her body had grown leaner, her movements quicker, and the soreness in her muscles, the burn in her lungs, made her feel something and left her wanting more.

On Mondays and Wednesdays, she'd hit the kickboxing class at five, followed by the bootcamp at six-thirty. Sometimes, she stayed behind for extra training with one of the coaches, focusing on her punches. After Coach Joe finished teaching in the Dojo, he'd join them for some training. She hadn't quite figured him out yet. He was funny and approachable, but when it came time to learning, he was all business. There was a certain presence about him, almost fatherly, that made her want to say "yes, sir" whenever he spoke.

On Tuesdays and Thursdays, DonnaMae arrived early so Coach Che could work with her before the beginners' boxing class. This week, he had tested her for the advanced class, and she had passed with ease. The advanced classes involved real sparring drills, so she needed to buy a mouth guard. Still feeling unsure about jumping into sparring, she decided to hang back, watch the advanced class tonight, work on the heavy bag, and officially start next week, and she would buy a mouth guard this weekend.

Fighting off her fatigue, DonnaMae grabbed her bag and headed into the gym.

"Hey Mae, you're early," Coach Che called out as the door swung shut behind her.

"Yeah," she shrugged, dropping her bag at her feet, "I was struggling to keep my eyes open while studying, so I figured I'd come in and try to master the speed bag."

Che leaned back in his chair, a grin spreading across his face. "You ready for the advanced class tonight?"

"Not quite." She chuckled, brushing a hand through her hair as she glanced over at him in his tiki-bar-style office. The setup always made her feel like she could walk up and order advice like a drink. "I still need to buy a mouth guard. I'll just hang back and watch tonight."

Che raised an eyebrow and crossed his arms, his smile widening. "Mae, you've been hanging back and watching since you joined this place." He stood up and walked over to the tall cabinet in his office.

"I just want to be prepared," she said, shifting on her feet. She took a hesitant step towards him, figuring she might as well ask about the speed bag while she was there. "Do you have anything going on right now? Maybe you could —"

Before she could finish, Che tossed something at her. She dropped her keys and caught it with both hands, fumbling a little before securing it in her left hand. She glanced down at the small black rubber half-circle. "There you go," he said.

DonnaMae tucked her right hand into her pocket, careful not to draw attention to it. It was tightly taped beneath her wraps, and she wasn't ready to explain why. "What's this for?" she asked, flipping the rubber piece back and forth in her fingers. She could only assume it was a mouth guard, but it looked nothing like she had imagined. It was thin and soft.

"It's on the house. I buy them in bulk so my guys have extra if someone forgets one. Next time it's two dollars."

Staring at the black half-moon in her hand, DonnaMae's nerves flared. "So, uh... am I just supposed to —"

"You can use it as is for now, just for a few light contact drills, nothing too serious," he said with a quick shrug. "Tonight, toss it in boiling water for about 60 seconds, then bite down to mold it to fit."

She glanced back up at him, feeling a bit out of her element. "Oh, ok... I had no idea," she said, holding up the mouth guard, inspecting it closely. "I remember the football guys with those huge mouth guards hanging off their helmets, but this just feels... so small."

Che chuckled. "They might look different, but trust me, this one's all you need for now."

"Thanks, Coach," she said, offering him a quick smile before heading into the gym. She was grateful for the mouth guard, but the idea of joining the advanced class tonight wasn't exactly what she'd planned.

In the locker room, she re-wrapped her hands, layering a bit more padding over her right knuckles. Last week, she'd noticed a girl sporting purple wraps, and while the thought of having a bright color had seemed cool then, right now, she was glad for her plain black ones. They'd do a better job hiding any blood.

She checked the time on her phone as she crammed the rest of her stuff into her bag. Only fifteen minutes until class started. Tossing her phone inside, she rushed out to grab one of the better jump ropes before they were all gone.

The gym was already coming alive with guys shadowboxing, jumping rope, and hitting the speed bag. Coach Che was tonight's instructor, and he was already in the ring, running mitts with a guy with short red hair.

As the night went on, more guys trickled into the gym. Only three other girls were in the beginner class, and just one girl was part of the advanced class, and she was there for the workout, not to learn to fight. She never did the sparring.

DonnaMae grabbed her jump rope just as the bell turned yellow, signaling the last thirty seconds. She launched into high knees, driving them up towards her chest, pushing herself to her limit. When the bell finally rang, she paused, breathless. *Well, that's one way to warm up, she thought, her heart racing.*

DonnaMae had started wearing long-sleeved shirts to protect her arms. But she hardly got those whip lines from the jump rope anymore. She had the basics of jumping rope down and could even do high knees with little trouble. It was still tougher than she'd expected, but she enjoyed it more than running. So far, they'd only run outside once during class, just to the half-mile marker and back. She'd been the last person to return, and that didn't sit well with her, so she added running to her list of things to work on.

After three rounds of shadow boxing, Coach Che lined everyone up. A heavy silence filled the room, broken only by the sound of labored breathing. All eyes fixed on Che as he started pairing people off.

The guy next to DonnaMae had an oniony scent that reminded her of pulling fresh bulbs from her grandpa's garden, only much stronger. She turned her head for a breath of fresh air, half-considering suggesting to Che that he put free deodorant in the guys' locker room. Or maybe she'd just buy them all their own stick.

Once everyone was paired up, they spread out around the room. One partner wore the red mitts with white focus dots (small targets), daring each boxer to aim for dead center. The other partner tightened their gloves, raising them to guard their face, ready to strike.

"One!" Coach's voice cut through the room. A flurry of jabs snapped out as gloved fists struck mitts, each hit landing with a satisfying popping sound. "Two!" Che called. A cross, a heavier impact that sounded more like a thud. With each call, fists found their marks, echoing off the walls. After three rounds, they switched places. DonnaMae braced herself as her partner's punches met the mitts, her arms absorbing each strike, muscles burning from the weight.

The bell blared, kicking off the next round. Coach Che cranked up "Hella Good" by No Doubt, its beat blending with his commands as he barked out combos. Each number blurred into a storm of strikes, the sound of punches overpowering the song. For the final push, Coach called everyone down for a brutal burn-out exercise, designed to drain every last ounce of energy. DonnaMae's muscles quivered, her body protesting, but she forced herself to keep going. She sprawled to the floor, jumping up with a quick jab-cross into her partner's mitts while they held a squat. When time was called, they switched and then finished with a round of abs.

DonnaMae stretched out on her mat after finishing the last round of Rocky sit-ups, feeling the burn in her abs. She glanced up as a group of guys for the next class walked in. A flutter of nerves stirred in her. She stood up to put her mat away, trying to shake it off. Her partner today had been Kim, the one girl who regularly stayed for the advanced class. Kim was older, experienced, and really good. DonnaMae hoped that Coach Che would pair them up again.

She had planned to stay late, so she'd packed a peanut butter and jelly sandwich just in case, but as she stood in the locker room holding the sandwich in one hand and her mouthguard in the other, she hesitated. This class wasn't just about hitting the bag — she might actually get hit tonight. The thought of throwing up her sandwich mid-round wasn't appealing. With a sigh, she shoved the sandwich back in her bag. Her stomach grumbled with hunger as she wrapped her fingers tightly around her mouthguard. She picked up her gloves and turned to leave, when Kim walked in.

"I hear you're staying for the next class, kid," Kim said, walking over to her pink gym bag on the floor next to the lockers.

"Yeah, Che gave me this and said I was staying." DonnaMae held up the mouth guard and shrugged her shoulders.

Kim laughed. "Right. Don't worry, you're with me tonight. I don't do contact. I wear mine just in case one of those asshats slips up, but we're not hitting each other in the face."

DonnaMae felt her whole body relax. "That's great news, I was so —"

"Don't think that means I'll be going easy on you. This is advanced boxing, kid, be ready to put the work in. I've seen you watching the classes. You know what to expect." Kim dropped her bag back down, popped her mouth guard in, and headed towards the door. She gave DonnaMae a light tap on the shoulder with her gloved hand as she passed and mumbled something that sounded like "Free your mouth here."

She was gone before DonnaMae realized she had said "See you out there."

DonnaMae glanced back down at her mouth guard and shoved it into her mouth. It was incredibly uncomfortable. She bit down and moved it around on her teeth. She started to push her hand back into her glove when a sharp, searing pain shot through her knuckles. "Awwgh," she groaned, jolted by the reminder of how raw her right hand was. The wraps had crusted over her knuckles, and as she pressed the glove on, it tugged painfully, creating a tearing sensation. Taking a deep breath, she bit down hard and pushed her glove on, wincing as she tightened the velcro around her wrist. At least she knew it would go numb after the first few punches. There was something satisfying in forcing herself through this pain. Every punch was a choice, a step towards her own strength. Unlike the pain she hadn't chosen that haunted her dreams, this was hers to create, and hers to control.

Coach Che was running both classes tonight, and by the time they were into the first round of boxing, DonnaMae was feeling her groove. Kim wasn't holding anything back. She called numbers faster than DonnaMae had ever punched.

"One, one, two, five," Kim shouted. DonnaMae circled and started to throw and then paused as Che put his hand on her shoulder mid-throw of her right hand.

"You're pulling your punch with your right hand," Che said, pulling her hand back towards her face.

DonnaMae stood frozen. She was not a fan of being touched, let alone by a man that close to her with his hands on her. He was talking, but she couldn't hear anything he was saying. She didn't want to feel this fear, so she closed her eyes and bit down hard on her mouth guard, then opened her eyes, exhaled, and turned her gaze towards Che, trying to stay calm. "What?" she asked, trying to not spit at him with her mouth guard in.

"Throw your right hand again, but punch her mitt like you are trying to punch through it and then pull it back to your face... quickly," Che said.

DonnaMae stared at the mitt and just beyond it she saw an image of him and his beady little eyes, peering through his glasses at her. Acting on instinct, she punched her right hand forward, connecting with a snap to the mitt. Pain surged through her fingers, causing her to wince.

"Good! Now pull it back to your face. Always protect your face."

She threw again, feeling the impact of her punch landing squarely on the target, the pain satisfying as she quickly pulled her glove back to her face.

"Again, but this time five in a row," Che said, stepping behind her and placing his hands on her shoulders.

DonnaMae didn't freeze under his touch. This time it ignited her and she unleashed five more punches, and each landed perfectly.

"Damn, ok kid, nice," Kim said, dropping her arm and shaking it out after DonnaMae's last punch.

Che gripped his hands on her shoulders. "Nice job, you are built. Have you ever thought about fighting?"

"No," DonnaMae said and pulled her hands up, readying herself to go again. Then she paused. "Wait, what? Like, actually fighting?" She somehow managed to get her words out and keep her mouth guard in.

"Yes! Let's chat after class." Che gave her a good job pat on the shoulder and told them to keep going.

DonnaMae pushed the thought out of her mind, determined not to let it distract her focus. He had just recommended that she become a fighter — she couldn't look bad now.

After class, DonnaMae kept her hand wraps on as she walked out of the locker room and headed into Che's office. It was late, and the thought of having to study before bed felt impossible. Exhaustion pulled at her to go home and sleep, but she wanted to hear what Coach Che had to say about fighting.

"Coach, you wanted to chat after class?" she asked, walking up to his tiki-bar-style office.

Che looked up from some papers and smiled. "Mae, you did good tonight," he said, motioning for her to come in and take a seat at her desk. "What'd you think of advanced boxing?"

As she entered the office, she couldn't help but giggle at the beach mural gracing the back wall. Everyone left here with bruises and aching muscles, while this place looked like a vacation spot. "So, you think I could fight?"

Che laughed, leaning back in his chair. "Yes, I do. I've been watching you in here. You learn quickly, work hard, and you're strong. The real question is, do you want to —"

"YES!" DonnaMae cried. "Wait, I mean, I'll have to call my dad and ask. Not because I need his permission, I'm eighteen. But, you know, he pays for my school and stuff, so I should probably — wait, how much does it cost?"

"I think calling your dad is a great idea," Che chuckled at her excitement. "Before we get into all that, how about you come in, train, and try out sparring first? See if you've got what it takes to take a punch. Lots of people think they wanna fight, but it's a different story when you get hit."

DonnaMae's eyes grew wide. "Ok, so what do I have to do to train?"

"It won't be easy," Che said, standing up from his desk. "You'll be the only girl fighter, which means you'll be sparring with the guys."

"Oh, I can handle that," she said. "I was raised around all guys, drove race cars with all guys. Oh, sorry, I cut you off again."

Che smiled. "It's alright, you're excited, but you also look exhausted. Take the next few days off. We'll start training on Monday. Come in early before class, and we'll start with footwork."

DonnaMae stood up, the smile on her face impossible to hide. "Thank you, Coach. I won't let you down."

As she turned to leave, Che called after her, "And maybe stop and pick up some Epsom salt for that hand. Soak it when you get home."

DonnaMae glanced down at her right hand, noticing the dried, crusted blood on her fingers for the first time. *How did I not see that?* She wondered, before answering with a grin, "Yes, Coach."

CHAPTER 41

...

DonnaMae moved through her classes on autopilot, her mind lingering on last night when her coach asked her about becoming a fighter. During a break, she stopped by the cafeteria, filled a cup with hot water, and slipped in a tea bag from Cadlers; a small taste of home. The warm, familiar flavor stirred a sense of homesickness, bringing back memories of mornings at Cadlers with her friends. She found an empty corner table and put on her headphones without music to keep anyone from trying to chat. That Cassie girl was nowhere in sight, sparring DonnaMae from any awkward small talk she wasn't ready for.

With a sigh, she pulled out her textbooks and notebook, letting herself sink into the words and formulas while her mind half-wandered into imagining what it would be like to train as a real fighter.

In her last class, DonnaMae couldn't help but glance at the clock every few minutes, counting down until she would be free to call her dad and tell him everything. She had been too tired last night to talk, and after her bath it was too late for anything but sleep. Today was a short day, and thankfully she had the afternoon off from the gym, Coach's orders.

She called her dad on the drive home, spilling every detail about her coach's offer and the idea of fighting for real. Her dad's words matched her coach's: "Try it out first, and we can go from there." But she could tell he was excited, the spark in his voice lighting her fire even more. This wasn't like racing. This was something different, something she had found for herself, not something that ran in her family, but her own discovery. And it was something her dad could come to watch her do.

Crisp fall air greeted DonnaMae as she stepped out of her truck, her boots crunching on a thin layer of leaves blanketing the ground. Her body ached, but she welcomed it. She curled her hand into a fist, inspecting her knuckles. The scabs had hardened. A faint bruising remained, but the pain was a shadow now. Opening the door to her apartment, she felt a rush of energy. She was home for the day, but she wanted to be at the gym training, not home studying.

She pulled her books and flash cards out of her bag, but as she settled in on her bed, the sound of wind rustling through leaves outside kept drawing her attention. Feeling restless, she thought maybe another cup of hot tea would help. She left her room and headed to the kitchen, mixing in a little shadow boxing as she went, dancing around the kitchen in her socks, dodging imaginary punches until the kettle whistled, her cue to rest. She fixed her tea and went back to her room. Unable to resist the urge to train, she set her cup on her nightstand, tied her hand wraps around her ankles, and began practicing her footwork around her room. Alternating between three minutes of footwork and three minutes of flashcards, she felt satisfied at her creative combo of physical and mental practice. On her fifth round, she heard a knock on her half-closed door.

"Hey, is there a—" Paul pushed open the door and paused at the sight of her bare feet tethered together. "What are you doing?" he asked with raised eyebrows and a half laugh.

"I'm studying. What does it look like I'm doing?" DonnaMae said, shrugging with her hands in the air.

"What are you studying? Cause that looks like you're studying how to kidnap yourself. Or —" He laughed again, waving his other idea off. "Yeah, never mind, let's stick with that." Paul shook his head.

"I'm working on my footwork. And did you know the human nervous system is made up of three basic parts: the central nervous system, the peripheral nervous system, and the autonomic nervous system? And right now, I'm learning all about the central nervous system and how you are probably missing parts of yours." DonnaMae shot him a quick smile.

Paul rolled his eyes. "Well, I was coming to give you your mail," Paul flung an offwhite envelope like a frisbee across the room. It landed on her bed. "And I was going to watch the first *Rocky* movie and I wanted to know if you wanted to take a break from — umm — whatever this is —" Paul gestured towards DonnaMae and the mess of flash cards and shoes she had laid on the floor as a makeshift boxing ring, "— and watch a non-Disney movie with me. I made way too much popcorn and —"

"You had me at popcorn. I'm starving." DonnaMae didn't even stop to look at the mail or untie her feet. She pushed past Paul and shuffled down the hall towards the kitchen, grabbing the Peanut Butter M&M's to add to the popcorn, before joining Paul in the living room. She chuckled to herself, thinking of Ella covered in melted chocolate every time they ate this.

DonnaMae had watched *Rocky* once before, but this time it felt different. She saw the story from a whole new perspective. She watched how Rocky's feet moved and how he threw combinations, jab cross, jab, jab cross. It took everything in her not to get up and start throwing the combinations right along with him.

DonnaMae hadn't even stepped into the ring yet and she was already filled with an energy she had never experienced before. She wished she could go to the gym right then and start fight training. She wanted to go for another run and bring hand weights and punch with every step. She wanted to be able to do the speed bag just like Rocky. Hell, she wanted to train so hard that she'd know when she stepped into the ring she would win. She knew it was just a movie, but the way Rocky could take a punch and never give up hit home with Donna-Mae. She felt like she and Rocky had something in common; she had taken hits her whole life. But now here she was, getting back up and fighting, not just to be in a ring, but to get her life back.

The credits rolled, and DonnaMae stared at the screen. If Rocky could do it, so could she. She could step into the ring with a bunch of guys and throw punch for punch with them. She could still be a girl and train like a guy, and she would. And she would fight to get herself back.

"Earth to DonnaMae? You ok?" Paul's voice echoed through the living room, catching her attention.

"Yeah, I was just contemplating the movie and my fight training," she said with enthusiasm. "I'm really excited about beginning my training."

"So, is that a yes or no to watching the next movie?"

"Oh, I didn't even hear you ask me that." She laughed. "I want to tell you yes, but I should get ready for my test on Monday. Maybe after a while we can watch another one for a study break?"

Paul smiled and stood up. "Sounds like a plan. I have shit I need to get done today anyway, and," Paul glanced back down at her feet, "you should also probably untie those before you do anything else."

DonnaMae jumped up from the couch, landed in her boxing stance, and threw a quick jab cross in the air off to the side of Paul's face. "Are you kidding me? Did you not just watch the same movie as I did? I'm going to sleep in these! Footwork is the foundation and I am —"

Paul laughed. "Ok, ok, have fun with that," he said, waving her off as she bounced back and forth on her toes. "Just don't jump around too hard, or our downstairs neighbors will complain."

"Light on your feet is key, float like a bee, sting like a — wait, I have that backwards. It's float like a..." she trailed off as Paul walked out of the room laughing.

DonnaMae shuffled her way back down the hall to her room. Walking through the door, she laughed at the sight of her flash cards scattered everywhere. She bent down to pick them up. *Damn, so much for not being sore,* she thought, giving in to the ache in her legs and collapsing to the floor. While she freed her feet from the wraps, her attention shifted to the thick anatomy book in front of her. The thought of a hot Epsom salt bath accompanied by a not-so-entertaining read seemed like a marvelous idea.

DonnaMae rose to her feet slowly, her body feeling as if it had aged to eighty over the last hour. With her book tightly clutched in one hand, she used the other to grip the bed, struggling to pull herself up from the floor. She grabbed her hidden supply of chocolates tucked away in her nightstand and headed to the bathroom.

Warm and relaxed from her bath and ready to call it a night, DonnaMae pulled her covers back from her bed. The envelope Paul had given her fell to the floor. She paused, picked it up, and carefully opened it. Inside, she found a letter.

Mae,

Happy Fall, can't wait to see you soon! We're all so excited for Thanksgiving and the annual alumni dance! Everyone is coming home, and we're all getting ready at Izzy's new place. We keep missing each other, so I figured I would write you and let you know our plan.

School was a whirlwind of activity, and I'm having a blast. Classes are challenging but fascinating, and keeping me on my toes. Not going to lie, there are tons of hot guys in all my classes, but I'm playing the single life. It's great to be back home, though. There's something special about our hometown that makes everything feel perfect this time of year. Well, except maybe the corn maze. I don't plan on going this year. I still can't believe your brother talked us into doing the haunted one last year, and that guy at the end with the chainsaw, and me peeing my pants! YIKES! Thank goodness for your jacket to wrap around my waist.

Anyway, I just love our hometown. I'm pretty sure this is where I will end up one day, with kids and a...... hahaha, I guess I have to date for that part.

Anywho, I stopped by Cadlers the other day and Fran asked how you were doing. She said she misses seeing you around and hopes you're settling in well. She told me that she thinks of you often and sends her love. It was nice to see her and to have her famous Monster Cookie.

Please let us know if you're coming home for the holidays. We all want to hear all about your new adventures and how you are doing. The girls said they can't get ahold of you either. We all miss you and hope you are doing well and just being your crazy busy self. The annual alumni dance is just around the corner, and it won't be the same without you there.

I miss you, Mae.

Love,

Ella

DonnaMae read the letter twice, feeling a pang of homesickness. She missed her friends deeply and was drawn to the idea of being with them, the way things used to be. But the thought of returning home stirred emotions she wasn't ready to face yet.

Guilt weighed on her. She had avoided going home — she was unprepared to face her past and the people who knew her best. She had found it easy to avoid their calls and had called back at the worst time of day so she could just leave a voicemail. If they answered, she said hi and talked for just a few seconds and then pretended like her call dropped or she ran out of minutes. The shame of her past built a wall, and the longer she stayed away, the higher it became and the easier it was to hide behind it. The idea of attending the alumni dance was even more daunting — Charles would certainly be there, and she couldn't bear the thought of encountering him, just thinking of his name made her whole body shiver.

DonnaMae folded Ella's letter and slipped it back into the envelope before setting it aside. She laid on her bed, staring at the ceiling. Maybe tomorrow she would write back and say she couldn't go anyway because she was training now and could not afford to take time off.

CHAPTER 42

December, 2002

December twenty-first. DonnaMae stared at the calendar, the red circle around the date glaring back at her. Tomorrow marked twelve years since her mom had passed; the day her whole world flipped. She could still remember that morning like it was yesterday, every detail etched in her mind. It was the kind of memory she kept going back to, like pressing a bruise, knowing it would only hurt. With Christmas right around the corner, she braced for the ache that would come.

She used to love this time of year — her dad had always tried to make it fun, likely masking his own pain from losing his wife around the holidays. But now, Christmas felt more like a reminder of everything she'd lost, everything she didn't want to be around, couldn't be around. She had finally settled into a new routine, a life that kept people at a distance and silenced her thoughts, but now the holidays were here to mess everything up.

She dreaded the way people would look at her, their pity unhidden. *Oh, you're going to be alone for the holidays?* The question she hated. But being alone was her choice, just like on Thanksgiving, when she had chosen to be on her own and actually had a pretty decent day. Well, mostly.

Paul and the rest of her family had tried convincing her to come home, but she'd told them she had training the next morning, which she couldn't miss. It wasn't entirely a lie. It was just a turkey burn boot camp at the gym, but it counted as training. Plus, she needed to log some volunteer hours for school, so she took on organizing the registration for the school's fundraiser turkey trot. It didn't require her to attend the event or interact much with anyone — she just had to get everything set up early that morning. That was the excuse she gave, and it had worked.

She'd picked up a turkey dinner from a local holistic grocery store: a turkey thigh, stuffing, and mashed potatoes, simple to put in the oven. She knew how to make gravy, thanks to her dad, who made gravy out of everything. After her morning of volunteering, she came home, put the turkey in the oven, set the potatoes aside in a pot ready to warm, and grabbed out the can of cranberry sauce, the good kind with real cranberries. Then, she'd soaked in a hot bath.

When she got out, the apartment smelled like burnt plastic. When she'd opened the oven, she was met with a cloud of black smoke setting the alarm off. She'd opened the doors and windows, fanned the smoke away, and pulled out her shrink-wrapped-in-melted-plastic turkey. She'd assumed the tray was oven safe, like the old TV dinners she remembered from when she was a kid. She was wrong. With all the stores closed, her Thanksgiving dinner had been reduced to a sad mix of potatoes and cranberry sauce.

As she'd dumped the ruined food in the trash, she'd spotted a Chinese takeout menu. Chow mein and chicken fried rice were the perfect solution. She'd ended her Thanksgiving with takeout and a binge session of season one of *Gilmore Girls*. Not a bad day after all. It wasn't often that she wasn't training or studying or on the move one way or another.

But Christmas was going to be harder to avoid. With two weeks off from school, everyone was heading home for winter break. Izzy, Ella, and Hazel had already sent DonnaMae letters and phone calls, asking when she'd be back. So far, she'd managed to avoid a direct answer, throwing out vague "I don't knows" and "lots going on." But really, she didn't have anything, and Paul knew it. He bugged her about being here alone for a week. "We live in an apartment, not the dorm rooms, I will be fine," she had told him. And truthfully, having the apartment to herself sounded nice.

Maybe she'd just go home for Christmas Day, drive in, stay the night, and head back on the twenty-sixth. That way, she'd still have time to bring flowers to her mom on her birthday, but not enough time to visit anyone but family. It could be a quick visit, a round trip from her dad's house right back to her new life, and with Christmas being on a Wednesday it worked. But just thinking about it left her feeling exhausted and overwhelmed. She walked away from the calendar, packed her gym bag, and headed out the door.

"Last Christmas" by Wham! drifted through the kickboxing gym lobby, feeling out of place to DonnaMae. Garlands draped the mirrors, and a wreath hung on the door, all reminders of the season she would rather forget. She and Paul hadn't even bothered with a tree in the apartment. All she wanted was for this season to pass quietly, to make each day feel as close to normal as possible, but the lights twinkling around the doorway were not helping.

She was the first student there, just as she had been every day for the past three weeks since her coach had asked her if she wanted to fight. Coach Che was at his desk on the phone. He nodded as she walked by and she waved back before peering into the Dojo, hoping to find her other coach, Joe. The room was empty. She paused, taking in the quiet Dojo. Then it hit her. It was Friday; no karate classes, only fight night. She'd been so wrapped up in thinking about tomorrow that she'd forgotten what was coming today: her first sparring match. Tonight wasn't just about throwing punches — she was here to prove she could take them, too.

DonnaMae walked to the girls' locker room and dropped her

bag on the bench, taking a deep breath. She was the only girl who showed up for fight night, and tonight would be her first time actually stepping into the ring. Every inch of her body ached. Last night's mitt drills had gone on for twelve brutal rounds after two back-to-back classes. This morning in Anatomy, her hands were so sore she had to rely on her recorder for notes, barely able to hold a pencil. Thankfully, it was the last day of classes before winter break and there wasn't much note taking.

Over the past few weeks, her training had ramped up to a whole new level. Che had her working on footwork drills, tying her feet together with a rope so they couldn't go further than a hip's width apart. She pushed through intense mitt work, each punch expected to land exactly where Che wanted it or she had to throw it again. Joe took her through rounds of rapid punches, pushing her speed until her arms felt ready to drop, only to make her slow down and focus on perfect form right after.

She learned to brace against the hits, blocking shots with her arms and absorbing the rest through bodywork drills. Some rounds were all about blocking, her forearms bearing the brunt. Other rounds, she had to keep her hands raised high, breathing through the flurry of light punches Che threw her way.

Each day, she pushed through exhaustion, soreness, and the new aches that came with throwing a proper punch and dodging one. Tonight, it would all be put to the test. She wouldn't just be throwing punches, but taking them, facing an opponent, one of the guys.

There was no way she was going to let anyone know how sore she was. "If you're going to punch a guy, you'd better be ready to take a punch like a guy," her dad's words played in her head as she pulled her hand wraps and gloves out of her bag. She shoved the rest of her stuff into the locker and walked out to the hardwood floor.

"Back for more, huh champ?" Che asked, leaning against the bar used to practice kicks on the mirrored wall.

"Champ? I haven't won anything," DonnaMae said.

"And with that attitude, you won't!" Coach Joe said, walking in through the double doors to the gym.

Joe was still in his work clothes, holding his gym bag at his side. "You train like a champ, kid," Che said, a smile tugging at the corner of his mouth. "I don't think I've ever seen anybody work as hard as you. I got guys all over this place I wish had half the heart and drive you've got."

DonnaMae blushed.

"And after last night's drills, we're honestly both surprised you're here tonight," Joe said, tilting his head.

"But you guys said I could spar tonight. And no pain no gain, right, Coach? That's what you said." DonnaMae turned to Che as she started wrapping her hands.

"Right, champ!" Che said, walking over, picking up her half-wrapped hand and taking over.

"Right," said Coach Joe, "but, practice doesn't make perfect —"

"Perfect practice makes perfect," DonnaMae finished for him. "How do I get perfect if I don't practice and learn to push through when I'm tired? Besides who said I was tired anyway?" She pushed away any thoughts of exhaustion with a mental reminder of her reward she had waiting for her at home: She had upgraded her bathroom to a personal spa, complete with candles, relaxing teas, bath oils and lavender Epsom salt. Tonight's addition was a refreshing face mask and a new Jane Green book she'd found as a CD audio version, and as long as she didn't drop her disc-man in the bathtub she would be fine. "Today is the day we see if I have what it takes to be a fighter, not just train like one, and I'm ready to take a hit and give one back," DonnaMae said, smiling from ear to ear.

Joe just shook his head and smiled. "Ok, champ, let's see what you got."

She had come in a few times to watch fight night and just work the heavy bag, and to practice the speed bag. She hated that thing more — it made her feel so stupid, but she promised herself she would never give up, so no matter how many times she wanted to quit and walk away, she always got her three rounds in on the speed bag, even if it hit her more times than she hit it.

But tonight she was not going to be hitting a bag and watching. She was going to be sparring. The thought excited her, but also made her stomach churn. She suddenly felt like she was going to be sick and she hadn't even started to warm up yet. As DonnaMae took down the jump rope, she tried to shake off her growing nausea.

The first guy walked in. He was a little taller than DonnaMae, and maybe a few years older. He glanced at DonnaMae and then back to Che. "*¿Está luchando? ¿No está muy chica?*" he asked Che as he walked by towards the locker room.

Her coach laughed, "*¡Si, pero está muy brava! Mas vale que te cuides.*"

Wishing she had taken more Spanish classes in high school, DonnaMae waited for the bell to turn green, battling the knots in her stomach. She forced herself to focus on stretching, pulling her right foot behind her and then switching to the left as another guy strolled in, his massive frame taking up what felt like half the room. He wore a worn white t-shirt that clung to his dark skin, looking as if it had never been washed. She watched him greet Che with a handshake that shifted into a hug, every muscle in his arm flexing. It was clear he'd been away for a while. She had never seen him here before.

Another guy walked in, pale and tall with a shock of red hair, right behind Fernando, her partner from last night. Quick on his feet and clearly experienced, Fernando was solid, but she hadn't realized he was part of the fight team. Wait, was there even a fight team here? Her heart leaped as she wondered for the first time if these guys were actual fighters, or did they just show up on Friday nights to let off steam and pound each other? The thought churned her stomach even more. She was so new to all of this, so far from fully understanding the place and its people. Her hand grew clammy, slipping slightly as she gripped her shoe. She steadied herself as best she could.

"Mae, you going to jump rope to warm up, or just stand there stretching one leg?" Che yelled at her from across the room. The bell had rung, and she didn't even notice. She blushed and quickly started jumping.

"Alright," Che's voice drew the focus of every person in the room, "everyone gets in three rounds of jump rope and three rounds of shadow boxing to warm up. Then put your gloves on and do two more rounds of shadow boxing." He nodded towards Joe, "Coach Joe and I will come around and hold mitts for you individually."

While Che was talking, a few more guys trickled in. Joe was now on the bike warming up not too far from DonnaMae, so she slowly inched her way closer to him. There was something about him that made her feel safe, almost a dad-like feeling. He was strict and didn't put up with anyone screwing off in class — she had even seen him get so mad once he kicked someone out of his class, but he also had an heir of protection about him that comforted her and she wasn't sure why.

"Mae, tell me about your day," Coach Joe said as the bell rang yellow.

DonnaMae stopped jumping "What?"

"I didn't say stop jumping. In fact, yellow means faster. High knees, go, go, go!" he barked with his serious coach voice.

Confused, DonnaMae kicked it into overdrive and jumped as fast as she could, driving her knees higher towards her chest with every jump, and Joe pumped hard on the bike with her until the bell rang. DonnaMae slowed to a stop and sucked in a deep breath. "Sorry Coach, I —"

"When I ask you a question, don't stop what you're doing. Just answer my question."

"Yes, Coach." The bell rang again but she was already jumping. It seemed to be helping her nerves.

"Now tell me about your day while you jump," Coach Joe said again. "Talking while you work is good for you, remember?"

DonnaMae laughed at that. "Well, if there's one thing I'm good at, it's talking. Are you sure you want me to talk? My dad says once I start talking I don't know how to stop."

"Well, you only have two more rounds, so you had better start talking," Joe said, letting out a breathless laugh.

DonnaMae did just that — she talked through her two rounds of jumping and her three rounds of shadow boxing, and when it came time to burn it out for thirty seconds DonnaMae talked faster and pushed harder.

"Where is your mouth, guard?" Che asked when he walked up to DonnaMae, who was still talking and punching even though the bell was red.

"Oh, it's right here," DonnaMae tugged the mouth guard from the top of her hand wrap. She had tucked it there when she'd started talking. "Coach said for me to talk and I didn't want to spit all over him."

Che shot her a puzzled look, pausing as she caught her breath. "Stop for a sec," he said. "Catch your breath and put in your mouth guard."

DonnaMae slipped the guard between her teeth.

Che continued, crossing his arms as he sized her up. "We're doing mitts first. You'll be the first in the ring, and you're going with Fernando." He nodded towards the far wall, where a bunch of ragged, blood-stained helmets hung. "After mitts, grab some headgear that fits and get ready to spar."

Before she could react or question anything, the bell rang green.

"Hands up, Mae! Protect yourself at all times," Che ordered, tapping her head with the side of his mitt.

"One — one — two — three — slip — three — two," Che called, circling her, forcing her to adjust her footing with each step.

DonnaMae ran through the combo in her mind, then fired off the punches, each one landing squarely as she slipped his jab, just in time.

"Good. Again," he said, his voice calm.

This time, she moved quicker, throwing the combination and nearly slipping his punch before it even came. Knowing it was coming, her body was a half-second ahead.

"Good," Che said, his expression tightening into a slight grin. "But don't get too comfortable. It's not about knowing what's coming, it's about reacting. One more time."

She nodded, resetting her stance. This went on for half of the round and then he hit her on the shoulder with the mitt, "Go get ready to spar."

DonnaMae was out of breath but felt good. The ache in her arms had faded, and she was ready. Each step to the headgear, she felt her nerves kicking in. It was the same way she felt buckling herself into her race car, and sure enough, she had to pee, except this time her pit crew wasn't there to tell her to just drive fast and go after. Her uncle wasn't beside her, reassuring her that she'd do fine. This time, she was on her own.

She pulled a slightly bulky helmet from the rack. The outside was bright red, while the inside was a dull gray and smelled like dirty socks. Turning it over in her hands, she noticed faded splatters of blood along the cheek pads. The thing looked like something straight out of *American Gladiators,* except it was a little more horror movie than TV.

"You need help with that?" Joe's deep voice startled her from behind.

She turned to see him watching her with a half-smile. "Um, yeah... actually, I just need to use the restroom really quick." Right now, she wasn't sure if she needed to pee, puke, or if she was going to pass out. But she needed to go.

"Nah, those are just nerves. You'll be fine," Joe said, taking the headgear out of her hands.

"No, I —" Before she could say anything else, he was pushing the headgear onto her head, smashing her ponytail down so hard she thought it might rip out of her head. She winced and bit down on her mouth guard.

He then pulled her ponytail through the top of the headgear, pulled some straps on the sides, and then buckled it under her chin. "There, that should work. I'll be in your corner after each round. You'll sit on the stool I put out for you and I'll give you some water." He held out a bottle of water that had a long spout on the top. "We're going light, sixty percent, not punching to knock out the other person, just punching to learn."

DonnaMae was sure if she got punched in the stomach it was going to end the fight, and not because she lost, but because they were going to need to call for clean up on aisle nine.

Joe stepped on the bottom rope of the ring so she could climb in. By this time, all the fighters were around the ring, waiting to watch, and Che was in the other corner talking to Fernando.

"Ok, when you're in the ring, I might call things out. Try to shut everything else out so you can hear what I'm saying to you. Listen for my voice," Joe said as DonnaMae backed up against the red post in the corner of the ring.

Che stepped into the ring to join them. "Opponents, please, touch gloves," he said, waving them both forward to step in front of him.

Fernando reached both his gloved hands out in front of him and DonnaMae reached hers out to tap his.

"Take it easy, nice and slow the first round, just feel each other out. Work on footwork and light punching. Keep your hands up." Che tapped their gloves. "Back to your corners," he said, and he stepped out of the ring. He walked over to the timer and reset it.

If DonnaMae thought she was nervous before, that was nothing compared to how she felt now. "Let your fear fuel you," she whispered, exhaling slowly and shutting her eyes. "Feel my fear, use its energy to fight," she silently reminded herself.

The bell rang, Che yelled "Fight!"

Her eyes flew open, she jumped into her fighting stance and pulled her hands up to her face. She stayed on her toes and bounced around Fernando. She could hear everyone yelling "Punch!" or "One, two!" She circled left and he followed her, but he didn't move as much as she did. She focused on moving around the ring using her foot work. She stepped in close to throw a jab and took his right hand straight to the face. It wasn't a powerful punch. She didn't stop moving, she took the punch like it was nothing. "Hands up," she heard from somewhere, so she pulled her fists close just in time to block a hook to her head that made her teeth clinch hard on her mouth guard. *Damn, this was sixty percent,* she thought.

She moved around, in and out, and threw a jab, but Fernando slipped it and countered with a light right tap on her shoulder. She tried again, and the same thing happened. She went back to bouncing around him until the bell rang yellow and she knew that meant burn it out, but how was she supposed to do that in the ring? She circled Fernando and bounced around faster.

He didn't punch, he moved with her until the final bell rang.

She went back to her corner, out of breath, and sat down on the red stool. "Could you not hear me?" Joe asked, pulling her mouth guard out of her mouth as she gulped in air. And then, before she could answer, he squeezed the funny-looking bottle against her mouth, giving her water. "Slow down out there. You're going to burn yourself out. Try punching this time." Joe put the mouth guard back into her mouth and the bell rang. In what felt like the blink of an eye, the minute was over. She stood while he left the ring with the stool.

"Let's go, more punching this time, Fernando. How are we going to know if she wants to fight if you don't give her a little taste," Che yelled from outside the ring.

"But she's a girl," one guy called out from the side of the ring. "Our mamas raised us to not hit girls."

Fuck that, DonnaMae thought, stepping in towards Fernando and pulling her gloves up to her face. "Let's go!" she said through her clenched teeth.

DonnaMae sidestepped to the left and then to her right, just as Fernando's left hook connected hard with her head. The hook caught her off guard, causing her to stumble slightly. She had her hands up, so her glove took the brunt of the impact. She paused to shake it off and collect herself, causing her to lower her guard and leaving her wide open.

Fernando seized the opportunity, delivering a powerful punch straight to her face.

DonnaMae stumbled back a step.

"Come on, Coach, don't make him beat up the pretty little girl," she heard a voice laugh through the slight ringing in her ear. Her vision was blurred from the punch.

Fernando threw another blow to her side that knocked the wind out of her, buckling her forward.

"The poor thing has had enough. Girls don't belong in a ring." Another cackle from the sidelines.

A scene from the movie *Rocky* flashed through her mind. "Stand up and punch, Mae!" she heard her coach Joe yell.

So, she did. She snapped upright and threw a straight jab cross, bounced out of reach, and then back in and punched again. This time, she threw multiple punches to Fernando's head and then his body, and when he dropped his hands to protect his body she went for his head again. He fought back and she ate a few of his punches to get back in and work his body. Another hard blow to her mouth, blood dripped from her lip and curled on her tongue. She fired more than one back to make him pay. Every time he hit her, it gave her more energy to hit back twice as hard with twice as many punches. When she wasn't throwing punches, she was bouncing around the ring like a jack rabbit.

The sound of the guys yelling filled the air as she and Fernando exchanged punches, blow for blow.

Che seemed to appear out of thin air, forcefully wedging himself between them, breaking them apart and yelling, "Enough! To your corners, fighters, the bell rang."

DonnaMae backed up to her corner, ready to sit down, but there was no stool. Instead, Joe was stepping on one of the ropes to let her out of the ring. "Why — are we — stopping?" DonnaMae sputtered out between gasps.

Joe unbuckled her head gear and walked her over to the wall lined with mirrors.

Her body was taken over by a tingling sensation, her arms felt heavy as she pulled off her headgear and asked again, "Why did we stop?" She took another breath in, "I thought we were going three rounds?"

Joe turned towards the mirrors and tipped his head, motioning for her to look.

DonnaMae followed his gaze. Her white cut-off t-shirt was covered in splatters of blood, and when she looked closer, she could see it was all over her face, even matting parts of her hair. Her nose and lip were bleeding. She looked like she had just been in a fist fight with Edward Scissorhands.

"It's just a bloody nose," she said, lifting the hem of her shirt to wipe off as much blood as she could. "I've been getting them since I was five. I've had my nose cauterized six times," she laughed, "this is nothing."

"Do you get fat bloody lips all the time as well? And that will turn into a nice little black eye if you don't get some ice on it," Joe said, pointing at her left eye.

Che approached with a handful of paper towels. "Well, champ, you proved you can take a punch and still punch back."

"For your first time in the ring, you did great," Joe said, taking the towels from Che before Che went back to the fighters. "But you've got a lot to learn, and one big thing is control. You can't just bulldoze your opponent." Joe threw a glance over his shoulder. "I heard what the guys were saying, and it won't stop. There aren't a lot of girl fighters out there. You can't let it get to you, or start throwing wild punches." Joe held out a towel to her. "Boxing is like chess."

DonnaMae grumbled, taking a towel from his hand, pinching her nose, and tipping her head back. "I don't even know how to play chess." She let out a half laugh, "Trust me, I'm used to guys saying I can't do things."

"You don't have to know how to play chess," Joe said. "It's about being smart, planning two steps ahead, and waiting for the moment your opponent slips up. When they do, you make your move and take them down."

"So, what the hell have I been doing?" She tilted her head forward, giving Joe a questioning look. "I thought I was training like a fighter."

He chuckled, "You've been working out. Learning the ropes. Real training starts Monday."

DonnaMae huffed and turned towards the locker room. "Great," she mumbled under her breath.

***

DonnaMae lay in bed, a frozen bag of peas pressed against her swollen cheek. Her whole body ached like she had come down with the flu after a grueling workout. A bath had been too much effort. Even her shower had felt like a challenging task. She was glad that tomorrow held no obligations, no training, no classes, just a chance to sleep.

"You did good, champ. You have what it takes to be a fighter, that's for sure." Che's words repeated in her mind as she drifted off to sleep.

CHAPTER 43

...

After two days of rest and a handful of Epsom salt baths, DonnaMae felt surprisingly recovered. She was still sore from head to toe, and a faint black eye lingered just above her cheekbone, barely noticeable but still tender when she pressed on it. The ache in her face was a dull reminder of her first sparring session, but it didn't bother her much compared to Saturday morning when she'd felt like she had been run over by a semi truck. A flicker of nerves lingered as she thought about what her coaches meant by "real training." She couldn't help but wonder just how much harder it would get.

She hopped out of her truck into a crisp winter morning. The air was chilly, but the sun warmed her skin. Pulling her thick blonde hair into a ponytail, she felt a thrill spark through her. Sparring had stirred something deeper, something different from what the boxing classes had ignited. It was like the freedom she felt racing down the track. But this time, it wasn't about escaping. She was fighting, not just for the sport in the ring, but to reclaim herself: Not the girl she had been before, but someone newer, stronger. Someone who wouldn't be pushed around.

She slammed the door shut, tightened her shoelaces, and

decided a run would be the perfect warm up before training. It was beautiful outside. It hadn't rained all weekend and was not supposed to rain for the next few days, which was rare this time of year in the Pacific Northwest. DonnaMae laced her keys between her fingers, making a fist around her canister of mace. Her thumb traced over the trigger as she whispered, "One day, I won't need you," with a smile before setting off at an easy jog.

DonnaMae noticed a group of high school kids making their way along the trail, their laughter and chatter filling the air as they strolled towards whatever winter break adventure awaited them. It had been a while since thoughts of the after school program crossed her mind. She missed the kids, the programs built from scratch, and her friends there. The memories tugged at her heart, but her reality felt miles away from them.

She still loved getting letters from her friends, and once in a while, she would hop on a call, long enough to hear their voices and catch up, but keeping it light and surface-level before finding a reason to end the conversation. She wasn't strong enough to face them, not strong enough to let them see the failure she felt she had become. The thought of disappointing them, of being a burden, made it easier to stay distant.

Lost in thought, DonnaMae nearly missed the one-mile marker and was surprised by how easy the run felt. *Three miles sounds good,* she thought, remembering the mile-and-a-half turn-around up ahead. Her body felt alive, the soreness turning into an energy she hadn't felt in weeks. Her smile grew. A sense of lightness filled her, carrying her forward.

As DonnaMae rounded a bend, she caught the faint sound of a scream that made her heart skip a beat. At first, she wasn't sure if she'd imagined it, but then it came again, louder, sharp and clear: "STOP! DON'T!"

Her pulse quickened.

The scream came again, louder. "I said STOP!"

DonnaMae picked up her pace. It was a girl screaming. *Stop, don't! Please stop.* The words echoed in her ears. The crash of the ocean roared in her ears, drowning out all other sounds. In the distance she could see a girl with long dark hair yelling at a taller, boyish figure. Her lungs burned as she sprinted past the half mile point, closing in on them.

The girl reached up and pushed the boy. He grabbed her arm.

DonnaMae opened her mouth to scream, but nothing came out. They were on a patch of grass in front of a parking lot, a low brick wall separating them from the trail. *Stop, Don't!* the sound of her own voice was so loud in her head. She tightened her grip on the mace, sizing up the wall to jump it. She had to help. She had to save that girl. She ran faster and leaped over the wall, landing like she was running the one-hundred meter Olympic hurdle, and with the next step her leg buckled and she tripped over nothing, landing face down in the grass.

"Are you ok?" the girl knelt down next to DonnaMae. "Jake, go get mom. She might be hurt."

Go get mom. Go get mom... they're just siblings, DonnaMae thought, finally allowing herself to take in a much-needed deep breath. "I'm ok, I just thought, I... " she trailed off. *Please stop!* The words still rang in her ears. She quickly pushed up to sitting and looked around.

"Miss, are you sure you're ok?" the girl asked, her gaze fixed on DonnaMae's leg.

DonnaMae followed her stare and saw the rip in her pants and the blood trickling down her knee. She wasn't standing in grass, she was standing on a gravel path, and she had landed on rocks. She felt a little dizzy. "It's just a minor scrape. I'm fine," she managed to get out. She spotted a drinking fountain in the clearing and pulled herself to her feet. "I just needed a drink. Thank you for asking." Pain shot up her leg as she walked to the fountain. *Walk it off,* she told herself. *You are fine.*

The water came out of the fountain slowly and she took a drink, her lungs feeling like she had walked out of a burning building full of smoke. She coughed and took another drink. Then, cupping her hands, she filled them with water and splashed it on her face, then her knee. It was a pretty good gash, but she would not let it stop her. Rolling up the leg of her pants and stopping on the cut, she created a makeshift bandage and tourniquet at the same time. She smiled at her quick fix, but the smile faded fast when she got a gut feeling that someone was watching her.

With a sudden shiver, she hurried back to the safety of the trail. *Shit, two miles to get back, she thought.* The pain had already faded some, and she went from a walk to a light jog, but the fear had not faded. With every step anger simmered inside of her. The roar of the ocean was back in her ears and she picked up her pace. She wanted to feel her lungs burn, she wanted to feel pain, something other than fear. Her pace quickened, and the image of his slithering hands and beady eyes haunted her thoughts. She pushed herself faster this time, throwing punches as she ran, pulling each punch back tight to her face, protecting herself in the only way she knew how. Her coach's voice pushed its way though the sound of the ocean, "One, two, three... good. Again." Her leg throbbed and her lungs were on fire, but she would not stop.

DonnaMae nearly collapsed by her truck, gasping for air as her hand touched the door as if she had just won a marathon. Her hands were marked with imprints from gripping her keys and mace tightly. Fumbling with the keys, she struggled to unlock the truck door, her hands trembling with exhaustion. She opened the door and sank into her truck, locking the door behind her. She closed her eyes and breathed to calm herself.

As she sat in her truck, DonnaMae began wrapping her hands, pulling the fabric tight over her knuckles. She could feel the anger simmering under her skin.

When she entered the gym, she didn't acknowledge anyone, making her mood known as she headed straight through the double doors into the training area. Gloves on, water bottle in hand, and mouth guard secure, DonnaMae made a beeline for the heavy bag, desperate to release her anger. All she could picture was him, his face, his words, and she wasn't sure if she was more furious with him or herself.

Before the bell even sounded, her fists were already landing hard and fast against the bag. Each punch carried a wave of rage, a frustration she couldn't control. How had she let him into her mind again? With each blow, she fought against the hold he still seemed to have on her life, anger growing hotter with every strike.

By her third round, DonnaMae's arms felt like lead with every punch, her muscles burning as she struck the bag with everything she had. Sweat streamed down her face, stinging as it dripped into her eyes, but she didn't stop to wipe it away. She pushed through the discomfort, blinking back the tears that threatened. She fought through the ache in her knee, the fire in her shoulders, and the pain in her heart.

"Who are you fighting, champ?" Che asked, steadying the bag.

She didn't respond, she just kept punching.

"The bell is red, that means stop."

She ignored him and kept throwing.

He stepped in front of her next punch and caught it with his hand. "Slow as molasses," he said.

She threw another punch, this one she knew was faster.

He caught it, "Molasses," he said again, holding her fist still.

"Errrr," she groaned, trying to wrench her hand free, but he held her steady.

"You going to tell me who you're fighting?" he asked again, his voice low.

DonnaMae stared blankly at the bag, her mind somewhere else entirely. Words from her dad ran through her mind, *"There are some things we just can't talk about... time will heal all pain."* She knew he thought she was weak, that she had disappointed him by letting this happen. She should just let it go, just sweep it under the rug, like everyone else wanted her to. She knew this was all her fault, and so did everyone else.

"Mae?" Che's voice pulled her back. He gently lowered her gloved hand.

"No one," she said through clenched teeth.

Che tilted his head, eyeing her rolled-up pant leg. "Then, you want to tell me about your new fashion statement?" he asked, nodding to her knee.

She shrugged. "I went for a run and tripped over a rock and it was bleeding, so I stopped the bleeding and ran back."

She was a horrible liar, so she just stopped talking so he could fill in the rest. Che didn't press her, but she could tell by his expression that he sensed there was more to the story. "There's a first aid kit in the office. We should clean that up."

DonnaMae nodded.

"But first," he said, "if you're going to fight a heavy bag, you're going to do it right." He motioned for her to step back towards him. "Put your hands up and move with the bag." He pushed the bag towards her. "When it comes towards you, practice maneuvers like slipping, ducking, or sidestepping to avoid the bag."

Che pushed the bag again and she sidestepped out of the way.

"Good, keep your hands up." He stopped the bag. "Now, when the bag moves away, use the opportunity to close the distance with footwork and throw a combination of punches." He pushed the bag again and stepped out of the way.

The bag swung back and forth and DonnaMae moved with it, letting her body relax and feel the movement.

"Hands up," he said again. "Do six more rounds like this and then come see me and we will fix you up." Che turned to walk away, then paused, "And if you don't keep your damn hands up, I will duct tape them to your face. Once you get this down, we'll go over how to work the heavy bag when it's not moving." He turned back to face her. "Then we'll learn how to not fight it like you're trying to kill it with rage." He turned and walked away, leaving her with her hands held tight to her face, moving back and forth with the heavy bag.

CHAPTER 44

February, 2003

DonnaMae sat on her bed in her apartment, a chill seeping through her window as she gazed over the frost-covered ground outside. She wrapped her fuzzy blanket tighter around her shoulders and took another bite of oatmeal, savoring the warmth as it melted in her mouth. Fresh-cut apples and a spoonful of her grandma's apple butter filled each bite with a cozy sweetness that brought a smile to her lips, the taste carrying her back to her grandparents' kitchen.

DonnaMae had made the difficult decision to go home for Christmas. It was a quick trip, long enough to see her family on Christmas Day and to visit her mom's headstone with a bouquet of sunflowers for her birthday.

The sunflowers were the reason DonnaMae had decided to go home. She'd stopped at the store to get more Epsom salt and was looking for a good bar of chocolate when she stumbled upon a clearance aisle filled with fall decorations. There, she'd found the most beautiful bouquet of sunflowers she had ever seen. The sunflowers were perfect, with large, golden-yellow petals and rich brown centers. Even the ribbon on them had a Mickey Mouse charm hanging from it. They'd seemed meant to be, and impossible for DonnaMae to resist. She'd taken it as a sign, and, forgetting about the chocolate, headed home with the flowers to call her dad and let him know.

The drive through her hometown had felt overwhelming, but once inside her parents' house on Christmas Day, she'd had the chance to relax a little, reconnect with her family, and share stories about her boxing. Her brother was living with a new girlfriend. DonnaMae wasn't a fan of her. Her thick makeup and flashy clothes seemed foreign to DonnaMae, and not her brother's type. But DonnaMae also didn't know the girl at all, and that hit DonnaMae with more sadness because her whole family was changing and she knew nothing of it.

Her little sister Adeline was growing up so fast, and DonnaMae ached, feeling like she was missing it. Adeline had been excited to show DonnaMae all about the Irish dancing she was learning. She danced around the house the entire day, her shoes with metal soles tap-tapping with every jig.

The scents of Elise's holiday baking wafted through the house amid laughter, a bittersweet reminder of what DonnaMae had missed on Thanksgiving.

Though it was nice to be home, her heart grew heavier instead of lighter. Her family members' lives had moved forward, untouched by the chaos that had unraveled hers. Where her dreams had stalled, theirs thrived. No one asked how she was really doing. It was as if everyone just went on pretending like nothing had ever happened, and she should too.

DonnaMae had spent the evening at her grandparents' house, choosing to sleep there so she could be farthest away from any chances of running into Charles, and to be close to the graveyard where her mom was buried. It made for an easy escape the next morning. She didn't drive around town to see the lights or soak in the usual holiday cheer. Instead, she filled her heart back up with love and conversation from her grandparents, aunts, uncles, and cousins, who knew nothing of her past struggles, making it easy to pretend things had not changed. They wanted to hear everything about her new adventures, and oohed and awed over all her stories about the gym and boxing and what her new school looked like. The kids thought the cereal dispensaries in the cafeteria were the coolest part. They played the card game hand and foot and drank hot chocolate until the late hours of the night.

On her way out, DonnaMae had stopped at her mom's grave. On the headstone, a large sculpted Mickey Mouse head stood out with its bright white eyes and oversized black ears. The headstone's surface was smooth and polished with, "We love you, Mom" and "Love you forever, your loving husband" engraved on it.

DonnaMae set her oatmeal aside on her nightstand next to her steaming cup of tea. She picked up an envelope and flipped it between her fingers. The morning sunlight filtered through her blinds, casting a soft beam of light that hit the white envelope. Hazel's familiar handwriting spelled out her name with a heart at the end. The letter was a welcome distraction from DonnaMae's textbooks and study notes scattered on her bed.

She carefully opened the letter. Hazel's cheerful handwriting filled the page:

Mae,

I missed you so much over the holidays. We all did. It wasn't the same without you around, but we've been keeping busy. Guess what? Izzy's boyfriend is amazing. We all loved him!

And I met someone at school. I wanted to tell you in person but this will have to do for now. His name is Michael... And, no, it isn't Michael Jackson, I knew you'd want to know that, haha. But he does like music of all kinds. He makes me think of you, how he seems to know all the songs.

The girls and I have been talking about renting a beach

house or planning a big get-together in June! We're all in need of a late night beach fire hang out. You have to come home for this!

We can't wait to see you and catch up. It's going to be great having you home and having some fun together over the summer. Maybe I will be able to talk Michael into coming that weekend so you can meet him. Let me know what you think and I will have my dad book us the house.

Sending you tons of love and hugs,
Hazel

DonnaMae re-read the letter, emotions swirling inside her. Images of the beach house she had stayed in flashed in her mind. She felt a lump in her throat, a scream that wanted to escape. She swallowed hard.

She wanted to be laughing at Hazel's small joke about Michael Jackson, and to be excited for the idea of reconnecting with her friends around a beach fire.

DonnaMae sighed, folding the letter carefully and placing it back in the envelope. She was still trying to build a new version of herself, one who was stronger and more resilient. She wasn't ready to face her friends yet.

CHAPTER 45

April, 2003

DonnaMae's punches cut through the air, each movement revealing the strength she had built over months of relentless training. She stared at her reflection in the mirror, eyes fixed on the toned lines of her arms. They were lean and powerful, muscles standing out with each jab, and her shoulders had broadened, giving her a presence she hardly recognized. Her once-soft frame had been sculpted into something stronger, more resilient. She was no longer the woman she used to know.

Focused on her breathing, she matched each exhale with a punch. Pain was a familiar companion now, a low hum beneath her skin that she could ignore. DonnaMae had learned to welcome that burn in her shoulders, to use it as fuel rather than a deterrent. Her mind was clear and centered.

"Mae!" Che's voice broke her focus. He was standing in the doorway, a small bag slung over his shoulder and a stack of mail clutched in his hand.

With a quick glance at her weights, DonnaMae set them down by the wall and approached him.

"Nice. I see you've stepped it up to the three-pounders," Che said, a hint of approval in his voice as he eyed the weights she had been using.

"I've been mixing it up between all of them, like you suggested," DonnaMae said, her smile broadening with a touch of pride. "And then adding a burnout with no weights when the bell rings to work on my speed, like Coach Joe does."

Che grinned, clearly impressed. "Very nice!" He gestured for her to follow him as he turned away from the door and headed towards his office. "Two things," he said, his tone shifting to a more serious note as DonnaMae followed him to his office, "your paperwork came today. I just need you to sign your contracts and USA boxing passport." He set the mail down on his desk with the USA Boxing stamped envelope on top.

Joe half-jogged over. "Are you excited?" he asked, out of breath. "She's only had one fight, but it sounds like it will be a good lineup."

"WHAT?!" DonnaMae whipped her head towards Joe and then back to Che.

"We hadn't gotten that far yet," Che said with a chuckle.

"I have a fight lined up?" DonnaMae glanced again between the two of them. "Already?"

"Oh!" Joe scrunched up his face, "I'd better get back to my class." He disappeared back into his dojo before she could say anything else.

"She's a few inches taller than you," Che said, "but the weight class is one thirty, so you won't have to cut any weight for this fight, and —"

"CUT WEIGHT?" DonnaMae had never thought about that before. She'd known the wrestlers did it in high school. When she was a cheerleader, she thought it was so dumb the way they would starve themselves and suck on candy all day and spit out the juice to stop them from eating.

"Yeah, we'll cross that bridge if we have to, but you're pretty short, so we probably won't ever really have to worry about it." Che chuckled to himself again.

"Were the two things my paperwork and I've got a fight lined up?" DonnaMae paused, glancing down at the paperwork. "When is this fight? Am I even ready?"

"You're sparring every week and have been training for over six months. The fight is Saturday, June fourteenth, so we have two months to get you fight-ready." Che pulled out a flier for the fight and set it down in front of her.

DonnaMae's stomach churned. *June fourteenth!* That date. She knew that date. She knew that date all too well. The day her life was shattered.

She shook her head to clear her mind and looked at her shoes. Her dad had just bought her new boxing shoes. Today was her first day wearing them. She stared past her shoes, past the ground, down into nothingness. She needed this fight. She needed to win this fight. She needed her dad to be proud of her. She needed to show him that she wasn't just a weak little girl. But why June fourteenth? Was the universe trying to tell her something? Was she really just a pathetic, weak little girl? Was this all just a waste of her time?

She felt like every time she moved forward, started coming back to life, he was right there to knock her back down.

Che cleared his throat, drawing DonnaMae's attention. "Number two was this," he said, holding up a giant roll of silver duct tape.

"Huh?" she raised an eyebrow at him.

"I told you if you didn't keep your damn hands up I was going to tape them to your face."

"Seriously?" she exclaimed, eyes wide as she stared at the duct tape. She had to hold back a laugh, thinking of when she was a kid and her dad used to duct tape her and Allan's legs together and set a timer to see how fast they could escape while he worked on cars in the garage. They'd wriggle free and then beg to be taped up again, determined to beat their record. Now, the irony wasn't lost on her, she was about to be duct taped again, but this time, it was meant to keep her restrained, not to find a way out.

"Go get your gloves on," Che said, then added in a sinister voice that made her burst into laughter, "after you sign on the dotted line."

"Duct tape and signing my life away," DonnaMae laughed. "You do realize how horrifying you sound?"

Che just let out an evil laugh, making DonnaMae roll her eyes at how childish her coach could be.

For the next week, every time she came in, Che stood at the door waiting with the duct tape. She would put her headgear on, hold her gloved hands up to her face, and he would wrap duct tape around them, locking her hands into place. It was defense drill after defense drill, from ducking and slipping a rope tied from one end of the gym to the other, to standing against a wall while Che threw tennis balls at her head.

"If you can dodge this ball, you can dodge a punch," or "Keep your eye on the ball and move" were some of his favorite things to yell at her. She had a bad habit of closing her eyes, he said, and this was the fastest way to learn to keep them open. At first she thought her coach had lost his mind, but after getting hit with the ball more than she would ever admit, it started working. Thankfully, her hands were taped to her face, so most of the time the balls hit her gloves or headgear.

Soon, she was moving with grace as she danced around the ring, dodging each punch like a pro. Che's punches came fast and hard, but she slipped past jabs and hooks, her upper body weaving and ducking effortlessly. The tape kept her hands glued to her face, forcing her to rely on her instincts and agility to avoid the blows.

Che pushed her to her breaking point, working her so hard she was sure she might pass out, throw up, or even die before she ever got the chance to fight. He introduced her to drills she had never even heard of, each one more grueling than the last. She flipped massive tires down the alley, tires that seemed bigger than she was, only to be handed a sledgehammer and told to pound away until her arms could no longer lift the weight. When she was spent, he made her punch his bare palms with her raw knuckles, driving her past what she thought was her limit.

Just when she believed she had nothing left, when her arms felt like they were slogging through mud, he demanded more. He forced her to push beyond boundaries she hadn't known existed. Every time she thought she was broken, that she couldn't get back up or train another second, Che was there, telling her she could, and somehow she did. In those moments, he wasn't just breaking her down — he was building her back up, stronger than before.

Joe focused on her technique and made her practice perfect. He gave her skills that only someone with his years of experience could. He taught her how to not just fight in the ring but how to throw a real punch without gloves, and how to be seven steps ahead of her opponent. How to look for an opening and take it, how to never give her opponent the chance to know what she was going to throw next. If she created a habit of stepping every time she punched, he saw it and broke it. He kept her on her toes. He made her throw a hundred fast punches with just her right arm, and then fifty more that only counted if they were perfect.

When she was exhausted and thought she had nothing left to give, they made her spar. She fought every guy in the gym. The other fighters began to develop a newfound respect for her, acknowledging her skills and determination. She might have been the only girl fighter, but she was one of them now.

CHAPTER 46

June, 2002

DonnaMae was one week out from her first fight. This was a week of light training and then no training two days before. She had rewarded herself with a long, hot Epsom salt bath, a book, and some chocolate every night. Her room was a crazy mess of dirty clothes, flash cards, school books, and paper everywhere. Most nights she would pass out on the floor with half a sandwich in her hand, face down on her books. She had taken to recording all her classes and would listen to her lectures on runs, in the car, or even in the shower, but she still had to read and study. Reading was hard enough with all the words being scrambled up half the time. Adding heavy eyelids just made it that much harder. But she knew if her grades dropped below C's her dad would put a stop to boxing.

C's were like B's and B's were like A's for her. She had to bust her ass and study harder than anyone in her class to just get a C. Her dad said that if DonnaMae's mom were alive, she would have been hell bent on DonnaMae getting A's, but he understood DonnaMae's struggles because he was never good at school. DonnaMae had no idea how he'd managed to graduate, because her mom had taught him how to read after high school, and even now, he still struggled. Despite everything, DonnaMae couldn't deny that her dad was one of the most intelligent people she knew. There was no puzzle he couldn't solve and no problem for which he couldn't find a solution. Whenever she needed help with her schoolwork, she always called on him. By the time she'd finish explaining the problem to him and he'd break it down for her, she could figure it out in her own way. Her dad's mindset always filled her with hope and made her realize that being dyslexic was not a setback, but a strength that allowed her to approach challenges differently than most, giving her an advantage in having to think outside the box. With her brother and dad sharing the same unconventional mindset, she felt a little less weird.

DonnaMae turned on her bath and checked the water temperature before walking over to answer her phone.

"Hello!" Izzy's cheerful voice filled the receiver. "Mae, it's me. I'm just trying to finalize our plans for next weekend. Hazel mentioned you hadn't said if you were coming to the beach house yet."

DonnaMae shook her head. Not again. It felt like the girls were playing a game of tag with her about the beach house Hazel's dad had rented, which, ironically, was the same weekend as June fourteenth. She was starting to think she was cursed with this date.

"Izzy, I have my fight next weekend," DonnaMae said with a forced laugh. She had made sure they all knew about her fight, not just because it was her reason for not going on the beach trip, but also because she really wanted them to be there. She needed them there. She missed them all so much, and even though they had no idea what June fourteenth meant to her, having them there after shutting them out for the past year was what she needed. She wanted them to see her strong and thriving, not the weak, pathetic girl she had been trying to hide from them.

"Mae, we're all coming to watch you fight," Izzy said.

DonnaMae didn't even realize she'd been holding her breath

until she released it. She couldn't contain her excitement. "You are?"

"Of course! All of us. And then we're going to the beach for a few days." Izzy paused, and the line went silent. "Mae, join us. We can head straight there and have a bonfire that night on the beach to celebrate. The break will be good for you."

DonnaMae's heart swelled at the idea. She loved the thought of a bonfire on the beach, but was she ready for the beach, let alone a beach house? Her friends knew nothing about the shame that had driven her away from them in the first place. She didn't want them to look at her with pity. They knew her as the girl who drove race cars and changed oil on stage in a beauty pageant.

"Ok, how about this: If you win, you go to the beach. If not..." Izzy's voice trailed off into silence. "Nah, you'll win. Looks like you're going to the beach."

DonnaMae mulled it over. Winning would not only prove to everyone that she wasn't weak, but it would also prove to herself that she could fight for herself and protect herself. "Deal!" DonnaMae almost shouted into the receiver, adding a laugh to make it sound less intense.

She could hear Izzy clapping her hands through the phone. "Oh my gosh, really? I'll ask my brother if he can load the truck with wood and have it ready for us to pick up on the way to the beach."

DonnaMae smiled at her friend's excitement. "Right," she teased, "so your brother can hide a snake in the wood to scare the hell out of us when we unload it." Izzy's brother was one of the nicest guys DonnaMae had ever met, with a heart of gold, but he loved his pranks. DonnaMae laughed out loud at the thought of him buckling over with laughter after pranking them.

"Right, good call, well he —" Izzy was cut off by someone yelling at her in the background. "Love you, Mae. I gotta go. See you in a few days!"

"Love you too, Izzy. Can't wait!" DonnaMae hung up, feeling

like she had just added even more to this fight than she could have ever imagined.

She sank into her bath and closed her eyes. This time she didn't have a book, a face mask, chocolate, or anything that could be a distraction. She focused only on her boxing, fighting meditation. Coach Joe would make her lie on the dojo floor and visualize fighting in the ring. She shut out all sounds, all distractions, and only saw herself in the ring standing alone. She found her coach's voice and let them call out combinations and she visualized herself throwing each one. The ring was empty. She had tried, but she couldn't see her opponent. She shuffled around the ring. The room was dark, she focused on her breathing and the only sound came from her coaches' voices. She mentally reached for an imaginary opponent, to visualize every move and strategy as if they were in the ring together.

"My beautiful Mae."

DonnaMae sat straight up in the tub, eyes flying open and water splashing everywhere. His voice was so close and so real she pulled her hands to her face and looked around the empty room. She knew he was not there physically, but he was. He was there. He was still taunting her.

"No! You are not welcome here," she whispered.

She closed her eyes again and slid back into the water. This time she let herself see him. She recognized him, and as she peered into his beady little eyes she whispered, "You don't scare me, not anymore."

Tonight she let him be her opponent. She zoned in on him, staying calm, listening to her coaches call combination after combination, following their instructions.

She punched him. He didn't bleed. He dissolved piece by piece. She knocked him out of her ring and he shattered like glass out of her thoughts with each blow she threw. She was winning, and he was no longer standing in front of her.

The once-warm bath water had turned frigid, sending a chill

down her spine. DonnaMae shivered, returning to reality with a smile on her face.

"Bye," she whispered into the chilled air around her. She stepped out of the tub, pulled the plug, and watched him, and his hold on her, swirl down the drain.

CHAPTER 47

June 14th, 2003

DonnaMae, with Joe and Che at her side, approached the high school gymnasium beneath a gray, overcast sky that the sun hadn't had time to burn off yet. The weigh-ins for DonnaMae's first fight were scheduled six hours before the main event later that afternoon, giving them plenty of time to head back to Che's house after the weigh-ins to relax and braid DonnaMae's hair into corn-rows to keep it out of her face, and to bring some calm before the storm of her debut fight. The parking lot stretched out before them, its surface a patchwork of worn asphalt and scattered potholes. There were only a few parked cars, making the place seem almost deserted, as if they might have arrived at the wrong venue.

The school building loomed ahead, a large structure of faded brick that reminded DonnaMae of home, its high windows glowing with golden light. DonnaMae pulled her fitted jacket tighter against the brisk breeze and glanced around the nearly empty lot. That familiar fear crept in. She quickened her pace to catch up with Joe and Che.

"How many girl fights are there tonight?" she asked, her voice breaking the quiet as they neared the entrance.

"Just yours, champ," Che said, turning back to tousle her soft blonde curls, sending them spilling into her face.

"Coach, you're messing up my hair," she said, cutting short a half laugh to smirk and side-eye her coach. "I'm going for a beautiful badass, look!" she said, flicking one of her long curls back over her shoulder. She had gotten up extra early that morning to curl her hair and was wearing her silver hoop earrings. Nothing too fancy, no make-up. She was going to be fighting that evening, so makeup would be overkill, but she wanted to feel girly. Her smirk turned into a smile at the thoughts of her grandma's words: "Go show this world what women can do, just don't forget you are a girl doing boy things, not one of the boys." DonnaMae often just thought of herself as one of the boys, but when it came time to do things like this, she went the extra mile to remind herself she was a girl and she wanted the world to know it. She couldn't have her hair down for the fight, but she could have it down for the weigh-ins.

Joe reached out and put his arm around her shoulders. "Mae, if you keep that mindset while you're in the ring, the other girl will never get a punch in and you'll walk out with your hair looking just fine."

Mae laughed. "No Coach, my hair will be in cornrows, and at that point I won't care anymore."

"Never stop caring about your hair," Che said, reaching up and running his hand over his shiny bald head. "One day it might just be gone and you will wish you cared more."

They all laughed.

Che stopped when he reached the gymnasium's doors a few steps in front of them. "You all ready for this?"

DonnaMae walked up to the doors without hesitation and yanked them open. "It's now or never baby!" she said, walking through the doors, then instantly scrunching up her face. "Oh man, it smells like an old gym locker in here," she whispered over her shoulder to her coaches.

At first, it was so quiet that she wondered if they were in the wrong place. But then she noticed a young man, approximately her age, approaching them. He had a sun-kissed complexion and tousled, dark brown hair. She couldn't tear her gaze away from his chiseled physique, every muscle flexing as he effortlessly shook out his shirt and pulled it on. He flashed DonnaMae a brief smile before shifting his gaze beyond her to her coaches. "Weigh-ins are down the hall, mate. Good luck tonight," he said with a nod, and kept walking right on past them.

"I think he was talking to me," DonnaMae laughed, though she knew he clearly wasn't. His gaze had swept right past her to Che, dismissing her for her non-fighter appearance.

As they walked down the hall, the sound of chatter grew louder the closer they got. Soon, a group of men appeared before them, some of whom were undressing down to just their boxers before taking turns stepping up on a scale while a man in a white shirt recorded their weights on a clipboard. After that, another man in a white shirt took them off to the side and seemed to be interviewing them. He had a stethoscope hanging around his neck. She figured he must be a doctor of some sort.

There were a few girls scattered in the mix, but none of them looked like they were fighters. Not that DonnaMae did, she realized, so they might be.

"Um, do I have to weigh-in with all these guys in my underwear?" DonnaMae asked, stepping back into her coaches. As the memory of standing in her underwear in front of her whole history class crossed her mind, she couldn't help but laugh. *What's the difference between underwear and a swimsuit?* Ella's voice echoed in her mind.

"What's so funny?" Che said, scanning the room and then landing on DonnaMae.

"I'm wearing regular underwear and a sports bra, so I guess it's not a big deal, right?"

"No! We'll find out where the girls are doing weigh-ins," Joe snapped in his father-like voice and marched over to the guy holding a clipboard.

A few minutes later, he returned. "Well, I think we shook things up a little. They actually have no idea what to do about a girl weigh in and —"

Before he could finish, an older lady with a clipboard walked up behind him. "DonnaMae?"

"Yes, that's me," DonnaMae said, stepping forward as the lady continued talking.

"Come with me to the ladies' room, we will take your weight. You can keep your underwear on, but that's all. After we're done, you will go straight to the doctor for a screening to get cleared, then you are free to head out." She paused and glanced over her clip board one more time. "Ah yes, and I will need your USA Boxing Passports," she said, looking past DonnaMae to someone standing behind her.

DonnaMae turned to find a figure wearing long dark shorts and a baggy black hoodie with the hood up. They kept their head low, eyes on the floor as they pulled a USA boxing passport from their hoodie pocket and handed it to the lady with the clipboard. DonnaMae noticed their short, stubby nails with black nail polish on them.

Her heart slammed against her chest as Joe stepped beside her and handed her passport to the lady with the clipboard.

"Thank you," the lady said as she took the passport and walked to the bathroom, the other girl following like her shadow of death.

"Both our passports," DonnaMae whispered to Coach Joe. "That's her." That hooded figure was DonnaMae's opponent.

"Yeah," Joe confirmed. "Go weigh-in. We can't go into the ladies' room, you're on your own."

DonnaMae smiled at her coaches, waved, and swallowed back any fear she felt creeping up as she followed the two women into the bathroom.

During the weigh-in, DonnaMae stood in nothing but her

bright pink underwear, her curly blonde hair so long it hid the fact that she wasn't wearing a bra and silver hoop earrings. She couldn't tear her eyes away from her opponent, who sported black spandex shorts resembling men's boxers, a shaved head, and an array of tattoos adorning even her scalp. As the girl turned her head, a cascade of earrings reflected the light down both of her ears. When she turned around to face DonnaMae, DonnaMae quickly glanced at the ground, but not before noticing the many piercings decorating the girl's face: a lip ring, an eyebrow piercing, and a hoop in her nose.

DonnaMae's stomach tightened as she came face-to-face with the girl, who stood taller than her, had two times the amount of muscle, and who seemed to have an unsettling fondness for pain. Just the thought of getting a tattoo made DonnaMae feel queasy, and this girl had at least twenty.

"All piercings must be removed before the fight," the woman with the clipboard said.

"Oh, I only have my ears pierced. I can take them out now, sorry, I don't train with them, I just, well, I…" DonnaMae's voice turned into a nervous babble as she scrambled to take out her earrings.

Her opponent locked eyes with her, a sinister grin forming on her face as she let out a low, mocking laugh. She swiftly gathered her things, pulled her hoodie over her head, and stormed out of the room without even taking time to put her shorts back on over her boxer-ish underwear things she was wearing. It was like she was showing that she didn't give a fuck.

DonnaMae came out of the locker room, fully dressed, and spotted her coaches casually leaning against the wall across from the ladies' room. Her legs felt like they might give out from under her. "Did you see her?" she asked, sounding ten times stronger than she felt.

"I don't think she was going for the beautiful badass look," Joe laughed.

"I think she is just a badass. Did you see all her tattoos and piercings and..." this time fear escaped in her voice, "I think she likes pain."

"Good, then give it to her," Che said, coming forward off the wall and throwing his arm around DonnaMae's shoulders. "Let's get you a light meal and get that hair in those braids you were talking about."

Joe walked up to her other side. "Didn't anyone ever teach you not to judge a book by its cover?"

DonnaMae sighed and shook her head. She knew they were just trying to help, but she was pretty sure she was going to need to go to the bathroom soon. Her nerves were in full effect. "I think we might need to stop and get some Pepto-Bismol," she said with a laugh, but she wasn't joking. She honestly felt like she was going to shit her pants or throw up.

"It's just nerves, champ, you'll be fine," Che said, giving her a smile

All she could think was, *Your wife won't be fine when I have to sit on the toilet the whole time she's putting my hair into cornrows.*

***

DonnaMae sat on a chair backwards facing Coach Che. Her hair in tight cornrows, the braids pulling her blonde hair close to her scalp, her arms rested on the back of the chair while Che wrapped her hands, his movements precise and deliberate. Joe stood beside her, making her feel safe, but it was Che who had her attention. This wasn't the normal wrapping on her hands, this was the real thing — the kind of technique used by professional fighters, where every twist and pull of the tape had a purpose.

Che began with a layer of gauze, wrapping it gently around her knuckles to create a cushion that would protect her hands during the fight. His hands moved with the confidence of someone who had done this a thousand times, but each wrap still felt personal, as if he was tailoring it just for her. The gauze cradled her knuckles in a soft, protective layer, and she could already feel the difference.

Then came the tape. Che worked it around her wrists first, pulling it tight, but not too tight. The crisscross pattern he created was almost like a piece of art. As he continued covering the knuckles, her nerves slowly crept up on her. She was suddenly aware of her surroundings. She could hear the dull roar of the crowd outside, the muffled sounds of punches landing, and the occasional cheer breaking through the thick air. The tension was building and her stomach was starting to churn again, and she couldn't shake the slight tremble in her fingers.

She wasn't cold, but her whole body felt like it was vibrating with nervous energy. Her eyes darted around the room, taking in the cracked mirror, the battered folding chair her coach was sitting in and the other ones lined up against the wall behind him. The room felt smaller by the second. It felt like the walls were closing in on her.

The door creaked open and DonnaMae's dad stepped inside. She looked up, catching his eye, and tried to give him a reassuring smile. Without a word, he slipped off his hooded sweatshirt and draped it over her shoulders, the worn fabric instantly warming her. The hood fell over her head, and she pulled it forward slightly with her free hand, letting it hide her face. It felt like a shield against the fear that was creeping in, trying to take her down before she even got into the ring.

"You're shivering," her dad said softly as he knelt down beside her.

DonnaMae glanced at him, her smile faltering. "I'm ok," she lied, trying to sound confident.

He placed a hand on her shoulder, his touch steady and comforting. He stood next to her and watched as her coach finished wrapping her hands.

Che finished and smoothed the tape with his thumbs, ensuring everything was just right.

DonnaMae's hands felt solid, like they were encased in something strong and unbreakable. She flexed her fingers, testing the wraps. "Wow, thanks, Coach," she said, standing up.

As Che started packing up the supplies, her dad stepped towards her and pulled her into a tight hug. She closed her eyes, breathing in the familiar scent of him, the warmth of his embrace wrapping around her like a blanket. For a moment, her fear subsided, replaced by the steady beat of his heart against her cheek. Her dad was here, and she was once again a little girl safe in his arms.

"I am so proud of you, Mae," he said, his voice thick with emotion. He stepped back from the hug, meeting her eyes. "In life, you're gonna get knocked down. And that's ok." He paused. "Mae, you got knocked down, but you didn't get knocked out. You have a choice, Mae. You can stay down or you can get back up." His eyes glistened with unshed tears. "Mae, you got back up, and now you're kicking ass. I am so proud of you." His voice cracked at the end and he quickly cleared his throat.

DonnaMae felt her throat tighten, the tears threatening to spill over. She nodded, swallowing hard as she blinked them back. "Thanks, Dad," she said, her voice almost a whisper.

He squeezed her shoulder one last time before stepping back again to leave. "Win or lose today, Mae, remember that you have already won something bigger." He smiled. "Love you forever and always, kid." He blew her a kiss and walked out of the room, leaving her to refocus on the fight ahead her.

DonnaMae flexed her wrapped hands, feeling the strength in them, the determination that her dad's words had sparked. The fear was still there, lurking in the corners of her mind, but it didn't feel so overwhelming now. She had stopped shivering. She could feel the warmth of his sweatshirt around her, his words echoing in her mind. You have a choice. Get back up. And she would. No matter what happened in that ring, she knew she would always get back up. She had too much weighing on this fight to give up. She needed to win this fight.

"Mae!" Joe's voice pulled her out of her trance. She pulled her eyes off her hands to look at him. "I know your hands look cool, but let's put them to use and get you warmed up." Joe held up two focus mitts, ready for her to punch them.

DonnaMae pushed her arms through the sleeves of her dad's sweatshirt, raised her fists to her face, and readied her stance.

The gym was packed shoulder to shoulder with people, but the path in front of DonnaMae was cleared out and a straight shot to the boxing ring. Her dad's sweatshirt was still draped over her shoulders, her hands now gloved up, and she was warm and ready to step into the ring. Walking out for her first fight, with her dad's hoodie over her shoulders it felt like he was walking out with her.

"Fighting out of the red corner —" the announcer's voice boomed.

"That's our cue," Che said, talking over the announcer before DonnaMae even heard her name.

Shannia Twain's "Man! I Feel Like a Woman" blared so loudly that it drowned out DonnaMae's heartbeat, which pounded in her chest with such intensity that it threatened to knock her out before she even reached the ring. This was her song. She let Shannia's voice take over and drown out all the screams and catcalls from the crowd. She bounced on the balls of her feet like she was in the ring and threw a few punches as she walked, keeping her body moving. They stopped at her corner and the ref smeared vaseline on her face, checked her mouth guard, and then yelled the rules to her over the music.

Che stepped up to the ring just like when they were sparring and held the rope down with his foot while DonnaMae climbed in. "Go walk the ring and say thank you to the judges and then come back," Joe directed, pulling the hoodie off her shoulders and revealing her red tank top with a thick white band that said "Mae" on it.

While she walked through the ring, DonnaMae surveyed the crowd until she spotted her friends and family. Just as the crowd settled to hear her opponent being announced, her brother caught her eye and yelled, "Kick her ass, Mae!" Heat rushed to her cheeks as she quickly thanked the judges and retreated to her corner, now feeling embarrassed.

Mae stood toe to toe with her opponent while the ref went over the rules one more time. "Protect yourself at all times," he said.

The fight begins when the bell rings, she reminded herself over and over, not when we touch gloves, not when I step into the ring, not when I walk out with my song blaring. Not when the crowd was screaming and cheering me on. The fight begins when that bell rings and the ref yells fight.

"Touch gloves," the ref said, and they did. "To your corners." But he didn't step out, he stayed in the ring with them.

DonnaMae closed her eyes and let out a slow breath to calm her nerves. "Ok Mom, this is for you. Let's break some 'no girls' rules," she whispered, tilting her head up towards the ceiling.

The bell rang, and her eyes snapped open.

"FIGHT!" the ref yelled, and the crowd went crazy.

DonnaMae stepped forward, feeling the rough canvas of the ring beneath her shuffling feet, her hands held tight to her face. She never threw the first punch; she found her footing and watched her opponent, taking them in. But right then, her nerves had her feeling scattered, making it difficult to focus. Her actions felt all over the place. She bounced around with lightning-fast speed, in and out, too quick for her opponent to land a punch. Her opponent was heavy on her feet and moved slowly. DonnaMae slowed down and matched her opponent's speed. She threw a few punches, but they all slipped by, none connecting. Her legs were shaky, and she felt weak with nerves. Her need to fight was absent. It didn't feel like she was in a ring fighting — at that moment, it felt like she was just on a stage in front of hundreds of people, prancing around. The bell had rung, fight had begun, but not for her.

They danced around each other, and finally the girl stepped in. DonnaMae's right hand was down, leaving her open, and she took a hard straight right hand, followed by a left jab and then a hook to the body. She stumbled back. The sting from the punches ran through her.

The ref, close by, watched as DonnaMae took another blow to the body. This one buckled her, and she gasped for air. Darkness teased the corners of her vision, and the ref put his hand out, stopping her opponent from taking another blow.

DonnaMae snapped back, blinking away the blur from her eyes, the world tumbling back into focus. Her limbs and breath returned as if she had remembered how to use them. Her head spun slightly as she bounced back on her toes, shaking out her arms and legs, now ready to support her. Her heart thundered as she circled her opponent, ready to fight.

It was like a switch had been flipped inside DonnaMae, her bell had finally rung. Her reaction wasn't to step back and run from the pain, but to run right into it and start giving it back. *If she likes pain, give it to her,* her coach's words filled her thoughts. *She's here to kick my ass, and I'm not about to let that happen,* she thought as she stepped forward, swinging like her hands had been caged and her opponent had just let them loose.

DonnaMae moved around the ring with wild energy, darting in and out, throwing punches with reckless abandon. The two squared off, locked eyes, and began to circle each other. "Come on," DonnaMae growled through clenched teeth, her rage burning inside her, "that all you got?"

Her opponent responded by stepping in and throwing punches.

DonnaMae took every punch, blocking some and not feeling the others. Then she retaliated harder and faster. The crowd grew louder, and she heard her brother in the distance, "Make her your punching bag, Mae!"

And so she did. She threw everything she had learned out the window and made this girl her punching bag. Anger raged through her and flew out her fist with every punch. This girl was taking hits for everything. DonnaMae was no longer fighting a girl, she was fighting her fears, her life, she was fighting Charles and everything he had taken from her that she wanted back.

Blood splattered from both of them. The bell rang, signaling they had ten seconds left in the round. DonnaMae held her breath and bit down hard on her mouth guard. She was taking blow after blow and letting the pain of it fuel her and she was giving it right back twice as hard. They stood toe to toe, throwing punch for punch, until the ref jumped in between them, breaking them up as the last bell rang, signaling the round was over.

DonnaMae practically jogged back to her corner, surprised when Coach Che nearly threw her down onto her stool, clearly pissed.

"What the hell are you doing out there?" Joe yelled at her. Blood dripped down her face and was splattered all over her gloves.

Che poured water on her face and in her mouth and cleaned her up. "You have to slow down and focus," he said. "We know you can take a punch, but you don't need to."

"What?" she practically yelled. Her anger reared inside her. She was fighting for her life out there, they had no idea! All she could see was red. Her ears were ringing and her heart was pounding.

"You might be landing hard punches, but you're taking just as many," Che said.

"Do you hear my voice?" Joe said right into her ear.

She didn't respond.

Che put water in her mouth and told her to swish and spit into the bucket he held up in front of her.

"DO YOU HEAR MY VOICE?" Joe asked again, this time yelling and placing his hands on her shoulders.

He had her attention. "Yes, Coach," she said. "I hear you."

"Then hear me in the ring. Focus, use what you've learned. Don't fight angry, fight smart."

She thought about what he was saying and she remembered the first day he had said that to her. She was angry and she knew it. Her dad's words played back through her head: *No matter what, you already won.* She counted backwards in her head and calmed herself down. She thought of all her hard work and training. She had trained for this.

The bell rang and Che put the mouth guard back in her mouth. "You got this, champ. You don't need to eat the punches to give them." He stepped out of the ring and DonnaMae stood while Joe pulled the stool out of the ring.

"This is your ring, Mae. Don't get your ass kicked in your ring. Own the ring."

DonnaMae let out a little laugh. Her coach said the dumbest shit sometimes, but it worked, she knew what he meant.

"Fight with technique, not anger this time. She won't see it coming," Joe said by her ear before she stepped forward.

"Fight!" the ref yelled, and this time DonnaMae didn't pounce in. That was what her opponent was waiting for her to do.

DonnaMae circled left and then right, she jabbed a few times to find her range and then she waited, and when her opponent came in just like she had last time, ready to bulldoze, DonnaMae slipped and threw a right to the body, ended with a left hook to her head, and quickly shuffled out. She slowed down her breathing and focused, shutting everything else out. All sounds disappeared. Suddenly it was just her and her opponent, the real opponent, the girl with the tattoos in the ring with her. She watched her opponent and picked her apart. She was slow and she threw punches that DonnaMae could time and slip to get in without getting hit. Her opponent had slowed down. DonnaMae was quick on her feet and she had fast hands when she wanted, but she also had one hell of an overhand right. If she could just figure out when to throw it, she could knock her out.

Coach Joe's voice broke through her silence. "Combo three, throw Combo three."

They had combinations of punches that were numbered so no one else knew what a fighter's coach was telling them to throw. Joe was telling DonnaMae to throw a jab and cross a hook. She moved around her opponent to try and see what her coach was seeing. Just as Joe yelled "Now!" she saw it. Her opponent was dropping her hand, and as she did, DonnaMae let her hands fly. Jab, cross, and then the hook landed perfectly and hard to her opponent's temple.

The girl with the tattoos rocked back and stumbled.

"Finish it!" DonnaMae heard both her coaches belt at the same time. The sound of their voices gave her a new surge of energy and she came in hot, jabbing her way in and finishing with a strong overhand right.

She felt like someone had hit the slow motion button as she watched her opponent go down just as the ref stepped in and pushed DonnaMae back and started to count.

The ref stood up, waving his hands in the air, calling the fight. She had just won in the second round by knockout.

Slowly, the sound of the roaring crowd grew louder as DonnaMae let all the outside sounds back in. Her coaches where both in the ring hugging her. She could see her friends jumping up and down yelling and screaming.

She had won!

CHAPTER 48

…

The car barely came to a stop before DonnaMae jumped out and let her feet sink into the sand. Her shoes and sweatpants were off before the car even pulled onto the beach. She was already in a full-on sprint, pulling her shirt over her head as she ran towards the ocean, when she heard Hazel yell after her, "Wait for me!"

But DonnaMae wasn't slowing down. This was her ocean. She loved her ocean. She had missed her ocean. She had not been to the beach, her favorite spot in the entire world, in exactly one year. The ice-cold water gave her a jolt as she ran through it, not stopping as she splashed water everywhere and then dove in and swam, letting her ocean take her in while taking in her ocean all at the same time. She felt the saltwater heal all her wounds as she bobbed up for air and let the waves carry her. She could stand up and touch the ocean floor, but she didn't want to. She wanted to just be one with the ocean, she wanted to be the ocean once again.

One year ago today, Charles had taken everything from her. Everything: her job, her friends, her family, her confidence, her strength. He had taken it all, even her ocean. For a year, the sound of crashing waves had filled her with fear. But not anymore. Riding the waves, she enjoyed the ocean's sounds and the laughter and screams of her friends joining in.

"Thank you," DonnaMae whispered. "I'm sorry for being so mad at you. That night you saved me, you helped me escape." A tear slid down her cheek as she said, "Thank you" one more time.

"You're welcome," Hazel said, splashing DonnaMae with water and jumping in next to her.

Ella screamed, and they both turned to see Izzy pulling her into the ocean. She was only up to her shins and for Izzy, that was a win. Ella never got in the ocean.

That evening, the fire crackled as flames danced along the logs of a bonfire and the wind blew. Pinks and oranges covered the sky as the sun started to set. DonnaMae and her friends gathered around the crackling fire, sitting on driftwood logs they had found and rolled towards the warmth. It was like they had never been apart. It was like nothing had changed. They laughed and sang and Hazel played the guitar. Ella poured the hot chocolate and Izzy added the peppermint schnapps.

DonnaMae leaned back and let a smile take over her face as she took it all in.

"What are you thinking, Mae?" Hazel asked, drawing everyone's attention to DonnaMae.

"I won!" DonnaMae turned her gaze up towards the ocean and she physically felt the weight of Charles lift off her shoulders. "I won!" she said again.

"Hell yeah, you did, you made that bitch your punching bag," Izzy said, throwing a marshmallow at DonnaMae. "And the darker it gets, the less beat up your face looks." She laughed.

"Heeeeeeeyyyyyy!" DonnaMae said, throwing the sand-covered marshmallow back at Izzy.

Everyone laughed. DonnaMae hadn't even thought about how she looked or felt, all she could think about was that she had won.

I won, I won! The words sang in her head with the laughter of her friends. But what her friends didn't know was her secret she had kept from them, her secret that she had let come between them, the secret that she had just won a lot more than a fight against some girl tonight. She was winning her fight against the man who had taken everything from her, and she was no longer going to let him win. This was her life, these were her friends, and this was her beach and no one was taking that from her ever again. DonnaMae's gaze drifted back towards the ocean.

I was once a girl trying to please everyone else, letting everyone walk all over me. The day I stepped into that ring, I cast aside that girl and I will be damned if I let her reemerge. A smile danced on her face.

*I **AM** the ocean, embodying strength, beauty, and freedom.*
I WON!

The end

Epilogue

The familiar scents of sweat and Pine-Sol greets me as I unlock the gym door. It's not often I get here before Coach, but today I'm early, ready to work up a sweat before the girls arrive for their class.

Today kicks off our summer program, and I'm thrilled. My professor at the college helped me connect with nearby middle schools, and now we're launching self-defense programs for girls. But this isn't just about learning to throw punches, it's about creating a place where these girls can be themselves, ask hard questions, and most importantly, feel supported.

As I toss my keys onto Coach's desk, a Far Side comic on his daily calendar catches my eye. Two dogs sit on a couch, but it's the bold date that grabs me: June fourteenth, the date that once haunted me, the date that changed everything. But today, two years later, I'm smiling as I tear off yesterday's page and toss it in the trash.

I'm not the person I used to be. A year has passed since my first fight, and with a record of four wins and one loss, I've learned that heart matters more than anything. It's about not giving up when things get hard, it's about learning from your failures. I'm no longer hiding from who I am or who I want to become. I'm learning to love me first. I might not have all the answers yet, or have a grand plan, but that's ok. I'm embracing the uncertainty, rolling with the punches — hell, I'm throwing them. Boxing has given me a confidence I never knew I had. It's taught me to face the world head-on, to take the hits, and if I get knocked down, to remember I'm not knocked out. I get to choose to get back up, to keep fighting.

And the best part? Now, I get to teach others to do the same.

$$Our\ Wave$$

A MESSAGE OF SUPPORT AND HOPE

After reading this book, you may find yourself experiencing a range of emotions or realizations. For some, engaging with stories about trauma, including sexual assault, may bring clarity to personal experiences that hadn't been fully processed. This can be an illuminating yet deeply emotional moment. Whatever you're feeling—confusion, anger, sadness, or numbness—please know that these are natural responses, and you're not alone.

If you've realized you've experienced sexual assault, it's important to remember that what happened was not your fault, and healing is possible. You deserve support and compassion on this journey. Taking steps toward healing can feel overwhelming, but there are resources available to help you navigate this process.

One organization I'm proud to support is **Our Wave**, a platform dedicated to providing a safe space for survivors to share their stories, ask questions, and connect with others. They also offer valuable resources to aid in healing. You can learn more by visiting **ourwave.org**, where you can share your story anonymously or find support from a compassionate community.

Additionally, if you'd like to help Our Wave continue their impactful work, please consider making a donation on their website. Your contribution helps create a stronger network of support for survivors everywhere.

Healing takes time, and there's no one "right" way to move forward. Be kind to yourself, and know that there is hope, strength, and resilience within you. Together, we can support one another and build a brighter future.

Book Club Conversations

DIVE DEEPER INTO DONNAMAE'S JOURNEY WITH THESE THOUGHT-PROVOKING QUESTIONS AND TOPICS FOR DISCUSSION. PERFECT FOR YOUR NEXT BOOK CLUB MEETING!

1 Themes of Loss and Resilience

- How does DonnaMae's loss of her mother shape her relationships with her dad and brother?
- In what ways does she demonstrate resilience throughout the story, and how does it evolve over time?

2 Family Dynamics

- DonnaMae's family is central to her story. How do the different family members help or hinder her personal growth?
- Discuss the impact of her father remarrying. How does DonnaMae's relationship with Elise and Adeline add complexity to her story?

3 The Role of Betrayal and Recovery

- How does the betrayal DonnaMae experiences affect her perception of herself and others?
- Discuss how boxing becomes a form of healing and empowerment for DonnaMae. Why do you think this was a meaningful outlet for her?

4 Friendship and Support Systems

◦ DonnaMae forms unexpected friendships throughout the novel. How do these relationships impact her ability to navigate the challenges she faces?

◦ How important is her "Crew Chief" in the story? Who in DonnaMae's life would you consider part of her "pit crew"?

5 Identity and Self-Discovery

◦ DonnaMae struggles with finding her place in a world full of expectations and change. How does she redefine her identity over the course of the novel?

◦ What does her transition from grief to empowerment say about the process of self-discovery?

6 Moments of Humor and Lightness

◦ Despite its serious themes, the novel includes many moments of humor and heart. Which scenes stood out to you the most, and why?

◦ How do these moments of lightness balance the heavier topics?

7 The Role of Community and Healing

◦ How does DonnaMae's small-town environment contribute to her experiences, both positively and negatively?

◦ What role does community play in her healing process?

Read on for an excerpt from
Mary Lou

Mary Lou

I watch as my husband puts the keys into the ignition and starts the car. He seems to be moving in slow motion. The motor turns over and the car starts. The lyrics to the Rolling Stones song "You Can't Always Get What You Want" fill the car.

Seriously? This song, right now? You have got to be kidding me! Before the third refrain can escape the speakers, I reach over and turn off the stereo. I turn the heater on full blast. I am freezing. The chill of the hospital seems to have followed me to the car and I can't shake it.

I stare hard at the dashboard as I feel the car go into reverse and back out of the parking spot. It still feels like we are moving in slow motion. All I want to do is get out of this cold, dark parking garage and away from this damn hospital.

Quiet replaces the sounds of the Rolling Stones, and I play the lyrics in my head. Except it's not the words of Mick Jagger, it's the words of the doctor. "There is nothing we can do." And now it's playing like a broken record.

I can see my husband trying to talk to me out of the corner of my eye, but I don't know what he's saying and there is no way in hell I am about to look at him.

My song, "There is nothing we can do, you will have to choose," drowns out all other sounds. I feel like I can't breathe, like the darkness of this parking garage is closing in around me. The sterile, damp smells of the hospital will not leave me. I need fresh air.

My hand fumbles along the door, trying to find the crank for the window, trying to find air. We finally pull out of the darkness and into the light, and I crack my window. I turn my gaze to the sky and take in a long, deep breath. A light dusting of clouds follows us as we drive down the road. The hospital grows smaller in the side-view mirror and my body relaxes. We drive past farms with fields full of cattle and sunflowers lining the fences. The sunflowers draw my attention, giving me a distraction. It's the flower my dad planted for me in our yard growing up, symbolizing happiness, loyalty, and longevity. I reach up and wrap my fingers tightly around my locket. Some sunflowers have their heads bent, their lives coming to an end. Some are still in beautiful full bloom, even though their future is sitting right next to them.

My eyes fill with moisture, and I look up, trying to blink away the tears. Twisting my necklace around between my fingers, feeling its familiar detail slide beneath my thumb, I close my eyes, hearing my dad's voice sing, "You are my sunshine."

I take another deep breath. I need to stay strong. I must stay strong. That's why I can't look at him. If I look at him, I will break. "There is nothing we can do. You will have to choose."

"Let's just go home for now and pick up the kids later," my husband says, pulling me out of my thoughts.

"I think that's a good idea," I reply, opening my eyes but keeping my gaze out the window. I can tell he wants to say more, but for once I don't think he knows what to say.

The sky grows dim as a patch of clouds covers the sun, bringing the cold, hard chill back. I pull my sweater tightly across my shoulders as we turn around the corner to our home.

We pull into the driveway, from what feels like the longest car ride of my life. Neither of us gets out and we just sit there. I can feel him looking at me. I can't look back at him. "How do I choose? How do we choose? How does anyone choose?"